TO RISKS UNKNOWN

Douglas Reeman was born in 1923 and left school at the beginning of the war when he volunteered for the Navy, having always had the greatest admiration for the Navy as a career and wishing to secure a war-time commission. After a period in destroyers he made a final 'home' in small craft, and saw service from the Atlantic to the North Sea and from the Icelandic waters to the Mediterranean.

After the Normandy invasion he was based with our naval forces in Germany, where he remained for a year after the war until he left the service. Following the war he served with the Metropolitan Police for nearly five years, mostly in the East End of London, attached to the C.I.D.

He has also been a welfare worker and short-story writer, but has always maintained his contact with the sea as a keen yachtsman and a member of the Royal Naval Sailing Association, coupled with regular tr[...] as a reserve officer.

Also in Arrow by Douglas Reeman

Douglas Reeman

TO RISKS UNKNOWN

ARROW BOOKS

Arrow Books Ltd
3 Fitzroy Square, London W1

An imprint of the Hutchinson Publishing Group

London Melbourne Sydney Auckland
Wellington Johannesburg and agencies
throughout the world

First published by
Hutchinson & Co (Publishers) Ltd 1969
First paperback edition
Arrow Books February 1972
Second impression May 1973
Third impression August 1974
Fourth impression November 1976
© Douglas Reeman 1969

Made and printed in Great Britain
by The Anchor Press Ltd
Tiptree, Essex

ISBN 0 09 905570 8

For Benbow
with love

Contents

When duty calls to risks unknown,
Where help must come from thee alone,
Protect her from the hidden rock,
From War's dread engines' fatal shock:

Naval Prayer Book

Author's Note

In 1943 Britain and her Allies had reached a turning point. There was to be no more retreat, no more pride in mere survival, but an all-out effort to carry the war to the enemy's territory, to seek and destroy him on his own ground.

From captured bases and makeshift harbours in North Africa the men of the Navy's Special Force were to be the probes of each major attack. They were an odd collection and as varied as their ships in which they carried the war far beyond the enemy's defences. But theirs was a strange war where stealth and individual cunning took precedence over tradition, where almost overnight the amateurs had become the professionals.

The whole panorama of war—and especially of war at that time—was made up of individual episodes. No one can tell how much difference each made to the whole, or indeed if some were necessary at all. This is the story of one such episode, of a ship and of the eighty men of her company.

1 For Special Service

REAR-ADMIRAL PERCIVAL OLDENSHAW stood with his arms folded and stared pensively through his office window at the rambling expanse of Portsmouth Dockyard. It was a very grey day, and although it was well into May it could have been mid-winter. The sky was hidden by low, dark bellied clouds, and the roofs of dockyard sheds and the crowded steel hulls of moored warships shone dully in a steady and persistent drizzle.

The admiral was a small, nuggety man with a face like tooled leather. He was bald but for a few wisps of grey hair, and the bright rectangle of decorations on the left breast of his impeccable uniform showed that he had seen the best part of his service long before most of the ships below him had been built, and before their companies had been born. In fact, he had retired from the Navy soon after the First World War and was well past seventy, and but for his stubborn and dogged persistence, his constant visits to the Admiralty and letters to all and sundry, it was likely that he would still be fretting in retirement.

In his heart he knew well enough that their lordships had allowed him to take over his office more to keep him quiet than with any hope of adding much to the war effort. On the sign outside his door it stated, 'Flag Officer-in-Charge, Special Operations'. In 1940 when that sign had first appeared it had been something of a sad joke, and as months dragged into years it was all but forgotten. But the admiral was not a man prepared

to rest behind a title or a desk. If his active service had ceased
with the memories of Jutland and the Dardanelles, his mind
and keen brain were as exact and as demanding as ever.

With Britain wilting under defeats and reverses on every
front, and the Battle of the Atlantic rising to a peak of new
savagery, he had set about making his small command into a
real and important force. The country was on the defensive in
those early days, and any raid on the enemy's coast, any sort of
pinprick against his far-flung lines of communications, was
needed desperately to maintain morale, to give the British public
the belief that somehow, somewhere, they were hitting back.

Now it was 1943, and the admiral sensed that a turning
point had been reached. It was more of a feeling than anything
he could put into words, but it was there. The catastrophes of
Dunkirk and Norway, of Greece and Singapore, were behind
them. Defensive war was out. The time had come to hit back,
and hit hard.

He swung round impulsively and stared at the room's two
other occupants. Seated at a wide desk his Operations Officer,
a fat, heavy-jowled commander, was leaning on one elbow and
leafing idly through a file of incoming signals. The admiral suspected that Commander Hallum was still suffering from the
effects of a heavy lunch at the naval barracks, and was merely
going through the motions to cover up his discomfort.

At another desk a plain-faced Wren officer was studying a
folio very intently, her eyes moving back and forth along each
line, missing nothing, remembering even the smallest detail.

The admiral's eyes softened slightly. Second Officer Frost was
like his right arm, he thought. She was always there, always
ready to do what she could no matter how late or how long it
took. He wished he could get rid of Hallum and replace him
with another Wren like Miss Frost. It was not that the admiral
saw himself as a ladies' man, but having Wrens around him
made him feel both young and fatherly at the same time. Also,
unlike Hallum, they had enthusiasm, and that was a quality
which rated very high with the admiral.

He cleared his throat crisply and both pairs of eyes lifted
towards him. 'It is now fourteen-thirty precisely. In half an
hour I will go to the north-west corner of the dockyard.' He

glanced briefly at Second Officer Frost. 'Have I forgotten anything?'

She played with one corner of the folio on her desk. It was a new one, and on the cover was printed, '*H.M.S. Thistle. For Special Operations, Eastern Mediterranean*'. Then she looked up at the large coloured chart which covered one complete wall of the office. The Mediterranean, from Gibraltar to the Lebanon, every mile marked by battles lost and won, with names like Malta and Tobruk, Alamein and Crete, which needed nothing more to fire the imagination.

She said slowly, 'H.M.S. *Thistle* is still in her basin, sir. The new guns are fitted now, and the radar people will be finishing their work tomorrow forenoon.'

Hallum said sourly, 'It's Sunday tomorrow.'

The admiral spared him a wintry glance. 'I don't give a bugger if it's bloody Christmas! I want that ship ready for sea within three days!' He calmed himself and added, 'Please continue.'

The Wren officer nodded. She no longer blushed at the admiral's expressions. They were part of him. Like his medals, and his rudeness to unwilling staff officers. And his offhand kindness and humanity which he tried hard to conceal.

She said, 'The new commanding officer should be aboard now, sir. He came through the dockyard gates forty-five minutes ago.'

The admiral nodded, satisfied. He never asked where or how she got her information. But somehow she managed to keep him informed of everything, sometimes before the Commander-in-Chief, and usually with more detail.

He walked to the big chart and stared at it for several minutes. Then he said, 'Ninety per cent of the Navy's role in this war has been purely defensive. Protecting convoys and shipping routes. Defending the Army, and defending itself.' He reached up and touched the southern tip of Italy with one wizened hand. 'Well, we know that in a matter of weeks we'll be changing all that. We've got 'em out of North Africa now. The next step is Sicily and then Italy, and on and up into the enemy's under-belly!' Without realising it he had raised his voice. 'At the moment we've got all our people scattered over

the ground. Combined Operations, Commando, the Special
Boat Squadron, Long Range Desert Group, and all the rest.
Too many, doing too varied tasks. We must have unity of
effort, a fluidity of purpose.' He nodded. 'And we *will* have it.'

Commander Hallum watched the admiral's narrow shoulders with weary resignation. It was quite obviously not going
to be a quiet afternoon. The admiral was showing unusual
excitement. For the past weeks signals had been flashing back
and forth at an unprecedented rate. From the admiral to his
senior officer in the Mediterranean. From Commander-in-Chief
to Commander-in-Chief. From the sunshine of Alexandria to
the grey bleakness of Liverpool, and back to the passageways
of Admiralty in London. It was quite beyond Hallum,
especially as the only outcome of all these signals and demands
had at last arrived in Portsmouth in the shape of the small
corvette *Thistle*.

The *Thistle* was a Flower Class corvette, and from the moment her keel had tasted salt water at a Belfast shipyard in
1940 had been thrown into the Battle of the Atlantic as a
convoy escort. She was in fact just another corvette. There
were dozens of them. Small, hastily constructed ships built to
an emergency programme, with little thought of comfort for
the men who manned them.

Hallum had seen her enter Portsmouth harbour just two
weeks earlier. She seemed so small as she passed down the lines
of sleek destroyers and lordly cruisers, and from bow to stern
carried the marks of hard use, the scars of the hardest battle
of all. Her crude dazzle paint was stripped away by wind and
sea, her chubby hull streaked with rust and marked by dents
and scrapes, souvenirs from mooring in pitch darkness or going alongside a sinking merchantman to snatch a handful of
survivors from the grip of death itself.

But the admiral had seemed as pleased as Punch. If the Admiralty had placed the *Rodney* or the *Howe* under his personal
command he could not have shown more excitement. To the
rest of the world the battered little *Thistle* might be just one
more survivor from the Atlantic, but to Rear-Admiral Oldenshaw she was exactly what he wanted.

Hallum realised with a start that the admiral had moved

back to the window. He said hastily, 'What about her new captain, sir? From what I've read in the folio he seems a bit of a has-been.' There was no reply, so he hurried on, 'He's a regular officer, and yet all he's been offered is this clapped-out corvette.'

The admiral said distantly, 'I arranged that appointment, Hallum.'

He let his eyes move slowly across the dockyard and rest on the towering outline of Nelson's flagship *Victory*. Against the dullness and the grey steel the old three-decker's black and buff hull made a fine patch of colour, her tall side shining in the rain like polished glass. Nelson, he thought. There was a man. But even he had fools like Hallum to contend with.

'Lieutenant-Commander Crespin has an excellent record. Up to the time of his last command being sunk he was on constant active duty. Most of that service was in the Mediterranean, with an independent command. He is a man who can think for himself, Hallum.' He did not hide the contempt in his tone. 'I know his record. I feel almost as if I had met him. The man who commands the *Thistle* for me has to be one like Crespin, and they are not easy to come by.'

Hallum saw Second Officer Frost's brief smile and said angrily, 'Well, I suppose both the ship and her captain *will* be expendable, sir!'

The admiral ignored him. 'I don't want some complacent career officer, nor do I require a hare-brained amateur strategist. I need a man who cares. One who gets things done.' He frowned, irritated with himself for rising to Hallum's anger.

'Ring for my car. It is time to go aboard.'

*   *   *

Lieutenant-Commander John Crespin stood quite still on the edge of the dock and stared down at the ship below him. He did not remember how long he had been there, nor did he re- call getting out of the car which had carried him from the harbour station. Behind him on the puddled road his aban- doned suitcase marked where he had left the car and walked the last few yards to the dock.

No ship looked at her best when suffering the indignities of a dry dock, and the *Thistle* was even worse than he had expected. Resting on chocks at the bottom of the high-sided basin, supported on either beam by massive spars, she looked the picture of dejection. A few dockyard workers were sloshing through the remaining inches of oily water below her rounded hull, and others were slapping on paint from various precarious perches, indifferent both to their accuracy and the rain which pelted into the dock with increasing vigour.

Although Crespin was used to small ships the corvette *Thistle* seemed minute against the wet concrete and towering gantries around her, and he was conscious of a growing despair which even the prospect of getting away from the land could not dispel. She was two hundred feet long from her chunky bows to her rounded, businesslike stern which would not have looked out of place on a deep-sea whaler. The upper deck was a tangle of welding gear, nameless pipes and abandoned packing cases, and power lines snaked ashore from every hatch to add to the general confusion of a hasty refit. There was not much in the way of superstructure. Just a square, boxlike bridge, a squat funnel and one stumpy mast, the latter forward of the bridge which was most unusual practice in naval vessels. On the forecastle the *Thistle*'s main armament, a four-inch gun, was trained haphazardly to starboard with somebody's boiler suit hanging from the muzzle, and from amidships Crespin saw a sudden flare of welding torches where some workmen were putting finishing touches to the additional gunpower. This was in the shape of two sets of twin Oerlikons, one on either beam. There was already a two-pounder pom-pom above the small quarterdeck and the ship's original Oerlikon just abaft the funnel.

Crespin bit his lip and then started to walk towards the steep brow, at the inboard end of which he could see an oilskinned sentry watching his approach with neither emotion nor interest.

He reached the top of the brow and faltered, feeling slightly sick. After everything which had happened, because of, or in spite of it, he had arrived here. This was to be his new command. Perhaps the last thing left for him to do.

He forced the growing despair to the back of his mind and rested his hands on the wooden rails of the brow. It was nearly six months since he had set foot in a ship. Six months of waiting and hoping. Of rising hope and overwhelming uncertainty. As if to jar his thoughts alive he felt the pain in his right leg. At first he had believed that once the wound had healed he would be the same as before. He had been wrong. He was not the same, nor could he remember what sort of a person he had been up to the time his last command had been shot from under him. The memory of the sleek motor torpedo boat, the creaming bow wave, the very excitement of even the most normal manœuvre made him starkly conscious of the comparison made by the ship at the foot of the brow. Like a racehorse and a bedraggled mule, he thought vaguely.

The gangway sentry waited until Crespin reached the deck and then levered himself away from the guardrail to salute. It was a tired gesture.

Crespin said quietly, 'Where is the first lieutenant?'

The seaman ran his eyes over the newcomer before replying. Crespin was wearing his raincoat and displayed no badges or rank. Only his rain-soaked cap proclaimed him to be an officer, and in the dockyard they were two a penny.

He said at length, ' 'E's in the wardroom, sir. 'Oo shall I say 'as called?'

Crespin eyed him coldly. 'Just fetch my case from the dockside. I'll find him myself.'

The mention of a suitcase and the coldness in Crespin's tone seemed to transmit a small warning. There was a ring of permanence about it, and with one more quick salute the man scampered up the brow and vanished.

Crespin found an open hatch and lowered himself down a steel ladder to the deck below. He almost collided with a cheerful-looking man in a blue suit and bowler hat. He was carrying a sheaf of papers in one hand and a mug of tea in the other. He eyed Crespin and grinned.

'If you're one of the new officers you'd better get yer gear stowed.' He winked. 'I hear the Old Man's coming aboard shortly, so you'd better get cracking!'

He was still chuckling as Crespin groped his way down a

small passageway past a cabin labelled 'Captain' and towards another marked 'Wardroom'.

Old Man was right, he thought. Crespin was twenty-seven years of age, but he certainly *felt* old.

He pushed open the door and met the gaze of another officer who was standing on the far side of the wardroom by an open scuttle. He was a veritable giant of a man. Tall and broad, with his thick dark hair almost brushing one of the motionless deckhead fans. He had a heavy but competent face, and Crespin saw that on the sleeves of his unbuttoned jacket he wore the interwoven gold lace of a lieutenant in the Royal Naval Reserve.

Crespin said, 'You must be Lieutenant Wemyss. I'm Crespin.'

The first lieutenant showed a flash of surprise and then annoyance. 'I'm very sorry, sir. I was not expecting you until this evening.' He spread a pair of massive hands. 'It's just that it's been like hell here. Dockyard maties all over the show, and half the incoming signals bogged down in some office or other.'

Crespin smiled. 'No bother. I didn't want any unnecessary fuss.'

He threw his raincoat across one of the battered-looking armchairs and removed his cap. He could feel Wemyss' eyes following each movement but he did not care. Then he caught sight of himself in a bulkhead mirror above the small sideboard. No wonder Wemyss seemed wary, he decided.

There were deep lines around his mouth, and his grey eyes were just that bit too steady, so that he seemed to be glaring at his own reflection as if he hated it.

He turned his back on the mirror and saw Wemyss' glance fall to the single ribbon on his jacket. The Distinguished Service Cross.

Wemyss relaxed slightly. 'Well anyway, sir, welcome aboard. It's good to have a commanding officer again. Our last one, Lieutenant-Commander Saunders, had to leave immediately we reached Portsmouth. He's taken command of a brand-new destroyer at Rosyth.'

Crespin watched him guardedly, but there was no hint of a question in Wemyss' remark. Yet he might well wonder why a regular officer, a man with a coveted decoration at that, should be given this command. A reservist would have been good enough. Wemyss himself could have had it.

He asked flatly, 'Have you been aboard long?'

Wemyss shrugged. 'Since she was built. I started as the junior sub-lieutenant and dogsbody and I've been with the old girl all the time in Western Approaches. When we were told of this new stunt, about the ship being taken over for special service and so forth, I thought to myself I'd like to stay with her. She's become a habit, I guess.'

Crespin sat down in a chair and rubbed his eyes. He was suddenly conscious of the bulky envelope in his pocket, the orders he had read and re-read a dozen times. Special service. He still did not really understand what it meant. To him and this ship.

He said, 'Well, what is the state at the moment?'

Wemyss seemed to welcome the sudden crispness in his tone and replied with equal formality.

'As soon as we handed over to the dockyard a fortnight ago most of the hands were returned to Western Approaches, sir. We have twenty of the original company, consisting of most of the key men, the coxswain, signals and W/T, and, of course, the chief. The coxswain is over at the barracks now mustering the new men, about sixty all told.' He smiled gravely. 'I shudder to think what we'll get. Whenever you ask for volunteers for anything a bit vague you're liable to get some strange birds, sir. Chaps trying to dodge bastardly orders, or avoid getting sent to some ship they *know* is bad.' He looked around the wardroom. 'The two new subs will be joining ship in the dog watches. I don't know them either!'

'You will.' Crespin wanted to go to his cabin. To find a small piece of privacy in this ship which would soon be alive and depending on him to keep it so. Eighty officers and men crammed inside this small hull. In the wild Atlantic it must have been a nightmare.

He asked suddenly, 'How was it in Western Approaches?'

Wemyss seemed to consider it. 'Grim. I know the papers tell us that the Battle of the Atlantic is turning in our favour. It looked bad enough when I left it, all the same. Forty ships started on our last convoy. Twenty-two reached the Bar Light Vessel at Liverpool!' His eyes were distant. 'I was second mate of a collier running out of Cardiff before this lot started. I've never got used to watching merchant ships being massacred. It's such a waste. Such a bloody waste!'

Crespin nodded. The next few days would show what sort of a man Wemyss really was, but the first impression was a good one. He was about thirty-three at a guess, and gave an immediate sense of complete reliability. Above all, he was a professional seaman, and in today's Navy that was rare enough, God alone knew.

He said, 'We'd better get started, Number One. I'll go through the confidential books and so forth later. Right now I want all the signals and the exact state of the dockyard altera-tions. After I've gone over that I'll want your check of stores and ammunition and a rough outline of the new watch bill if you've got it.'

Wemyss watched him gravely. 'I've got it, sir.'

'Good.' Crespin stood up and then winced as the pain lanced through his leg.

Wemyss said quietly, 'I heard you'd been wounded, sir. Are you feeling all right now?'

Crespin swung on him, his mouth already framing the angry words. Instead he heard himself reply calmly, 'I'm all right.' He hesitated. 'Thank you.' Then he turned and left the ward-room.

Lieutenant Douglas Wemyss stared at the closed door for a full minute and then shrugged. He finished buttoning his jac-ket and then felt the pockets to make sure he had left nothing lying about. With dockyard men running wild all over the ship you could not be too careful.

He thought suddenly of Crespin's barely controlled resent-ment when he had asked about his wound. Embarrassment? He shook his head doubtfully. Crespin did not seem the kind of officer who had much time for personal feelings of that type. But it was quite obvious to Wemyss that the *Thistle*'s new captain had some burden which was far heavier than taking a command. He had only smiled once during the whole inter-view, and in those brief moments Wemyss had seen a picture of what Crespin had once been. Youthful, even boyish, with a touch of recklessness which was appealing. Then the guard had dropped behind those grey eyes. It was as if Crespin intended to keep his secrets to himself.

Wemyss glanced quickly around the untidy wardroom and then patted the ship's crest at his side. He grinned. He knew from experience that in a ship this size it was hard to keep even a thought secret for more than a minute.

He heard some dockyard workmen laughing beyond the door and set his face in an impressive frown before leaving the wardroom to hurry them along again.

One thing was sure. Crespin was not the sort of captain who would tolerate slackness. Not from anyone, he thought grimly.

*   *   *

Crespin pushed aside the bulky folio of stores and modifications and leaned back in his chair. The cabin was small and almost square with one scuttle through which he could see the rain-slashed wall of the dock. There was a bunk along one bulkhead with a reading light and a well-worn telephone, so that even in harbour the captain could be contacted with minimum delay. At sea Crespin knew he would be lucky if he ever left the bridge, and then only for catnaps in the tiny sleeping compartment attached to the chartroom.

There was nothing in the cabin to give a clue to the previous occupant. But above the small bulkhead desk was a framed photograph of the *Thistle* in heavy weather, obviously taken from a larger and more stable ship in some convoy or other. Her bows were right out of the water and her after part was so deluged in breaking spray that she appeared to be sliding sternfirst towards the bottom.

He thought of Wemyss' one word in answer to his question. Grim. It was a bad understatement, he thought.

But whatever might lie ahead, the *Thistle* was his ship now. And his home. The last thought came to him so violently that he half rose to his feet and then slumped back again, unwilling to allow his tired mind to explore further than that.

After leaving the naval hospital Crespin had gone home. He had known it was a mistake, but something had drawn him there in spite of his inner warnings.

It was an ordinary semi-detached house in the Surrey suburbs of London. Like countless others whose owners had before the war been content with the quiet and unexciting, but nevertheless pleasant, way of life. They caught the same train to town and came back together. They passed non-controversial comments to one another across neat garden hedges on Sunday mornings, while some, the more prosperous, polished the family car. Crespin had been born in one of those houses and had gone to school locally, as did all the other boys.

From the first time he could remember having any sort of definite ambition he had wanted to go into the Navy. He loved ships and everything about them. His father had no experience of such things, and in any case wanted him to follow him into a safe job at the bank. His mother merely wanted him to be happy. Neither was very much help.

Maybe they just let Crespin try for a scholarship entry into the Navy merely to get it out of his system. Whatever the reason, they stood back and awaited results. To everyone's surprise, not least Crespin's, he passed his entrance exam to Dartmouth with room to spare. And at a time when most young gentlemen selected for Dartmouth College were either the sons of serving officers or from influential families it was no small victory.

His parents forgot their fears and showed their pride whenever Crespin came home on leave. It was a fine career, a new dimension, and in their eyes Crespin had suddenly moved to unreachable manhood.

Then everything changed when the Germans marched into Poland. At the time pain and personal grief seems unending, but now looking back to that first year of war it was strange to realise how quickly everything had altered.

His father had set off for London on the usual train. His usual *Daily Mail* under his arm, his sandwiches hidden in his cardboard gasmask container. He was never seen again. There was an air-raid outside Waterloo Station, one of those sneak daylight ones which came and went in seconds, before the warnings had even had time to set up their sinister wail. Many other ordinary men and women died that morning, but it was no consolation to Mrs. Crespin. There was nothing to show for it. No body, and not even a witness. Just oblivion.

Crespin was first lieutenant of a small destroyer at the time, and when he eventually managed to get home he found his mother terribly aged and like a stranger. He had felt something like guilt. After all, he was trained and paid to fight. They were not. He learned much later in Greece and Crete that war was quite impartial when it came to exacting its dues.

His mother never really accepted her husband's death. One day she was walking with a neighbour, making her way to join one of the food queues at the local shops, when she looked up and said, 'There's George! It's my husband!' Before her friend could stop her she ran across the road. The driver of the lorry had no time to apply his brakes and she died instantly. Later the neighbour told Crespin that his mother had a smile on her face as they carried her away. The first smile since her husband had died. The worst of it was that the man she had seen was not a bit like Crespin's father. He had been at the funeral and Crespin had seen for himself. He had returned to his ship, leaving the house and everything else to be sold and to be wiped from his memory.

Why then had he gone back this time? Perhaps like his mother he still clung to the idea that things would somehow return to normal if only he believed it hard enough.

The house had looked the same, but smaller and shabbier. And to his surprise he had found it full of soldiers, like most of the rest in that familiar, tree-lined road. A beefy sergeant had ushered him inside and had gone about his affairs rather than intrude on Crespin's brief visit.

Only the wallpaper was the same. In his old room where he had first read avidly about life at sea he had even found the brighter patches on the wall where his old pictures had been carefully hung.

It would have been better to keep the old memory as it was. He knew that now. But now it was too late. Never go back. Nothing is ever the same.

He jerked from his brooding thoughts as someone rapped on the door and then jerked it open. It was the same gangway

sentry, but this time his face was working with excitement
and alarm.

'C-Captain, sir! The first lieutenant's respects, an' there's an
admiral comin' aboard!'

If the Holy Ghost had appeared on the quarterdeck he could
not have looked more confused.

Crespin picked up his cap. That is all I need. Aloud he
snapped, 'Next time wait until I tell you before you barge in!'

He brushed the seaman aside and stepped into the passageway. It was already too late. On the steel ladder he could see a
pair of black-stockinged legs which were soon, if clumsily, followed by their owner, a very plain-looking Wren officer. Then
came Wemyss, muttering excuses and apologies for the mess
and the gaping workmen. And finally the admiral.

For a moment they all stood chest to chest in the narrow passageway, then the admiral cocked his head on one side and
said cheerfully, 'Rear-Admiral Oldenshaw. Glad to meet you,
Crespin.' He pushed between them and strode energetically
into the wardroom, his gaze swinging from side to side as
if searching for intruders.

Wemyss ushered the Wren to one of the chairs and then
stood by the door. The admiral's pale eyes regarded him unwinkingly and then he snapped, 'You can carry on, Number
One. I know all about you, what!' Wemyss withdrew with
unseemly haste.

Crespin stared at the little man with surprise and growing
anger. He looked as old as time. God, when would they stop
giving jobs to these ancient warriors just because of the un-
written old pals act?

He said curtly, 'I am sorry I was not on deck to receive you,
sir.'

The admiral squatted on the edge of the wardroom table and
smiled. 'My fault. Quite deliberate I'm afraid, Crespin. Dislike
ceremonial, except in its right place. I came to see you, not
some bloody wooden-faced guard of honour!'

The Wren coughed quietly and the admiral nodded. 'Quite.
Mustn't get carried away, eh?' He looked round the untidy
wardroom. 'Small ships. Salt of the earth.'

Crespin replied, 'The refit seems up to date, sir. The main

intake of new men will come aboard as soon as we've got our own power connected up again. At the moment they're in the barracks.'

'Know all that, Crespin. Made all the arrangements myself, as a matter of fact.'

Crespin clenched his fingers until the pain steadied him a little. 'And I have read my orders, sir. If the refit is completed I will sail for Gibraltar on Tuesday.'

'It had better be completed!' The admiral eyed him thoughtfully. 'When you were last in the Mediterranean you commanded the 71st M.T.B. Flotilla. Before that you were in destroyers. You've seen a lot of combat, and you've a damn good record. So you're probably feeling sorry for yourself because you've been given command of this battered little warrior, eh?' He held up a wrinkled hand. 'Don't bother to argue, your face is full of resentment!' He chuckled. 'Fact is, I arranged that, too. I needed a captain for his brains, not his rank.'

The Wren officer, who had been touching a ladder on one of her stockings with a forefinger, said suddenly, 'The admiral means that you were chosen for your experience. Not because you happened to be available.'

Crespin felt the cabin swaying, and it was all he could do to stifle his anger. 'Thank you, sir.'

The admiral did not smile. 'You really are resentful, Crespin!' He folded his arms and regarded the other man with a fixed stare. 'Very soon now the Allies will be landing on enemy soil. Italy will be an obvious starter, but the war cannot be won until our men are in France and then Germany itself. Therefore, whatever we succeed in doing when we invade Italy will be watched and calculated by the enemy. We will be at grips with the real foe. North Africa was too remote for ordinary people's minds to grasp. It was too far away. So when we set our men down on Italian shores it is essential that we get the full co-operation of every living soul who has been living under Nazi oppression. Patriots, terrorists, I don't care who they are, just so long as they can hate Germans and pull a trigger!'

Crespin thought of the *Thistle* as he had first seen her in the open dock. So far he could see no role for her at all.

The admiral must have read his thoughts. 'You know the Aegean, Crespin, and the Adriatic, the thousand and one places where the enemy's lines are stretched to the limit. As soon as the Allies start making progress these island people and their friends on the mainland will start to revolt. They will cut supply roads, shoot down enemy patrols, and generally cause havoc behind the German lines. The Hun will *have* to take valuable troops to quell these uprisings, and so our advance will go all the faster. More important, it will show the peoples of France and Holland what *they* can do when the day comes to invade Hitler's coveted West Wall, eh?'

'How can you be sure of all this, sir?'

The admiral's answer was swift and biting. 'I've not exactly been sitting on my arse for the past three years, for God's sake!' Then he smiled. 'I've got people out there now. In Yugoslavia and the Greek Islands, and more to send when they're needed.' He became serious again. 'That is why I asked for a corvette. A destroyer is both too large and too vulnerable. And you know better than most that M.T.B.s are too damn noisy for this sort of game.'

Crespin had a sudden and vivid picture of the burning torpedo boat, the screams and curses of his men dying around him, the bullets and scalding tracers ripping the waters apart and tipping the spray with scarlet. It was no game, as the admiral had implied. It had been sheer bloody murder!

The admiral stood up and consulted an ancient gold pocket watch. 'Just get the ship to sea, Crespin, and pull these volunteers into one fighting unit. You've done it before, otherwise I wouldn't be here, and neither would you. At Gib you'll get fresh orders, and by that time I'll know a bit more of the next phase of things. It's not going to be easy for you. Nothing worthwhile ever is. But you'll know that what you're doing is important, maybe even vital. By harrying the enemy's communications and working with our terrorist friends you'll be taking the pressure off the main battlefront.' He peered at Second Officer Frost. 'We'll leave now, eh?'

Crespin said quietly, 'Thank you for being so frank.' He found that he meant it.

Rear-Admiral Oldenshaw grimaced. 'Thought I was a silly

old fool, didn't you? Imagined I'd dropped you this command because you could both be spared, wasn't that the case? Well, you may still be right if I'm proved to be at fault. So stop worrying about the ship's capabilities and get on with the job. It's probably just what you need after what you've been through. In this kind of war you've got to fight with what you've got. Not what you'd *like* to have. My God, when I first went to sea as a young cadet we went straight to the China Station to fight pirates, and *that* was in a sailing ship! The *Thistle* may not be a thoroughbred but she's proved her value already.' He turned towards the door. 'The main difference, however, is that this time *you* will be the pirate!'

Crespin followed them up the ladder to the gangway. Wemyss had mustered a small side party and they saluted as the old admiral followed by the tall, unsmiling Wren made their way up towards the dock wall.

Crespin saw the unspoken question in Wemyss' eyes but said, 'Carry on, Number One, and let me know when the two officers come aboard.' Then he retraced his steps to the quiet of his cabin.

The gangway sentry said, 'Must be nice, sir. Bein' an' admiral an' that?'

Wemyss smiled faintly. 'War is like the cinema, Pim. The best seats are high up and at the back!'

Then he turned on his heel and walked forward towards the forecastle. He too had a lot to think about.

2 A Mixed Bunch

TUESDAY dawned clear and surprisingly cold, but by the time the ship's company had completed a hasty breakfast there was some hazy sunlight which, if nothing else, gave a hint of spring.

Crespin stood on the deserted bridge and stared down at his command. It was hard to realise that she was the same rust-streaked vessel he had first seen in dry dock. The previous evening had been a mad whirl of activity, with the *Thistle* being warped from the dock to lie alongside a portion of reserved jetty to await her supplies and the rest of her fittings.

Now she was ready. Her crowded upper deck was clean and neat with guardrails in position and lines flaked down as per instruction book. Crespin guessed that Wemyss had checked each item himself so that his captain's eye would find no outward offence at least. And the great mountain of stores which had been waiting on the jetty had vanished as if the ship had gobbled up every item herself. Food, supplies, ammunition, liferafts and all the small ship clutter of war were now out of sight, jammed, coaxed or lashed throughout the hull until needed.

They had taken on a full load of fuel, and there was still a tang of oil in the crisp air to mingle with that of new paint, the last of which had been slapped on in almost complete darkness.

The tannoy speaker squeaked and then a voice called, 'Clear lower deck! All hands lay aft!'

Crespin stood back a little to watch as his new company appeared as if by magic. They flowed down either side to congregate in a packed mass around and above the tiny quarter-deck, while petty officers and leading hands made a quick check to ensure that nobody but the essential watchkeepers was absent.

The final men had come aboard the previous morning. Most were strangers to one another. They had yet to be welded into a useful company. They were in working rig, blue overalls and regulation caps, but nevertheless it was possible to see that individuals were already visible amongst the jostling, chattering press of figures.

The seasoned seamen wore dangerous-looking knives in hand-made leather sheaths and chatted very little. They knew it was far too early to make assessments. The 'Jolly Jacks', a breed found in all ships, were clad in overalls scrubbed and bleached until they were almost white, to give the outward impression of 'old hands'. Here and there were small companionable groups, friends made at the barracks where the draft had been assembled. There were also other men, isolated and alone in spite of the crush around them. The men with personal and secret reasons for leaving the land. They must be watched, Crespin thought.

Heads turned curiously as the two new sub-lieutenants appeared on deck and walked aft together. To look at they could not have been more unalike. Shannon, the senior of the two, who was to be the gunnery officer, was dark, tense-looking, and would, Crespin thought, be very attractive to women. Sub-Lieutenant Porteous, on the other hand, was fair, pink and overweight. He was appointed depth-charge control officer, but aboard this corvette his duties could be anything which was thrown his way. Crespin knew that before joining the Navy Porteous had been a new and junior barrister. He could well imagine it. Surprisingly, he had failed to get a commission on two occasions, and had spent eighteen months in an East Coast escort vessel. Both were temporary officers. Hostilities only.

There was a clatter of feet on the ladder and Petty Officer Joicey, the coxswain, appeared at the bridge wing and saluted.

Joicey was a regular. He was stocky, almost square, with

bright red hair and a harsh Cockney accent. Wemyss had already described him as a first-class petty officer, and like himself had been aboard the corvette from the beginning, which
he had originally joined as a leading seaman. But Crespin had
seen for himself that Joicey was one of those petty officers
who were the backbone of the Service. During the hectic days
since he had stepped aboard Crespin had seen Joicey everywhere and at all times of the day and night. He never seemed
tired, nor did he allow others to be.

Good coxswains were in great demand, and one with Atlantic experience stood a better chance than most of getting
quick promotion in some other ship, larger and more comfortable than *Thistle*. The previous captain had written a glowing
recommendation to this effect. Wemyss had told Crespin why
Joicey was still here doing the same job as before, but with a
disordered and untested company.

Joicey had fallen in love with a Liverpool girl. They had
been married during one of the *Thistle*'s brief rests in harbour.
All the ship's company had been there, and the captain had
helped to pay for the wedding reception out of his own pocket.

Two convoys and several thousand miles later the *Thistle*
had wended her way back to Liverpool. Even the twin towers
of the Royal Liver building, a landmark so familiar to all returning sailors, were masked in smoke. The German bombers
had done their work well. So well that when Wemyss and
some of the others had gone to the graveyard with Joicey there
was one great mass burial with Joicey's young wife just a name
on an alphabetical list in the padre's hands.

He had not faltered as far as his duties were concerned. If
anything, he worked twice as hard. But Wemyss said that he
was changed far beyond things as impersonal as daily routine.

Now he stood framed against the pale sunlight and the grey
ships at his back.

He said, 'First lieutenant's respects, sir. Lower deck is
cleared.'

'Very good, Cox'n. I'll come down.'

Joicey followed him down the steep ladder, and then Crespin
paused in the shadow of the port boat davits.

'Well, what do you think of them?'

Joicey's eyes were blue and very bright. He stared past Crespin's shoulder, watching an ambulance wending its way between the dockyard cranes.

Then he replied, 'A mixed bunch, sir. Some are born skates, in an' out of detention barracks more than in any ship. A few are good enough 'ands. Others are as green as grass. Straight from their mothers' arms an' filled with ideas of death or glory!' He sounded contemptuous.

Crespin eyed him gravely. 'And you? How do you feel about it?'

Joicey's glance moved momentarily to Crespin's face. 'Dropping depth-charges on U-boats is all right. But it's slow an' very uncertain, sir. If you're lucky you'll get an oil slick an' a few bits of flotsam. If not, just a few gutted fish.' His eyes hardened. 'Not like when our poor bloody merchantmen get swiped by one of their tin fish. You can see *them* burn and fall apart well enough!' He seemed to pull his thoughts together. 'Me, sir? I just want to kill Germans. But this time I want to *see* 'em die!'

Crespin walked the rest of the way in silence. He did not see the men springing to attention, nor did he notice the quick glances of curiosity and uncertainty from all sides as he climbed up on to a depth-charge rack and returned Wemyss' formal report.

He said, 'Tell them to stand easy, Number One.' But his mind still lingered on Joicey's words, the desperate hurt in his eyes.

Then he looked above the watching faces, past the canopied guns and the gently flapping ensign. There was a faint haze of smoke above the squat funnel, and he could feel the ship moving gently against her moorings. She was impatient to go.

He said, 'This is the first time I have seen you all together. It may be some time before I get another chance.' He saw some exchanging knowing glances, and here and there a man nudged his new friend. 'Most of you don't even know yet what sort of thing you volunteered for. Some perhaps are unaware even why they volunteered at all. You have been kept in the dark because so far as the rest of the world is concerned this is just another corvette, one more overworked escort. And it must go on believing that.' He had their full attention now. 'I know

that many of you came to the *Thistle* because you merely
wanted to get away from something else, some even because
they were unfitted to hold down anything they had attempted.'
His tone hardened. 'I am not interested in your past, nor in
your motives. All I ask is that you work together as a team.
Doing a job is not enough. A badge on a man's sleeve may say
one thing, but until I have seen actual results of proficiency of
a very high standard I will not be satisfied.'

Crespin could sense a different reaction around him. Some
looked openly worried, others resentful and defiant. It could
not be helped. This was no picnic, and it was as well to
start off on the right foot. It was rarely the popular way to
begin.

'I will keep you informed as much as I can of what is happening. If you have any worries then speak to your officers or
heads of departments. For believe me when I say this is not
just another overworked escort. We are sailing to do a hard
and dangerous job. A lot of things we are called to do you may
not like. I don't suppose I will either. But it has to be done,
and done correctly, if we are to see England again.'

Along the jetty he could see a line of seamen leaning on the
guardrails of a smart destroyer, watching the little corvette
and no doubt wondering what her captain could find to make
a speech about.

He added slowly, 'We leave harbour in one hour. Nobody
will set foot off this ship again until we have reached our first
destination.'

From the corner of his eye he saw a black Humber staff car
moving slowly past the ship, a smart Wren driver guiding it
carefully over the dockyard railway lines. In the back was a
small, shadowy figure, and he guessed it was the little admiral
taking a last look at his pipe-dream.

He glanced along the upturned faces once more. Soon the
men would emerge from behind these masks. He said curtly,
'Carry on, Number One. Dismiss the hands and get them to
work. We will proceed to sea as ordered.' That was all.

The men sprang to attention, and as he walked between
them Crespin could feel the warmth of their bodies, as if the
whole crew was one living, breathing being.

At the back of the crowd he stopped beside a tall, gangling seaman. 'What is your name?'

The man stared at him with something like fear. 'Trotter, sir.'

Crespin eyed him calmly. 'I've seen you before somewhere. Have we served together?'

'No, sir, never!'

Crespin nodded and walked quickly towards the bridge. The man's reply was too quick, too eager. Perhaps he had been conscious of the general hostility around him and wanted to show that the new captain had no ally amongst the lower deck. And yet . . . there *was* something vaguely familiar about him.

He almost collided with the *Thistle*'s chief engineer. Chief Engineroom Artificer Magot, known by his subordinates as 'The Maggot', affectionately or otherwise as the situation dictated, was very thin and stooped. He was also one of the dirtiest men Crespin had ever seen which, strangely enough, was rare in his branch. But when he had taken Crespin on a tour of his gleaming domain below decks he soon gave proof of tremendous reliability and something akin to love for his engine. At best *Thistle* could muster sixteen and a half knots. Yet Magot seemed to look on his charge with no less pride than the chief engineer of the *Queen Mary*.

'You wanted me, Chief?'

Magot wiped a greasy paw on his boiler suit and blinked his eyes several times. He seemed to dislike the bright light, and Crespin imagined that he hardly ever came on deck unless absolutely necessary.

'Well, sir, I just wanted to say that the engine's never run sweeter. I dunno what they told you about this ship, sir, but whatever anyone says, the old engine's as good as new.' Magot's conversation was normally carried on by lip-reading. Trying to speak above the roar of his machinery was quite impossible. Now his voice was so quiet that Crespin had to lean forward to hear him.

He said. 'Thank you, Chief. Was that all?'

Magot nodded, apparently satisfied. 'Just wanted you to know, sir.'

Crespin smiled in spite of his crowded thoughts. 'I appreciate that.'

As Crespin walked towards the bridge a round-faced stoker thrust his head through the hatch at Magot's feet. 'Told 'im, 'ave you, Chief?' He was grinning.

Magot rubbed his chin, leaving another smear. 'Too early to say yet. He *seems* all right, but once they gets to sea you gets a changed man. Then it's full ahead for this an' full astern for that, or "Give me more speed, Chief!" ' He sighed. 'No appreciation, that's the trouble!'

The stoker shook his head. 'Shame, annit!'

Magot took a swipe at the grinning stoker. 'I'll give you shame, you useless bastard! Get below and check them valves like I told you!'

Magot took a last glance at the water lapping alongside and then climbed over the hatch coaming. As far as he was concerned they could *have* the sea. His nostrils dilated as the smell of oil enfolded him like a cloak.

Engines now, you knew where you were with them.

*   *   *

Crespin walked slowly on to the port wing of the bridge and stared for several seconds at the seamen milling around the forecastle deck. It looked a terrible tangle, but there was a good leading hand in charge, and if Sub-Lieutenant Shannon was in any doubt what to do he should be safe in his hands.

There was a sort of nervous expectancy pervading the whole ship. A few moments before everyone aboard must have been aware of the surrounding ships, the age-old stone of the dockyard, a sense of permanence.

Then the pipe: 'Special sea dutymen close up! Hands to stations for leaving harbour!' had changed all that.

The gangway had vanished, and goaded by the leading seamen and Petty Officer Dunbar, the chief bosun's mate, the men had at last sorted themselves into some kind of order. Mooring wires were slackened off, and between the hull and the high jetty was a widening strip of oily water.

Wemyss had already reported: 'Ready to proceed, sir.' He

was standing beside the voice-pipes, his heavy features quite expressionless, and probably wondering what his new captain would make of getting under way in a strange ship.

Crespin had to admit to a sensation of apprehension. The *Thistle* had but one screw, and there was a stiffening north-west wind to push the ship playfully back alongside the jetty whenever inclined. A dockyard tug had already inquired if he needed assistance, but had hauled off immediately in response to Crespin's curt 'Negative!' Nevertheless, the tug still hovered nearby, almost guiltily, and half concealed behind a massive cruiser, staying close by just in case.

Crespin glanced at Leading Signalman Griffin who was standing beside him and staring unwinkingly at the dockyard tower. Griffin had two good-conduct badges and was one of those signalmen who had seen and done everything. Being stationed on the bridge he was privileged to eavesdrop on his officers, to hear their doubts and petty differences as well as their confidences, but true to his kind he kept his opinions to himself.

Crespin said, 'Signal the tower. Request permission to proceed.'

He turned his back and walked to the forepart of the bridge as Griffin's lamp began to clatter. A diamond-bright light answered immediately, and Griffin reported, 'Affirmative, sir.'

Crespin breathed out slowly. They must all be up there watching. Oldenshaw, his unsmiling Wren, and God knows who else.

'Ring down stand by.' He ran his fingers along the toughened glass screen and felt the deck beneath his feet begin to vibrate with renewed insistence.

He caught Wemyss' eye and remarked quietly, 'Well, Number One, here we go!'

Wemyss showed his teeth. 'I'm not sorry, sir. A bit of sunshine'll be very welcome.'

Crespin looked away. 'Let go aft!'

The order was repeated, and from the quarterdeck came a sudden flurry of activity as wires were slacked off, while on the jetty two bored dockyard workmen released the great spliced eyes from their bollards and dropped them in the water.

Crespin saw Sub-Lieutenant Porteous, flushed and obviously over-anxious, cup his hands and yell, 'All clear aft, sir!'

Wemyss sprang across the bridge like a tiger. 'Not yet! Wait until you've got 'em both aboard! They'll wrap around the screw if you don't watch out!' He came back breathing heavily and lapsed into silence.

Crespin nodded. Wemyss was more anxious than he thought.

'Slow ahead.' Crespin craned forward and watched narrowly as the jetty began to sidle past. The long wire spring which ran from the forecastle to a bollard almost level with the quarterdeck lifted and tightened until it was like a steel bar. Unable to go any further ahead because of the restraining wire, the bows moved inwards towards the jetty. To his relief he saw Petty Officer Dunbar and a handful of men already waiting with heavy fenders at the point of impact, so that when the hull snubbed against the jetty the stern automatically began to swing outwards into the stream. Wider and wider, until the ship stood out from the wall at an angle of forty-five degrees. Even the eager wind was unable to stop the *Thistle* from swinging clear.

Crespin licked his lips. They were as dry as dust. 'Stop engine. Let go forrard.' He waited, counting seconds as first the head rope and then the much-tested spring were hauled dripping through the fairleads and the forecastle hands slipped and cursed amidst the coils of greasy wire which seemed to fill the deck from side to side.

'Slow astern.' Crespin had seen Shannon right forward by the jackstaff. He had not made Porteous's mistake so perhaps Wemyss' anger was useful.

Gently and then more confidently the little corvette slid sternfirst away from the jetty. All at once the towering gantries and dockside sheds lost their individuality. They were part of the harbour's general panorama. Something remote.

Crespin readjusted the glasses around his neck. 'Stop engine. Slow ahead.' He watched the wind ruffling the water of the anchorage as it cruised to meet him. 'Starboard fifteen.' He paused. 'Midships.' They were moving. He heard Joicey's voice from the wheelhouse and knew that the coxswain would need no other orders until the ship was clear of the harbour. He said abruptly, 'Hands fall in for leaving harbour, Number One!'

With her ensign blowing out stiffly to the breeze and making a small patch of colour against her new paintwork the *Thistle* moved purposefully towards the entrance. On her forecastle and quarterdeck the hands were fallen in, their bodies swaying in unison as a destroyer surged past, her backwash lifting the *Thistle* like a dinghy and throwing spray high over the weather rail.

Petty Officer Dunbar and the bosun's mates stood just abaft the bridge, and while the corvette thrashed past one senior ship after another the air was tortured by the shrill twitter of their pipes as the *Thistle* paid her respects to her betters.

On and on, with Joicey guiding her from one marker to the next. Past anchored ships and imposing buildings which wore the flags of admirals, and which replied to the *Thistle*'s feeble piping with bugles that sounded almost patronising.

There was the entrance. Old Portsmouth to port and the grey walls of Fort Blockhouse, the submarine base, to starboard. Between them, like penned water in a massive dam, lay the open sea.

Crespin said, 'As soon as we are clear we will exercise action stations, Number One. Go round the ship and check every man yourself. There might not be much time later on.'

When he looked again the harbour mouth was passing on either beam, and from the huddled houses on the Point he saw two women waving. Women must have waved like that when the *Victory* sailed for Trafalgar, he thought.

He snapped, 'Secure for sea. Fall out harbour stations.' He saw Shannon waving back towards the town and added sharply, 'Tell Shannon to get those wires properly stowed, Number One! It's like a bloody road accident down there!'

Behind his back Griffin looked at the bridge messenger and pursed his lips.

High on the dockyard signal tower Rear-Admiral Oldenshaw lowered his binoculars and wiped his eyes. The wind was very keen up here and made him feel his age.

The dockyard had done a good job, he thought, although whether the *Thistle* would have sailed on time without his bullying was another matter.

He lifted the glasses again and watched intently as the little corvette turned slowly around the jutting wall of Fort Block-house, the weak sunlight lancing along her side and showing at a glance that she was already lifting and rolling to meet the open water outside the harbour. She appeared very small indeed, and strangely vulnerable.

Behind him he heard Second Officer Frost say quietly, 'She looked very well, I thought, sir.'

The admiral nodded. 'Crespin handled her perfectly. That's why I sent that tug along. I just wanted to see if he'd accept any help.'

She smiled sadly. 'I guessed as much, sir.'

Oldenshaw handed the glasses to a signal rating and said testily, 'Lost sight of her now. Let's get back to the office, eh? Crespin will be at Gib in a week and there's a lot to fix up before then.'

*   *   *

Fifteen hours after her departure from Portsmouth found the *Thistle* some twenty miles south of the Lizard, that last jutting tusk of Cornwall and therefore the final view of England, had it been light enough for anyone to see it.

The corvette was heading almost due west, and the wind which had freshened considerably throughout the day was making her progress both uncomfortable and painful. As each rank of white-crested waves cruised out of the pitch darkness the ship would lift her bow with something like tired resignation before reeling over and down into the waiting trough, her stern rising almost clear of the water as the sea thundered along her weather side and broke across the streaming deck as if to catch and destroy anyone foolish enough to be making the treacherous journey from one part of the ship to the other. It was a savage, corkscrewing motion, and the experienced men aboard knew it would get worse once the ship had clawed away from the last lee of the land and started to head south into the Atlantic and across the fringe of the dreaded Bay of Biscay.

A few minutes before midnight Wemyss and his watchkeeping companion, Sub-Lieutenant Shannon, clambered into the upper bridge and groped their way from one handhold to the next, each man waiting for his eyes to get accustomed to the leaping wilderness of spray beyond the glass screen.

Wemyss went immediately to the chartroom to see the captain, and Shannon, having discovered Porteous still clinging to the voice-pipes in the forepart of the bridge, made his way across to him.

'Where the hell are we?' Shannon had to shout above the din.

Porteous gestured miserably with one hand. 'Just passed the Lizard. Course is two-six-zero, and we've reduced speed to ten knots.'

Shannon listened to the voice-pipes chattering in the darkness as the men stumbled on deck to begin the middle watch. He said, 'And I suppose you've been sick again?'

Porteous shook his head. 'I'm all right if I stay on deck, Mark.' He sounded doubtful. 'But I hope it doesn't get any worse.'

'It will.' Shannon seemed angry.

Porteous said, 'The captain let me run the watch practically on my own. I did quite well really. Just once when we altered course around two trawlers, then he had to help me.'

'I suppose you put the wrong helm on?'

Porteous stared at him through the gloom. 'Well, yes, as a matter of fact.'

Shannon turned as a bosun's mate said, 'Middle watch closed up at defence stations, sir. Able Seaman McDiarmid on the wheel.'

Shannon nodded curtly. 'Very well.' To Porteous he added, 'I suppose Wemyss is gassing about us to the C.O.'

'I like the first lieutenant.' Porteous staggered as the deck canted over with a sudden lurch. Then he added, 'He's so, er, helpful.'

Shannon shrugged. 'Well, if you need help, I imagine that's all right.'

Porteous watched him worriedly. It must be nice to be so independent and confident, he thought. Yet there was something unreal about Shannon's attitude. He seemed to have a constant guard up, and was quick to show resentment to any criticism.

Porteous thought back over the day and felt vaguely satisfied in spite of his several glaring errors. As he had wandered around the upper deck or shared his watch with the captain he had a feeling that at last, at long last, he had found his rightful niche in things. None of his tasks had been too difficult so far, and there always seemed to be someone nearby like a petty officer or leading hand if he appeared about to commit a real breach of discipline or seamanship. Only on the bridge did his old feeling of apprehension and doubt return to dog his every move. When it came to passing a helm order or making a fix on some vague and swaying buoy or beacon he got that same fear he had somehow made a mistake. Even when he was proved right he could find little consolation and put it down to luck rather than ability.

He said, 'By the way, the signalman of my watch comes from Putney, just a few streets from my home. He's a very nice lad, and used to deliver our newspapers.' He shook his head. 'Amazing, isn't it?'

Shannon caught his arm and whispered tightly, 'That's another thing. For God's sake stop chatting to the ratings the way you do. They won't respect you for it. They'll more likely think you're soft.'

Porteous looked at the deck. 'I'm sorry.'

'And stop apologising for everything!' Shannon broke off as Wemyss and the captain appeared at the rear of the bridge.

Crespin walked to the gyro repeater and peered at it for several seconds. In the shaded light his face looked much younger and showed no trace of tiredness, although he had been on and around the bridge the whole time.

He saw Porteous and said, 'Better get below, Sub. You're up here again in less than four hours.' He seemed to sense the tension and added calmly, 'You did quite well today. Keep it up.'

Porteous stared at him. 'Thank you, sir. I—I will, sir!'

Crespin's teeth showed briefly in the compass light, then he said, 'I'm going to turn in, Number One. Call me when you alter course at 0300. Or for anything unusual.' Then he was gone.

Wemyss walked to the voice-pipes, his long legs splayed out to hold the deck as it lurched from one angle to another. Then he glanced at Shannon's outline against the screen. 'All right, Sub?'

Shannon shrugged. 'Thank you, yes.' He waited until the duty signalman had moved to the opposite side and then asked quickly, 'Will we be going into action as soon as we reach the Med, Number One?'

Wemyss yawned. 'I've not been told. The captain will tell you when he's ready, I imagine.'

Shannon did not notice the gentle rebuff. 'He seems a bit edgy, don't you think?' He waited for a comment, but Wemyss remained silent. 'But I suppose that if half I've heard is true it's not surprising.'

Wemyss wanted to shut him up, but something in Shannon's tone made him prick up his ears. After all, Crespin was certainly not confiding in him beyond the necessities of duty. That was unusual aboard the *Thistle*.

Shannon continued, 'He was leading some motor torpedo boats along the North African coast. They were jumped by German E-boats and shot to pieces apparently, and our captain had to swim for it.'

Wemyss broke his silence. 'It happens.'

'Maybe, but this time the survivors were machine-gunned in the water, several hours *after* the boat was sunk. Crespin managed to get ashore with three survivors, and one of them died later.'

'Go on. Get it off your chest.'

Shannon sounded angry. 'Well, that's about all of it. The captain and his two remaining men had to walk across open desert for three days. They were eventually found half dead by an army patrol.'

A light winked feebly through the leaping spray and Wemyss said sharply, 'Check that buoy on the chart, Sub, and be quick about it. Fixes will be hard to get in this weather.'

When Shannon had gone he walked to the front of the

bridge and hoisted himself into the steel chair which was bolted
to the deck for the captain's use at sea. He had been wrong to
let Shannon rabbit on about the captain, he thought. Crespin
was hard to reach and his suffering probably explained that.
But deep down Wemyss believed there was more to it than
that.

He settled more firmly into the chair, his ears recording the
familiar shipboard sounds without conscious effort. The
monotonous bleep, bleep from the asdic shelter, the scrape of
feet from invisible watchkeepers and the steady vibrating beat
of the engine. Like a thousand other times, and always the
same sight through that salt-caked glass screen. The common
enemy.

Again his thoughts returned to Crespin. He was quick to find
fault, but he could still take time to drop a word of praise when
it was most needed.

Like his remarks to Porteous, for instance. Wemyss smiled
in spite of the leaping spray which had already turned the
towel around his neck into a sodden rag. Porteous was so
awkward and bumbling. He tried hard enough, perhaps too
hard, but how he came to be here, or even in the Navy at all,
was quite beyond understanding. Wemyss had learned that
Porteous's father was a judge. Probably just as well, he
thought. Without backing of some sort it seemed unlikely that
he would find any job at all.

He heard Shannon's voice, low-pitched and threatening as
he laid into one of the lookouts. He was another sort of man
entirely. Wemyss was rarely given to snap judgements but he
guessed that Shannon's resentment came from some sort of
inferiority complex. Taking it all round it was a very rum
ship's company indeed, he decided.

A voice-pipe muttered, 'Permission to bring up a fanny of
kye for the middle watch, sir ?'

Wemyss craned over. 'Carry on.'

And so the *Thistle* went back to war.

3 Briefed to Attack

ONE week after leaving England, almost to the exact hour, *Thistle* dropped her anchor in the busy roadstead beneath the protective shadow of the Rock. After the rain and greyness of Portsmouth dockyard and the savage squalls which had dogged them across the Bay of Biscay it seemed to the corvette's small company like entering another world. Everywhere was bustle and a great show of purpose and preparation. There were stately troopships, their rigging bedecked in khaki washing and decks crowded with half-naked soldiers whose skins were already changing from pink to pale tan. There were cruisers and destroyers with at least two battleships, and the waters of the crowded harbour were churned and criss-crossed by countless launches and pinnaces as if to emphasise the importance of this, the gateway to the Mediterranean.

But it soon became obvious to everyone aboard that if the *Thistle* was momentarily with part of a great fleet she was not of it. A launch came alongside with fresh despatches, and almost before the weary seamen could feast their eyes on the shore the corvette was moving again, this time to an oiler. While all hands turned to and rigged fuel hoses, Crespin was whisked away in the launch with hardly enough time to change into another uniform.

Wemyss had seen him over the side and had asked, 'Any orders, sir?' He had gestured towards the white waterfront buildings which shimmered in a heat haze as if coming alive.

'A drop of liberty would do our people a world of good.'

Crespin had stared at him for a few moments. 'No leave, Number One. As soon as we've taken on fuel we are to move out to the anchorage again.' He had felt like adding that there was nothing he could do about it anyway. It was all in the despatches. But something in Wemyss' eyes made him keep his resentment to himself. He had merely added, 'They can buy their damned souvenirs later. When they've achieved something.'

It had been unjust, and as he sat moodily in the launch's cockpit he knew he was only voicing his own disappointment.

The lieutenant who had come out in the boat said, 'Nice little ship you've got there, sir.' He was smartly dressed in whites and looked as if he had never set foot aboard a ship in his life.

Crespin eyed the other officer calmly. 'I suppose *you* don't know what's happening?'

The lieutenant stared at him and then grinned apologetically. 'Sorry, sir. Hush, hush, and all that.'

Crespin relaxed slightly. *As I thought. He knows damn all.*

But it was good to be back in the Med. He had half-expected to feel the rebirth of fear, but so far he was all right. And the clear sky, the healthy-looking sailors aboard the anchored ships and, above all, the crushing burden of defensive tolerance you found in England which was so alien here made it seem like a homecoming.

His escort appeared to assume that Crespin's silence was a kind of rebuke, and ushered him ashore and into the waiting car without another word.

As the vehicle ground slowly through the narrow streets past gay cafés and open-fronted shops, Crespin marvelled at the normality of it all. The only thing you really noticed was the absence of women. But the streets were jam-packed with servicemen of every kind and of many nationalities.

Wemyss had been right all the same. After the hasty departure from England and the voyage south his men could do with a sight like this.

The *Thistle's* company had settled down quite well, too, in spite of the terrible weather and the uncertainties which al-

ways came with a new venture. And the little corvette was
not the best sort of ship for starting from scratch. There was
never enough room. Men ate and slept herded together in a
single messdeck, which did nothing to improve tempers.
Stokers and seamen, signalmen and quartermasters, each used
to their own ways, were expected to live in each other's pockets, so that men only just in their hammocks for a few hours
sleep were awakened by others being called for duties elsewhere, cursing and staggering against the swaying hammocks
while the ship dived and reeled through every maddening
gyration.

The weather had been bad, although it was hard to see it
with the same eyes through the window of a slow-moving
car. In the wardroom it had been uncomfortable enough, with
chairs lashed together when not in use and everything damp
and jerking about with a mind of its own. In the crew's quarters it was much worse. Water slopping around the steel deck
while the men sat hunched at their tables trying to eat food
already cold and flavourless after its precarious journey from
the galley.

The *Thistle* had kept well clear of land and away from the
convoy routes. Her purpose had been to reach Gibraltar and
not to get involved in the affairs of the Atlantic. If ships could
think, then she must have wondered at the behaviour of her
masters. Even when the W/T office had reported a heavy U-
boat attack on a convoy barely thirty miles away Crespin
had held down his personal feelings and had maintained his
set course.

There had been one disturbing incident to mar the short
voyage. Or two if you stopped to consider the aftermath.

Four days out, with the weather beginning to change in their
favour, they had suddenly sighted a man in the water. It had
been quite impossible of course, for the corvette had the sea
and sky to herself. But as Crespin had rubbed the sleep from his
eyes and run quickly on to the bridge he had seen the lonely
figure for himself. Not a corpse drifting and forgotten from
some massacred convoy, eyeless and without meaning like so
many in the past, but a living, and at that moment, wildly
excited human being.

The *Thistle*'s off-duty hands had lined the rail while a scrambling net had been lowered and three strong seamen climbed to the waterline to haul the gasping survivor aboard. He had been all in, and would doubtless have died within hours. *Thistle*'s stubby silhouette must have looked like something from heaven in his red-rimmed eyes.

It was later, when the survivor's speech returned to his salt-swollen tongue that they all realised what they had found. He was a German.

Wemyss, who spoke the language quite well, had announced flatly, 'He's off a U-boat. He was watchkeeping on the conning tower two nights ago when a great wave swept right across the bridge. His safety harness snapped and he went over. His mates never saw him go.'

It should not have made any difference. Men killed in action were taken for granted. Captured ones hardly raised comment any more. But this particular German made all the difference in the world. Maybe the *Thistle*'s company wanted to make their first useful gesture, as if to prove themselves, to start the record the right way. Or perhaps the battered little corvette had fought the bitter Atlantic battle for so long that she could not bring herself to accept this pitiful symbol of that savagery.

Whatever the truth of the matter, Crespin had been shaving in his sea cabin on the following morning when Lennox, the Leading Sickberth Attendant, had rushed in hardly able to speak coherently.

'The Jerry, sir! I can't understand it, but . . .'

For a moment longer Crespin had imagined the German had died. It was not unknown for survivors to recover only briefly from their ordeals and then die without any visible reason.

Lennox had made another effort. 'He's *gone*, sir!'

The ship had been searched from stem to stern. But the German had indeed vanished. One minute sleeping in the sickbay, the next oblivion, as if he had been imaginary.

Wemyss had suggested doubtfully, 'Perhaps he had some kind of brainstorm, sir? Or maybe being in the drink alone knocked his mind off balance and he . . .'

Crespin had interrupted. 'He just walked away, eh?'

Wemyss had shrugged. 'Well, I don't like Germans, sir, but I don't like what you're suggesting either!'

'And neither do I, Number One. But like it or not we've got a bloody murderer in this ship, maybe more than one.'

Wemyss had said thickly, 'It's a bad beginning.'

Crespin jerked from his thoughts and realised the car had stopped outside a tall building, the plain unmarked entrance of which was guarded by two marine policemen.

Three minutes later he was sitting before a large desk in the presence of a Commander Gleeson, a harassed-looking officer who dryly announced himself as 'Rear-Admiral Oldenshaw's man in Gib.'

Then he leaned back in his chair and placed his fingertips together below his chin. He looked rather like a schoolmaster running the rule over a new boy.

'So you're Crespin, eh?' He nodded briskly. 'A good trip?' He did not pause. 'That's all right then.'

Crespin said quietly, 'I've made a full report. We picked up a German survivor but lost him the following day.'

Gleeson's eyes hardened. '*Lost* him, for God's sake?'

'Overboard.'

Gleeson seemed very relieved. 'Oh, is that all. Thank heaven for that! For one second I imagined he'd escaped or something.'

Crespin watched him impassively. You callous bastard. Aloud he said, 'Well, it's all in the report.'

'Quite so, Crespin.' He shuffled some papers on his desk. 'Now there's a bit of a rush on, so I'll be brief. You're going to Sousse, and you're sailing tonight at 2300. Suit you?'

Crespin tore his mind away from that gasping, sodden survivor and all that his disappearance implied. Half to himself he said, 'North-east coast of Tunisia, about nine hundred miles from this room. At cruising speed I can be there comfortably in four days, sir.'

Gleeson did not look up. 'Then you'll have to do it *uncomfortably*. I want you there in three, right?'

Crespin clenched his fingers tightly. 'I think I know my ship's capabilities, sir.'

'So do we! That is why she was chosen for this work.' Gleeson's voice was smooth. 'Do what you have to, but get there in three days. You'll report to Commander Scarlett at Sousse and he will brief you.' His lips curved slightly in a smile. 'Stop thinking of possible breakdowns or getting your own back on senior officers who are too stupid to understand, and just remember this is important, *damned* important.'

Crespin stood up. He wanted to get away, for he knew he might say something to Gleeson which both of them would regret.

The commander eyed him calmly. 'I know what you've been through. I was here when it all happened. Bad luck.' It was the same tone he had used for the missing German. 'But this is a different sort of war you have come to join. Methods are not so important as results. Get to Sousse and let off steam there if you like. I should think that you and Commander Scarlett will get on like a house on fire.'

Crespin picked up his cap. 'I don't think I know him, sir.'

Gleeson walked with him to the door. 'You will, Crespin. Of that I am quite sure!'

The interview was over.

*　　　　*　　　　,

At the prescribed time *Thistle* weighed anchor, and once clear of the harbour limits altered course to the east. Crespin walked out to the port wing of the bridge and stared back at the Rock. As it fell further and further astern it seemed to rise from the sea like a symbol of that other world before the war. The town below the great natural fortress was a mass of glittering lights, some of which ran up the side of the Rock itself as if to reach for the stars in an unending necklace. Without looking over the rim of the bridge he knew that most of the off-duty seamen were also staring back along the corvette's sharp wake.

How different it must seem to most of them, he thought. At home, and all over Europe, the lights had gone out for the duration. At night the only ones you ever saw were bursting flak or the glow of burning buildings.

He turned his back on the dancing reflections and walked into the bridge. 'Very well, Sub, you can inform the chief that I'm ready to increase speed now. I want revs for fourteen and a half knots.' He saw Porteous's pale outline by the chart table and could almost feel him digesting his order before he passed it down the handset. It was just a formality, for Crespin had already told Magot what was expected of his department if they were to reach Sousse on time.

Magot had regarded him with something like hurt before saying, 'If you *say* so, sir. If it's really necessary.' He had craned forward so that Crespin had been able to smell the encrusted oil and dirt on his boiler suit. His tone had suggested that perhaps Crespin might still change his mind.

Crespin had said, 'I do, and it is, Chief !'

Magot had vanished through his hatchway muttering to himself, and was no doubt down there now watching his dials and cursing the lack of consideration from the bridge.

Porteous came back breathing hard. 'The chief says he'll do his best, sir.'

Crespin smiled to himself. Porteous's embarrassed air implied that Magot had also said other, less repeatable things.

At midnight Wemyss and Shannon appeared to take over their watch.

In the airless chartroom Crespin said, 'It'll be a change to be able to hug the North African coastline without being shot at, Number One.'

Wemyss leaned on the chart, his big hands encompassing the Western Mediterranean as he studied the pencilled lines and bearings. 'Can I ask you what we're going to Sousse for, sir?' He did not look up.

Crespin listened to the watchkeepers handing over their duties, their voices muffled by the increasing beat of the engine. 'I don't know myself yet. A Commander Scarlett is coming aboard as soon as we get there. He seems to be the man in charge.'

'I see.' Wemyss sounded strangely relieved. 'At least we'll be *doing* something again.'

'You've not heard anyone mention that German, Number One ?'

Wemyss looked up, caught off guard. 'No, sir. But I'm keeping my ear to the ground. There's been a good bit of speculation on the lower deck, of course, but most of the lads seem as baffled as we are.'

Crespin eyed him gravely. 'Don't just look on the lower deck. Grudges have been known to appear elsewhere.' He glanced at the bulkhead clock. 'I'm going to turn in.'

But with the door of the tiny sea cabin closed behind him he knew he would not be able to sleep. With the ship blacked out and deadlights screwed over every scuttle the compartment was like an oven. Even when he stripped off his shirt and stood directly beneath the deckhead fan he could find little relief. Corvettes had been designed mainly to face the Atlantic, where a lack of ventilation was often a real advantage. The dockyard's hasty additions to the air ducts were anything but adequate for the fierce sunlight of the day and the oppressive humidity in the overcrowded cabins and messdeck.

Perhaps that was why he had made another dig at Wemyss' opinions and attitude over the missing German. Wemyss was everything a first lieutenant should be and he was an excellent seaman. But when it came to other matters, outside the actual running of the ship, he seemed unwilling to be drawn, as if by shutting his mind to the problem it would automatically cease to exist.

Crespin knew otherwise. Somewhere between decks, or standing his watch right now beneath the great canopy of stars, was a murderer. Perhaps in his own mind this man, whoever he was, had already justified his action. But a man who could kill secretly and with such cool judgement was a menace to everyone around him. The more reasonable his deed might appear in his mind, the more dangerous he would become.

Crespin threw himself on his back and stared up at the darkness. And it had sounded from what Commander Gleeson had said at Gibraltar that the unknown killer would soon have plenty of opportunity to act again, if he had a mind to.

He felt the engine vibrations coursing through the bunk and imagined Magot cursing him from his private world of noise and pounding machinery. Some of the vibrations seemed to aggravate the wound in his leg, and with a groan he rolled on to his side, the effort making the sweat break out across his bare chest and run freely beneath his armpits.

It was strange that he was going to Sousse. It had been less than fifty miles from there that his boat had been surprised and sunk. The agonising weeks in hospital which had followed, the dazed and jumbled recollections of screaming men and blazing fuel had, strangely enough, become clearer now, so that he could piece the events together in his mind like a complicated jigsaw. But it was more as an impartial onlooker than as one of the three survivors. Very few actual faces stood out in the pattern. Without effort he could still see the small patrol of soldiers rising from behind a sand-dune like one more cruel mirage, their unshaven faces changing from watchfulness to surprise and then compassion as Crespin and his delirious companions had stumbled at their feet. They had been carrying the other sailor all day and did not even know he had died somewhere along the haphazard path which Crespin had taken, with only the mocking strip of sea and the blazing, relentless sun to guide him.

There had been one other face, but that was more vague and could have been part of the nightmare. In hospital, tossing and sweating in his bed, Crespin had relived the actual moment a thousand times, when with his men he had been swimming and floating under the stars surrounded by a patch of fuel and a few pieces of flotsam. All that remained of the M.T.B.

Crespin remembered swimming around the widening circle of bobbing heads, calling encouragement, threatening and pleading, doing and saying anything which might make them hold on to life and hope until daylight. A patrol would find them. If not some of his own flotilla, then one of the patrolling destroyers, or even a reconnaissance seaplane.

Then, it must have been two hours later, Crespin still could not remember, they had heard the low, throbbing note of high-speed engines. Some of his men had little red lamps on their lifejackets, and they held them above their heads, yelling and cheering as the unseen craft drew nearer and nearer. A few of the men were sobbing with relief and did not care if the approaching craft was friend or foe. It just meant rescue, and that was more than enough.

Crespin pressed his face into the damp pillow and tried to recall exactly what happened next. But all he could really remember was the eye-searing beam of a searchlight and the sudden stammer of machine-guns.

The cheers had changed to cries of anger and fear and then to terrible screams as the boat had reduced speed and had moved methodically through the struggling figures while the guns had slashed the water into a bloody carnage.

The fact that Crespin had been swimming around his men probably saved his life. The boat's bow wave swept over his head, forcing him under and filling his lungs until he thought he was drowning, and when he eventually rose gasping to the surface he had seen the boat's flat stern right over him, so that he had to fight with all his remaining strength to kick clear of the whirling screws.

Then, and this was where reality became confused with the nightmare, he remembered a face. It was leaning over the boat's guardrail, arctic blue in the searchlight's reflected glare, and seemed to be shouting. Or it could have been vomiting.

Crespin closed his eyes tightly. The man, whoever he was, had good cause to vomit. The sea had been alight, and in the dancing fires Crespin had watched his remaining men, some of them too badly wounded to swim at all, while they were devoured by the spreading pool of flames. The last to go had been an eighteen-year-old midshipman. It had been his first patrol. Crespin could still hear his shrill cries. It had been like a woman screaming in agony.

The burning fuel had flickered and died, and as if satisfied the boat had cut her searchlight and with a roar of engines had faded into the darkness.

When daylight had at last come Crespin had discovered that the land was only a mile away. At the time it had seemed endless, and when he and the remaining three men had crawled up on to the burning sand the impossibility of their position had been almost too hard to bear.

Now, looking back, it was even harder to understand why the commander of that patrol boat had done what he had. He must have known exactly what he was doing. Must have wanted to do it. For if he had been unwilling to burden himself with prisoners he could have left them to fend for themselves, knowing that the land was within their reach. After that they could have managed for themselves as far as he was concerned, but at least his conscience would have been clear.

Crespin sat up on the bunk and shivered. The sweat on his body felt like ice water. It was mad to go on like this. It was over. Finished.

But as he pulled a blanket over his shoulders he knew in his heart that he would never forget. Nor could he find it within himself to forgive.

Eventually, worn out by his tortured thoughts, Crespin fell back on the bunk and was instantly asleep.

*   *   *

The small Tunisian port of Sousse seemed shrouded in a permanent dust cloud through which the sun only just managed to penetrate. It was hardly surprising, for it had been one of the last vital supply routes for the retreating Afrika Korps, a final toe-hold in North Africa, and although it had been in Allied hands for almost two months it still looked desolate and ground down by the machinery of war. But amidst the ruined buildings and along the waterfront with its ravaged houses and cratered jetties there was an air of purposeful rejuvenation. Troops and vehicles slogged through the swirling dust, while sappers and bulldozers pushed away the wreckage of past battles and laid a foundation for the next one. It was a clearing-up process. North Africa was cleansed of the enemy, and Rommel had gone. The remnants of his desert army were either captured or had managed to escape across the Strait of Sicily, where, if they had avoided being bombed or torpedoed on the journey, they were no doubt licking their wounds and awaiting what must be an inevitable invasion of their own territory.

After exchanging signals with a red-faced and overworked berthing officer the *Thistle* groped her way alongside a burned out Italian storeship and stopped her engine. It was a poor berth, but with the harbour littered with wrecks and filled almost to overflowing with the victors, they were, as the red-faced officer implied, lucky to get one at all.

As at Gibraltar, the build-up of power was impressive to see. Warships of every kind, landing craft and supply vessels, while overhead friendly aircraft maintained a regular umbrella to ensure that the preparations remained undisturbed.

Crespin leaned over the bridge screen and watched as Petty Officer Dunbar clambered along the other ship's scorched and splintered deck and supervised the final arrangement of mooring wires.

They had done it. Three days, with hardly a complaint from Magot, and not a single hour wasted in repairs or faults.

It would probably turn out to be an anticlimax. Crespin knew his Service well enough to expect this sort of thing. In the Navy you did everything earlier than necessary. If you went to sea it was always at the crack of dawn, or in the dead of night when the hands were too tired even to think properly. It must be left over from the days of sail, he thought, when their lordships were always worried in case the wind died and their ships were still far from their prescribed stations.

Wemyss climbed on to the bridge and saluted. 'Ship secured, sir.'

'Thank you. Well, I don't imagine that our people will want any leave *here*, Number One. The place looks a bit the worse for wear.'

Wemyss grinned. 'There's always somewhere left where you can find a bit of pleasure, sir.'

Crespin wondered what Wemyss considered as pleasure. It was hard to picture him doing anything else but his job.

Leading Signalman Griffin interrupted his thoughts. 'Beg pardon, sir, but there's a motor boat heading this way.'

Crespin nodded. 'Very good. Man the side, Number One. This must be Commander Scarlett.'

He climbed stiffly down to the main deck feeling the sun beating across his neck. God, this Scarlett did not waste any time. He must have been sitting in the ruins with his glass trained on the harbour entrance.

He paused and glanced swiftly around him. The seamen working on the upper deck were stripped to their shorts, and some were already looking sunburned, while others displayed a goodly selection of tattoos. The ship was cluttered with mooring wires and clothing hung up to dry. And the new paint could not hide her old scars and dents. But for all that she looked tough and competent, and he felt vaguely satisfied. Yet when he had learned of his appointment his spirits had dropped so low that he could never imagine himself feeling anything but resentment. But the *Thistle* had a character all of her own. It was useless to compare her with a thirty-knot M.T.B. or a graceful destroyer. Like her design her personality was uncompromising. She seemed to say, Well, here I am. Take it or leave it.

Crespin turned as Wemyss said quietly, 'There are three passengers in the boat, sir. Two of them seem to be soldiers.'

Crespin was already looking at the tall figure standing very straight-backed beside the boat's coxswain. He was dressed in khaki shirt and slacks, and as far as Crespin could see wore no badges of rank at all. But on his head, tilted at a somewhat rakish angle, was a brightly oak-leaved cap. So he was obviously Scarlett.

The boat sighed to a halt alongside, and almost before the bowman had hooked on the commander heaved himself aboard, returning the salutes from the side party and gripping Crespin's hand in a firm clasp in what appeared to be one movement.

He was over six feet tall, lean and very tanned. From beneath the peak of his gleaming cap his eyes were blue and restless, so that as he spoke they were moving around the upper deck, missing nothing, as if working independently for their owner.

'Crespin? I'm Peter Scarlett. Damn glad you made it on time.' He had a more resonant voice than Crespin had expected, and when he smiled he seemed very conscious of it, and Crespin suspected that nothing this man did was ever to no set purpose.

Scarlett gestured to the two soldiers. 'Major Barnaby and Lieutenant Muir. They've come along to look over the ship.' He did not explain what he meant but hurried on, 'Where can we talk?'

Crespin led the way down to his cabin, and was glad to see
that Wemyss had had the presence of mind to prepare it at
such short notice. The scuttle was open, and someone had
tidied up the littered desk and had placed some clean glasses
on a tray and a jug of tepid-looking water.

Scarlett laid his cap carefully on the bunk and glanced
around the small cabin. Without the cap he looked older, and
Crespin put his age at about forty. He had thick wavy hair
touched with grey, and this, added to his strange uniform and
the pistol-holder on one hip, gave an unreal, even theatrical
impression which, Crespin guessed, was no accident.

'I expect Gleeson filled in some of the details when you
paused at Gib, eh?' Scarlett's eyes fell on the glasses. 'Scotch
for me, if you have it.' He waited until Crespin had found a
bottle and added briskly, 'I heard about your trip from the
U.K., the missing Jerry and so forth. You mustn't blame yourself, you know. These things can't be helped.' He downed the
whisky in one swallow and breathed out noisily. 'Good stuff.
I've just been in Algiers swapping yarns with our American
friends. Got back an hour ago, as a matter of fact. A relief to
see you alongside, I can tell you.'

Crespin refilled the glasses carefully. 'I understand that I
am to serve directly under you, sir?'

'Correct.' Scarlett regarded him over the rim of the glass.
'Why, are you a bit peeved about it?'

Crespin stared at him. 'I don't quite understand, sir?'

Scarlett threw back his head and laughed. He had excellent
teeth. 'Good God, I suppose they forgot to tell you!' He became serious again. 'I'm R.N.V.R., old chap. One of those
bloody temporary fellows!' He could not stop the grin from
spreading again. 'So you see, Crespin, the normal scheme of
things has been reversed.'

Crespin felt the whisky like fire in his empty stomach. This
must be another of Oldenshaw's strange prodigies. But it was
unusual to find temporary officers either so senior or so important. He knew that many of his contemporaries would have
hated to serve under a part-time sailor. Perhaps that was why
he and not one of them had been chosen to command the

Thistle. If that was so, then the little admiral's knowledge was even more vast than he had imagined.

He said flatly, 'I know plenty of regulars whom I wouldn't trust in command of the Gosport ferry, sir. I have also met reserve officers whom I would place in a similar category.'

Scarlett wagged the glass. 'Spoken like a man! Well, we shall get along all right. I run the outfit here, and all you have to do is get this ship in the right place when and where I tell you.'

Crespin saw Scarlett's eyes rest meaningly on the bottle. It was a third empty already and it was still only ten o'clock in the morning.

He asked, 'Those two soldiers. Do they have anything to do with us?'

Scarlett nodded. 'Very much so.' He seemed to relax slightly as Crespin refilled his glass. 'I was just coming to that, as a matter of fact.' He glanced at his watch and downed the glass in two swallows. 'I left word for your officers to join us in the wardroom, I hope you don't mind. It saves me saying everything in duplicate, what?'

Crespin smiled. 'I'll lead the way, sir.' Inwardly he resented being kept in the dark. In front of his own officers he would hardly be in a position to ask questions without undermining his own authority. But there seemed to be no second motive behind Scarlett's words. Maybe he wanted to show that as far as he was concerned everyone involved in his scheme was being treated as an equal. Crespin imagined that Scarlett was, above all, the sort of man who needed to inspire confidence, just as he needed plenty to drink.

He found his officers and the two soldiers standing in a silent and somewhat self-conscious group.

Wemyss said, 'I've sent the steward away, sir. I hope that was what you wanted?'

The question was directed at Crespin and Scarlett's brows dropped slightly in a brief frown.

But his voice was as crisp and breezy as ever. 'Well, gentlemen, let's get on with it, shall we?'

The major took out a chart and unfolded it carefully on the wardroom table. It showed part of the North African coast with Sicily and the Italian mainland at the top. There were several pencilled arrows and figures and a whole jumble of dates and references which Crespin could only guess at.

Scarlett said, 'It's getting near time for the big push.' He tapped the land mass of Sicily with one finger. 'Next month we will launch an invasion here. Operation Husky, as it is called in higher circles. After that we will have a crack at Italy, so this first invasion must go like clockwork.' The finger moved south and stopped midway between Sicily and the African shore. 'Now, as some of you know, there are three Italian islands here. The biggest is Pantelleria, which Mussolini in all his wisdom chooses to call the Italian Gibraltar. The others, Lampedusa and Linosa, are important, but without the main one's support will not give too much trouble.' He looked round the intent faces. 'If the Sicilian invasion is going to work first time, as it must, our chaps will have to be given round-the-clock fighter cover. On the approaches, over the beaches, and right up to the time the jolly old pongos can capture a few airfields for themselves.' Here he shot the two soldiers a beaming smile, and Crespin saw the major reply with a dour twitch of the lips which might have meant agreement or irritation.

But Scarlett was warming to his theme, and Crespin could see little beads of sweat running down his cheek as he added, 'Pantelleria has just the airfields we need, but more than that, if we don't take them *before* Operation Husky begins then Jerry can use this base just as we used Malta against him. In fact, it seems unlikely that our people could cope. I am informed by the C.-in-C. that an all-out sea attack will be made on Pantelleria on June 11th, and the R.A.F. is already doing a bit of softening up in that direction. However, the island is a real fortress in every sense of the word, and there is always the chance that it might be able to hold out, just as Malta did.' He took a sharp breath. 'This is where we come in. Before the final assault on Pantelleria, or Operation Corkscrew as it is officially to be known, we are going to carry out a party of our own!'

Crespin glanced at the others. It was amazing the way Scarlett bandied around items of secret information. Either he was as confident as he sounded, or he had great faith in security arrangements. He saw Wemyss staring at the chart, his mind obviously busy with the problems of navigation and making a safe approach. Porteous was craning over his shoulder, his expression just a bit too intent and serious, like one who has hardly understood a word but is certain that others will explain it later on. Shannon was watching Scarlett, his shoulders straight and firm as if he was on parade or facing an enemy broadside. His eyes were very bright, and Crespin felt that Shannon wanted to show that he at least was ready to follow Scarlett to the end if so required. The two soldiers on the other hand seemed almost disinterested. Their task obviously started only if the Navy played its part first.

Scarlett had his hands firmly on his hips as he said, 'This ship will make an approach from the north-east and will cover a landing party under Major Barnaby. He will have thirty men, each one an expert in his trade, and his mission will be to blow up the fresh-water reservoir on that side of the island. Without water in bulk the garrison in Pantelleria will be less inclined to put up a long resistance, and, furthermore, as the reservoir is under the guard of German troops, its destruction will make the Italians less inclined to knuckle under the Jerry command when we put the pressure on.' He flashed a smile around him. 'Any questions?'

Wemyss looked up from the chart. 'It's a difficult approach, sir. If they've got a good radar unit we will be clobbered before we get within a mile of the place.'

Scarlett looked at him searchingly. 'Good point, Number One. But the island's radar is not too hot from all accounts, and is directed mainly towards the south. The part where we will be working is well protected by high cliffs and shallows. The enemy seems to think it safe enough from his point of view.'

Wemyss said doggedly, 'But if he *has* got good radar there, sir?'

'Well, we shall just have to make the best of it.' Scarlett turned away from Wemyss and asked, 'Anything else?'

Crespin said quietly, 'Is there any information about local naval patrols, sir?'

Scarlett sighed. 'Our bombing has driven most of the heavy stuff away to Sicily. There are a few armed trawlers, I believe, but I will give you the latest gen on those when we get closer to zero hour.'

He stood back against the white bulkhead and studied all of them intently. 'This is damned important for us, gentlemen. It is our first real operation of value in the Mediterranean. I intend to see that we do not make a mush of it.' His glance fell briefly on Wemyss. 'In this game you've got to think fast and boldly. It's no place for barrack stanchions and people who are afraid to act for themselves. No use dripping over lack of detailed plans, or waiting for someone to wipe away the tears when it gets a bit dicey.' He slapped his palms together and Porteous jumped nervously. 'Just remember that the island's defences are only as strong as the weakest men there. In this case, the ruddy Eye-ties. If we can smash their water supply and rub the Jerry's nose in the dust as well, we shall be well on the way to success.'

He took Crespin's arm. 'Walk with me to the launch. I just want to fill in a few details before I send your final orders aboard.'

As they left the wardroom followed at a discreet distance by the two soldiers, Shannon said, 'Now *there* is someone who is getting things done!'

Wemyss grunted. He had taken a firm dislike to Scarlett.

Porteous said vaguely, 'He has quite a record, I'll give him that.'

The others looked at him and then Shannon asked, 'Do you know him?'

Porteous flushed under the combined stare. 'I've *heard* of him. He's already got a D.S.O. and D.S.C.'

Wemyss unbuttoned his shirt and muttered sourly, 'Then he's either got a lot of our blokes killed or he's managed to survive longer than most!'

Shannon's thin face darkened. 'Well, what else do you know?'

'He's been building a sort of private navy down here for some time. Running stores to Tobruk, carrying out raids and that sort of thing.'

Shannon bit his lip and stared through the open scuttle. 'Well, it just shows that given half a chance even the Admiralty can see that temporary officers are as good if not better than regulars!'

'Well, yes.' Porteous faltered and then blurted out, 'Of course, he is a *very* influential man. Before the war he was a big stockbroker in the City, and was pretty famous as a yachtsman *and* mountaineer. He's not *exactly* typical, would you say?'

Wemyss turned away, unable to watch Shannon's anger. You had to hand it to Porteous, he thought. Soft he might be, but when he did pluck up courage he certainly had all the right words.

On deck Crespin stood beside Scarlett and watched the soldiers jumping down into the waiting launch.

Then Scarlett said softly, 'I want you to make a good show of this operation.'

Crespin did not look at him. 'I shall do what I can, sir.'

'I am sure you will, old boy.' Scarlett straightened up to leave. 'I just have a thing about people I've not worked with before.' He faced Crespin and his eyes were for once quite still and devoid of warmth. 'It does not follow that because a man has reached a certain rank or appointment at a time when a battle starts that he is equipped in any way for fighting it. I've got very high standards, and I expect everyone under me to reach them.' A quick smile broke the hardness on his features. 'Still, I'm sure *you* will be all right.'

He touched his cap in a casual salute and dropped down to the boat.

Crespin watched the launch curving away towards the waterfront and realised that his hands were shaking badly. So it was not as he had imagined it at all. He had thought the *Thistle* to be a last-chance command, all that he was fit for after his experiences. Now it was quite obvious that he might not even be good enough for *her*, if what he had seen in Scarlett's face could be believed.

He knew he was getting edgy again, and he tried to hold back the sudden flood of despair and resentment with something like physical force. He looked at the ship with her bridge

and upperworks shimmering in the heat as if burning from
within. He had not wanted her, nor did he have any feeling
which he could mark down as either pride or enthusiasm. But
the thought of losing her, just like that, was almost more than
he could bear, and the realisation filled him with anger and
disbelief.

4 The Raid

CRESPIN withdrew his head and shoulders from beneath the oilskin hood across the bridge chart table and walked to the gyro repeater. In those few minutes while he had studied the chart and memorised the final bearings and soundings he had almost lost his night vision, so that he had to wait, forcing himself to stand beside the compass until he could see the black edge of the bridge and the endless flow of pale stars beyond.

Then he crossed to the voice-pipes. 'Starboard ten.' How loud his voice sounded. 'Midships, steady.' From the corner of his eye he watched the luminous compass card ticking round. 'Steer two-three-zero.' His busy mind barely recorded Joicey's acknowledgement from the wheelhouse, and he was more conscious of his heart pounding noisily against his ribs.

Scarlett had certainly chosen his night well. As black as pitch and with a faint haze across the sky which made the stars seem very far away.

He glanced at his watch. Ten minutes to midnight. He wanted to go back to the chart table, to make one more check, but he instantly dismissed the impulse. It was pointless now, for across the bows, stretching away on either hand was the blacker, more solid shadow of Pantelleria. It was about the same size as the Isle of Wight, yet when Major Barnaby had spread his chart on the wardroom table just two days ago it had looked so small and meaningless, a mere grit against the greater land masses above and below it.

Now it was here, and very real indeed. The *Thistle's* engine
was throttled down to dead slow with hardly enough revolutions to give her steerage way, yet with each passing minute
the shadow of land seemed to swell in size as if to reach out
and enfold the little ship and crush the life out of her. The
small radar repeater beside the voice-pipes added to the impression. The distorted outlines seemed to writhe like phos-
phorescent weed, the picture further twisted by a mass of
back-echoes, so that it looked as if the island was alive.

The sea was dead calm, not even an occasional whitecap
to break its oily swell. That was another reason for such a
slow approach. Any sudden burst of spray from the ship's
stem would be seen instantly by any watcher on the shore.

Wemyss' big figure crossed the bridge silently like a cat.
'Getting close, sir. I make it about a mile.'

He was speaking in a hushed whisper. It was strange how
the nearness of danger made men do that, Crespin thought.
And how much louder the ordinary shipboard noises seemed
to have become in the last few crawling minutes. A flapping
halyard was like the crack of a whip, some lookout's nervous
cough a thunderclap.

Crespin plucked at the front of his shirt. In the lifeless air
and after the sweat of the day it felt like a damp rag.

'Go to the chart room, Number One, and tell Commander
Scarlett. Then get aft and keep an eye on the soldiers. I don't
want any noise when the rafts go over the side.'

Wemyss' outline melted into the darkness and once more
Crespin was very conscious of the tension around him. The
ship had been at action stations for hours, and he could almost
feel the gunners straining their eyes into the darkness, their
hands clammy with excitement and apprehension on triggers
and ammunition hoists.

Up to this point everything had gone smoothly. Maybe it
was the very impudence of Scarlett's plan which had made
it so.

That first night in Sousse the soldiers and their four sausage-
like inflatable rafts had come aboard without warning or
ceremony, materialising out of the burned-out freighter alongside almost before a startled quartermaster could call a chal-

lenge. They were very professional looking, with the quiet, dangerous appearance of men who had spent much time doing this sort of thing, who needed no advice on how to go about it.

The next morning the *Thistle* had sailed, outwardly at least as extra escort to a small eastbound convoy, and then under cover of darkness she had turned north and increased speed, alone once more.

Crespin had seen little of Scarlett, who had spent most of his time in close consultation with Major Barnaby or sleeping in Crespin's unused cabin. When he did see him he always looked cheerful and unruffled, and his general appearance of confidence seemed to have transmitted itself to everyone aboard. How much of it was bluff, Crespin did not know, but if Scarlett had nothing else he certainly had charm, and he used it expertly.

He heard feet moving on the gratings and when he turned he saw Scarlett and the two army officers groping their way around the side of the bridge. Against the night sky the two soldiers appeared to be headless, and then he realised that both men had blackened their faces.

Scarlett breathed out loudly and said, 'A damn good night for it.' Then he glanced at Crespin. 'How long now?'

'Fifteen minutes, sir. I have passed the word for the rafts to be ready for lowering.'

Scarlett peered at his watch. 'Running late. We'll get cracking now.' He did not wait for any comment but turned to the soldiers. 'All right with you, Barnaby?' He could have been discussing a cricket score.

The major nodded. 'I'm not bothered. There's no wind so it should take us about thirty minutes to paddle ashore.' He nudged the lieutenant who walked away without a word. 'I hope our chap in Pantelleria is there to meet us.'

Scarlett's teeth gleamed in the darkness. 'He'd better be!'

Wemyss clambered on to the bridge. 'All ready, sir.'

Scarlett said dryly, 'Well, Number One, we got here without any fuss, didn't we?'

Wemyss replied calmly, 'It may be noisier on the outward passage, sir.'

Crespin broke in, 'Tell the chief bosun's mate to rig some more fenders alongside. We must cut down noise as much as possible.' He knew Wemyss would have attended to it already, but he also knew that he had to be kept away from Scarlett at this moment. Scarlett seemed to enjoy prodding at Wemyss' caution, but it could break into something unpleasant and unmendable.

Scarlett watched the first lieutenant stride away and then remarked, 'He's a good man, you say?' He sounded doubtful. 'Well, I suppose you should know, eh?'

A tall sergeant peered over the bridge coaming, his eyes like small lamps in his black face. 'Mr. Muir says we're ready to go, sir.'

Like the rest of the soldiers the sergeant made a formidable sight. On his head he wore a rough stocking-type hat, and his body was hung around with ammunition pouches, grenades and a lethal looking commando dagger, while across his shoulder he carried a Thompson sub-machine-gun with the easy familiarity of an old friend. All the soldiers wore rubber-soled shoes, and Crespin almost pitied the first dozing enemy sentry to be awakened by one of them. He would not have very long to think about it, that was certain.

Barnaby touched his small moustache and stared at Crespin. 'Pick us up if you can, Captain. But don't hang about. It'll be rough when the balloon goes up.' He chuckled. 'And go up it will, to an unprecedented height, I shouldn't wonder.' Then he was gone.

Crespin moved to the voice-pipes. 'Stop engine!'

The deck gave a small shudder and then began to sway gently as the ship idled aimlessly across the offshore current. From aft there came a few splashes and one small scrape of metal, but nothing more.

The rating at the quarterdeck telephone looked up. 'All clear aft, sir.'

'Very good.' Crespin felt ice cold. It was too easy. 'Slow ahead. Port fifteen.' To Scarlett he added quietly, 'That Major's a cool customer.'

Scarlett heaved himself into the steel chair. 'Doing his job.' He sounded almost disinterested. Then he said, 'Take the ship to the nor'-east. If Barnaby gets ashore without trouble he'll be in position by 0200 and we can make the pickup an hour later.' He ran his fingers along the screen. 'As you know, there's an air strike laid on to get the Eye-ties on the jump, and in the general confusion Barnaby ought to be able to get clear.'

Crespin studied his pale outline, noting the change in his attitude and tone. Scarlett was not excited, but there was a sort of elation, a brittleness which gave the impression he was only holding himself in check with effort.

He said slowly, 'If he runs into trouble before he can get to the rafts we may have to get close inshore, sir.'

Scarlett's fingers stopped their little tattoo for just a few seconds. 'If *that* happens, Crespin, I shall decide what is best for us to do.' He turned his head slightly and Crespin saw that he was grinning. 'I need a lot from you, but advice I can manage without, do you follow me ?'

Crespin opened his mouth and then closed it again. The operation was very important, especially to Scarlett. So there was some justification for his sudden irritation. Yet at the back of his mind he seemed to hear a warning, as if he had seen Scarlett for the first time. As he really was.

He heard Wemyss moving across the bridge. 'Everything all right ?'

Wemyss nodded. 'No trouble, sir. They went off paddling like bloody demons!'

Crespin glanced at Scarlett's shoulders. 'We shall soon know now, one way or the other.'

The first lieutenant followed his glance and replied quietly, 'And to think that I believed the *Atlantic* was rough!'

Crespin walked to the opposite side of the bridge and lifted his glasses. It was still completely black. No sudden burst of tracer, no alarm flares to break that brooding shadow of land. Things, he reflected, would get a lot rougher before much longer.

*   *   *

If the slow approach inshore to discharge the small landing party was a test of nerves, the waiting was far worse. With her

engine stopped the *Thistle* lay about a mile clear of the long
tentacles of jagged reefs which marked the actual landing
place, her hull rolling uncomfortably in a gentle but regular
offshore swell which had also managed to swing her beam on
to the island. The slow swaying motion meant that regular
checks had to be made on loose equipment, ammunition belts
and even the discarded cocoa mug which might slide off a ledge
and so arouse some sleeping dog ashore that in turn would
wake its owner.

An hour passed and nothing happened to break the eye-
straining tension. Scarlett had remained on the bridge chair,
rocking with the hull and completely silent. He could have
been asleep or so immersed in his thoughts that the mounting
strain had somehow passed him by.

Crespin stood on the port grating and moved his glasses
slowly along the screen, covering every yard of mocking darkness. In his mind's eye he could see his ship, the men at their
stations, the blind gun muzzles and the small huddle of figures
on the quarterdeck who waited to haul the returning soldiers
to safety. Down in the engine room Magot would be squatting
with his stokers, his eyes staring at the great dial, waiting to
open the throttles and drive the little ship to his captain's
bidding.

Scarlett broke the silence. 'What's the time?'

Crespin said, 'A few minutes to two o'clock, sir.'

Scarlett spread his arms wide and yawned. 'Things will be
starting anytime now.' He stood up and massaged his legs
vigorously. 'The reservoir is well protected from the air which
is why the R.A.F. have drawn a blank in the past. The planes
have to make a very low approach and are easy targets for
flak.' He stiffened and held up his hand. 'Did you hear that?'

Everyone on the bridge froze. Very faint at first, and then
with increasing power like surf on a rocky shore came the
murmur of far-off aircraft.

Scarlett nodded. 'That will be the little diversion.'

Across the long expense of black water Crespin heard the
sudden wail of a siren and imagined the enemy gunners running to their weapons, wiping the sleep from their eyes and
cursing as they fumbled with shells in the pitch darkness.

Wemyss said, 'Let's hope Major Barnaby's crowd don't get caught in the raid.'

Scarlett half turned and looked at him. 'The bombers are going for the harbour at the other end of the island. No fear of that.'

It was strange to stand back as a spectator and watch the next act being played like this, Crespin thought. The bombers droned unhurriedly over the island, their course marked by small, vicious shell-bursts and occasional streams of bright tracer. The latter soon fell quiet, and Crespin guessed that the bombers were content to fly well out of range of small weapons. After all, they had no special target in mind this time.

Minutes later the bombs started to fall. They were too far away to be seen or heard as individual explosions, but the humid air trembled to a constant grumble like thunder, while the mist beneath the stars flickered and then gleamed more steadily to a pale red glow.

Scarlett groped for his watch and muttered, 'Come on, Barnaby! Get your bloody finger out!'

Crespin was beginning to share his impatience. Barnaby's raiders must have got to their positions without being seen, but perhaps some unforeseen obstacle had blocked their final approach, or worse, they had got lost in the darkness. Aerial photographs and intelligence reports were all right in their way, but it was something else entirely to be blundering around amidst rocks and bushes, expecting at any second to walk into a hail of bullets.

And there was not much time. The bombers were only making one sweep before they turned and flew back to Malta. If Barnaby had failed to plant his explosives by the time the raid ended he would find himself in serious trouble.

He turned his head to watch as a small, arrow-shaped flame moved slowly away from the black hump of land, like some earthbound comet, to glide above its own reflection until both were joined and instantly extinguished.

Leading Signalman Griffin murmured, 'One of the bombers has gone for a Burton, sir.'

Crespin saw Scarlett twist round, an angry retort probably

forming on his lips, when all at once his whole face lit up and the glass screen by his side shone with sudden brightness, so that for a few more seconds Crespin imagined a second aircraft had plummeted alongside and exploded.

When he looked abeam he saw a great tongue of fire, deep red like blood, which seemed to shoot straight up from the very top of the island. Then the explosion reached the ship, preceded by a great surge of warm air, and the ship trembled violently in its path.

Scarlett yelled, 'They've *done* it! They've blown the water supply!'

Caution was momentarily forgotten as voices passed the news along the gun positions and to the men below decks. Someone was laughing, and another sound came up the wheelhouse voice-pipe. It was Joicey humming a little tune which seemed all the more macabre because of the angry glow from the shore.

Scarlett said, 'Give them ten minutes and then head for the pickup. There'll be so much bloody chaos ashore I shouldn't wonder if Barnaby gets back without losing a man.'

Crespin nodded and moved to the voice-pipes. That was quite likely. Sentries, who seconds before had been watching the impartial havoc across the distant harbour would certainly be unprepared for the sudden collapse of the great damned mass of water.

The picture faded from his mind as a voice-pipe intoned, 'Radar . . . bridge!'

Wemyss bent over the tube. 'Bridge.'

It was Willis, the new Leading Radar Mechanic who had joined the ship with the additional equipment.

'I'm getting a strange echo about four miles astern, sir.' In the sudden and oppressive silence his words boomed around the bridge. 'I thought it was one of those back-echoes from the shore.' He faltered and then said firmly, 'Would you have a look on your repeater, sir?'

Crespin lowered his head into the small hood around the repeater screen. Behind him he heard Scarlett say savagely, 'Why in hell's name didn't he see it earlier?'

For a while he saw nothing new on the dancing mirage of

luminous weeds. Then he held his breath. Willis was right. Dead astern there was something. It was motionless and seemed to be almost rectangular, although the shape was hard to fix in the strange flickering light from the screen. But whatever it was, it was too far out to be part of any land.

He snapped, 'What do you think it is, Willis?' He knew the operator was a well-trained man. He must have heard Scarlett's angry comment and might keep silent when he was most needed.

Willis replied, 'It's not very large, sir. But whatever it is, it must have come around the headland,' he paused, 'and then stopped where it is.'

Scarlett said, 'Are we going to stand here all bloody night?'

Crespin looked at him. 'Willis is right, sir. What bothers me is the speed at which it, or they, got to that position.'

A bridge lookout called, 'Flare, sir! Port beam!'

A pear-shaped green light hung above the glowing fire on the island and then dipped slowly behind a ridge of hills.

Scarlett said softly, 'Well, the enemy's on to Barnaby by the look of it.' He swung round violently. 'Did you say "or *they*"? I thought there was only one echo!'

Crespin replied calmly, 'Could be two ships alongside each other.'

Willis's tinny voice broke in excitedly, 'That must be it, sir! One vessel a bit larger than the other, and both stopped!'

Crespin peered at his watch. It would take all of thirty minutes to find Barnaby, even supposing he had managed to get clear. By that time the unidentified ships, whatever they were, would realise what was happening, and pinned against the reefs with the island behind her *Thistle* would be a sitting target.

'So much for your bloody radar!' Scarlett was showing his anger.

And so much for your damned intelligence reports! Aloud Crespin said, 'We will have to engage them, sir.'

Scarlett peered over the screen as two small explosions blossomed briefly against the black wall of cliff. 'Grenades,' he said. Then he looked towards Crespin and added, 'In your opinion we should attack them before we go in for Barnaby?'

It was surprising how calm Crespin felt. His limbs were completely relaxed and his breathing seemed quite normal. It was a kind of latent madness, biding its time, waiting until . . . he stopped his mind from going further and snapped, 'It *is* my considered opinion!'

Scarlett seemed more composed again. 'Very well. But if you're wrong we may have to leave Barnaby to swim home.'

And if we're sunk trying to pick up the soldiers, what then? Crespin replied, 'I don't see any alternative, sir.'

'Maybe.' Scarlett climbed on to the chair. 'It's your responsibility.'

Crespin smiled at Scarlett's back. There was never much doubt about that.

He shut the possibility of failure and recriminations from his thoughts. 'All engine orders will be passed by voice-pipe, Number One. The telegraph can be heard for miles at night.' It was an exaggeration, but probably necessary. 'And pass the word to all positions to be ready to open fire instantly.'

Wemyss was standing very still, his body rising and falling easily with the deck.

Crespin added, 'Then tell Porteous to prepare for a depth-charge attack. Minimum settings, right?'

Wemyss faltered. 'It's risky, sir. Might blow the stern off.'

'Have you never dropped a charge at minimum depth setting before?'

Wemyss seemed to shrug. 'Once, sir. That was an accident.'

'And the stern is still attached.' Crespin turned away as more dull explosions echoed across the water.

He had committed himself and the ship. It was final. He felt his breathing getting faster. That was better. It was dangerous to be too relaxed and cocksure.

'Slow ahead.' There was an answering flurry of foam from aft. 'Hard aport!'

Joicey's answer seemed very close. 'Engine slow ahead, sir. Thirty-five of port wheel on!'

Crespin had his face inches from the ticking gyro. Round and further round, until it looked as if the bows were already touching that black wall of cliffs. How deceptive it was, but a quick glance at the radar repeater told him that the reefs were not so distant, and when she completed her turn the ship would be less than a cable clear. But turning towards the open sea would be too dangerous. If either of the strange ships carried effective radar they would see the corvette instantly. This way ensured that the back-echoes from the land would help the labouring *Thistle*, as they had once deceived her.

Willis again. 'Radar . . . bridge. Both echoes still in position, sir. No change.'

Crespin felt the sweat running beneath his cap and splashing across the back of his hand.

'Midships! Steady!' Between his teeth he added, 'Tell Shannon that the target is dead ahead and to stand by to fire starshell.'

Joicey sounded completely engrossed. 'Steady, sir. Course one-nine-zero.'

Wemyss appeared at his side. 'I've told Shannon, sir.'

There was a clank of steel from the forecastle and Wemyss swore savagely. 'Jesus, what the hell is he doing?'

Crespin ignored him as he stared now at the radar repeater. The jagged shape had turned slightly, perhaps caught in the same offshore current. But suppose it was a false echo? Every swing of the *Thistle*'s screw was taking her further and further away from the pick-up point, and even now Barnaby might be coughing out his lifeblood, as his own men had once done while they waited to be saved.

'Six thousand yards, sir.'

'Very good.' Crespin licked his lips. They felt like dust. He could not wait any longer. At any second he might be seen, and there was still so much to do.

He heard himself say, 'Full ahead!'

Magot must have been waiting like a runner under the starting pistol, for the ship seemed to bound alive as the shaft quivered and sent the screw whirling and seething like a millrace.

Crespin dragged his shirtsleeve across his eyes, counting seconds, feeling the ship shaking around him as the revolutions mounted and the bow wave fanned out on either beam in a giant, creaming arrowhead.

'Fire star-shell!'

The four inch lurched back on its mounting, the bang of the explosion sending a sharp shockwave over the bridge like a wind. Seconds later the shell burst with eye-searing brilliance, so that the whole of the seascape changed from sullen blackness to the stark unreality of a film negative. The headland and outflung rocks shone like ice, and the sea which parted in a hissing bank of foam across the corvette's bows gleamed from a million reflecting mirrors in the eerie light of the drifting flare. And there, directly in the path of the glare, lay the two vessels.

Crespin jammed his elbows on the screen and tried to steady his glasses against the ship's violent vibrations. The nearest ship seemed to be some sort of trawler, short and sturdy, with a black funnel and a tiny wheelhouse, but beyond her, and overlapping at either end, was a lower hull, the sleek bows of which shone in the drifting flare like burnished pewter.

He yelled, 'Open fire! The furthest ship is an E-boat!'

Through the quivering lenses he could see the tiny figures which seconds earlier had been standing like stricken waxworks running across the decks, tearing at mooring lines which held both craft together.

Vaguely he heard Shannon yelling, 'With semi-armour piercing! Load, load, load!' His voice was high-pitched and excited. There was the clang of a breechblock and almost instantly the earsplitting crack as the gun opened fire in deadly earnest.

Crespin snapped, 'Port ten!' He must give the other guns a chance. 'Midships!' There was a dull explosion and somebody cursed on one of the voice-pipes.

Shannon shouted, 'Over! Down two hundred!' Another pause. 'Shoot!'

Crespin felt his stomach muscles tighten. Here it came. The lazy, cruising balls of tracer which lifted over the trawler, so deceptively slow until they reached the apex of their climb. Then they seemed to come whipping down with the speed of light, tearing the mind apart with the screech and clang of bursting cannon shells and the wild shriek of ricochets.

Now came the answering fire from the starboard pair of Oerlikons, sharper and faster, the red tracers licking across the dancing water, intermingling with those of the enemy before tearing into the unmoving craft with the force and speed of a giant bandsaw. The steady thud, thud, thud of the pompom, and then another Oerlikon, until the whole night was torn in shreds by noise and violent flashes.

Faces stood out around the bridge, crude and alien in the shifting glare, and from every direction voices seemed to be calling and cursing in a mad chorus.

Crespin heard the enemy's shots hammering against the bridge plating, and ducked as something shattered a glass screen and whipped past his neck like a heated iron.

The enemy was still motionless, but firing with increased vigour now with at least three sets of guns. Maybe the men had died before they could cast off, or perhaps . . . Crespin swung round as a man screamed behind him. In the flare's dying light he saw one of the bridge lookouts staggering against the chart table, tearing at his chest, his hands like claws. In the strange glare his chest seemed to be covered with molten black glass, which spread even as he watched and ran down across the gratings between the man's kicking feet.

Griffin caught the man as he fell and some of the blood splashed across his own face as he yelled, 'Dead, sir! Got the poor bugger right in the throat!'

Crespin turned away. 'Pass the word aft! Stand by starboard side depth-charge!'

Scarlett twisted on the chair as if it was restricting him like a cage. 'Look at that crafty bastard! No wonder he didn't cast off!'

Crespin did not answer. As the *Thistle* surged down on the two rocking vessels he could see quite easily what had happened. The E-boat was using the other craft as a shield, and as the bursting tracers ripped and exploded against wood and metal he saw that the shield was no more than a fishing boat. There was no time to wonder at her presence here, or what the E-boat had seen fit to investigate. In the stabbing gunflashes he

could see the handful of figures crouched along the sagging
bulwark and several inert shapes scattered around a crater
where the wheelhouse had stood before one of Shannon's shells
had found its mark.

Wemyss yelled, 'Those poor devils will be cut to bits!'

Crespin flinched as splinters clanged against the steel plates
beneath his elbows and screamed away into the returning
darkness. The E-boat's commander was no fool. He had been
taken completely by surprise by the *Thistle*'s sudden onslaught,
but provided the corvette maintained her course and furious
speed he was better off to stay where he was.

The flare was almost gone, and to fire another Shannon
would have to stop using his gun for its true purpose. By the
time he reopened fire *Thistle* would be past and she would
cross directly over the E-boat's bows and her waiting torpedoes.

Wemyss could stand the hammering of gun-fire and the
merciless business of killing, but he was no torpedo-boat officer.
Crespin knew far better than he what would happen if the
E-boat was allowed to unleash her salvo against the *Thistle*'s
unprotected flank.

A bell jangled and a man called hoarsely, 'Depth-charge
ready, sir!'

The flare vanished, but the intermingling tracers were more
than enough to pick out the scene. Somewhere aft a gun had
jammed and from below the bridge a man was sobbing, 'Oh,
God, help me! *Help me!*'

Crespin gripped the screen, feeling the sweat running in his
eyes and across his spine. He saw a man on the fishing boat
holding up a shirt like a white flag, and another, it looked like
a boy, leaping overboard in a pathetic effort to save himself.

Wemyss murmured, 'God forgive me!'

Crespin dropped his hand. 'Fire!'

There was a brief thud, and some of the watching men saw
the depth-charge hurtle from its thrower before splashing almost gently within yards of the fishing boat and the madly
thrashing figure alongside.

The depth-charge sank to a distance of fifty feet only before
exploding.

Crespin had carried out such attacks against small surface craft several times, but at thirty knots he had been well clear before the explosion came. This time it seemed to be almost alongside. It was more of a feeling than a sound, and Crespin found himself falling against the voice-pipes as the deck gave a convulsive leap and then swayed right over away from the blast. But even then it was possible to see the towering column of water which appeared to rise higher and higher until it hung over the ship like a towering iceberg. Then with a hissing roar it subsided, while the reeling bridge became a blind, coughing wilderness of struggling men and a cascade of water which seemed to taste of charred wood.

Crespin hauled himself back to the screen. There were several small islands of fire swirling around in a great maelstrom of seething water, and what appeared to be the bows of the fishing boat. There were faint patches of white joining in the grotesque dance, which looked like dead fish, but Crespin knew they were fragments of men.

Shocked and dazed the gunners scrambled back to their weapons and the tracers reached out astern, further tormenting the grisly remains and lighting up the bridge and funnel so that they looked red hot.

Crespin shouted, 'Cease firing! *Cease firing!'*

But the guns continued to fire, and he heard his men yelling and calling to each other like maniacs.

As he threw himself on the bellpush below the screen he saw Scarlett's face shining in the flashes. He was laughing, or shouting, Crespin could not tell in the din around him. But as he found the button he felt Scarlett's fingers on his wrist like steel and heard him yell, 'Let them shoot if they want to! It'll do 'em good!'

Crespin tore his hand away and pressed the button hard. As the cease-fire gong rang tinnily around the ship first one, and then reluctantly, the rest of the guns fell silent.

Crespin hardly trusted himself to speak. He walked to the voice-pipes and felt his shoes slipping in the dead seaman's blood. It was thick, like paint.

'Port twenty!' He was sick and near to collapse and could

not understand the empty calm of his own voice. 'Midships. Steady.'

Joicey was breathing heavily. His face must be right against the mouth of the voice-pipe so that he should not miss an order in the noise and roar of battle.

'Steer zero-one-zero.' The compass dial was swimming in a mist. 'Half ahead.' He made himself look round. 'Report damage and casualties.'

He saw Griffin looking over the broken screen as the ship plunged back along her original course, brushing aside the smouldering flotsam and leaving the rest hidden in merciful darkness.

Petty Officer Dunbar clattered up the bridge ladder and stared around as if surprised to find the bridge still standing. 'Three men wounded, sir. One badly. 'E was aft on the quarter-deck and got a splinter in 'is thigh. Oh an' a stoker broke 'is collar-bone when 'e fell off a ladder in the boiler room.' He saw the dead man beside the chart table and sucked his breath noisily. 'Then there's this one o' course, sir.' He sounded different. Relieved, exalted, sickened, it was impossible to say.

Crespin took a handset from a messenger. 'Captain speaking.'

Magot's voice seemed to come from miles away. 'Nothin' very bad down here, sir. Some leaks from that, er, explosion.' He paused. 'I thought we had been tinfished, sir.'

Crespin dropped the handset. The stench of blood seemed to be all over him. 'Get this man off the bridge.' He saw Dunbar and Lennox the S.B.A. covering the dead seaman with an oil-skin. He wanted to find compassion or disgust. But all he could think of was the unknown stoker who had broken his collar-bone.

'Light in the water, sir! Two points off the port bow!'

His legs moved automatically. 'Slow ahead! Stand by with scrambling nets!'

Somewhere, in another world it seemed, a single gun fired and a shell whimpered across the sea to explode with a muffled roar. Pantelleria's coastal artillery had fired at last, but to no purpose.

'Stop engine.' Crespin felt the side of the bridge pressing

against his chest as he leaned out to watch the soldiers being pulled aboard. There were only two rafts and about half the men who had started out. He screwed up his eyes and tried to clear his brain. Less than four hours ago? It was a lifetime..

Major Barnaby climbed heavily on to the bridge and glanced at the silent figures around him. 'Lost fourteen chaps, including Mr. Muir. Several wounded, too.' He sighed. 'But still.'

Scarlett asked harshly, 'Did it go all right?'

Barnaby seemed to come out of his daze. 'Fair enough. We killed a few Jerries, I should think, and the rest are probably having a good drink before the last of it runs into the sea.' Then he laughed. It was a toneless, empty sound.

'All clear aft, sir.'

'Very well.' Crespin was still watching the soldier. 'Full ahead. Starboard fifteen.' He waited. 'Steady. Steer three-three-zero.'

Wemyss crossed to his side. 'Sir, I think . . .'

Crespin did not turn. 'Keep your thoughts to yourself please. Work out the new course. We will change in thirty minutes.'

When he did look again Wemyss had gone into the chart room and Scarlett and the soldier had disappeared.

Somehow he managed to get into the chair and for several minutes sat staring at the water creaming away on either side of the stem. The raid had succeeded, and no doubt when daylight came Scarlett's promised air cover would be there to see them safely back to base. Scarlett was efficient. Like Gleeson at Gibraltar who had said that results were more important than methods. Like himself, who had deliberately murdered helpless fishermen with no more thought than if he had been crushing a beetle.

There was a step beside him and Petty Officer Joicey's stocky shadow moved on to the grating.

'I've been relieved on the wheel, sir.' He looked over the screen. 'I thought you might like a wet?' He held up a large mug.

Crespin took it with both hands and felt the hot metal shaking uncontrollably against his teeth. It was thick cocoa laced with neat rum. He felt it searing his stomach, holding him together.

'Well, 'Swain, what did you think of that?'

Joicey shrugged. 'I didn't see much from down there, sir. But what I 'eard suited me very well!' Then he took the empty mug and walked back to his wheelhouse. Crespin could hear him whistling.

When he looked over the screen again Pantelleria had vanished.

5 Run Ashore

LIEUTENANT DOUGLAS WEMYSS pushed open the sagging door of the building labelled 'Officers' Club' and strode purposefully through the noisy mass of uniformed figures who crammed the main room from wall to wall. Three air force officers staggered to their feet, and before anyone else could make a move Wemyss wedged himself at the small table and gestured to Porteous who was staring round the place with a mixture of surprise and awe.

Sousse had taken such a battering in the desert fighting that it was, Wemyss supposed, fortunate to have any building left in one piece. But this place was pretty bad, and even the bright tablecloths and red-fezzed waiters could not mask the dinginess and mauling of battle. Union Jacks and giant pictures of Churchill hung everywhere, but served more to cover up splinter holes and cracks left by the bombing than with any sense of patriotism. It was strange to think that such a short time ago officers of the Afrika Korps were probably sitting at this very table below pictures of their own leader.

Porteous laid his cap beside him and said, 'God, it's *hot* in here!'

It was, too. The air was thick with tobacco smoke and a dozen aromas of cooking, and with every window and bomb hole sealed against possible air attack the atmosphere was overpowering.

Above the roar of voices and the clatter of glasses Wemyss realised that someone was singing, and when he stared over the heads at the next table he saw a girl standing on a small dais, the words of her song all but lost in the din. She was dark-skinned, but looked more Greek than Arab, and she was singing in French. As her mouth moved to the accompaniment of a three-piece orchestra her eyes wandered around the crowded room and were, he thought, incredibly sad.

He turned his back and signalled to a harassed waiter. To Porteous he said, 'I've a flask of brandy in my hip pocket. We'll just use the local hooch for washing it down. I don't fancy falling dead from drinking meths, or whatever they use here.'

Porteous nodded absently. 'If you say so.'

Wemyss studied him thoughtfully. Ever since the action with the E-boat he had hardly said a word. For a whole day after returning to Sousse the *Thistle* had laid alongside the old freighter replenishing ammunition, covering the new collection of scars and arranging for the burial of their first real casualty.

Now most of the ship's company were ashore, free from the crowded life between decks for the first time since leaving England.

Wemyss felt the raw alcohol burning his stomach and said, 'Aren't you glad you're ashore and not O.O.D. like Shannon?'

Porteous came out of his trance. 'I keep thinking about those people in the water.' He looked at his glass. 'I've never seen a dead man before. Just relatives, and they were in their beds.'

'I know.' Wemyss wondered what he was doing here with Porteous. At the same time he knew he was glad he had brought him instead of Shannon. Maybe it was because he and Porteous were poles apart. Wemyss was a professional, with little left over except for simple enjoyments of the land. Like this miserable hole, for instance. Porteous was out of his depth, a born bumbler, who tried hard but was as vulnerable as an injured sparrow.

He said roughly, 'We did what we had to. It was us or them. And I must say you got your lads organised well enough when the moment came.'

Porteous's eyes were wretched. 'Leading Seaman Haig did most of it. I heard the order, but I just stood there watching that fishing boat.'

Wemyss thought of Crespin's cold anger on the bridge, his sudden withdrawal into himself. He replied gravely, 'You weren't the only one.' It was no use. They were getting morbid.

He asked suddenly, 'Tell me, what made you volunteer for this caper?' He held up the glass. 'And don't give me all that crap you gave the interview board.'

Porteous smiled for the first time. 'I suppose I was desperate really. The only thing I've ever achieved in my life was getting this commission.'

Wemyss stared at him. '*What?* And you a barrister with an influential father and God knows how many others in the family before you!'

'Exactly. I never felt that I'd got where I was on my own. My father is a hard man in some ways. Even when I joined up it was the wrong thing as far as he was concerned. A waste of time, he said. They'll always need lawyers, but you'll be just one more junior officer, and not a very good one at that. And he wanted me to enter the Guards when at last he realised I was determined to go. All my family have been in the Brigade.'

Wemyss watched him with new understanding. Porteous was not boasting. It was just another relative fact as far as he was concerned. But to Wemyss it was another world. University, the Guards, judges and barristers all came under the category of 'they'. All the same, he was glad to be spared Porteous's obvious uncertainty. Wemyss had made his way up the ladder by a much harder route. As a young apprentice he had sailed out of Liverpool for the Far East with a tough skipper who placed more faith in his fists than in the Merchant Shipping Act when it came to matters of discipline.

Porteous blurted out, 'I suppose I wanted to prove myself *to* myself more than anything. But it doesn't seem to be working here either.'

Wemyss touched his arm. 'Look, my lad, I'm ten years older than you in age but about a hundred in experience. I've knocked around and done a lot of things, and to be fair, I've not had your chances or your background to help me. After this lot's over I'll be lucky to get a job in anything but some clapped-out old tub, while you'll be up there at the Old Bailey with people hanging on your every word and a dirty big Rolls-Royce and chauffeur waiting to whisk you to your club as soon as you've got some poor devil hanged or acquitted. But don't think about that, or what's gone before. This is now, and maybe tomorrow, and what you're doing is important, believe me it is! Leading Seaman Haig probably knows more about depth-charges and eye-splices than you'll ever learn in a month of Sundays, and so he should. He's been in the Andrew for damn near seven years. But if things get really tough, and I mean tough, you'll be the one he comes to for his orders. You'll be the chap who decides if he is going to live or die. Either way, that's all right. But make sure it's to some useful purpose, see?'

Porteous nodded gravely. 'I'll try, Number One.'

'You do that!' Wemyss grinned, both at Porteous's serious face and at his own words. Pompous bastard, he thought. Must be getting stoned. He added, 'In most other ships you could probably sink out of sight until you knew all the answers. In the *Thistle* it's more difficult. And if Commander Scarlett has any say in the matter it'll get *more* difficult rather than easier.'

A tattered Arab sidled between the tables and stopped by Wemyss' massive shoulder. With a furtive glance at the nearest waiter he whipped out a bundle of grimy photographs and hissed, 'Here, Captain, you like good time? You want pretty ladies?'

Wemyss took the top photograph and then pushed it across to Porteous without a word.

Porteous studied it for a full minute. 'Well, *really*!'

Wemyss grinned. 'Obscene, isn't it?'

'It's not the obscenity that annoys me, Number One. It's the very *impossibility* of it!'

Wemyss threw back his head and roared with laughter. 'If only your father could see you now! He'd be proud of you!'

Porteous smiled shyly. 'I think I'm ready for the brandy now, if you don't mind,' he said.

*   *   *

Crespin lay back in one of the battered wardroom chairs with his feet propped on another, his shirt open to catch the churned air from a deckhead fan. The ship was very quiet, with only the lap of water and the creak of fenders against the wrecked freighter to break the silence. If he opened the ward-room door he would hear the occasional shuffle of feet from the quartermaster at the gangway, or the muffled sounds of music from the messdeck where the duty hands listened to the nostalgic voice of Vera Lynn, wrote their letters home, and more to the point, awaited the return of the libertymen who would no doubt need to be lifted into their hammocks after a night ashore.

But he kept the door closed because he wanted privacy. He had stayed in his small cabin alone until Shannon had called on him to report that six of the *Thistle*'s stokers had broken up a café in the town and were being held very firmly by the military police. It had been a good excuse to send Shannon ashore to get it sorted out, and another to quit the cabin, the sides of which seemed to be crushing in on him like a trap.

He reached out for his glass and knocked it on to the carpet. Breathing hard he leaned over and retrieved it, the effort making him sweat more freely than ever, and poured himself another glass of neat gin. The water jug was empty and the bitters were out of reach on the sideboard, and he was too tired to ring for the steward. Too tired, and probably too full of gin to make the effort, he decided.

He wondered vaguely what Wemyss and the others were finding to amuse themselves. Probably the same as himself. Wemyss had obviously wanted to take him ashore with him, if only to break the tension which had built up between them. But it was not Wemyss' fault. There was no single, sensible reason which could be put into words, even if he wanted to.

A man slipped and fell heavily on the deck overhead and he heard Dunbar's voice, harsh and unfeeling. ' 'Ere, give me that bottle, you drunken bastard!' There was a brief scuffle and the sound of a splash alongside. Then Dunbar again. ' 'Ad a good run ashore, 'ave you? Come back full to the gills and poxed up to the eyebrows, I shouldn't wonder!' There was some sort of mumbled protest. 'Well, get forrard on the double and turn in afore I put you on the first lieutenant's report!' The culprit's unsteady feet shuffled away and Dunbar followed him with, 'An' get yer 'air cut!'

The petty officer was probably seething at being kept aboard while his mates enjoyed themselves, Crespin thought.

He looked around the deserted wardroom, the litter of magazines, tattered and out of date, the coloured picture of King George, its glass cracked after some Atlantic gale, and all the companionable homeliness of a small ship, where men were thrown together and had to make the best of it.

What stories this place could tell. And what of the officers who had sat as he was doing with the ship resting in harbour? Some promoted, some killed, but all part of the ship's history.

He took another long drink. It was sour and burned his stomach lining like fire.

His thoughts were getting jumbled again. Now he did not know whether it was the Pantelleria raid or its aftermath which was making him take refuge in the bottle. It was all mixed up in a vague panorama which came and went like the picture in a radar screen.

The scene in the makeshift cemetery, with his men looking clean and strange in their best uniforms. The coffin covered with a Union Jack, the firing party with Shannon in charge, and his own words as he read the burial service. But what did it all mean?

Then the decoded signal which he had read very slowly in his cabin. Maybe that had been the one thing to throw him off balance. The final attack on Pantelleria with a full naval bombardment and air attack had been carried out, Operation Corkscrew as Scarlett had described it, and after a brief parley with the Italian commander the garrison had surrendered. The Italian acceptance of defeat had finished with the words, 'due to lack of water'. It should have made it all worthwhile, should have blotted out the rest of the picture and made every death necessary and unavoidable.

But when Scarlett had made a brief visit to the ship to inform him that she would not be needed for a day or so, that last belief had been shattered.

He could see him now sitting calmly in the chair where his

feet now lay, his head on one side as he stared at Crespin with something like amusement.

'Oh yes, the *water*. Well, of course, that was just to save face, old boy. Actually there was plenty of drinking water on the island in other storage places, and they could have held out much longer if they'd got the stomach for it!'

'Are you saying it was a waste of time, sir?' He could remember exactly the bitterness in his voice.

'A waste? Certainly not!' Scarlett had been very emphatic. 'But the Eye-tie admiral in command knew damn well what would happen to him later if he pushed on with his defence, especially as his country is bound to come on to our side as soon as we invade it in force.' He had paused. 'No, our little raid gave him the *excuse*. Surrender with honour and all that clap-trap, and after the final bombardment he was able to come out like a true gentleman.'

Crespin closed his eyes and tried to work out how many had died because of the required gesture. Half of Barnaby's men, the able seaman on the bridge, that bomber crew and, he swallowed hard, God alone knew how many on the fishing boat.

But it certainly did not worry Scarlett, so why should it bother him in this way? After all, he had been trained to carry out orders without question, had been taught to accept that it is better to lose men obeying wrong instructions than to save lives against the wishes of superiors.

Perhaps after all he resented serving under a temporary officer, just as Scarlett had implied on their first meeting. That would be an acceptable reason for the way he felt, but he knew instantly it was not so.

When he had watched helplessly as his own men had been shot and burned alive by the unknown launch he had called curses of such depth and depravity that he had imagined he would hate his enemies and would kill with no more thought of humanity in war. He had been wrong about that, too. The enemy was faceless, and was better left so. The only real hatred he stored in his heart was for that one man who butchered his small crew so thoroughly, and he was probably dead himself by now.

The door was jerked open and he saw Petty Officer Dunbar watching him anxiously, his cap beneath his arm.

Crespin asked, 'Well, what is it, P.O.?' He made another effort. He hardly recognised his own voice and his words were slurred together like some music hall drunk. 'Are the liberty-men coming aboard?'

Dunbar's eyes moved swiftly from the empty bottle to his face. 'Beggin' yer pardon, sir, but Commander Scarlett is comin' aboard.'

Crespin lurched to his feet, almost knocking over the chair. This was the last straw. There was to be no respite from Scarlett even now. He caught sight of himself in the mirror, wild-eyed and dishevelled, his unruly hair tumbled across his forehead, his shirt patchy with sweat.

He was glad he had been drinking so heavily now. He would tell Scarlett exactly what he thought of him and to hell with the consequences.

Dunbar said cautiously, ' 'E's got a lady with 'im, sir.' He jerked his head towards the deck. ' 'E's got the quartermaster 'elping 'er over the old freighter right now, sir.' He sounded vaguely outraged.

Crespin stared at him. 'Lady? Freighter?' He was not making sense, and the realisation made him suddenly furious.

There was a scuffle of feet on the ladder and the sound of a woman laughing. Scarlett too, booming and full of high spirits.

Dunbar sucked his teeth. 'I *could* get an officer off the guard-boat, sir, if you don't feel up to . . .'

'What's all this?' Scarlett's voice made Crespin's head ring. 'Who's not up to anything?'

He stepped over the coaming, gleaming white in freshly laundered shirt and shorts, his face shining as if from a cold shower. But Crespin was staring at his companion. She was a Wren officer, also in white, with a single blue stripe on her shoulder. She had jet black hair pulled back severely into a bun, and was young and extremely attractive, although she was staring at Crespin with something like amazement.

Scarlett's smile was still broad, but appeared fixed and un-moving. He said, 'Well, Penny, this is John Crespin, the, er, captain.'

Crespin reached out to take her proffered hand and all but fell headlong over the chair. He saw her mouth twitch slightly in a suppressed smile and felt even angrier at their intrusion. More than that, he felt ridiculous.

Scarlett sat down carefully. 'Third Officer Forbes has flown in from Alexandria. She's been working for our people there and has now been seconded to *us*.' He shot the girl a quick grin and she returned it readily. Like a conspirator, Crespin thought.

He replied, 'I didn't know you were coming, sir.'

The girl said quietly, 'I said it was unfair to barge in like this.'

Scarlett glanced at Crespin and asked, 'Why not throw out a bit of hospitality?' He sat back comfortably. 'We'll celebrate, eh?'

Celebrate? What the hell was he talking about? Then Crespin's eye fell on Scarlett's shoulder straps. Was he that drunk? No. There were *four* stripes there now!

Scarlett let his smile fade and nodded gravely. 'Yes, Crespin, a little promotion for services rendered.'

Crespin moved to the hatch and pressed the pantry bell. It took Barker, the steward, several minutes to appear, buttoning on his white jacket and wiping crumbs from his mouth, and in that time Crespin made a last effort to pull himself together. Behind him he heard Scarlett and the Wren conversing together in low tones, and when the girl laughed he felt himself flushing, guessing that they were probably discussing him.

Well, let them, he thought savagely. Scarlett's war was going very well. His promotion was proof of that, and his attractive companion was probably another sort of reward which went with it.

Scarlett said, 'We shall be moving again soon. Things are happening in high places, and with any sort of luck we should be having another crack at the enemy before we're much older.'

Crespin watched Barker padding round the carpet pouring drinks and no doubt soaking up this information for his own uses.

The girl was studying him gravely. She had brown eyes, very large, and beautifully shaped hands.

She said, 'We saw some of your men in town, Captain. They seemed to be enjoying themselves.'

Crespin knew it was a peace offering, but his mind was still hanging on Scarlett's words. More work. Another raid perhaps?

He said at length, 'They've earned it.'

Scarlett beamed. 'There you are, Penny, what did I tell you? He's a true example of the straight-laced professional! Understatement and no flannel, that's him!'

There was a violent thud followed by a string of obscene curses and the sounds of feet across the steel deck overhead. The libertymen were returning.

Scarlet stood up. 'Better be off, old chap. Just wanted to share the good news.' He became serious. 'We must get together. Have a little party. Good for you, you know.' He winked at the girl. 'That's right, isn't it, Penny?'

She watched Crespin gravely. 'Thank you for the drinks, Captain.' She held out her hand and this time Crespin did not stagger. She added, 'I expect we will meet again soon.'

Scarlett guided her through the door where Dunbar was still hovering with a giant flashlamp. By the ladder he paused and said softly, 'I know this isn't the time, old chap, but do try and get a grip on yourself.' The grin came back. 'Not quite the thing, eh?'

Then he was gone.

Slowly and deliberately Crespin walked back to the chair and almost fell into it.

Barker asked timidly, 'Anything more for you, sir?'

Crespin replied slowly, 'A clean glass, if you please.' Then as the steward padded away he said vehemently, 'Damn him to bloody hell!' Then he stood up, and as Barker returned with a fresh glass he brushed past him and walked unsteadily to his cabin.

*   *   *

Not far from the waterfront, in a position which afforded a good view of the harbour during daylight hours, was a small restaurant. Most of the metal-topped tables were deserted at this late hour, and the owner, a massive, shaven-headed Turk, was standing with his back to the kitchen door wearing a look of patient resignation.

Joicey, Magot and Leading Signalman Griffin sat around their table in contemplative silence, for they were so full of red wine and vast portions of rich curry that any attempt at conversation took considerable effort.

It had, on the whole, been a good 'run ashore', for each of the three men had been too long in the Service to waste time in the irritating preliminaries of sightseeing. As Magot had pointed out more than once, 'All these wog places is the bloody same, so let's have a good blowout and be done with it.'

The *Thistle*'s chief engineer certainly looked satisfied. Even in his shoregoing clothes he carried the mark of his trade, for his white cap cover bore one defiant streak of grease and his shirt looked as if it might have been hung on a steam pipe to dry.

He said suddenly, 'There was times when I thought we wouldn't get our run ashore at all.'

Griffin grimaced and poured some more wine. 'When that depth-charge went up I thought the old girl was going right over.'

Magot scowled. '*You* thought! You should'a been in the bloody engine room! It was like being hit with a bleeding sledge-hammer!'

Joicey smiled quietly as he rolled his glass between his fingers. Magot was looking old, he thought. Poor old bugger, he should have been well out of the Navy by now, but because of the war he had been recalled almost before he had got the feel of retirement.

He asked, 'What d'you make of the skipper, Griff ?'

The signalman shrugged. 'Search me. One minute he's a ball of fire and the next he's as broody as a nun in the family way. But he sure knows how to handle a ship. I'll give him that.'

Joicey's eyes were dreamy. Without effort he could hear Crespin's orders in the voice-pipe, could sense his own hold over the ship as he spun the polished spokes of the wheel and waited for the steel sides to cave in on him. Once as the ship had rolled over to the exploding charge he had actually seen water pouring out of the voice-pipe's bell mouth, as if the *Thistle* was already plunging to the bottom. But always Crespin's voice had been there, crisp and definite, with no inkling of doubt or fear. Yet every man was afraid, Joicey knew that well enough. Fear was the spur, not senseless bravery and empty patriotism. Out of fear came hatred, and from it the strength to hit back at the bastards, and keep on hitting.

He made himself relax slightly, for he had found his fingers about to crush the glass like a paper bag.

He said abruptly, ' 'E's a good 'un. Not like that big 'eaded twit Scarlett.' He grimaced. ' 'E's just the sort to drop you *right* in it!'

Griffin grinned. 'All officers are awkward, 'Swain. They're put on this earth to make things difficult for the likes of us.' He drained his glass, 'Still, it could be worse.'

Magot grunted. 'I don't care for that young Shannon. A cold little bastard that one.'

Joicey nodded. 'Too right. 'E's even jealous of poor Mr. Porteous.'

'Then he must be daft!' Magot's eyes were glazed. 'The day they let bloody civvies sew on a bit of gold braid was a bad one for the Andrew.'

Joicey smiled. 'An' what was *you* before you joined? A bleedin' rabbit?'

Magot stared at him. 'I've bin in this regiment so long now I forget what I was, and that's the truth of it.'

Three Australian soldiers who had been sitting at the other occupied table rose in unison and marched steadfastly towards the street door. The Turkish proprietor made as if to stop them and then fell back into his original torpor.

Griffin said, 'Those Aussies didn't pay. Why didn't that big bastard say something to 'em?'

Magot showed his uneven teeth. 'Would *you*? Did you see the size of them squaddies? They'd take him apart if he tried.'

Joicey was fumbling with his money. 'Proper thing, too. A

few weeks ago that bastard was serving Jerries in 'ere! If I 'ad my way 'e'd be in the cage with the rest of 'em!'

Magot was not so drunk that he could not see the danger in Joicey's eyes or hear the tightness of his voice. Almost gently he said, 'Never mind. His daughter'll probably catch a dose off one of my stokers!'

Joicey looked at him and then grinned. 'Let's get back, shall we? Old Jim Dunbar'll be needin' a bit of 'elp by now.'

Picking up their caps they strode into the darkness and soon merged with the throng of figures which headed down towards the harbour and the waiting ships.

*   *   *

Sub-Lieutenant Mark Shannon stopped in a doorway and lit a cigarette. For a few moments he stood breathing deeply and inhaling while he waited for his muscles to relax and the flood of anger to disperse. He had just been to the military police post where the six stokers had been held for escort. It had been horrible and disgusting, and all the more so because of the watching soldiers. The military policemen had seemed genuinely amused by the stokers and stood grinning like apes while he had addressed the culprits.

The stokers had been battered and bleeding, their uniforms stained with drink and vomit, and one of them was so far gone that he had sunk to his knees in the middle of Shannon's speech. And all of them had been totally unrepentant. It was sickening, and so damned unfair.

He crushed out the cigarette and turned into a narrow street, his direction marked only by a lane of stars between the houses where the low roofs seemed to reach out and touch as if for mutual support.

No matter what he achieved, no matter how hard he worked, there was always the let down at the end of it. Shannon never spoke to anyone of his past life, for in truth he was genuinely ashamed of it. His upbringing in Manchester where his father, a big, shabby man, worked in one of the great cotton mills, and his mother fought an everlasting battle to keep her tiny terraced house from falling into total decay. He could not understand how his parents managed to appear so content with their existence, and his mother's persistent hopes for him to 'settle down' and get a safe job like his father did nothing to help.

He had at least managed to avoid the mill, and after leaving school had become a shop assistant in one of the larger stores, where his dark good looks made up for his total lack of interest in the work. Day by day he watched the rich tradesmen and their wives across the counter, and the county people who came into town once a month to do their shopping, and out of his constant envy grew a burning determination to break away, to assert himself in his rightful place.

The war had been a godsend, and having volunteered for the Navy, which if nothing else would take him well away from Manchester, he settled down with a determination and a devotion which left his instructors baffled.

When serving as an ordinary seaman aboard a destroyer he had maintained a constant guard against any sort of companionship or intimacy which was offered by his companions. He said and did nothing which might show his superiors that he was one of the crowd and not of their sort, a potential officer.

In the end he had been recommended, and at the officers training establishment at Hove had again applied the same zeal as before, sharing nothing with his companions, avoiding the possible failures, and mixing only with those who could help him attain his goal. When others went ashore to relax Shannon stayed with his books and his manuals. When they avoided extra duty, he was always there, smart and willing. He had to succeed, and he did, with room to spare.

At first it had been unnerving to sit and drink with the very people he had once served and envied. But he was a good learner and was also a good listener. He even managed to overcome his northern accent, and unlike some junior officers he was ready to go on learning. For to Shannon it was only a beginning.

His last home leave had been a failure. Instead of being proud of his visible achievements his parents had been moist-

eyed and clinging. His father had even wanted to take him
along to the Working Men's Club. He was that proud. Even to
think of it made Shannon come out in a sweat.

His first appointment to a fleet destroyer based at Scapa
Flow had been another let down. Swinging around the buoy,
with occasional dashes to sea as escort for a battleship or carrier. But no action, and no possible chance of further recognition.

When the call for volunteers for special service had arisen
he had been the first to see it. His commanding officer, a grave
and unassuming man, had studied him for some minutes and
had recommended him without protest or congratulation. He
was probably glad to see the back of him, Shannon often
thought. Most likely jealous of the success he had had in Rosyth
when there had been a cocktail party aboard. The other officers
had had to be content with their wives for the most part.
Shannon had knocked them sideways with two smart girls
from the dockyard typing pool. He could see them looking at
him now. The women with envy. The officers, well, they just
looked.

He thought about the *Thistle* and felt the blood pumping
through him as he relived the short action with the E-boat.
Never in his life had he imagined it would be, like that. It was
sheer, breathtaking excitement, the noise and the vivid colours
of tracers and shell-bursts making his body quiver as if from
elation or some overwhelming sexual satisfaction. It made up
for so much, and even helped to overcome the disgust he felt
for the captain for not showing some of Scarlett's pride in the
action. And Porteous, he was no better. He should never have
been given a commission. He probably got it because of his
father's influence. There could be no other reason. Fat, soft
and stupid. How the men must laugh at him behind his back.
It was humiliating, and no better than the stokers he had just
left.

But Scarlett, now there was a man. He seemed to thrive on
every challenge, to be head and shoulders above anyone he
had ever known.

Well, he would show all of them, and Scarlett would be the

one to help him. It just needed the moment, and that was
bound to come. On his way to the M.P.s' post he had seen Scarlett driving a jeep with reckless speed over the rutted road, a
laughing Wren officer beside him, her teeth shining with
excitement and obvious pleasure. That was the way to live.
The only way. People did not respect weaklings and those
who touched their caps.

A figure stepped from a deep doorway and reached out for
his arm. 'Pardon, m'sieu, but I can make the introduction to a
fine and lovely girl. My daughter, m'sieu, very pure, jus' sixteen. You would like her, m'sieu?'

Shannon stared at him wildly, caught off guard. That was
the one experience still lacking, but the thought of ending up
with some terrible disease pushed the tantalising picture of a
young girl with dark, rounded limbs far to the back of his
mind.

He snarled, 'Get away from me, you dirty bastard! I'll call
a patrol if you're not out of my sight in three seconds!'

He strode on, his breathing fast and uneven. Who did he
think he was speaking to, for God's sake? Some stupid sailor?
He could wait his time. Someone like Scarlett's young Wren,
for instance. He quickened his pace, his mind already busy on
this new possibility.

Behind him the man in the doorway shook his head sadly
and continued his vigil. He would not have long to wait.

                    *   *   *

The following morning found the moored *Thistle* going
about her daily routine with only a procession of defaulters
as evidence of the hangover from the night before.

Wemyss watched as Joicey marched the last man away
from the little table which had been erected on the quarterdeck. Fortunately there was only the one serious case. The rest
were either charged with being drunk and fighting, drunk and
malicious damage in one café or another, or just plain drunk.
The last one had almost got away with it, and but for a last
minute lapse as he climbed aboard would be none the worse
for his experiences.

Joicey's face had been inscrutable as he had read out the offence, his eyes fixed on the bared head of the offending rating.

'Finch, Able Seaman, sir. Urinatin' on the quarterdeck.'

'Anything to say?' Wemyss wondered how *he* would have answered.

'Don't remember nothin', sir.'

It was strange the things that sailors got up to, he thought.

Then he saw Crespin coming towards him and drew in his stomach. The captain looked pale and strained, and if half of what he had heard was true, had good reason for it.

He saluted formally. 'Defaulters dismissed, sir.' He bit his lip. Crespin's face was quite impassive. Like a mask.

'I'm afraid there's a deserter, sir.'

Surprisingly, Crespin remained unmoved. 'Probably overstayed his leave, Number One. Sleeping it off somewhere, I expect.'

Wemyss shook his head. 'I doubt it, sir. He went ashore alone, and some of the lads saw him cadging a lift on an army lorry.'

Crespin nodded absently. 'Well, inform the authorities. He can't go anywhere from here.' He paused. 'Who was it, by the way?'

Wemyss watched him steadily. 'Able Seaman Trotter, sir.'

'Trotter? I can't place him.'

'The man you thought you recognised in Portsmouth, sir.'

Crespin swung round. 'Are you sure?'

Wemyss nodded. He could not recognise this mood at all.

'Well, find him, Number One. Use the duty watch if you like, but *find* him!'

Wemyss stared helplessly at the mass of shimmering buildings along the waterfront. 'I'll do what I can, sir.'

Crespin seemed to be speaking his thoughts aloud. 'If a man deserts he must have a reason. And until I know what it is you'll go on looking, understand?'

He turned on his heel and Wemyss watched him walk towards the bridge.

What had got into him now? he wondered. Any deserter

was a damn nuisance, but more danger to himself than the ship. And in a company like this one it was only to be expected.

He saw Porteous wandering aimlessly below the boat davits and called, 'Here, Sub, I've got just the job for *you*!'

6 Scarlett's Circus

AFTER a few days of fruitless search and enquiries the hunt for Able Seaman Trotter was called off, and with the sudden arrival of fresh orders he was all but forgotten as once more the little corvette prepared for sea.

Tied up as she had been to the listing wreck in Sousse harbour she had somehow faded into the backwater of preparations for invasion and battle, and it was with something like relief that Crespin studied his brief instructions and destination. While the Allies continued to mass men and shipping for what would certainly be the largest amphibious operation ever undertaken, the invasion of Sicily, the orders for *Thistle* seemed to indicate that she, at least, was to be pointed in the opposite direction.

Crespin could not ask Scarlett for further information as he had flown out of Sousse two days earlier, accompanied as always by Third Officer Forbes, who was now officially known as his Operations Officer, although on the *Thistle*'s lower deck her real role in things was viewed with a more earthy appreciation and no little envy.

So beneath a cloudless sky the *Thistle* left harbour and sailed east, her destination Benghazi some thousand miles deeper into the Mediterranean.

Benghazi had never been much of a place, and after months and months of bitter fighting with the tide of desert war swaying back and forth across and around it like an iron juggernaut it would be even less hospitable than Sousse. But the four days

it took the ship to reach there had a marked effect on her company. The placid sea, a sky empty of prowling aircraft and a
busy daily routine did more to pull the men together and build
up a new camaraderie than Crespin had dared to hope.

The ship had a kind of jaunty independence which transmitted itself to her company, and her imposed isolation
strengthened rather than dampened the spirits of even the most
pessimistic men aboard. The stark memories of Pantelleria
faded with the ship's wake, and some men probably believed
that the top brass no longer knew what to do with the *Thistle*
and that she would play out her existence, detached and unreachable, until the end of the war.

Within an hour of the anchor splashing into the clear water
below the town nearly everyone aboard knew that any such
belief was an illusion. Crespin went ashore in the motor boat
to find Scarlett, and after searching amidst the ruined buildings for someone in authority was driven at high speed in a
Bren carrier by a giant Australian corporal who punctuated
his savage gear changes with questions about the war, the next
supply convoy, women, and the possibilities of taking on the
Thistle at cricket, while Crespin clung to the hot metal side of
the vehicle, half blinded by dust and almost too shaken to
reply.

On the outskirts of the town the Australian slewed the Bren
carrier to a halt and pointed towards two large canvas tents.

'There you are, Cap'n! That's where your fellah hangs out.'
He grinned and mopped his face. 'We've had him here before,
of course. The lads call this outfit Scarlett's Circus!'

It was certainly a strange place to find part of the Royal
Navy, Crespin thought. Around the two tents were scattered
vehicles of every size and make, British, Italian and German.
The only thing they had in common was that they were all
wrecks, salvage from battlegrounds which had been towed to
this point on the map to resemble one great junk yard.

A few half-naked seamen were busy with acetylene burners
on some of the wrecks, and others were checking over piles of
salvaged weapons and freshly cut slabs of armour plate as if
they were building their own arsenal, while a fierce, red-
bearded R.N.R. lieutenant strode from one party to the next

issuing orders and looking over the finds with the zeal of a scrap-dealer.

He saw Crespin watching him and hurried across, darting a suspicious glance at the Australian before saying, 'Glad to see you, sir. I'm Moriarty, engineer officer of this outfit, God help me!'

Crespin smiled. 'I was just wondering what you were doing.'

Moriarty nodded soberly. 'You may well ask. Commander, pardon me, I mean *Captain* Scarlett is no easy man to work for. But to give him his due he doesn't spare himself either.' He pushed his cap to the back of his head. 'I've been up here for weeks, and the Army has been helping quite a bit to collect all this stuff from the desert.' He waved vaguely towards the sea. 'Scarlett has got his private fleet here, too. An old Greek schooner with an engine straight out of the ark, a caique, an armed motor launch which had been abandoned on a sandbar after being shot up by the Luftwaffe, and which *I* had to put together with my own hands, and an armed yacht.' He sighed. 'The latter is the best of the bunch. It belonged to a French colonial official and was taken over by the Italians. Then Jerry commandeered it from his gallant ally and converted it to a patrol boat, and *we* captured it when Rommel did a bunk.'

Crespin grinned. 'And where does all this hardware come in?'

'I've got to turn this gallant little fleet into a suitably protected fighting force. A bit of armour here and there, a few guns which my lads have begged, borrowed or stolen, and a certain amount of divine belief in indestructibility!'

'Ah, Crespin.' Scarlett appeared through a flap in the nearest tent. 'Getting up to date, eh?'

Moriarty's smile faded and he turned and hurried back to his men.

Crespin said, 'Quite a going concern here, sir.'

Scarlett was dressed in khaki drill again and looked even more tanned than before. He said absently, 'I flew in just in time. The Army has been getting a bit slack. But I jollied 'em along and they've lent me some sappers to bring in some more gear from the desert.' He watched the sweating seamen. 'Just a few more days and I'll be ready.'

He turned and Crespin followed him into the tent. It was tall and cool after the dusty heat outside, and after the chaos and disorder of the abandoned vehicles appeared almost clinically neat. Piles of crates and cases of ammunition, blocks and cordage, spare canvas and coils of wire, everything numbered as if in a naval barracks. It was certainly impressive.

Then Crespin saw the girl. She was sitting at a trestle table, a hand over one ear, as she spoke quietly into a field telephone. She was wearing khaki slacks and an open-necked shirt, and her jet-black hair was no longer neat but speckled with sand and dust.

'Nice to see you again, sir.' She sounded as if she meant it.

Crespin grinned. 'What does it feel like to be here? Surrounded by thousands of lonely soldiers?'

She grimaced and gestured towards the piles of ammunition cases. 'I feel safer with these sometimes!'

Scarlett sat down in a canvas chair and said, 'I've not got you here just to admire the view, Crespin.' He was smiling, but sounded vaguely annoyed. 'There's one hell of a lot to do, so you must get cracking right away.' He ticked off the points on his fingers. 'You've heard about my special boat squadron from Moriarty, I gather. He's a garrulous bastard, but quite a good engineer. Well, the boats are almost ready, and when we eventually get to grips with the enemy, up in the Adriatic and so forth, they'll be worth more than all your precious destroyers and cruisers. They can sneak in and out of the islands and inlets, drop partisans and guerillas, and generally play merry hell!'

Crespin eyed him calmly. 'That'll be a while yet surely, sir? We've got to take Sicily first, and then there'll be Italy.' He paused, seeing the annoyance growing on Scarlett's dark features.

'I'm coming to that!' Scarlett stood up and walked rapidly across the sand. 'I want your ship to start training. I have laid on a good programme for you, so get down to it as of now.'

'Training? I'd have thought that a bit unnecessary, sir?' Crespin thought he saw the girl give a slight shake of the head, but he did not care. It was amazing the way Scarlett managed to get under his skin. Now he was making him rush to the defence of his ship like an anxious hen to a chick. The realisation only made him angrier.

Scarlett said smoothly, 'Yes. I want you to get used to working at night. Rendezvous with landing parties which I will arrange along the coast. Practise berthing and disembarking men in complete darkness until your people know their jobs blindfolded. And I want you to make your officers change round with their work, so that even if you get your head shot off someone can take over instantly.'

'How long have I got for all this, sir?' Crespin kept his voice level, but it was not easy.

'Two weeks at the outside. If you're no good by then you're no use for the sort of thing I have in mind, right?'

A petty officer in filthy overalls peered into the flap and said, 'Beg pardon, sir, but we've just hauled in another crate of nine millimetre ammo. Shall I get my lads to put it in here?'

Scarlett stared at him. 'Do I have to do everything around here? God, man, *use your initiative*!'

The petty officer flushed. He was elderly for his rank and had probably been in the Navy for twenty years or so, Crespin thought.

Scarlett snatched up his cap and sighed. 'Very well then. I'll come and have a look.' He paused and shot Crespin a meaning glance. 'Initiative and guts. That's all I need in this unit!' He stamped off calling for Moriarty.

Crespin pulled his pipe from his pocket and began to jab tobacco into the bowl with quick, angry thrusts, aware that the girl was studying him across the trestle table.

She said quietly, 'He's been working pretty hard, you know.'

Crespin struck a match and said harshly, 'And so have a few million others!' He relented slightly. 'Is it always like this?'

She sighed and spread out her arms. 'Usually. Captain Scarlett uses his authority to get what he wants, and he sometimes treads on a few toes in the process. But it is for a good purpose, and most people seem to understand that in the end.'

'And I suppose that if his charm fails he sends you in to tip the balance?'

She did not drop her eyes. 'You could put it like that.' Her lips puckered in a smile. 'Men really are rather horrid!'

'Especially with each other.' Crespin blew the smoke towards the roof of the tent and watched it hang motionless. 'I'm sorry if I was rather rude just now. It's not your fault.'

She did not reply directly. 'Captain Scarlett has had a lot of experience in managing people, you know.' She ran her eyes over Crespin in a slow appraisal. 'He's a good bit older than you are, and comes from a different sphere of things.'

Crespin stared at her. She was summing him up, giving her considered assessment. A mere girl, who due to somebody's influence or favour was in a position to make a game of this sort of thing.

He said coldly, 'You think I'll be good enough then, do you?'

She looked at him calmly. 'I cannot answer that, sir, now can I?'

At that moment Scarlett reappeared in the tent. He said, 'Well, that's settled.'

Crespin looked from one to the other. It was just as if the whole interview had been stage-managed before he had arrived. After he had gone Scarlett and the girl would exchange notes to see if he had measured up to the task in hand, like a schoolboy applying for his first job.

He said shortly, 'Perhaps I can return to my ship, sir?'

Scarlett nodded. 'Certainly. Time ashore is time wasted as far as I am concerned.' Then he smiled warmly. 'We can start getting down to work after lunch. That'll give you time to warn your people what to expect, eh?'

When he left the tent Crespin found that the Bren carrier had disappeared without waiting for him. Or perhaps Moriarty's men had sawn it up for scrap. Either way he would be damned if he would ask Scarlett to lend him some transport. By the time he had found his way back to the jetty he was sweating, tired and still seething with anger.

If the interview had been a strain, the days which followed it were a living nightmare. Scarlett had chosen his location well, for whereas Benghazi had once been a hinge in the desert campaign for Englishman and German alike, it was now a backwater, and he was able to put his strangely assorted force through its paces with nobody but an amused and critical army garrison to break the isolation.

True to his word he had the ship going through every conceivable manœuvre and situation, some of which he seemed to dream up on the spur of a moment. Once he sent a brief summons for both Crespin and Wemyss to report to him ashore, then immediately sent a signal to the ship ordering it to weigh anchor and patrol a mile offshore.

The approaches were littered with wrecks, and handling the ship was no easy matter. Crespin had been forced to stand in helpless silence while the *Thistle* had edged this way and that, her squat funnel pouring smoke as her screw thrashed from ahead to astern, churning up sand and weed until it looked as if she was already aground.

It seemed as if he was always in open conflict with Scarlett, always making excuses for his ship, so he held his tongue and watched the *Thistle*'s efforts without a word. She had managed to scrape her side against one small wreck, but had at last reached deeper water without further mishap. It turned out later that it was due more to Joicey's efforts on the wheel than to any coherent orders from the bridge.

Under cover of night they had made several mock landings and pickups from vague chart references, and had fought off sudden attacks laid on by 'hostile' forces, enthusiastically played by the local troops, who were not averse to using their fists as well as thunder-flashes and carefully aimed rocks.

Sometimes Scarlett accompanied them on manœuvres, and without warning would point at an officer or rating and yell cheerfully, 'You're dead!' Then he would peer round and shout, 'Come on then! Who takes over? Jump to it!'

The only one to escape from direct interference was Magot, but as he squatted in his engine room and watched the crazy demands of his telegraph dial he found little comfort from that.

Crespin's early resentment hardened over the days into a determination which he found almost alien to himself. From disordered and dangerous manœuvres it seemed to change into a personal conflict between him and Scarlett, with neither speaking openly of it, yet each pressing the other to fresh limits at every opportunity.

Towards the end of the second week Crespin had to admit that the methods, though crude and dangerous, were certainly having a marked effect on his ship. During lulls or around the wardroom table there was never any lack of speculation or discussion about what might happen next, and even Porteous, a ready target for Scarlett's boisterous barrage, seemed to have found a little more confidence. He had certainly lost weight.

Shannon went about his duties with a fierce determination which left him spent and morose by the end of the day, and Wemyss had been heard to say more than once, 'If the Jerries don't kill us, that bugger will!'

And then it was suddenly over, and they looked at each other as if wondering where all the days had gone.

With the ship swinging gently at her anchor and the town shining eerily beneath a pale crescent of moonlight Crespin went ashore to collect his orders. This time he went in an army jeep, but when he reached the site he imagined for a few moments he had taken the wrong road. One of the big tents had gone, and apart from a sentry there was no sign of life at all. Only the stripped remains of salvaged vehicles stayed to mark the extent of Scarlett's efforts, like bones from some nightmare feast.

He found the girl sitting alone in the remaining tent, crouching beside a hissing pressure lamp, her hair shining in the glare like polished glass.

She looked up and smiled. 'As you can see, sir, the circus has moved on to the next village.'

Crespin sank down into a chair, the strain and prepared guard slipping away like steam. She was a very attractive girl. Again he felt the nagging sensation of envy.

She said, 'Captain Scarlett has flown off to Algiers to see the Americans.'

Crespin nodded. 'In his private plane, I suppose.'

'Not exactly.' She was tapping her teeth with a pencil, her eyes shining with quiet amusement. 'The Americans put one at his disposal.'

Crespin glanced around the tent. All packed up and crated,

he thought. And the girl was sitting there alone in the desert. One more fragile possession to be collected when and where Scarlett decided.

He felt suddenly reckless. 'Are you leaving soon?'

She pouted. 'Yes. Back to Sousse.' She pushed a bulky envelope across the table. 'I was just waiting to give you this. You're to return to Sousse immediately and await instructions.'

Crespin watched her. 'So we're off again.'

'I don't know exactly what's to happen next. But it certainly looks like the big invasion.'

Crespin picked up the envelope and weighed it in his hands. Slowly he said, 'When we get to Sousse.' He paused. He was on dangerous ground. 'There may be a few days before we move again.'

She gave no indication of her thoughts. 'Maybe.'

'I was wondering if we could meet? Have a drink perhaps?'

She studied him gravely. 'In Sousse?'

'Yes.'

She looked at the end of the pencil. Considering it. 'When the cat's away? Something like that, d'you mean?'

Crespin could feel his shirt clinging to his skin. Almost violently he said, 'No, I didn't mean something like that!'

She smiled, showing her teeth. 'All right. Yes, it might be fun.'

Crespin stood up. Somehow she had retained the advantage. He said awkwardly, 'I'd better go now.'

She nodded, her eyes distant. 'Just when we were getting acquainted.'

Crespin knew she was laughing at him again, but he did not care. He said, 'I'll try to be sober next time we meet.'

Then he walked out into the moonlight, feeling better than for a very long time.

*   *   *

Two days out from Benghazi there was a sudden change in the weather, and by the time the *Thistle* had reached the protective coastline of Tunisia it had worsened considerably.

Gone was the blue sky and placid water, the drowsy heat and
steady motion which many of the ship's company had come to
accept as permanent features of the Mediterranean, and while
the north-westerly wind mounted to a full gale the sea changed
to a wilderness of short, savage waves which threw the corvette about with no less vigour than the Atlantic.

On the afternoon of the fourth day Crespin stood on the
grating at the port side of the bridge and watched with narrowed eyes as the ship moved slowly towards her new berth
in Sousse harbour. He was thankful that it was no longer
alongside the old freighter, for with only one engine at his
disposal manœuvring in the strong gusts was no easy matter.
Twice he edged the bows towards the jetty and each time the
stern swung away before the cursing line-handling parties
could get their mooring ropes ashore, where despondent and
dripping in spray some native workers waited to receive them.

Wemyss shouted, 'The harbour looks pretty deserted now,
sir!'

Crespin nodded. It was true. Apart from an elderly cruiser
and some support ships the *Thistle* had the pick of moorings.
The landing craft and destroyers, the encamped troops and the
gathered clutter of invasion equipment had been spirited away
as if by magic. As the girl had said, it would not be long now.

He watched the bows edging towards the jetty once more
and saw a burly seaman poised like a statue, a heaving line at
the ready, while from aft he could hear Porteous calling
anxiously to his own men as the tossing triangle of water les-
sened between the ship and the land.

'Stop engine!' Crespin leaned out over the screen and saw
the line snake across the rail to be caught by some half a dozen
yelling Arabs. The eye of the wire headrope followed jerkily
above the water and was eventually dropped around a massive stone bollard, and from the quarterdeck there came fresh
confusion as two lines fell short alongside before a third was
seized and made fast.

He snapped, 'Full astern!' The deck trembled violently as
the screw thrashed the water into a great gusher of white froth
and slowly but surely pulled the stern round, lending its
weight and power to the straining seamen who skidded on the

wet deck and threw themselves against the tautening wires.

'Stop engine!' Crespin felt the hull sidle against the waiting fenders and give a final convulsive shudder. To Wemyss he said, 'Not the easiest place in the world to get into.'

But Wemyss was still staring over the screen. 'Look at that, sir!' His tanned features split into a grin. 'Now that is what I call a *proper* reception!'

Crespin followed his stare and saw a jeep pulling to a halt almost opposite the ship. A seaman was at the wheel, but there was no mistaking the slim figure beside him. She was still wearing khaki slacks and shirt and on her head, barely held in place against the eager wind, a bright yellow sou'wester. She was peering up at the bridge, her eyes squinting against the blown dust and sand, her shirt already blotchy with spray.

Some of the seamen were already swarming ashore to secure the springs and breast ropes, and more than one stopped in his tracks to whistle with appreciation until herded away by Petty Officer Dunbar.

Wemyss said, 'She's a damn pretty girl. I don't know what use she is out here, and I don't much care. I just know it's always good to see her.'

Crespin saw Dunbar giving the girl a hand to climb aboard the maindeck, his normally severe face split into a smile of welcome. Like Wemyss he seemed to look on her as part of *their* world now. Crespin knew Wemyss was watching him and wondered if his face displayed some of his own feelings. During the voyage back he had thought about her a good deal, but the suddenness of the confrontation had momentarily unnerved him.

He said, 'I'm going below, Number One. When the ship is properly secured you can dismiss the hands and send them to tea.' He knew that his words were both unnecessary and stupidly formal. Wemyss' broad grin was no help either. He added sharply, 'And make sure the gangway staff are properly in the rig of the day. I don't want some bloody reprimand from that cruiser because the ship looks like a day excursion to Southend!'

Wemyss saluted smartly, 'Aye, *aye*, sir!' But he was still grinning.

When Crespin reached the deck he found the girl standing below an Oerlikon mounting, talking with Magot. Crespin saluted. 'This is unexpected. But I'm very glad to see you.' Magot stood his ground, shifting his eyes from one to the other.

Crespin asked, 'Was there something, Chief?'

Magot wiped his hands on his overalls and muttered, 'It can wait, sir.' With obvious reluctance he moved back to the engine room hatch, where two stokers watched the girl with unwavering admiration.

She said, 'Sorry to drop in like this.' She looked around the upper deck. 'It looks different this time. More businesslike!'

Crespin watched her. She seemed tense, less confident than at their last meeting.

He said, 'Come below. You must be wet through.'

The wardroom was very quiet after the wind and activity of the upper deck. He watched her as she tugged off the sou'-wester and brushed away some strands of hair from her face.

'I'll get you some tea,' he said awkwardly. 'Then we can talk.'

She turned and faced him squarely, her eyes troubled. 'I'm very sorry. But this is an official visit.' Her words seemed to fall like stones in the damp air. 'Captain Scarlett flew in this forenoon.' She studied the changing emotions on Crespin's face. 'So there it is.'

'I see. Thank you for coming anyway.' He could not disguise the bitterness. 'It's as well you warned me. I might have come barging in on *you* for a change. I wouldn't want to upset things between you and Scarlett.'

Her lips parted slightly and for a moment she looked as if he had attempted to strike her. Then she gave a small shrug and pulled a sealed envelope from inside her shirt.

'These are your new orders, sir.' She was in control again. 'You're to sign for them, if you please.'

Crespin stared wretchedly at the envelope. 'What is it this time?' He did not really care. He had made a wrong move again and the change in her tone made him suddenly ashamed.

She walked across the wardroom and stared thoughtfully at the ship's crest. 'Operation Husky is to start on the tenth of the month. It's all there in the orders. The combined British and American forces are to invade Sicily's south-east section, stretching about one hundred miles from Syracuse to Licata.' She turned slightly to watch him as he flattened the closely typed pages on the table. 'General Eisenhower and the C.-in-C. are already in Malta, and the whole invasion fleet is waiting for the order.'

Crespin's eyes moved rapidly down the pages. Rendezvous points, recognition signals, landing beaches and objectives, it was all there. He asked quietly, 'Don't they know about the weather?' The invasion date was four days away, and if conditions stayed like this it could be a living hell for the landing craft and their cargoes of men and tanks. Due to the speed of the military build up most of the landing craft had been used for ferrying troops, and the young officers who commanded these unwieldy vessels had little experience or training in the actual business of beaching on a defended coast. In this sort of weather some of them might capsize before they reached the beaches. Others could miss their objectives altogether.

She said, 'There isn't any choice, sir.' The *sir* turned in Crespin's heart like a knife. 'The met people say that it could blow itself out in a couple of days. By that time it would be too late to change anything, even if the weather got worse. Some ships might not get their recall in time and go ahead on their own. Others could get scattered and picked off by the Luftwaffe.'

Crespin did not need telling. This invasion was a must. It was the pattern upon which Europe's fate would be decided.

He turned over a page and stopped. There was an addition typed in red and headed: 'Attention of Commanding Officer, *Thistle*.'

Before he could start reading she crossed swiftly to his side and laid one hand directly across the paper. When he turned she was watching him, her eyes apprehensive and unhappy.

She said, 'The enemy must know all about the preparations for the invasion. He's had plenty of time. Our people have to have all the help they can get.' She made no attempt to remove her hand, nor did she take her eyes from his face. 'Captain Scarlett put this plan to the C.-in-C. and the Americans. Both have agreed that it is possible, even desirable,' she faltered, 'under the circumstances.'

Crespin took her hand and gently moved it aside. Her fingers
felt smooth but ice cold. He could feel her eyes watching him
as he read through the remainder of the orders.

Then he said dryly, 'A diversionary action, I think they call
it.' He felt vaguely light-headed. 'It doesn't allow much time.'

She stood back. 'Is that all you've got to say?' Her voice was
trembling.

'What else *is* there to say?' Crespin looked round the shabby
wardroom feeling suddenly trapped. 'I'm to take this ship to a
point north-west of Sicily and cover a raid with a force of
marine commando. Scarlett's intelligence officers have assured
him that the local Sicilian "underground" is ready to launch
an attack from inland to coincide with ours, so that the Germans will have to withdraw some pressure from the southern
beaches.' He pushed the papers across the table. 'Always
assuming, of course, that Jerry hasn't got the whole place
covered as it is!'

'What are you going to do?'

'Do?' Crespin stared at her. 'I don't have any choice in the
matter!'

Wemyss stepped quietly into the wardroom, his smile
fading as he saw the expressions on their faces.

Crespin said, 'We're getting under way again at 2100. I shall
speak to the ship's company before that time, but I'll fill you
in on details right now.' He gestured towards the table. 'Sit
there and read that lot. It'll give you something to think
about.'

Across Wemyss' shoulder he studied the girl and said, 'I take
it you have to get back?'

She nodded. 'I'm late already.'

Crespin walked with her into the passageway, conscious of
her nearness, the touch of her arm against his sleeve as he
guided her to the ladder.

She stopped suddenly and faced him. 'I'm sorry about this.
I really am.'

'I was looking forward to that drink, too.' He tried to move
his mouth into a smile but it would not come.

'I didn't mean that!' Her eyes flashed in the grey light.
'When I heard what you've been asked to do I wanted to hide.

Then I thought it would be better if I brought the orders myself. I had to see you before you left.'

Crespin listened to the whine of wind against the moored
ship. So it was as bad as that?

He said quietly, 'I'm glad you came. I mean it. Otherwise
I'd have thought . . .'

She interrupted, 'You'd have thought what you *did* think.
That my relationship with Captain Scarlett was something
more than official.'

Overhead a voice called wearily, 'Hands to tea! Men under
punishment to muster!' Another world. The ship living her
separate, controlled existence, as if nothing else mattered.

He said, 'If I get back perhaps we can keep that date?'

She nodded firmly, and he saw that her eyes were shining
with something other than the reflected light.

'*When* you get back! And I shall hold you to it!' Then she
turned and ran quickly up the ladder.

Crespin followed her and watched as she climbed down the
brow and into the waiting jeep. She looked very small against
the background of bombed buildings and angry clouds. As the
jeep moved away into the swirling dust she turned and shouted
against the wind. He could see her white teeth, the hair flapping rebelliously from under the oversize sou'wester. She could
have been calling good luck, he thought. Or goodbye.

He turned and walked slowly towards the bridge, his mind
dragging itself reluctantly back to those orders.

When he reached the deserted bridge he glanced down at the
place where the seaman had died. That man, and the one who
had deserted, would be well out of it, he decided bitterly.

Then he crossed to the chartroom and slammed the door behind him.

Perhaps the inexperienced officers who commanded the
landing craft were better off after all. They at least would go
into battle knowing nothing of the odds against them.

He opened the chart and stared for several minutes at the
craggy coastline before marking the point of the proposed
gesture with a small cross.

In his mind's eye he could picture the place quite well
enough, although he had never been within a hundred miles of

it. Small, rocky and backed by high, featureless hills. A place where people had scraped a bare living since time began without knowing why.

He picked up a pencil and parallel rulers and began to work. In a few days they would have something to remember, he thought bitterly. It was to be hoped that they would appreciate it.

7   Better to be Hated

FAR from improving, the weather got steadily worse, and within twenty-four hours of leaving harbour the *Thistle* was crashing into the teeth of a great north-westerly gale. The short, steep waves were replaced by long ranks of towering rollers with savage-looking crests which broke across the reeling ship in a continuous procession and even burst high over the bridge.

She was accompanied on the first part of the journey by a powerful new fleet destroyer, for to give her sudden disappearance from Sousse some recognisable purpose to any interested enemy agent the stage had to be properly set. The destroyer had taken on some impressive wooden crates a few hours before sailing, each left on the jetty just long enough to be noted, and clearly addressed: 'Flag Officer in Charge, Gibraltar. Naval Stores'. Once, on the first day out, a flimsy Italian seaplane had dived out of the clouds to be met by a few sporadic bursts from their anti-aircraft guns and had immediately returned to the safety of the clouds, no doubt satisfied that this was just a small unit of enemy ships en route for the Western Mediterranean. So perhaps the clumsy precautions were justified after all.

Few aboard the *Thistle* cared much one way or the other. Watchkeeping was sheer misery, and below decks for a brief respite it was even more wretched. For crammed between decks were two hundred Royal Marine commando, complete with their ammunition and weapons, scaling lines and

numerous other bundles of nameless equipment which made
movement from one part of the ship to the other almost impossible. Only once before in her lifetime had the little corvette carried nearly that number of passengers. Wemyss recalled that during a particularly bad Atlantic winter when the
Thistle had been tail-end Charlie on an eastbound convoy she
had picked up the survivors of some ten torpedoed merchantmen. One hundred and twenty to be exact, so this new
situation was even worse. Everywhere you went you seemed
to fall over sleeping marines or stacks of weapons, and all the
while the ship rolled and staggered, dived and lifted her bows
to the scudding clouds as if to tear herself apart.

Watching the big destroyer from the upper bridge gave
everyone some idea of what the *Thistle* must look like. The
ship showed her bilge keel, and then her upper deck as her
masts and superstructure swung back and forth across the
yellow-fanged waves in a sickening motion which increased
as both ships left the shelter of the land and butted out into the
open sea.

At the close of the second day the destroyer's signal lamp
blinked across the tossing water, 'Good luck. Give our love to
Mussolini.' Then with a rising surge of power from her forty-
eight thousand horsepower she headed away into the murk
and was almost at once out of sight.

Painfully, waiting for the right moment, the *Thistle* altered
course to the north-east, quite alone, a tossing fragment of grey
steel against the wilderness of empty sea. Only the chart
showed visible evidence of that other danger. Like the jaws of a
great trap the islands of Sardinia and Sicily lay one hundred
miles from either beam, a hostile sea, with Italy across the
bows as the final barrier.

But if the weather was terrible, it was also an ally. Not once
did they sight an aircraft or ship, for the enemy probably
assumed that no one in his right mind would take a ship alone
and unaided into these waters, expecially in this sort of
weather.

As Crespin lived out each day within the staggering world
of his bridge he felt inclined to agree with such reasoning. No

one in his right mind would have *sent* the *Thistle* in such conditions.

Slowly but surely he guided his ship around the north-west
corner of Sicily. It was as if the *Thistle* was held to the coastline by an invisible thread, as a child will hold a captive model
aircraft with himself as the centre of its flying circle.

Three days to the hour after slipping her moorings found
them a bare twenty miles north-north-east of Cape St. Vito, a
craggy prong of land which guarded the final approach to
Castellamare Bay and their objective.

Just twenty miles from enemy territory, but as Crespin
swung his glasses over the screen he thought it could have been
a thousand. There was no sign of land and the visibility was
next to nothing. It was a wild panorama of broken wavecrests
and bursting spray, the latter being so continuous that it might
have been tropical rain. They had a beam sea now, the most
dangerous of all, and although the hands had been at action
stations for several hours it was in name only. The four-inch
gun on the forecastle was abandoned, the crew hiding somewhere abaft the bridge, and as the sea thundered up and over
the side of the hull and sluiced greedily the full length of the
deck the gun stood alone and desolate like a half-submerged
rock.

Crespin readjusted the sodden towel around his neck. His
skin felt raw and chafed and his body bruised from the constant pounding.

Wemyss clawed his way to his side and shouted, 'Bang on
time, sir!' He was unshaven and red-eyed, and Crespin wondered how men could stand up to this sort of thing.

He nodded. 'As far as we can tell!' He ducked below the
screen as a towering wall of spray lifted over the bridge and
then smashed down jubilantly on the crouching men before
gurgling through the scuppers and cascading down the ladders on either wing.

He saw Shannon wedged in the opposite corner of the
bridge, his face raw from spray and wind, his lips set in a tight
line as he peered towards the starboard bow. He looked worn
out, but something was keeping him on his feet.

Crespin said, 'Check with the W/T again. We might get a recall in view of all this.'

Wemyss looked at him doubtfully. 'Too late now, sir. We'd have heard by this time if the invasion was off.'

'Check anyway.' Crespin moved his glasses along the screen. At most other times it would be as bright as noon. But it was growing darker every minute, and the clouds if anything were thicker and faster.

Wemyss came back shaking his head. 'Nothing, sir!'

'Very well. Take over the con. I'm going to the chartroom.' He held up his wrist and showed Wemyss his watch. 'There's no point in pretending that this raid is going to be called off, so we might as well get on with it.'

The small chartroom was so crowded with people that Crespin had to use his shoulder to open the door. The four marine officers and all the senior N.C.O.s had somehow managed to get inside, and the air was almost nauseous with tobacco smoke.

The senior officer was a major named Cameron. He was extremely tall and as thin as a stick, and his narrow, rather haughty face was dominated by a bushy moustache and a pair of small, penetrating eyes. His green beret was set at an exact and regulation angle on his head, and in spite of the discomforts of being a passenger he had managed to shave, as had the rest of the marines present. Up to this moment Cameron had been content to remain just one more piece of cargo. Resigned was probably a better word, Crespin thought. Now, or in two hours' time, their roles would change. Major Cameron certainly gave the impression that he was more than able to cope, no matter what was waiting for him and his men.

Crespin stared down at the chart. The bay towards which the bows were pointing was about fifteen miles across, with the cape of the nearest headland reaching out towards them like a spiked mace. It was a terrible coast. Steep cliffs and end-less reefs, with neither light nor beacon to make the approach any easier.

Five miles inside the bay, hacked into the headland itself, was the objective, the tiny settlement of St. Martino. It could not be called a port or a village, for there was no real harbour or need for social habitation. In the great hills behind the inlet and connected to the rest of the island by a narrow gauge railway were several quarries. In peacetime they were mostly worked by convicts, the stone being used for buildings as far afield as France and Spain. Now the quarries were little used, for in time of war concrete had been proved more useful and less troublesome than the slow business of hewing out stone.

What made St. Martino different from the rest of this inhospitable coastline was its long pier. Coasters and schooners had used it to load their cargoes of stone, and the *Thistle* was about to use it for a more lethal business.

Major Cameron glanced swiftly around the watching eyes. 'We go alongside the pier and disembark in three parties as arranged.' He had a clipped, impatient voice, and Crespin judged that he would be a hard man to serve. 'First party will head north and seize the coastguard station. Second will go here,' he jabbed the chart with his finger, 'and blow up the railway track and all the equipment adjoining it.' A massive colour-sergeant was scribbling furiously in a notebook, and one of the young lieutenants was clasping and unclasping his fingers as he stared at the chart. Cameron said, 'Third party will cover the coast road and remain there until our Sicilian patriot friends take over.' He looked up sharply. 'Right?'

A round-faced lieutenant asked, 'Suppose these chaps *don't* turn up, sir?'

The major eyed him coldly. 'Well, we'll just have to manage on our bloody own, won't we?' He turned his head. 'Has anyone got anything sensible to say?'

No one replied, and Crespin was not surprised. Cameron looked at the bulkhead clock. 'Get to your men and prepare to disembark.' He cleared his throat. 'Just remember this. It is a raid we are carrying out, not a bloody suicide mission. I want plenty of noise and confusion, but no damned heroics, got it? We hit 'em and pull out.' He shot Crespin a brief smile. 'After that it's the captain's problem to get us away.'

They struggled through the swaying door and Cameron said flatly, 'I think they should have called *this* operation by some suitable name.' He pulled out his pistol, checked it and thrust it back into his holster. 'Operation Bloody Miracle would be pretty apt, don't you think?'

Crespin looked at the clock. He wanted to get back to the bridge, and imagined he could feel a slight easing of the ship's motion, as if she was already moving into the lee of that headland. But Cameron's sudden change of tone, the bitter hopelessness of his words, held him there.

'Tell me, what do you really think?'

Cameron shrugged. 'It could work, of course. I've been on many raids with far less preparation than this one. But we're so far away from help, and when we light the fuses we'll have the whole bloody island on our ears.' He pointed towards the southern coast of the island. 'The Americans are going to land here and here. In this weather they'll have their work cut out to reach the right beaches in one piece. Our little diversion should draw some of the Jerry armour our way and away from them. At least in theory it should.'

A handset buzzed and Crespin picked it from its hook. 'Captain here.'

Wemyss' voice was muffled by wind and sea. 'Ready to change course, sir.' He paused. 'Very dark now. Barely see more than a cable.'

'Very good, I'll come up.' He dropped the handset and looked at the marine. 'The main Allied invasion is scheduled to start in five hours, so we'd better get going.' He held out his hand. 'Good luck.'

The major studied him intently. 'Thanks. Just remember that if we get bogged down you're to pull out on schedule yourself. I said no heroics. It applies to you, too.' Then he smiled. 'Sometimes I think of Eastney barracks, the parades and the bloody colonel's inspections. How we used to wish for action and glory. I wouldn't mind being there now, I can tell you!'

A marine lieutenant poked his head round the door. 'All ready, sir.'

The major's face froze into an impassive mask. 'Right. Well, don't stand there gaping. What do you want, a bloody medal?' The man vanished.

The major looked around the chartroom and grinned. 'It's

better to be hated, you know. They don't miss you so much when you get your head shot off!'

Crespin watched him go and thought suddenly of Scarlett and the men like him who moved the flags on maps and decided who would live and die, and to what purpose. They never seemed to consider those who actually had to carry out their orders and translate the schemes into grim reality. Men like Cameron and his stolid colour-sergeant, and the pink-faced lieutenant who was so obviously afraid, yet more afraid of showing fear than of the unknown dangers ahead.

He sighed and wiped the lenses of his glasses before thrusting them inside his oilskin. Then he opened the door and made his way quickly to the upper bridge.

*   *   *

As the ship moved closer and closer inshore the wind fell away as if suddenly sealed off by a giant wall. There were no longer any leaping wave-crests to break the darkness, but a steep, undulating swell gave the ship an unpleasant corkscrew motion which made the helmsman's work all the more difficult because of the slow speed.

Crespin clutched the screen in the forepart of the bridge and swung his glasses slowly from bow to bow. They were less than a mile from the side of the headland and he could almost feel it like a physical force, but apart from the occasional splash of white foam around the pitching stem there was nothing to break the blackness or to give him some hint of his landfall. The radar was practically useless for this sort of thing, and it was madness to depend on it. The screen merely showed a wavering outline of coast distorted by a mass of back-echoes and nothing of any real value. What he took to be the small inlet was barely recognisable as such, and of the pier there was no sign at all. His brain told him that this was simply because of the towering cliffs at one side of the inlet which were enough to mask any such narrow object under these conditions, but his straining nerves kept playing tricks with his imagination so that it was even harder to concentrate on the final approach. Suppose the pier had been destroyed with just this sort of raid in mind? He could go on creeping forward until there was no room left to turn. He was still wearing the oilskin and could feel the warm sweat running down his body, yet he dared not take even a few seconds to remove it.

Around him he could hear the lookouts moving quietly at their stations, the occasional rasp of an ammunition belt on one of the bridge machine-guns as it swung against the steel plates. Everything was tense but normal, and this realisation added to his sense of apprehension. They all had such faith. He gave his orders, they obeyed. If they had any doubts or uncertainties in his ability, his translation of the facts at his disposal, then they gave no sign. But his mind was so crammed with stored details and preparations for this single moment how did he not know that he had forgotten some vital point? It was not unknown for a captain to get so keyed up, so immersed in the actual technicalities of his job, that he suffered a kind of mental blackout just when he was most needed.

And even if the first part of the plan worked, was it not just possible that the enemy was there, right now, waiting for him? In his mind he got a stark picture of the inlet, each ledge and piece of roadway ringed with waiting armour, the long guns already pointing at the uncertain, wallowing shape of the corvette.

He dashed the sweat from his eyes. It was no good getting like this. He heard the steering mechanism creaking again. Joicey was having great difficulty in holding his course.

He snapped, 'Up two turns!' He heard Wemyss' deep voice murmuring down the voice-pipe, the answering 'Revolutions seven-zero, sir!'

It was still dead slow, yet it felt as if the ship was heading for the hidden land with the speed of an express train.

A lookout said sharply, 'Light on the starboard bow, sir!'

Feet scraped nervously on the gratings and Crespin trained his glasses across the pale wedge of the *Thistle*'s forecastle. Nothing. The man's nerves were playing games with him. He stiffened. There it was. Very low down on the water. Two blue flashes.

He said, 'Starboard ten. Midships.' He saw the signal appear once more. 'Warn the side party. They'll have to be sharp about it. I'll not be able to stop.'

So Scarlett had been right about this, too. He seemed to have agents everywhere. Perhaps if the Germans had been able to invade England they would have had a whole list of ready-made spies there also. Traitors? Patriots? . . . It depended entirely on your point of view.

The small open boat bobbed out of the darkness like a sodden log. One minute it was well clear and the next it seemed to be wallowing directly under the ship's bows. There was a dull thud and few muffled shouts, followed by a steady scrape of wood against steel as it staggered sluggishly down the ship's side where Dunbar and his grappling hook were ready and waiting.

Wemyss was leaning over the starboard wing. 'Got 'em, sir! Just three men.' He half turned. 'What about the boat?'

'Cast it off!' Crespin could feel his hands shaking badly. 'It'd be a damn hindrance now!'

The newcomers eventually arrived on the bridge accompanied by the thin shape of Major Cameron. In the dark it was not possible to see them properly, but one of them, a man with long, greasy hair and a crude goatskin coat, had an odour of dirt and sweat which could be appreciated on every part of the bridge.

Cameron said, 'These are the leaders of the partisan group.' He gestured at the other two men. He rested one hand on the goatskin. 'This one is Lieutenant Coutts, Grenadier Guards.'

Crespin smiled in spite of his aching mind. 'You surprise me!'

Coutts pushed the hair from his face. 'Filthy, I agree, Captain. But rather necessary if one is to exist with these chaps.' He had a gentle drawl which made his appearance and his scent all the more grotesque.

Crespin asked, 'Is it all fixed up?'

'Almost.' Coutts was peering around the bridge. He had probably been away from this sort of atmosphere for a long time, Crespin thought. 'The partisans moved in on time and captured the coastguard post on the headland. They have, er, explained to the few local inhabitants that it would be prudent

to remain in bed tonight, no matter what they hear outside!'
He laughed quietly. 'This is, after all, bandit territory. The
folk around here are careful not to ask too many questions.'

Cameron asked impatiently, 'Where are the Germans, for
God's sake?'

Coutts looked at him. 'The nearest force in any size is at
Palermo, thirty miles away across the other headland. Then
there is the Italian garrison down at Trapani. That's only half
the distance, but the roads are pretty grim, and in any case
the old Eye-ties are not too keen on moving at night.' He
gestured at the two Sicilians. 'These gentlemen have a great
dislike for authority of any sort.' He drew his finger across
his throat and said, 'Mussolini?'

The taller of the men bared his teeth and then spat on the
deck.

Coutts grinned. 'Unreliable bastards. They were going to
kill me until I got some guns and ammo dropped to them in a
special airlift.' He saw Crespin's warning glance and added,
'It's all right. Neither of them speaks a word of English.' He
became serious again. 'When the Allies take Sicily we shall
have just as much trouble with them as the present manage-
ment, I shouldn't wonder.' He pulled a luminous watch from
his coat. 'Right now you should be getting a signal.' He followed Crespin to the front of the bridge. 'The pier is slightly
to the left. I'm having a light put at the outer end of it.'

Sure enough the light appeared. A yellow eye hanging
in space, but to Crespin it looked as good as any modern
beacon.

'Port ten. Midships.' To Coutts he added, 'What happened
to the coastguards?'

'They were local policemen actually.' Coutts sounded weary.
'They killed them.' He did not elaborate.

Crespin would have liked to turn the ship and go in stern
first. It would have made a better chance for a quick exit. But
there was neither time nor room, and with the sudden offshore current as well as the swell to contend with he headed
straight for the pier. There was to be no second chance, and
in spite of the massed fenders and coils of stout rope hanging
along her side to withstand the shock of impact he was almost

thrown from his feet as the hull lifted and then ground down on to the wooden piles of the pier.

There seemed to be dozens of people on the pier, all armed to the teeth, and hindering rather than helping as they collided with hurrying seamen and mooring wires, and then with the marines, who like an unpenned flood clattered over the rail and then surged towards the land with hardly a glance at the pitching ship which had brought them this far.

Coutts pulled out a Lüger and swung it carelessly in his hand. 'I'll go with Major Cameron and act as interpreter and so forth. The marines tend to be a bit possessive when it comes to acts of daring. We wouldn't want there to be any misunderstanding between them and our new-found allies, would we?'

Crespin watched the three figures scurrying after the rest of the raiding party. It was all so ridiculously casual and easy, yet here was the ship. Moored alongside an enemy pier within thirty miles of a German military outpost. To say nothing of what might be out on the roads.

Wemyss interrupted his thoughts. 'It's damn peaceful, sir.'

Crespin looked over the screen. Apart from a few seamen standing by each mooring wire the pier was deserted.

'According to Cameron's schedule that situation is about to be changed, Number One.' He was startled by the sound of his own voice. Cool, able to joke about it. It was strange how this madness got into you.

There was a violent explosion, the echoes of which rumbled around the invisible hills behind the inlet as if some ghostly battery was already opening fire.

Wemyss breathed out sharply. 'That'll be the railway line going up. The telephone wires'll be buzzing any minute now!'

Two more savage explosions followed in quick succession, the last one bringing a dull red glow which lit up the side of a nearby hill and brought the tang of scorched wood on the wind.

Crespin thought of the unfortunate Italian policemen. The partisans had probably cut their throats as they slept. Cameron would be annoyed when he found out about that, he thought. Not because he had a spark of feeling for the enemy, but because the partisans had wasted a valuable method of spreading

panic. They could have released them after the raid, and in
their eagerness to cover their own incompetence as St. Martino's guardians they would be sure to exaggerate the size of
the attacking forces.

A rattle of automatic fire crackled around the hills, followed
by sharp, thudding detonations as the marines brought their
mortars into play. They would be bombarding the bridge above
the inlet now. The vital bridge which linked the rough coast
road to Trapani, and along which the first enemy troops might
come.

Crespin found time to think of the poor inhabitants of this
dismal place. In peacetime they were preyed on by bandits
and bullied by an unfeeling authority which found it necessary to make them more afraid of them than of the men they
hunted. They probably payed some sort of unlawful tax from
their meagre living to the local Mafia, and were always caught
between the warring factions no matter what they did. Came
the war, and with it the troops and more harsh regulations
which they would barely understand. Finally came the Germans. The latter might bring law and order for the first time
in years, but the price was higher than threats or taxes.

The explosions were more varied and almost constant now
as the marines scampered from one act of demolition to the
next. Railway track, junction boxes and storage sheds were
being blasted skyward with far more explosive than was really
necessary. In one place about a mile along the coast road some
of the gorse and bracken had been set alight, and from the ship
they could see the dense black smoke streaming across the
dancing flames in an unbroken plume.

Petty Officer Dunbar appeared on the bridge. 'You wanted
me, sir?'

Crespin did not lower his glasses. 'Yes. Set the demolition
charges along the inner end of the pier. We'll blow it as we
pull out.'

He heard Dunbar hurrying away calling names into the
darkness. Blowing up the pier would not make much difference, but it all helped to keep his men from wondering
about what would happen when daylight came. It was amazing how excited they seemed now that the raid was in pro-

gress. Gunners called to one another, reporting the various explosions, airing their knowledge on ranges and the extent of each piece of destruction. It was more like a regatta than a serious raid.

It was nearly an hour before they heard aircraft approaching from the east. As the guns lifted skyward to track the invisible planes Crespin guessed that they were from the other side of the island, probably from Catania itself where a big build up of enemy bombers and fighters had already been reported by aerial reconnaissance. Well, it was a start.

It must make an impressive picture from the air, he thought grimly. Scattered fires and smoke which must appear all the more damaging in the strong wind.

Once an aircraft dived down low across the inlet itself, and Crespin could imagine the pilot straining his eyes into the darkness, searching for signs of an invasion fleet. Seeing none, and not being fired on from the sea, would most likely make him suspect that the enemy had made a landing in force with parachutists and gliders. Either way his report would soon reach the rudely awakened staff at his base, and the wheels would begin to turn. Whatever the purpose of this raid proved to be, it could not be overlooked, just as it would not be assumed to be a major invasion. Again Crespin found himself agreeing with Scarlett. The Germans would no doubt isolate the headland, the whole bay if necessary, and await the daylight, when they could mop up the impudent invaders at leisure. But to do this they would have to move men and tanks, which right at this moment in time were worth far more in the south where sandy beaches and gentler terrain would soon ring to the clamour of an Allied invasion.

Boots thudded along the pier and two marines climbed on to the bridge breathless and sweating from exertion. One was the young lieutenant who had been at the receiving end of Cameron's sarcasm.

He said, 'We've got all our objectives, sir, but things are getting out of hand with the bloody partisans.' He took another deep breath. 'It seems that there are two factions. One lot are bandits, and the others are a communist group from surrounding villages. The communists are okay at the mo-

ment, but the other mad bastards are all for striking further
south-east to the other end of the bay. It's something to do with
the mayor there, a matter of honour, or some such rubbish.'
He turned to his orderly who was already setting up a port-
able radio. 'Our lads on the headland caught a lorry-load of
Eye-tie infantry in their crossfire, but it's pretty safe from that
end.' He opened his map and flashed a shaded torch across it.
'The real problem is the main coast road from Palermo. Without the partisans to back us up we'll never hold it once the
armour comes for us.'

The radio crackled at their feet. 'Hello, this is Tango. Do
you read me? Over.'

There was no mistaking Cameron's terse voice or his obvious
anger.

Crespin took the handset from the marine. 'This is Harle-
quin. Receiving you loud and clear. Over.'

Cameron said, 'So he got there all right, did he?' Crespin
felt the marine lieutenant tense at his side. 'Well, listen to me.
We can hear tanks coming down the road. Can't say how
many, but could be a dozen or more. The road surface is quite
good, so they'll be up to us in about fifteen minutes. Can't
hold 'em with mortars, so I want a bit of artillery support.'
There was a rush of static, or it could have been Cameron
chuckling. 'Try a sighting shot on the road. We can give you
spotting orders from this hill. God, and what a hill! Like a
bloody bobsleigh run!'

The marine lieutenant said quietly, 'The place where the
road comes down to the bay is about four miles off your port
beam, sir.'

Cameron spoke again. 'Well, can you do it?'

Crespin said, 'Right away.' He stood up and ran to the forepart of the bridge. Below the screen he could see Shannon's
white cap cover and his crew standing idly around the four-
inch.

'Load with H.E., Sub! We've got a spotting team aboard
and another above the coast road!' He did not wait for a reply
but added to the watching marines, 'Carry on, Lieutenant. I
can't see it'll be much help, but do what you can.'

The marine grinned. 'When you've got nothing, sir, *any-*

thing's a help!' Then he ran for the ladder and disappeared towards the forecastle. Fifteen seconds later the four-inch crashed out like a thunderclap, the shell ripping across the black water like tearing silk.

Drifting smoke hid the explosion but the marine looked up from his radio and said, 'Short, sir! Up five hundred!'

And so it went on, with the gun banging out at regular intervals and the various changes of range and bearing coming back just as smoothly.

Once Cameron broke radio silence to say that one shell had started a miniature landslide and some of the tanks were held up beyond it. But four, maybe five were already through and on their way towards the inlet.

Crespin peered at his watch. It was only one o'clock. He shook the watch angrily, but it was not lying. It did not seem possible that so little time had passed since he had conned the ship alongside the pier. And there were still two hours at least before he could consider making a withdrawal.

A searing white flare burst above one of the hills, and Crespin saw the high cliffs, the grim hostility of the surroundings for the first time.

A long orange tongue licked out of the smoke and a shell screamed over the pier, making the waiting seamen fall flat on their faces. The flare was dying, but Crespin had already seen the low, squat shape rounding the bend of the road, its long gun muzzle swinging and then settling on its target.

Crespin crossed the bridge in three strides. 'Port Oerlikons open fire! There's a tank at red four-five!' He winced as another shell shrieked overhead to explode in the cliffs beyond the pier. All hell broke loose as the Oerlikons jerked into life, the bright tracers smashing through sheds and cottages alike, until with a roar some of them found and held the tank in a vortex of bursting cannon-shells. A great tongue of red flame licked out of the turret, against which Crespin could just make out a solitary, writhing shape before it fell back again into the tank's blazing interior. But another tank was already thrusting its ugly snout round the bend, the gun firing as it moved. To avoid its blazing consort it mounted the side of the road, gouging into a small dwelling house and smashing it into rubble with the ease of a man demolishing a child's sand castle.

Crespin yelled, 'Tell the four-inch to shift target! If those tanks get down here we're finished!'

He felt the deck jump beneath him, the scream and whine of splinters as a shell exploded against the hull. He heard Shannon yell, 'Shoot!'

Seconds later the four-inch shell slammed into the fallen building, setting it alight and hurling pieces of stone and wood into the air like leaves in a wind. Figures were running across the road, outlined against the flames, bent double with desperate urgency as the tank slewed around the side of the road towards them. Partisans or marines, it was impossible to tell, but before they could reach the next huddle of buildings the tracers came from the tank's machine-guns, streaking across the smoke and rubble and cutting down the running figures like puppets. Some were only wounded, and Crespin turned away as the tank rolled across them, grinding them into pulp.

The next shell caught the tank squarely in the side. There was a bright flash and a black object flew into the air, shining in the billowing flames before dropping back on to the roadway. It was the tank's gun-turret. Shannon was yelling at his men to reload, and as the drifting flare died on the hillside Crespin saw Porteous gripping the guardrail, his eyes fixed on the blazing litter of tanks and buildings as if he was mesmerised.

The marine at the radio said, 'First wounded coming back, sir.'

Crespin pulled his mind away from the burning tanks. 'Tell Lennox to take his stretcher party along the pier at the double!' To Wemyss he added, 'The other tanks will think twice about coming down here now!'

The glass screen shivered to fragments and one of the bridge lookouts fell back clutching his wrist. From aft an Oerlikon began to fire long bursts of tracer towards the hillside, but Crespin shouted, 'He's wasting his time! That was a sniper. The Jerries must be pushing infantry around the top of the inlet.' Another heavy bullet slammed against the bridge and ricocheted viciously into the darkness. Crespin watched the wounded man being helped down the ladder and snapped, 'Tell

Lennox to put the wounded in the wardroom. There'll be more room for them.'

The firing was getting heavier and closer. Rifles and machine-guns intermingled with the crump of mortars and grenades as hunters and hunted changed places on the steep hillsides and below the remains of the road bridge. Moving on the upper deck was dangerous, too. The hidden marksman was probably firing blind, but every few minutes one of his heavy bullets would clang against the steel or plough into one of the ship's boats, bringing curses and shouts of alarm from the waiting gunners.

The marine looked up, his eyes white in another flare. 'Major Cameron says he'll have to evacuate his hill in thirty minutes at the outside, sir. He's lost twenty killed and wounded, and the enemy are working round behind him right now.'

Crespin nodded. This was bad. If the Germans could take the hill from Cameron there was nothing to stop them using their mortars on the pier and the ship.

Wemyss seemed to read his thoughts. 'We'll be a sitting duck here, sir. The bastards will pound us to scrap once they get zeroed in!'

Crespin stared at him. 'Do you think I don't know that?'

He swung round as the marine said tonelessly, 'Those other partisans have run right into it, sir. The Jerries are cutting them down from two sides at once.'

Wemyss said savagely, 'Serve them right! Running off like a lot of bloody commandos!'

Crespin replied coldly, 'At least they were doing something!' To the marine he said, 'Call up the major and ask him if we can help.'

There was a long pause and then a new voice replied, 'We're pulling out! Can't hold it any longer!' There was a pause and they all heard the savage rattle of automatic weapons. The voice continued, 'This is Lieutenant Price. The major's had it!' The set went dead.

Crespin crossed to the starboard side and watched as the first of the wounded came along the pier. Staggering, hopping or being carried by the sailors, but all looking at the ship as if expecting a miracle. He recalled Cameron's words. It's better to be hated. They don't miss you so much when you get your head shot off! Now he was out there somewhere, lying with most of his small detachment.

Shannon called, 'I can't continue firing, sir. We might hit some of our people!'

'Well, keep shooting on the original bearing! It might make the enemy think we've still got something going for us!' He ducked his head as a bullet fanned his face like a hot wind. He shouted, 'And be ready to shift target to the road again if the tanks try another attack down here!'

Wemyss said stubbornly, 'Major Cameron is dead, sir. You are the senior officer now.'

Something snapped in Crespin's mind and he said harshly, 'What are you asking? Do you want me to pull out and leave these poor devils behind?' He saw Wemyss' face, impassive and sad in a drifting flare. 'Well, I was left to die once, Number One, and I'm not running for you, *or anyone else!*'

Tracers stabbed from behind a smoking cottage and some wounded marines scattered feebly before being cut down almost within reach of the pier. The Oerlikons opened fire, the shells clawing away the wall of the building, starting fresh fires and bringing down the sagging roof in a shower of bright sparks. The enemy gun fell silent.

Wemyss said, 'I was thinking of you, sir. You have your orders. No one would blame you now.'

'Orders are not meant as a substitute for common sense, Number One! A lot of good men have died tonight, and a lot more will go before we get out of this. So for Christ's sake let their deaths be to some bloody purpose!'

There was an abbreviated whistle and a loud bang. It seemed to be right alongside the ship, and as water cascaded across the port side Crespin saw the telltale whirlpool within twenty feet of the bow.

'Mortar!' He ran to the rear of the bridge. 'Get the damage control party up forrard at the double!' He knew Wemyss was still watching him, just as he knew his advice had been right.

Another mortar bomb exploded in almost the same place,

and again the hull jumped to the onslaught of flying splinters.

Crespin said between his teeth, 'Time check!'

Leading Signalman Griffin replied, 'Time check, sir. 0230 exactly.'

Crespin looked at him dazedly. They had done it. In less than half an hour the British and American landing craft would be grinding ashore, and this raid would be a tiny memory, if that.

He snapped, 'Signal a recall, Number One! Warn the engine room to stand by!'

He turned to watch as still more wounded struggled along the pier into the arms of the waiting seamen. A few marines, but this time they were mostly partisans, and in the glare of burning buildings and flares Crespin could see that some of them were wearing makeshift uniforms, all adorned with the red star. Whatever their true reasons, they had fought well, and had the discipline for this kind of war. The main body of the partisans, now dead or captured, had been more used to ambushing solitary lorries or sniping at policemen. Some would remember them as heroes. Most would give a sigh of relief.

'Take over.' Crespin pushed past Wemyss and ran down the ladder to the side deck. It was about level with the top of the pier, but the uneasy swell was making it hard for some of the wounded to climb across. He seized Porteous's arm and snapped, 'Go ashore, Sub! Get these people on board as quickly as you can!'

Porteous stared at him without recognition and then heaved himself over the guardrail where Lennox was standing amidst a litter of wounded figures yelling instructions to his assistants and anyone else who was fit enough to help.

A slim figure in a blood-stained shirt and carrying two rifles sank to his knees and almost fell between the piles and the grinding hull of the ship. Porteous caught him and lowered him gently to the rough planks. Now that Crespin had galvanised him into action it seemed as if his mind and hands could not move fast enough. With a sob he tore open the bloodied shirt, searching for the wound, and then rocked back on his heels as his fingers moved over the smooth curved skin underneath.

'It's a girl!' He looked back at Crespin. 'She's just a young girl!'

Then he seemed to get hold of himself, and with infinite care he placed a thick field-dressing across the angry wound below the girl's right breast. Once she opened her eyes and studied Porteous's intent face for several seconds. He looked up and saw her watching him. Saw her smile directly at him before letting her head fall back again on to the pier.

Porteous finished fixing the dressing and said gently, 'There. You'll be all right now.'

Lennox hurried past, his white jacket speckled with blood like a butcher's. He paused at Porteous's side and then said abruptly, 'I'm afraid she's dead, sir.' Then he ran on after the rest of his helpers.

Porteous stared down at the girl's face, unable to move. She was still smiling, but in the flickering glare of the fires he could see that her eyes were without understanding.

Blindly he staggered to his feet, and as he walked heavily after Lennox and into the drifting smoke Crespin saw there were tears running down his face.

It was Lennox's white jacket returning through the smoke which told Crespin that there was no point in waiting any longer. How many dead and wounded were still back there on the hillside and beside the road he could not tell. But he had done what he could, and more than was reasonable.

As a handful of marines came running back along the pier and more mortar bombs exploded in the deep water of the inlet the *Thistle* sounded her siren. Those who were cut off from the pier would know that there was no point in dying for nothing now. The wounded still lying in the gorse and staring at the indifferent clouds could wait and expect help, even from an enemy.

'Let go forrard!' Crespin heard the crack of the sniper's rifle but stayed where he was on the gratings. 'Let go aft!'

A seaman on the jetty released the eye of the headrope and then screamed as another bullet from the hidden sniper slammed him down. The crouching men on the forecastle watched with sick horror as they hauled in the wire and saw the dead seaman being dragged along the pier, one foot still entangled in it. Like so much meat, already without meaning or personality.

'Half astern!' The screw thrashed eagerly below the counter, and with gathering speed the little ship backed away, leaving the pier and a handful of corpses to settle back into the shadow.

A tank rumbled around the curve in the road and small figures darted amidst the ruins, lighting up their pitted walls with gunfire as they raced on to the deserted pier.

Crespin was staring aft, indifferent to the whimpering bullets as he gauged the distance and watched the stern thrusting steadily through the heaving water. Because of this he did not see Dunbar's demolition charges explode, and when he turned his head there was only a pall of smoke with a glowing red core to show where the ship had once been moored. Of the tank and the running men there was no sign at all. For the tank crew it must have been a quick death, he thought. Straight to the bottom of the inlet.

'Stop engine! Full ahead, starboard twenty!'

Another mortar bomb threw up a thin column close to the hull, and once more the bridge shook to the splinters. The side must look like a pepper pot, Crespin thought vaguely.

'Midships! Steady!' He lowered his eyes to the glowing gyro. 'Steer zero-zero-five!'

He felt sick and unsteady, but something was still holding him upright, his brain working with the regulated independence of the gyro.

'Report damage and casualties.' He swung his glasses back over the splintered screen. Isolated fires, almost hidden in the great bank of smoke. But no more shooting. Perhaps even now the same wires which had buzzed with the news of *Thistle*'s presence were screaming orders, recalling the troops who now stood by the remains of the pier.

He thought of Cameron and wondered what had become of Coutts, the Grenadier in a goatskin. Dead or captured? Or perhaps already on his way to some new breeding ground of espionage and sudden death.

Crespin lowered his head to the voice-pipe. 'Port ten. Midships.' He could feel the bows rising and falling with a livelier

movement as the ship pushed from the protective headland
and left the reefs somewhere astern. 'Steer three-five-zero!'

His head was getting heavier on his shoulders, and he knew
that if he climbed on to his chair he was finished. There was so
much to do before daylight. Repairs to the splinter holes, many
of which would be below the surface once the ship met with
rougher water. Even now he could hear the pumps thudding
away to control the seepage. Casualties would have to be ac-
counted for, replacements made for the more valuable men.
The dead gave no trouble. They just had to be buried. Back in
England there would be more telegrams to disrupt more lives,
with perhaps a medal or two to compensate the ones left to
remember.

The *Thistle* climbed slowly across a steep roller and lifted
her tail towards the clouds as she plunged down on the opposite flank. Crespin gripped the voice-pipes and stared at where
the horizon should be. Tomorrow might bring some fresh attack to test their battered resources. But at least they were at
sea. Away from the land and its stench of burning and death.

When Wemyss returned to the bridge he found the captain
standing in the same place by the broken screen, his body swaying easily with the deck beneath him.

He said carefully, 'The W/T office reports that the invasion
has started, sir. According to plan.'

Crespin nodded distantly. 'Good.'

'Do you think we helped, sir?'

Crespin turned to face him. 'I might be able to tell you that in
ten years' time.' He watched Wemyss pull his list of casualties from his pocket. 'My guess is that we will never know.' He
listened to the meaningless words and was conscious of
Wemyss' controlled breathing. *He thinks I'm a cold, unfeeling
bastard. If it was light enough to read that list I would not be
able to hold it. My hands are shaking so much that I . . .* He
checked his despair and said, 'I'll deal with that in a moment.
Right now I want to know about the damage to the hull.'

He saw Cameron clearly. *It's better to be hated. . . .*

Wemyss watched him without expression. *You poor bastard,* he thought. *You're breaking apart, but you'll never admit
it.* Then he cleared his throat and began his report.

8 The Welcome

THE *Thistle*'s return to Sousse lacked both the stealth and the deception of her departure eight days earlier, and as she crept cautiously towards the same jetty in the sweltering afternoon sunlight it seemed to the weary seamen on her upper deck as if the whole town had turned out to watch.

Crespin stood at the port wing and watched as the mooring lines sagged, tautened and then took the strain and cradled the ship against the jetty wall.

'Ring off main engine.' His voice sounded heavy with fatigue, and as he ran his eye around the bridge and forecastle he found himself marvelling at this safe return. There were splinter and bullet holes wherever he looked, and below on the main messdeck the sides of the hull were so punctured there was as much sunlight through them as came through the scuttles. And yet they had made it. In spite of bad weather and the holes along her waterline which at times had almost gained on the desperate efforts of the pumps, they had returned to base as ordered.

On the morning after the raid the bombers had found them. Three Ju. 88s in tight formation had swept out of the clouds, dodging between shell-bursts and tracer, intent only on the *Thistle*'s destruction. For thirty minutes the battle had raged without pause, the guns glowing hot as the seamen poured burst after burst into their attackers. But the corvette made a small target and the visibility was poor. But for these points, and the fact that the enemy needed every available aircraft

elsewhere above the invasion beaches, the ship would have
died there and then. There had been two very near misses, the
last shaking the hull so badly that several plates had started
and two stokers of the damage control party had been cut to
pieces by flying splinters. One of the bombers had been hit,
too, and had been last seen heading for land with a greasy
trail of smoke to lessen the chance of her ever getting there.
The others had followed. They had dropped their bombs and
had had enough.

Surprisingly, there were no more attacks, nor did they see
another aircraft until almost within sight of a friendly coast.
And then it had been a Catalina, its lamp flashing a welcome
and the wings almost brushing the masthead as it dived down
to get a better look at the lonely victor.

Crespin sighed and pushed himself bodily from the rail. He
could see the bearded engineer, Moriarty, and a large party of
men already hurrying to the brow, while along the jetty a line
of khaki ambulances waited patiently to clear the ship of her
dead and wounded.

And the people. It did not look like the same place. They
must have been in hiding before, he thought dully, for now the
sea road and the town beyond were thronged as if for a public
holiday. Shops and cafés were open again, and even the old
scars of battle could not hide the fact that Sousse was returning to life.

Then he saw Scarlett. He was pushing through the cordon
of soldiers, waving a greeting here, pausing by a man on a
stretcher there to murmur a few words and flash his famous
smile before striking on towards the brow.

Wemyss saluted. 'Ship secured, sir.' He was swaying on his
feet. Worn out like the rest of them.

Crespin said, 'Very well. Go and see Moriarty and give him
all the help you can. Thank God the hull's all right. I don't
imagine the resources around here are exactly up to Portsmouth.' As Wemyss turned to go he added quietly, 'And
thanks, Number One.'

Wemyss looked at him, caught off guard. 'Sir?'

'You did damn well. You all did.'

Wemyss' lined features creased into a smile. 'Thank *you*,

sir.' He looked at the squat funnel, which like so much of the ship was etched with bright-rimmed holes through which little trails of escaping smoke moved unhurriedly skyward. 'She did pretty good, too, I thought.' There was genuine affection in his tone.

Crespin heard Scarlett's resonant voice below the bridge. 'All right, are you, my boy? Good show! *Damn* good show!' He said, 'And make sure the last of the wounded get away, will you? I imagine I'll be tied up for a bit.'

Wemyss nodded and stepped aside as Scarlett heaved himself on to the bridge.

Crespin said, 'Mission completed, sir.' He should have been on the gangway to greet Scarlett, but his mind refused to care. He was half-asleep on his feet and his eyelids felt as if they were gummed together.

Scarlett returned his salute and gave a huge grin. 'Bloody good show, Crespin!' He waved at Wemyss who was trying to slip quietly away. 'Glad you made it, Number One!' Then to Crespin he added, 'What's the bill?'

Crespin studied him calmly. 'The ship lost five killed and ten wounded. The marines have brought back thirty of their wounded.' He paused, seeing Scarlett nodding with concern or polite interest. 'They also left seventy-five killed and missing behind.'

Scarlett rubbed his hands. 'Better than I'd dared to hope. Pity about Cameron, of course, but it's all part of the game.'

Crespin looked past him. Part of the game. It was no game. 'There's a good deal of damage to the ship. Mostly splinter holes, although we did get a direct hit from a tank gun on the port side.'

Scarlett nodded. 'So I saw, Crespin. So I saw indeed.' He was suddenly serious. 'I've already formed what I intend to say in my report, and I'm having an official photographer come down to get some pictures of the ship.' He saw the astonishment on Crespin's face and added brightly, 'No time for being coy or hiding the old light, what? It always helps to push a bit in this game, you know. Then when you make a real boob you´re got something for you in the balance.' He laughed loudly and waved to some marines who were marching down the brow, their steps dragging, their eyes glazed with strain.

Crespin said, 'I take it then that you're satisfied, sir?'

'Satisfied? I certainly am!' Scarlett rested his hand on Crespin's shoulder. 'I know how you must feel, how we *all* feel about seeing good men die. But look at it this way. If every single man had been killed and the ship sunk it would have been worthwhile. You have to weigh up the odds. Learn to use a force small enough to tie down a far greater number of the enemy. And small enough to be no crippling loss if the balance goes against it.' He patted his shoulder. 'But I'm being morbid. This is your day, and I'm pleased.'

He looked over the screen and continued briskly, 'Mostly superficial damage, by the look of it. Moriarty can fix it, or I'll know the reason why! We have to learn to improvise in this unit. Improvise and make do. If you think Sousse is crude, then just you wait until we really get going!' He tapped the side of his hooked nose. 'But that'd be telling, eh?'

Crespin let the words wash over him like spray. It seemed as it Scarlett would never stop, never go away.

Scarlett said, 'I shall be leaving for Malta tomorrow. With the Sicily invasion going so well we can't stand still, you know. Plans to make, possibilities to explore and all that sort of thing.'

'And my orders, sir?'

Scarlett seemed to consider the question. 'Get the ship repaired and restocked with everything you need. You'll not get a dockyard refit here so don't try and make a big thing of it. Patch up and splash on some fresh paint and she'll be as good as new.' He laughed. 'But I don't have to teach you these tricks, do I?'

Crespin did not answer directly. He was thinking of the blazing tanks, the seaman being dragged by his leg along the pier and Porteous with the dead girl. So many vivid pictures. Then he said, 'A month at the least, I should think.'

'What? You're playing games with me again, Crespin, because I'm a rotten old amateur, eh?' Scarlett's face seemed to be swimming in a mist. 'No, I'm afraid I can't have that, old chap. *Three* weeks at the most. I've already told Moriarty what I want, so don't try and get round him, there's a good chap!'

'She's not built for this sort of thing, sir. For that reason she needs extra care, otherwise something will go just when we need her most.'

Scarlett studied him sadly. 'There you go again. You must try to remember that your command is not a way of life, it's steel and guns, a *weapon*! And you must ensure that is how it stays.' He consulted his watch. 'Must be off now. Lot to do.' He grinned. 'Almost forgot. I'm recommending you for a bar to your D.S.C. I'll make out a list for you to sign of other possible decorations for your chaps. Oh, and that Sub of yours, Shannon, I'm suggesting that his second stripe is brought forward. It all helps to keep 'em happy, you know!' He swung round on the ladder and ran quickly to the deck.

Crespin gave him a few minutes and then walked slowly towards the ladder. He had hardly left the bridge for eight days and his legs felt unwilling to make the effort.

As he reached the deck he saw the hands already at work dragging the shore power lines inboard, along with all the clutter of welding gear and nameless pieces of steel plate. They looked dirty and unshaven, but worked as a team in a way he had not seen before. As he passed amongst them some looked up and grinned self-consciously, others merely stared at him with a mixture of awe and pride. The fear and the uncertainty were behind them, the future too remote to contemplate. They were safe in harbour, and every other sailor and bloody civvie in the port had come to see them. It was as simple as that. And to most of them, who had expected to be killed or taken prisoner, Crespin represented far more than the commanding officer of their battered little ship. He *was* the ship, her strength and her cunning rolled into one.

Crespin realised none of those things, but in spite of his troubled thoughts he was deeply moved by what he saw.

He climbed down another ladder and saw Barker, the steward, clearing the mess of soiled bandages and dressings from the wardroom, with every scuttle open to drive away the stench and pain of death. In his own small cabin he could not completely escape. There were two splinter-holes above his desk and blood on the carpet where a wounded stoker had been laid to die.

There was a tap on the door even as he rested his head on his hands. 'Well?' He could hardly get the word out.

It was Shannon. 'There's an officer of the Military Police here, sir. He's had a telephone call from Captain Scarlett.'

Crespin forced his brain back to work. It did not make any sense. 'Phone call? But he was with me a few minutes ago.'

Shannon stared at him. 'Nearly *half an hour*, sir.'

Crespin looked away. Half an hour. He must have been asleep on this chair without knowing it. 'What does he want?'

'It seems that our deserter, Able Seaman Trotter, is holed up in some house on the other side of town, sir.' Shannon seemed irritated. 'I told the Provost officer that he should have dealt with it, but it seems that Captain Scarlett thought *you'd* want to handle the matter.'

Crespin groped for his cap. Scarlett obviously considered that an arrest effected by the military might cast blight on the *Thistle*'s impressive return.

'All right, I'll come up.' He saw Shannon's eyes exploring the cabin and added, 'By the way, you're being promoted. It's not official, but you can take it for granted.'

Shannon was visibly shaken. 'Thank you, sir. I—I mean, thank you very much!'

Crespin eyed him emptily. That was odd. Shannon's voice had taken on a distinct northern accent. It was strange he had not noticed it before.

He could not bring himself to like Shannon very much, but he had certainly shown himself capable of keeping his head in action. He said, 'Well, let's get it over with.'

The M.P. lieutenant had small, gimlet eyes and an aggressive black moustache. He carried a leather cane under one arm, and threw up a salute which would have done credit to the Guards.

Crespin wondered what sort of a picture he made by comparison. Red-eyed, in a sweat-stained shirt with a face still stiff from salt-spray and smoke.

He said, 'Are you sure it's our deserter?'

The M.P. replied primly, 'No, sir. But Captain Scarlett has

been informed that it is. And acting on information received I have placed two of my men in a position near the house to await instructions.' He even sounded like a policeman.

He moved his boots noisily. 'I have a jeep on the jetty, sir.'

Crespin saw Porteous hovering by one of the working parties and beckoned him across. 'We're going for the deserter, Sub. He is in your division, I believe?'

Porteous nodded vacantly. 'Yes, sir.'

When they reached the gangway Wemyss said quickly, 'Would you like me to detail a proper escort, sir?' He shifted under Crespin's gaze. 'You could do with some rest.'

He was really implying it was odd to say the least for a captain to go looking for a mere deserter.

Crespin replied calmly, 'I'm just going for the ride, Number One. I've one or two items on my mind and this might help to clear them.'

He climbed on to the brow, and as the pipes twittered in salute he turned and looked along the exposed side of his ship. She had certainly been lucky. The wounds were bad, but by some miracle nothing vital had been touched. He thought of Scarlett's description. A weapon. Not a way of life. It was strange how deeply he could still feel those words. As if he had been insulted personally.

By the jeep the M.P. stopped to check his revolver, and Crespin said coldly, 'You won't need that, Lieutenant!'

'You can't be too sure with these chaps, sir.' The M.P. was frowning severely.

'In this war you can't be sure of any bloody thing.' Crespin climbed into the jeep and lapsed into silence.

Scarlett had said he was going to Malta. So the girl would be leaving, too. It would be interesting to see if she remembered her invitation.

With a jerk the jeep bounded forward, and both ship and jetty were swallowed immediately in a pall of churned dust.

It did not take very long to reach the house where the deserter was said to be in hiding. It was one of a terrace of tall, dingy buildings with flaking plaster and an air of general decay. Some of the windows had iron balconies which were linked to similar structures on the opposite side of the narrow

street by lines full of sad-looking washing, carpets and clothes
for which there was presumably no room to spare in this rabbit warren of rooms and apartments. Another police jeep was
parked at an intersection, and a tall M.P. snapped to attention
and saluted as they approached.

'I've sent Thompson round the back, sir.' He gestured towards a deeply shadowed doorway. 'This is the only other
way out.' He glanced curiously at the two naval officers. 'I
gather from the old ratbag who runs this joint that the sailor
is on the top floor. There's a brothel on the next landing, and
some of the girls have been keeping him supplied with food
and that.' He grinned. 'Other things as well, I shouldn't
wonder.'

The M.P. lieutenant plucked his moustache impatiently.
'We'd better go on up. We don't want a crowd gathering
around us.'

Crespin looked up and down the narrow street. Apart from
a dozing beggar in a doorway and two scavenging dogs it was
deserted. The teeming occupants were either down at the
harbour watching the *Thistle* or still enjoying their siesta, he
thought. The whole place stank of dirt and urine, and he found
himself wondering what would make a man exchange the
clean, ordered world of a ship for this. It was no solution, no
matter what trouble he had got into, and he would certainly
end up in detention barracks or the local jail.

He followed the two M.P.s inside and started up the great
sagging stairway with Porteous close on his heels. Each landing was more seedy than the one before, and only when they
passed a door which had been recently painted and bore the
words 'Off Limits to Allied Personnel' did he hear any sign of
life. What must have been a very old gramophone was playing
'I left my heart in an English garden', and they could hear
some girls giggling and what sounded like someone having a
bath.

The M.P. officer grunted, 'Always chasing our chaps out of
here. I'll bloody well close it if they don't toe the line.'

On the top landing there were only two doors, and the M.P.
lieutenant pointed with his cane. 'That must be the one.
There's a Greek in the other room.'

Crespin looked at him. He obviously came here quite a lot. Maybe that was why he kept the brothel off limits. So that he could have its dubious pleasures all to himself.

He lifted his cane and rapped smartly on the door. There was no sound in reply, and on the landing below the giggling and the scraping music suddenly fell silent.

The M.P. scowled. 'So we're being awkward, are we?' He rattled the handle adding, 'Locked, too!'

The corporal put his ear to the door and then yelled, 'This is the Military Police! Open the door or we'll bust it down!' Nothing happened and he added unnecessarily, 'He's not going to answer, sir.'

Crespin stood back watching the two policemen with sudden dislike. He should not have come. The preparations for breaking into Trotter's squalid world were both humiliating and embarrassing.

The corporal stood back and then thrust his shoulder hard against the door. It flew inwards with a splintering crash, and the M.P. lieutenant was inside the room, his pistol in his hand before Crespin could make a move to follow.

But it was in pitch darkness with just a few bright horizontal slits of sunlight from a shuttered window on the far side. There was no sound of movement and only the monotonous buzzing of flies broke the silence around them.

The lieutenant said wearily, 'The bastard must have gone over the roof. Open that window, Corporal, before I spew up!'

Feet shuffled on the landing, and Crespin could sense the other inmates of the building creeping up the stairway to see what was happening.

But Trotter had not gone over the roof after all. As the shutters banged open and a shaft of dusty sunlight cut across the littered room Crespin saw him sitting slumped sideways against a table, one hand resting on some crumpled papers, the other holding a long-barrelled Italian automatic.

Porteous said quietly, 'Oh Christ! He's blown half his head away!' He retched and then thrust a handkerchief against his mouth.

Crespin made himself walk across to the rigid figure in the

chair. Trotter's eyes were almost shut, the features contorted, frozen at the moment of impact. But in the filtered sunlight Crespin could see the narrow slits of reflected glare, so that it looked as if Trotter might be still alive and would suddenly open them wide and condemn their intrusion. But the right side of his head had almost gone, and Crespin had to swallow hard to restrain the nausea as he stared at the flies which covered the blood and shattered bone in a murmuring, eager mass.

The lieutenant said, 'Go down and phone for the meat waggon, Corporal.' He pushed Trotter's other hand aside with his revolver and held the paper up to the light.

To Crespin he said, 'It's easy for them to get hold of these guns, sir. The whole place is full of junk left behind by the enemy.' His eyes hardened. 'This is interesting. He started to make a confession.' He moved closer to the window, his eyes moving busily back and forth over the large scrawling handwriting. 'He says that he has not been able to sleep or eat because of what he *done*.' His lip curled with amusement. 'Not much of a writer, was he?'

Crespin snapped, 'Just read the letter! The grammar lesson can wait!'

The lieutenant flushed and continued reading in a strained tone. 'He says that it was murder. There was no other word for it. That he knows nothing can make it right, but that he had to get it off his mind.' He turned over the paper. 'Damn, that's all he's written!'

Crespin took it from his hand and stared at it. So it had been Trotter who had killed that German. To Porteous he said wearily, 'Is it his handwriting?' He just wanted to get away from this place.

Porteous nodded.

The M.P. lieutenant had recovered his dignity by now. 'Can you be sure, I mean, if there's no actual signature?'

Porteous said flatly, 'I'm sure. He was in my division. He came to me once to ask how to write an allotment form for his mother. I noticed his handwriting then.'

The M.P. eyed him bleakly. 'You're something of an expert, are you?'

Porteous looked at him, his eyes suddenly angry. 'I was a

barrister, Lieutenant. I'm used to this sort of thing.' He paused. '*And* policemen!'

The M.P. snatched the letter and folded it inside his wallet. 'That wraps it up then. Nothing more we can do here. I'll go and see if the ambulance is here yet.' He strode out of the room and could be heard snapping at the silent people on the stairs.

Crespin said quietly, 'Little bastard!'

Porteous clutched his arm. 'Look, sir, I don't know how to say this.' He swallowed hard, and in the shaft of sunlight his plump features were wet with sweat. He persisted, 'I remember Trotter's handwriting for another reason.'

Crespin faced him. 'Go on.'

'He was left-handed, sir.' Some of his confidence faded under Crespin's level stare. 'You can check with Petty Officer Dunbar, sir. He'll be able to confirm . . .'

Crespin walked back to the corpse. 'Left-handed, you say?'

Porteous would not go any closer. 'Yes.'

'This is a heavy automatic, Sub. Yet he's holding it perfectly in his *right* hand.'

Their eyes met across the dead man's bowed head. Then Porteous replied quietly, 'Exactly, sir.' He glanced towards the door. 'Shall I fetch the lieutenant back?' He looked wretched.

'No. It can't help Trotter now. And neither can we solve anything by warning whoever it was who killed him.' He saw the uncertainty on Porteous's face. 'He's got a mother, remember? To die away from home is bad enough. To be murdered is another thing entirely.'

Porteous nodded. 'I see, sir.'

They walked from the room, closing the door behind them.

At the main entrance they found an ambulance and several M.P.s writing busily in their notebooks.

The lieutenant said, 'I'll want a brief report from you, sir. All the usual stuff. But it's just a straightforward case. I expect you're well rid of him.'

The corporal said, 'Can I drive you back to your ship, sir?'

Crespin shook his head. 'Take Sub-Lieutenant Porteous. I'm going to walk for a bit.' He saw the corporal and Porteous exchange an uneasy glance.

Porteous said awkwardly, 'Is there anything *I* can do, sir?'

He shook his head. 'I'll be all right, Sub. Number One can cope well enough without me.'

Porteous saluted and climbed into the jeep. As it roared away he was still staring back, his face filled with concern.

Crespin pushed through a small group of chattering on-lookers and strode quickly away from the building. Porteous's legal mind was probably worried by what he had just seen and by the way Crespin had made him withhold what he saw from the proper authority. As he strode down the street Crespin was even surprised at himself. But his mind was too tired to cope, even though he repeatedly told himself that the pattern was clear to see, if only he could concentrate.

If Trotter had been murdered, why was it necessary for his killer to make it look like suicide? Murders were probably two a penny here, and one more would hardly matter. Trotter had been writing what amounted to a confession, and his killer had not bothered to destroy it before shooting him at point-blank range. He halted in his tracks, suddenly cold. Unless there had been another sheet of paper which he *had* destroyed? It must have been like that. A few more lines to betray another man, someone who had helped him to kill the German and throw him overboard. The man who had pulled the trigger.

Crespin strode on. That was ridiculous. No one else was ashore but himself and Porteous. There had to be another solution, if only he could work it out.

He eventually stopped in a small square, completely spent. He realised that the sun had moved right over the town and the square was almost in complete shadow. He must have been walking for an hour, yet he had hardly noticed it. Like a man in a dream, tied to his innermost thoughts.

He stared at a small, white-painted hotel which faced him across the square. A German eagle and swastika had been crudely daubed out above the door and a new sign stated it was for 'Officers Only'. Without consulting his notebook he knew why his feet had brought him here instead of back to the ship. He walked through the street door and saw a small soldier sitting behind a desk reading a tattered copy of *London Opinion*.

The soldier regarded him suspiciously. 'Sir?'

Crespin looked at himself in a large gilt mirror. He was suddenly near to panic. He must return to the ship. But there was no time. In a few more hours . . . He looked at the soldier and said sharply, 'Third Officer Forbes. Which is her room?'

The man ran his eyes once more over Crespin's stained clothes. Then he replied, 'First floor, sir. Second room on your left.'

As Crespin crossed to the stairs he picked up a brass telephone and cranked the handle. Bloody officers, he thought. If I came in here like that I'd be on a bleeding charge.

A voice said, 'Hello?'

She had a nice voice, so he could make an exception in her case. He said, 'There's a naval gentleman comin' up, miss. Is that all right?' He waited, listening to her breathing in his ear.

'A captain, is it?'

'Nah. Two an' a half striper, miss.' This time there was a definite intake of breath. Most satisfactory. He replaced the telephone and sat down again. After a moment he leafed through *London Opinion* until he found the full-length picture of a nude. It was quite easy to picture the girl upstairs like that. He recalled Crespin's dishevelled appearance and chuckled aloud. She'd soon send *him* packing. Untidy sod.

Crespin did not have time to press the bell before the door was pulled open and he saw her staring at him with a mixture of disbelief and surprise. She was dressed in khaki shirt and slacks and he noticed that her feet were bare and very small.

He said clumsily, 'I've come at the wrong moment by the look of it.'

Then she smiled and brushed a loose strand of hair from her eyes, the gesture so familiar in Crespin's memory, and said, 'I was packing. But do come inside. You look all in.'

Crespin found himself in a deep chair and watched her as she closed two suitcases and thrust them towards the door.

He said, 'Malta this time, isn't it?'

She nodded. 'But don't talk about that. Tell me about you. I was so happy when I saw the ship coming in. I watched you through the glasses. I felt I could almost touch you.'

'You were there?' Crespin studied her against the open window. 'I—I didn't know.'

'Of *course* I was there.' She stood with her hands on her hips watching him gravely. 'Did you think I'd miss it? I've thought about you a lot since you left. I've been keeping my fingers crossed all the time.'

She busied herself at the sideboard. 'I'm getting you a very large drink. I've only got gin, so don't grumble about it.' When she turned towards him he saw that her eyes were shining. Just as they had been aboard the *Thistle*.

'That will be perfect,' he said. He meant it.

'Actually I've been packing early.' She sat opposite him, her knees drawn up to her chin. 'I thought it might just be possible someone would want to take me to dinner, or something?' She put her head on one side, her mouth lifting in a smile.

'I'd like that very much.'

She stood up lightly and crossed to his chair. 'You really have had a bad time, haven't you? When did you last eat or sleep?'

Crespin said vaguely, 'I forget.' He tried to push the dragging weariness aside. 'It's not just that. I've just been to a house. To fetch a deserter.'

She nodded slowly. 'I heard that you were being told about him.'

He shook his head. 'I thought I'd met him before somewhere. I suppose if I hadn't been so clapped out I'd have sent someone else. In any case I was too late. He was dead. He'd blown his head off.' His tone was unnecessarily brutal, and he knew it was to cover a lie.

'I see. I'm sorry.' She poured another drink into his glass. 'I know I should care more than that.' She shrugged. 'But I am so glad you're safe that I can't think very clearly myself.'

He reached out and took her hand. He did not remember actually doing it. It just seemed to happen. She made as if to pull it away but changed her mind, standing very close, so that he could feel the warmth of her body.

He said, 'I've missed *you* very much, as it happens.' He half expected her to laugh it off, or change the subject for all time.

For a moment she said nothing. Then she replied quietly,

'You're in no shape to take me out to dinner, are you?' She did not allow him to protest. 'If you like we can have something here. There's a bath adjoining this room, so why not take advantage of it?' She smiled. 'You'll find a razor in there, too. I use it for my legs, but beggars can't be choosers!'

He squeezed her fingers. 'I'd like that very much. If you're sure?'

'I'm quite sure. I wasn't until I saw you again. But I am now.'

He stood up still holding on to her hand. 'When you go to Malta ...'

But she put her other hand across his mouth. 'That's tomorrow. This is now.'

The next instant she was in his arms and he was pulling her against him, feeling her mouth against his, the desperate longing flooding through him like fire.

Then she pushed him gently away. 'Go and have that bath. That's an order, *sir*!' But this time she could not look at him. 'When you're a bit more presentable I'll ring down for some food, maybe even a bottle of wine.'

He could see her breasts rising and falling under the shirt, could almost feel the tension in the room like a living force.

He tried to smile. 'I'll be as quick as I can.'

But they did not eat, nor did she ring for any wine.

When he left the bathroom the room was deep in shadows, and although the windows were wide open there was not a breath of wind to break the stillness.

She was lying on the bed, the silk cover pulled tight against her chin, her eyes watching him without expression. In the half-light she looked like a child, he thought. He sat on the edge of the bed and touched her hair. It was no longer restricted but lay loose across the pillow and felt very thick and soft.

Her voice was husky and less controlled. 'I have to go to Malta tomorrow ...'

He touched her mouth very gently. 'You said we were not to talk about tomorrow.'

'There's so little time. I just wanted you to know . . .' She reached out and gripped his shoulder. 'You *do* understand?'

He felt her fingers digging into his shoulders as if she was in pain as he pulled the cover from beneath her chin and threw it on to the floor.

Against the sheet her body was very tanned, except for her breasts which protected from the sun looked very white beneath his fingers.

She closed her eyes and gave a small cry. 'I don't want it to end!'

Then he was down and felt her mouth pressing into his, her tongue like a trapped animal. She reached round his shoulders, her nails biting into his flesh, pulling him down and down as her body arched to encircle and hold him.

When it was over he lay for a long time with his face in her hair, feeling her mouth moving against his throat in small, soundless words. Then he slipped on to his side, and as she cradled his face between her breasts he fell into a deep sleep. For once there was no dream to reawake the old memories. Just darkness, and an overwhelming sense of fulfilment.

As the window changed to a rectangle of bright stars the girl stayed very still, holding him to her, watching him as he slept until she, too, could watch no more.

9 Sailing Orders Again

CRESPIN'S estimation of the ship's damage and the time required to effect minimum repairs proved far more accurate than Scarlett's cursory verdict. Apart from the mauling sustained to the hull and superstructure there was extensive damage to electrical circuits, and Moriarty's frantic demands for spares were either ignored or delayed by far-off staff officers who obviously considered the needs of the armada in and around Sicily to have first claim on everything.

Perhaps like everyone else they had been more surprised than excited by the successes which had marked the whole campaign. There had been so many reverses and bloody set-backs in the Mediterranean war that the firm Allied advances from the beach-heads and the quick succession of victories had left the planners breathless. Only the Germans fought back with the same tenacity and vigour, while their Italian counter-parts surrendered and deserted in such vast numbers that the American and British troops were hard put to accommodate them. To set an edge on the enemy's reverses Rome Radio had announced that the King of Italy had demanded and received Mussolini's resignation, and had even gone so far as to dis-solve the Fascist party. The knot which had tied the Italians and Germans together for nearly four years of war was slip-ping, and once the Allies were able to land on the Italian main-land it would be finally broken.

Surprisingly, Scarlett received Crespin's weekly reports on progress without comment or complaint. He had no doubt

been anticipating another raid behind the enemy's lines, but
the swift Allied advance, the capture of ports and aerodromes,
made any such effort unnecessary.

So week followed week, with the ship's company and
Moriarty's mechanics working as best they could to put right
the damage. Crespin tried unsuccessfully to obtain permission
to dock the ship and carry out a fuller inspection of the lower
hull. It seemed that as far as the Navy was concerned the
Thistle was too small a unit to receive any sort of priority.
Thirty-eight days after she had backed away from the shell-
scarred pier and the blazing German tanks the *Thistle* was as
ready for sea again as she could be under the circumstances.
Her many wounds were covered, if not completely hidden, and
from stem to stern she gleamed with fresh paint and newly
acquired fittings which Moriarty had begged or wheedled from
a dozen dubious sources.

The delay of her return to duty had other, more beneficial
effects. The new men who had come from England to replace
the dead and badly wounded had time to settle down in their
fresh surroundings, while the rest took every opportunity to
enjoy the freedom of Sousse. Chasing women or drinking,
hunting for that indefinable something which all shorebound
sailors hope to find, yet would not recognise if they did, passed
away the time and helped to drive the old uncertainties and
fears well into the background.

No one ever spoke of the dead deserter any more, and most
could hardly remember what he looked like.

Even in the wardroom there had been one change. An additional officer had joined the ship during the second week, and
his arrival was greeted with pleasure, although for different
reasons. Sub-Lieutenant Jocelyn Defries was slim and
extremely fair, with almost Grecian good looks. For the previous nine months he had been in the submarine service, his
boat operating in the North Sea and Baltic, until after being
pinned on the sea bottom by enemy destroyers and depth-
charged for nearly twelve hours his nerve had given way. It
had been nothing dramatic, and outwardly it had not even
shown, but in that élite service the symptoms were as recognisable as they were dangerous. He had been informed he was

no longer suitable for submarines. It was just one of those things. Not that he needed to be told.

Defries was hard to draw out and seemed remote to a point of controlled detachment. But Porteous took to him from the start, and was doubly pleased to be able to unload some of the ship's paperwork, which as junior officer he had previously carried alone. The additional officer would also be a blessing as far as watchkeeping was concerned, and the duties could be more evenly divided.

Shannon on the other hand welcomed the young officer as one more junior upon whom he could use his newly acquired seniority. It was amazing how Shannon had changed since his promotion. He seemed to have grown in size, and aired his knowledge in a manner which was fast becoming both pompous and unbearably condescending.

Wemyss watched them all with amusement and tolerant good humour, for with Moriarty living as a temporary resident in the ship during the repairs he was able to leave the others to their own devices.

The day the last enemy resistance in Sicily ceased and the bulk of the German rearguard crossed the three miles of water to the Italian mainland, Crespin received his sailing orders. He did not really know what he had been expecting, for while the overhaul had been under way he had felt that his ship and her role were fast becoming redundant. If the Italian invasion, when it came, was as swift as the Sicilian one, it seemed unlikely that there would be anything worthwhile for Scarlett's Circus to perform. The *Thistle* might even be sent back to the Atlantic to serve out her time in the one battle which never seemed to flag.

But it was not to be, nor was he to go to one of the newly occupied ports in Sicily. His orders merely told him to sail forthwith for Malta and await instructions.

During the past weeks Crespin's thoughts had returned again and again to that one night he had spent with Penelope Forbes. Sometimes, after a bad day, he had imagined her with someone else, had tortured himself with a hundred possibilities and doubts. On other occasions it was hard to believe it had ever happened. And now, with the arrival of the coded signal, she was right back in the forefront of his mind. She would be there in Malta. With Scarlett. The realisation acted both as a tonic and a warning.

They slipped their moorings at dawn and by midday were some sixty miles to the north-east. Sousse lay astern, hidden below the horizon, and Crespin doubted if they would ever see it again.

The ship seemed pleased to be at sea again and thrust through the clear blue water with the indifference of one who has seen it all before. For unlike those she carried within her hull she had neither fears nor hopes, and her destiny lay in the hands of those who controlled her. That was the way of ships, and had always been so.

As Crespin sat on his steel chair on the bridge and watched the shimmering horizon swaying gently across the bows he wondered what Scarlett would find for them to do. A man of his energy and ambition needed action. It was to be hoped that his needs would not blunt his judgement. He heard Shannon muttering something down the voice-pipes to the helmsman and smiled to himself. Shannon's second stripe was a visible reward of that last raid. Scarlett's vague promises had otherwise amounted to very little as far as the ship's company were concerned. Crespin had received a bar to his D.S.C., but only one other decoration had been allotted for the rest. After some heart-searching he had decided to award the medal to Lennox, the S.B.A., for his work before and after the final evacuation of the raiding party. With only limited skill and few pieces of medical equipment at his disposal Lennox had more than proved himself. He accepted the award with more embarrassment than pleasure, but the rest of the ship greeted the choice with popular agreement.

Perhaps if Scarlett had taken part in the operation everyone aboard would have got a medal. Such things were not unknown. He knew he was being unfair, just as he knew the reason for it. Someone had once said to him that envy and jealousy always walked hand in hand with extreme joy. But he was not envious of Scarlett. If anything, a man with so much personal ambition was to be pitied. But he was in Malta, and so was the girl. He stirred uneasily on the chair. And there was no doubt in his mind that she admired Scarlett, perhaps even more than that. He could not find it in his heart to blame her. Scarlett was a man of influence and charm, and after the war he would have much to offer any woman. Whereas he . . . he glanced round the bridge. A peacetime Navy, pared down to the bones, with a nation so grateful to be at peace again it would soon forget the lessons of weakness and unpreparedness. He had often heard older officers speak of the bad times which followed the First World War, when even experienced and senior ones were thrown on the beach jobless, with no trade to help them face the new world which had rejected them and had forgotten the part they had played to save the nation from defeat.

He shook himself angrily. They had to win the bloody war first, and from where he sat it still looked as if there was a long way to go.

* * *

The long low room overlooking Valletta harbour was pleasantly cool after the sunlight outside, and as he sat in a cane chair listening to Scarlett's voice Crespin felt suddenly drowsy. Through an open window and between a gap in the sandbagged barriers he could see a triangle of blue water, the anchored warships and transports swinging above their reflections like scale models. For once it appeared safe from the constant and pitiless air raids which had been Malta's lot for so long.

Scarlett always seemed to be able to find himself comfortable headquarters, he thought, no matter where he chose to settle. What with the amount of bomb damaged buildings, the overcrowding of naval and military staffs on the island, it must have taken a good deal of influence to obtain this place.

The corvette had anchored just an hour earlier, and a curt message had brought him ashore almost before he had time to arrange for further fuel supplies to be delivered.

Scarlett seemed changed in some way. He moved about the room a good deal while he was speaking and his smile had not yet shown itself.

'So the repairs are satisfactory, are they?'

Crespin replied, 'As far as they go, sir. I would like to get her dry-docked as soon as possible to make a further inspection.'

Scarlett walked to his desk and fidgeted with some papers. 'Waste of time. Must learn to improvise.' He turned and looked at him. 'I could have done with Moriarty here. There's a lot to do. I can't deal with every damn thing myself.' He sounded angry. As if he was blaming Crespin and Moriarty for the amount of damage to the ship.

Crespin said, 'I thought we'd be going to a base in Sicily, sir.'

'Did you?' Scarlett sounded miles away. 'Well, that's a job for the footsloggers now. We've other fish to fry.'

There was a tap at the door and Crespin's heart gave a leap as the girl moved across to the desk. She looked cool and very calm, and the fact that she was properly dressed in uniform further added to an impression of remoteness.

She sat down and smiled gravely. 'It's nice to see you again, sir.' That was all.

Crespin felt Scarlett watching both of them and sensed a small warning in the girl's eyes.

He said, 'Good to be here.'

Scarlett ran his fingers through his thick hair. 'I've had some of our people over in Sicily for the last two weeks collecting captured enemy weapons.' He added bitterly, 'Battlefield clearance stores, as they are officially titled.'

Crespin watched him steadily. So that was why he wanted Moriarty. He had a sudden picture of the North African base, the litter of gutted vehicles and salvaged weapons.

Scarlett continued, 'I've been all over the damn place trying to drive some sense into the top brass. If it wasn't for Rear-Admiral Oldenshaw's support from England I honestly believe that some of these stupid dunderheads would get this force disbanded!'

Crespin tensed. He was right. Scarlett had been trying to enlarge on his successful raid but had found no takers.

Scarlett spread his hands with mock despair. 'Left to them this first success would just fade into a slow infantry war, all the way from the toe of Italy to Berlin. It could take years and years, and probably end in bloody stalemate!'

The girl said softly, 'You've a conference at sixteen hundred, sir.'

Scarlett stared at her. 'Oh yes. Thanks.' He pulled his thoughts together with an effort. 'Third Officer Forbes is just trying to get me off my hobby-horse.' He smiled at her and she bent over some clipped signals.

Crespin could almost feel the tension between them like a steel spring.

Scarlett said sharply, 'Anyway, I am not without some influence. I was able to make our point of view in the right quarter, but it was a struggle.' He walked heavily to a wall map. 'This is top secret, but I can tell you. I haven't any choice as it happens.' He rested his index finger on the toe of Italy. 'We are to invade here on the third of next month, with a second group of landings six days later further north to cut off and occupy Naples.' The finger moved up the coastline. 'That will be the big one, Operation Avalanche, smack into the Gulf of Salerno.'

Crespin hid a smile. Scarlett seemed to love these names they gave to the various landings.

Scarlett turned and rocked back on his heels. 'Now, when this starts moving the Hun is going to realise that we're really in earnest and going for the jackpot. He's going to pull troops from everywhere, just as he did in a small way to combat your little raid.' He took a deep breath. 'Intelligence has already reported heavy movements of armour and troops from all over Italy, and what is more to the point, from other occupied countries. Well, that's all fine and dandy for the countries in question, but it's no help to our forces. Winter will soon be here and the Army will have enough trouble fighting its way north through Italy, what with flooded valleys, roads washed away and so forth, without facing an enemy twice as powerful as it is at this moment.'

Crespin did not move. He could feel a fly crawling on his arm, could sense the girl's eyes on his face, but could not even turn his head. Scarlett knew exactly what he was going to say, but for once he seemed unable to say it.

He said calmly, 'When we have occupied the southern part of Italy, I assume you will start moving the special service units into the Adriatic, sir? After all, the Yugoslavs have already proved they are willing and able to fight the Germans, if only they can get the weapons.'

Scarlett studied him bleakly. 'You are so right. Unfortunately, we cannot wait that long. By the time we have fixed a line right across Italy the damage will have been done. We must hold up the enemy's movement of troops from the other side of the Adriatic, and that, as you so quickly observed, means Yugoslavia. We already have agents over there, and people who are doing invaluable work in liaison with the underground. But it is not enough, and this is where you come in.' He sat on one corner of the desk and swung his leg slowly like a pendulum.

'I want you to go to the offshore islands and meet some of these partisans and find out what they're doing.' He saw Crespin's unspoken question and hurried on, 'Not with your ship. That would be out of the question of course. I have a schooner ready and waiting in the harbour. It's full of battlefield clearance stores which will be far more use to the Yugoslavs than any of our gear. After all, anything they've got now is either German or Italian, so we must try and keep it that way.'

From the corner of his eye Crespin saw the girl staring at Scarlett with something like shock. So even she had not been told about this.

Scarlett was saying, 'I can give you some good men, but I don't have to tell you how risky this could be.' He leaned forward slightly. 'It's an important mission, otherwise I'd have sent some madcap lieutenant. Also, while you're there you can try and find a suitable and protected anchorage for the *Thistle*. For when we do move into that area in strength I want to hit the bastards where it hurts most!'

A smart marine peered through the door. 'The car's ready, sir.'

Scarlett waved him away. 'Well, Crespin, what do you say?'

'When do you want me to leave, sir?' Crespin thought he saw a flash of relief in Scarlett's eyes. 'I mean, if the Germans are as edgy as you say, it might be better to get a move on right away.'

Scarlett nodded slowly. 'Quite right. I am glad you see it my way. I've made arrangements for your ship to remain at her present moorings and a normal harbour routine to be carried out. Lieutenant Wemyss can run things here until you return, and this way we will excite as little attention as possible. One whiff of rumour about what you're up to and I'm afraid it would be serious. And I would be helpless to assist you in any way. You're on your own, and your judgement is what I'm depending on.' He laid one hand on Crespin's shoulder. 'What we're *all* depending on!'

He stood up and walked towards the door. 'You'll find the schooner ready to go. You can study the rest of the available details as soon as you get aboard.' He looked Crespin gravely in the eyes. 'Good luck.' Then he walked through the door calling for the marine.

The instant the door had closed the girl was round the desk and in his arms. For a long moment she pressed her face against his, her words broken and despairing. 'You *mustn't* go, John! Tell him it's too dangerous!'

He ran his fingers over her hair, the touch bringing back the memories and wiping away the pain of separation. 'I have to, Penny. You must see that!'

Then she pushed herself away and leaned back against the desk. 'You don't understand! He's been like a different person all these weeks. He's tried to get his own way, and when he couldn't fit in with the Sicily landings he nearly went mad.' She shook her head. 'But I never dreamed he would suggest your going in the schooner!' She pointed at the map. 'Why, we don't even know for sure which islands are in the hands of the partisans and which ones are occupied by the Germans.'

Crespin walked towards her and held her arms against her sides. 'I'll be all right. Someone has to go, and I'm the obvious choice if my ship is to be the one which eventually ends up there.'

She said, 'He's been trying to pump me ever since we got to Malta. I've not told him about us. I wouldn't dare. He's so possessive, so jealous of anyone who looks like challenging his position.'

Crespin grinned. 'I thought you admired him.'

'I did.' She shuddered. 'But now I don't know him at all!'

They both turned as the door opened a few inches. It was Scarlett, his face expressionless as he peered in at them.

He said, 'I just wanted to say that you can take the rest of the day off, Penny.' His eyes flickered between them. 'But I see you have already made your arrangements!' The door shut with a sharp click.

Crespin held her more tightly. 'Well, I imagine he knows about us now!'

She seemed to go limp and rested her forehead against his chest. 'I want the whole world to know. But I'm afraid of him, John. He's so ruthless, so filled with his own importance.' She clutched his sleeve. 'And I'm partly to blame, I know that now.'

Gently he lifted her chin and studied her. 'He wanted you, too, is that it?' When she nodded he said quietly, 'That's something I won't blame him for.'

She reached inside her pocket and he felt her thrust a piece of paper into his hand. 'I've got a room. I share it with a nurse, but she's away most of the time.' She was holding his arm so tightly that he could feel her fingers digging into his skin. 'I'll be there waiting. Please try and come to me before you leave.' She looked up at him, her eyes pleading. 'Say that you will try!'

He touched her face and felt the skin hot beneath his fingers. 'As soon as I can. And don't worry, I'll be all right.'

When he reached the crowded street he looked up at the window but she had gone. Then he touched the piece of paper in his pocket and walked quickly down the hill towards the harbour. Not only would he get back, but this time he had a good reason for surviving, he thought. The best reason in the world.

*   *   *

The schooner was about seventy-five feet in length and had, Crespin imagined, been afloat for the same number of years. She lay in a small silted inlet tied to a disused jetty, and looked as if she would topple on to her beam ends without its support.

She was scarred and filthy, and the tan-coloured sails which were so carelessly furled on her two masts were so patched that they must surely lose more wind than they caught.

But she was typical of the hundreds of such craft which scavenged an existence throughout the Adriatic and the Aegean. In peacetime you would find them as far afield as Gibraltar and Spain, although from their rough and ready appearance it was hard to know how they stayed afloat.

A bearded, surly-looking man in a torn shirt and canvas trousers watched Crespin climb down to the littered deck. He could have been a Greek or a Cypriot, but when he spoke he obviously came from some part of London.

He said, 'Leading Seaman Allan, sir.' He pointed at the hatch. 'You'll find the other officer below.'

Crespin nodded. It was a good beginning. As he climbed down the rickety ladder he was conscious of the mixed selection of smells. Paraffin and petrol, bad fish and tar, and an all-enveloping one of dirt.

The cabin was little more than an airless box. It was lined with crude bunks and lit by two oil lamps. An army officer was seated at a table, a chart spread out between a jumble of wine bottles, dirty plates and a huge chunk of cheese. He was wearing a washed-out suit of khaki drill and had a huge German Lüger strapped to one hip. As Crespin ducked between the low deck beams he stood up and gave a broad grin.

Crespin had been immediately aware of some familiarity and the grin clinched it. It was Coutts, the Grenadier in the goatskin, whom he had supposed dead or captured. He looked very much alive and had also been promoted to captain.

Coutts pushed a stool across the deck. 'Park yourself, old chap.' He saw Crespin's expression and laughed. 'The bad penny, you see, has reappeared!' He poured some wine into two glasses. 'Actually, it wasn't too difficult. I played "dead" and the Jerries were so enraged about what you were doing by the pier that they didn't bother to prod me with a bayonet to make sure.' He frowned briefly. 'There were plenty who were less fortunate.'

'But how the hell did you get away?'

'Walked, old boy. Just kept going until I ran into the

Americans coming in the opposite direction. They were harder to convince than the Germans but, as you see, I'm back in circulation again.'

The wine tasted sour but was very welcome nevertheless.

Crespin said, 'What do you think of our proposed jaunt?'

Coutts rubbed his nose. 'It's far too soon of course, but we'll just have to feel our way. I've been to Yugoslavia before, but things keep changing there. You're never quite sure who is a friend.'

There was something very reassuring about Coutts. He said, 'This boat has a crew of ten, and the skipper is a petty officer who used to be a trawlerman before the war. A bit rough, but damn handy in a scrap.'

Crespin leaned over the chart, his eyes taking in the details without effort. He asked, 'How did you get into this game?'

Coutts stared at the bottle. 'I've been in the Long Range Desert Group. One of my ancestors was a pirate, so I suppose I just wanted to follow him. And now that the desert's all cleared up again I've transferred my affections to this sphere of operations. I don't think I'll ever really settle down to Buckingham Palace guard duty after this!'

Crespin chuckled. It was hard to picture this long-haired character as a red-coated Grenadier.

At that moment the schooner's skipper dropped noisily through the hatch. Like the man on deck he was bearded and extremely tough. But he had a gentle Scottish accent and seemed to bring a breath of the Western Isles into the sordid little cabin. He also had a way of making a few words go a long way.

'Would be better to sail before five in the morning.' He dabbed the chart with a thick, grimy finger. 'The engine is a mite rough, but with this nor'-westerly we can get the sails on her.' He regarded Crespin with a pair of deep-set, dog-like eyes. 'T'would be right for you to stay in uniform, I am thinking. If caught you may be treated as a prisoner of war.' He shook a bottle and then poured himself a glass of wine.

Coutts grinned. 'Petty Officer Ross will get us there. He can smell his way!'

The skipper held up the glass to one of the swinging lamps

and grimaced. 'This wine is a thing now. A dram of Laphroiag would not come amiss, I'm thinking.'

Coutts pointed at the chart. 'I think we should head for this island. It is very small but quite close to the larger one of Korcula where we might make contact with the partisans.'

Crespin studied the island in silence. It was over six hundred miles away, deep inside the enemy held waters of Yugoslavia, and only twenty-five miles from the mainland itself.

Ross said calmly, 'It will take us a week. Maybe more.'

Coutts leaned back, apparently satisfied. 'We've a good motor mechanic aboard so the old engine might be all right.' He shot Crespin a meaning glance. 'If that's all right by you, we'll get under way in ten hours' time. That'll give me the chance to check the guns and ammunition and make sure it's all well hidden away from prying eyes.' He held up his watch. 'So if you want to go ashore for anything?'

Crespin looked around the cabin. These men, these preparations all made his own raid seem easy and secure by comparison. Yet there was no boasting, no false sentiment. Ross was sitting quietly on his stool puffing a rank-looking pipe, and overhead he could hear two of the schooner's crew stamping accompaniment to a mouth organ.

He stood up. 'I shall be back in four hours.'

When he had gone Coutts smiled and said quietly, 'Give her my love.'

Ross looked at him for a few seconds and then said, 'He seems a pleasant fellow to be sure.' His eye fastened on to Coutts' shoulder strap. 'Not like an officer at all.'

10 A Man Called Soskic

IN the dream the girl was lying motionless beneath him, her perfect body clearly outlined by endless darkness. But he was being pulled away, and no matter how hard he tried to hold her, those other hands seemed to be lifting him, dragging him free, while the deep shadow overlapped and covered her limbs like water.

A voice said, 'About time! You sailors can sleep through anything!'

Reluctantly Crespin rolled on to his side and opened his eyes. Barely inches away Coutts' face shone in shaded torchlight like an unshaven genie, with no more reality than the dream.

He asked, 'What time *is* it, for heaven's sake?'

'Nearly six, old son.' Coutts held out a chipped mug. 'Drink this, it'll bring the colour back to your cheeks.'

He propped himself on one elbow sipping the bitter coffee while his mind slowly returned to life and understanding. Apart from the torchlight, the small cabin was in darkness, and he could hear the schooner's crew snoring or turning restlessly on their bunks, while around him the hull creaked and shivered, the sea sluicing against the worn planks barely inches from his head.

Coutts said cheerfully, 'Dawn's coming up.'

Crespin peered at his watch. It was the fifth dawn since leaving Malta. For days they had pushed steadily north-east, using the sails and occasionally running the ancient engine when the wind looked like dying on them. It had been a strange and unnatural existence, with an overwhelming sense of loneliness and vulnerability as hour by hour they had watched the horizons and the sky expecting to see a prowling aircraft or a telltale smudge of smoke, any of which could spell disaster. On the third day they altered course almost due north towards the Otranto Strait, a forty-mile bottleneck which marked the entrance of the Adriatic. It was known to be heavily patrolled by sea and air, and with Italy on one side and Albania on the other it was generally described as impossible to pass. Even submarines, the only warships which had so far penetrated into these waters, had been hard put to get out again unmolested.

Coutts took the mug and put it on the table. 'Thought you'd like to come on deck and take a look at the land.' He grinned. 'It's quite romantic in the first light.'

Crespin pulled on his shoes and followed him up the ladder.

The sky was already much lighter, the breeze cool and refreshing, making the big sails crack and shiver above their heads as Coutts pointed across the starboard bulwark. 'Corfu!'

Crespin nodded. The island arose from the sea in a dark blue hump, the top of which seemed to shine with a faint luminous glow. Soon the sun would make its appearance, and once again the little schooner would be pinned down in the glare like a moth on a sheet of silk.

Coutts added quietly, 'It'll take about nine hours to reach the narrows and pass through the Strait.'

They had discussed that moment many times in the last few days. Any sort of bravado at this stage was asking for trouble, and to attempt a night passage, even with its higher chance of success, would kill their hopes completely if a patrol boat discovered them slinking past the coast alone and with no good explanation. It would be far better to be obvious. To sail close inshore and join the other traffic of schooners and caiques, rusty freighters and all the hotchpotch of vessels which plied back and forth along the Dalmatian shoreline.

With the roads and railways of their occupied territories under constant attack by roaming bands of partisans and bandits, the Germans made full use of every sort of sea transport available. It was easier to watch and protect. It was also easier to use if you wanted to avoid arousing too much interest.

Crespin said, 'We shall pass right by Valona Bay this afternoon.' He was speaking his thoughts aloud. The port in question was on the Albanian coast east of the heel of Italy, the guardian of the gate. It was known to be used as a German naval base from where many of their patrols sailed to police the narrows and the mass of islands which screened the Adriatic coastline almost from end to end.

Coutts yawned and spread his arms. 'It'll be September in a day or so. We'll have been at war for four years.' He grinned. 'I never thought I'd end up in a situation like this.'

Crespin studied him in the pale light. Coutts was wearing his smelly goatskin again, and in five days he had withdrawn to his old character, unshaven and long-haired, the picture of neglect and poverty.

He made Crespin feel like a complete interloper, as did the rest of the schooner's villainous-looking crew. They had insisted he should keep as smart as he could even at the expense of the scanty supply of fresh water. When he had protested Coutts had said coolly, 'You must look the part, old chap. It won't do for all of us to go ashore like a pack of bloody heathen.' Crespin had to be content with this explanation for Coutts did not elaborate on it.

Petty Officer Ross was standing straddle-legged at the wheel, his pipe jutting through his beard, his eyes switching between the compass and the sails. Crespin had hardly heard him speak more than a few words, and he noticed that the rest of the crew respected his self-imposed isolation.

That was the strange thing about all of them, he thought. There was no outward discipline or any sort of routine, yet each seemed to know what to do and exactly when to do it.

There was an able seaman called Preston, for instance. Crespin had spoken to him several times and marvelled at his tremendous range of knowledge, from politics to preparing explosive booby traps. He had a laconic, modulated drawl, and had in fact been to Eton. Unlike many Crespin had met he had not failed to obtain a commission or blotted his copybook to such a degree that his application had been turned down. He was one of the Navy's happy misfits, and had refused to accept the chance of being an officer so many times that he had at last been allowed to sink into his own particular way of life.

He was certainly a misfit. But Crespin knew others like him who had ridden astride two-man torpedoes deep into enemy harbours, or had been frogmen landed on defended beaches to clear obstacles and mark the way for a raid or an invasion. Their work was too secret and too dangerous to receive any publicity. They just got on with the job in their own way, as Preston was doing right now.

Coutts remarked suddenly, 'You know, it's not going to be easy. Your Captain Scarlett doesn't have much idea of these people we're going to see.'

When Crespin did not speak he added, 'When the Germans first overran Yugoslavia their methods were so brutal that many of the people turned against them out of sheer necessity. They went to the hills and hit back as best they could. Blowing up bridges, sniping at despatch riders, all that sort of thing. The Huns, true to form, responded with even crueller measures. They killed hostages, even wiped out whole villages to show the Yugoslavs they meant business.' He shook his head. 'But they misjudged these people very badly. They're tough and used to hard-living. They gave no quarter, and got none. The Germans have had to tie down whole divisions just to keep the roads open for supplies and communications.'

Crespin filled his pipe and lit it carefully below the edge of the bulwark. 'Well, what went wrong?'

Coutts shrugged. 'The usual thing. As the guerillas obtained more weapons and grew more successful there was growing unrest between their own groups. On the one hand you've got the partisans under Tito, and they're mostly communists like those chaps were in Sicily. And the others are the Chetniks. Royalists, for the want of a better description. When I was last in Yugoslavia, over a year back, it didn't matter so much. But now it's a different picture. Some say that the Royalists have actually been fighting Tito's chaps, and that a large proportion of them have even been helping the Germans. So the question is, which side do we help?' He stared intently through the smoke from Crespin's pipe. 'When I say *we*, I don't mean some silly old clots in Whitehall, I mean you and I!'

Crespin looked at the water sloshing against the hull. 'It will all depend on which lot we meet first, I suppose.'

Coutts smiled. 'Of course, if we run into the Jerries we don't have to bother. Things will all be decided for us!'

Ross snapped, 'Boat engines to the nor'-east!' He was craning his shaggy head, one hand cupped to his ear. 'Coming out from the land by the sound of it.'

Coutts moved like a cat. He whipped out his Lüger and placed it carefully beneath a coil of rope by the bulwark. Hidden but within easy reach.

'Roust out the lads, Skipper. I'll take the wheel.' To Crespin he said, 'You go to your little nest under the cargo. I'll give you a call if the patrol boat wants us to go aboard for cocktails!'

Crespin hesitated, feeling the instant tension of alarm and danger. He could hear the crew tumbling from their bunks, the snap of metal as a Sten gun was loaded and jammed into some hiding place where it could be found and fired within seconds.

Coutts said, 'Go on. There's nothing for you to do yet.' His tone was different. Clipped and final.

In the cabin he saw Preston taking a last look round to make sure there was nothing which might betray a casual inspection.

He said, 'I'll shut you in, sir.'

Crespin lowered himself down another ladder and through a coffin-like lid cut into the bilges amidst the piles of mixed cargo which covered the hidden boxes of ammunition and guns in a solid, entangled jumble. There were crates of dubious-looking wine and piles of dried fish. There were even rolls of barbed wire addressed to the garrison at Split, complete with an authentic German army despatch note.

Preston watched Crespin lie down in the cramped, airless space and grinned. 'One thing, sir. If we get blown up, you'll not need to move. You've got your coffin on already!' He was still chuckling as he jammed the boards into place and heaved something heavy over the top.

Crespin lay in the stinking darkness feeling a sudden sense of panic. He thought of his new sub-lieutenant, Defries, and wondered how he would react under these circumstances. Suffering the claustrophobic nightmare of a submarine in total darkness and under a barrage of depth-charges had almost broken his nerve completely. This would surely drive him mad.

Curiously, the thought seemed to steady him, and after a few minutes he was able to relax his body and ignore the pounding of his heart while he tried to listen to what was happening beyond his tiny prison.

It was more of a vibration than a sound at first, and again he felt the sweat pouring over his chest and soaking across his groin. It was like those old dreams, reliving the horror of that other patrol boat, so that his body began to contract, as if waiting for the rattle of gunfire, the smashing impact of bullets.

He heard muffled shouts and the clatter of rigging. Ross must be dropping his sails. Then the engines roared out, very loud, it seemed right against the side of his hiding place, and the whole hull shuddered and groaned, while the water between the two vessels was churned into a great maelstrom until with a final lurch they came tight together. The engines died, and in the sudden silence Crespin could hear the harsh bark of commands, the thump of booted feet on the schooner's deck.

It was impossible to know what was going on or how long it was taking. The sides of the hiding place were so low that Crespin could not move his wrist up to his eyes to see his luminous watch. The feet pounded up and down, with sharp, guttural voices intermingling with quieter, confused murmurings. But whatever was happening the patrol seemed to be carrying out an inspection. If nothing else it meant that the enemy was on a routine patrol. If they had been forewarned in any way of the schooner's real mission they would have taken stronger action by now. Crespin wondered if the false documents and carefully aged permits would stand a close scrutiny, or if they had been changed since the Navy's forgers had done their work.

He stiffened as another hatch banged open and feet clattered down a ladder almost directly above him. He could see the yellow glare of lamps through a slit in the planking just by his face, and felt dust and sand falling across his mouth as boots grated right over his hiding place.

A voice rapped out something in German, and he heard
Coutts muttering a reply in a hoarse, wheedling tone which
he hardly recognised. The German shouted an order and there
were more scrapes and bangs as some of the cargo was moved.

Crespin held his breath and waited for the planks to move
and the first surprise give way to the flash of gun-fire. He closed
his eyes tightly and tried to hold on to a picture of the girl as
he had last seen her. Like the dream, soft and naked in his
arms, shutting out the rest of the world in the fierceness of
their love.

Someone laughed and the feet halted again right above his
face. He could even hear the leather creaking as the German
swayed with the slow roll of the schooner's deck.

The lamplight dimmed, and seconds later the hatch was
closed again. Another age passed, and then with a roar of
power the patrol boat cast off and thrashed clear of the
schooner's side.

The planks moved and Preston peered down at him. 'Gone,
sir. I hope you are feeling all right?'

When Crespin reached the deck Coutts was standing beside the wheel a cheroot drooping from one corner of his
mouth. He held out his hand. '*Keep down*. The bastards might
still be looking at us!'

Crespin lifted his head slowly above the bulwark, conscious
of the sunlight on the milky water, the fresh smells of freedom and escape.

The patrol boat was already well away, her screws throwing up a mass of white foam beneath her counter, the bow
wave creaming across to make the schooner rock uncomfortably in her wake.

Coutts said slowly, 'They took some of the wine, the greedy
swine! But they were taking too long to check the papers. I
had to do something.'

Crespin turned towards the land. It looked very beautiful,
and shrouded in pale sea mist, unreal and unreachable.

He said, 'That was close.'

Coutts' eyes were still on the distant boat. They were cold
and filled with hatred. 'He stood so near I could feel his bloody
stomach rumbling. He'll never know how near he came to get-

ting a knife in his fat guts!' Then he seemed to shake himself from his thoughts. He held up the papers and grinned. 'And now we've got a nice new rubber stamp on these. In this war there's nothing like a rubber stamp for oiling the wheels of diplomacy!'

Crespin met his eyes and smiled. 'No matter which side you're on,' he replied.

Nine hours later, with her tan sails flapping in a gentle breeze and the old engine pouring out a cloud of rank fumes, the schooner edged past the fringe of Valona Bay. Here there were plenty of other such craft, and Crespin found himself wondering if some of them carried people like Coutts, on missions which were so vague and treacherous that there was neither yardstick nor guidance to ease their way.

By nightfall they were well into the Adriatic, with the coast of Yugoslavia reaching out towards the starboard bow like a black shadow. If there had ever been thought of turning back it had gone now. Crespin sat on the hatch-cover and watched the phosphorescence dancing away from the bows, and listened to Ross humming a strange, lilting little tune. They were all committed, and when he thought of the many miles which had rolled away astern he wondered if they would ever be able to return. Here, time and distance meant nothing. Survival just a word.

Yet as he listened to Ross and watched the stars on the dark, heaving water he knew he was glad to be here, even if he did not know the reason.

*   *   *

Six days after the German patrol had stopped and searched the schooner she dropped her anchor in the lee of a small island called Gradz. The chart showed a tiny village on the southern side, but as Crespin clung to a foremast stay and strained his eyes through the darkness he found it hard to believe that anyone still lived there. That anybody *could* live on such a place. The island was barely four miles long, and surrounded by tall, sheer-sided cliffs. Below them the sea rumbled and hissed, daring any craft to move closer inshore and face the necklace

of reefs which showed in the darkness in a broken line of
breakers. The cliffs seemed unending, yet he knew they were
in fact filled with steep inlets and coves, and he could hear the
sea booming across the nearest one like water in a cave.

The dawn could not be far away, but he was too tired even
to look at his watch. During the past days there had been so
many false alarms and disappointments that he no longer felt
any room for hope.

Around him the schooner swayed uneasily as she snubbed at
her cable, and he could hear two of the seamen in the bows
murmuring to each other as they peered into the choppy water
watching for the first sign that the little vessel was dragging
her anchor. For the sea was very deep here and the anchorage
totally unsuitable for any craft, let alone one hiding from an
enemy.

And that was how it had been all along. Groping amidst the
islands by night and hiding by day. Time and time again Coutts
had gone ashore with Preston in the small dory to visit some
village or to call on a tiny clump of fishermen's huts huddled
in a bleak inlet, and each time he had returned with little more
than a curt shake of the head. Nobody it seemed would talk, at
least not to him. Perhaps they were too frightened of reprisals,
or maybe they were so long weighed down by occupation and
war they had forgotten the meaning of resistance. They were
neither hostile nor suspicious. They just shrugged and then
waited for the schooner to leave. But it could not go on like
this. They were courting disaster, and sooner or later they
would be betrayed, or would stumble across another, more
vigilant patrol boat.

It was hard to tell what the schooner's crew thought about
it, but Coutts had withdrawn completely and hardly spoke to
anyone but Preston. He was restless and moody, and once when
Crespin had tried to draw him out he had snapped, 'You can
do your job when I've found these bastards. Until then for
God's sake leave me in peace!'

And now they were here. It seemed like the end of the line.
Beyond this rocky island lay the larger one of Korcula, and
beyond that the unknown strength of the German occupation
forces.

He shivered and banged his hands together. It was damp and extremely cold, and unless Coutts returned very soon the ship would have to stay where she lay, exposed and obvious to anyone who cared to come and inspect her.

Crespin walked slowly aft to where Ross leaned against the wheel, his unlit pipe clamped in his jaw.

'How long has he been gone, Skipper?'

Ross took the pipe from his mouth and tapped it on the spokes. 'Three hours. Maybe more.'

Crespin eyed him in the darkness. Ross sounded so untroubled by their predicament, even though Coutts might be lying dead, shot by some unexpected patrol or drowned in a capsized dory.

He said, 'It looks a pretty inhospitable place.'

'Aye.' Ross seemed to consider it. 'But there is a very fair anchorage beyond yon bluff. Deep water and good shelter on both sides. A place a ship could well make use of, I'm thinking.'

Crespin thought of the *Thistle* lying at her moorings at Malta. It was hard to picture her here, hiding amidst bare cliffs with the enemy almost within gunshot. He found himself wondering if the admiral at Portsmouth or the commander in Gibraltar, or even Scarlett for that matter, had any idea of the dangers and complications involved when they devised this mission.

Ross said suddenly, 'The Germans cannot be too happy about their work here. Can you imagine the difficulties of patrolling such an area?' He shook his head. 'It must be like putting one English policeman to patrol the Irish frontier, except that here there is also a problem of language.'

Crespin smiled. 'That's one way of looking at it.'

Ross shrugged. 'You have to feel your way in this sort of warfare. You must be *right* for it. Now take that poor fellow Trotter for instance. He was a sad one to be sure.'

Crespin stared at him. 'You knew him?'

'A passing acquaintance. In North Africa it was. Last year sometime, I forget exactly. He was working with the Special Service even then, but he was doing the work for the wrong reasons. He had made a failure of his previous life and thought this work would be more of an escape from his worries.' He sighed. 'I thought he might be killed, but not in the manner in which he has died.'

Crespin looked past him towards the heaving water. The wind was breaking the surface into short, angry crests, and he could feel the spray soaking against his legs like rain. But he was thinking of Trotter. It was strange how he kept cropping up.

He asked, 'That was the last you saw of him then?'

Ross nodded. 'As I remember. I never really knew him though.' He turned towards Crespin, his beard blowing out in the wind. 'But surely Captain Scarlett will have told you about him?'

'Captain Scarlett?'

'Surely.' Ross was getting restless, as if unused to so much talk. 'Trotter was one of his team in those days. He must have known him better than most.'

Crespin walked back to the foremast, his mind turning over Ross's information. What sort of a game was Scarlett playing? If Trotter's death made little sense, this latest piece of deception made no sense at all.

A seaman muttered, 'Dory's comin' back!'

Ross hurried from the wheel. It was amazing how quickly he could move when he had a mind to. 'Cover it with the Stens, lads!' To another he rapped, 'Stand by the cable in case we have to cut loose in a hurry!'

Preston's voice echoed above the wind and spray. 'It's all right! It's me!' It was hardly a correct approach, but there was no mistaking his drawling tone.

The boat banged alongside and a grapnel thudded into the bulwark.

Crespin stayed by the mast watching the dark heads rising above the pitching rail and wondering what Coutts would have to report this time. But the man with Preston was certainly not Coutts. He was short and shaggy, his thick jerkin criss-crossed with bandoliers and a heavy carbine slung across one shoulder.

Preston saw Crespin and said quickly, 'Be careful what you say, sir. I'm not sure if he speaks English or if he's just pretending to be awkward.'

The man shambled across the deck and peered closely at Crespin's uniform. He smelt strongly of woodsmoke and dirt. Then he nodded violently and gestured with his thumb towards the cliffs. Preston spoke to him for several seconds and the man replied in a short, guttural whisper.

'He says we are to enter the inlet, sir.' Preston sounded tired. 'He's not exactly forthcoming.'

'But where is Captain Coutts?' Crespin felt isolated and useless. 'What did you find?'

Preston stared at him. 'Oh, didn't I say? Well, we managed to find a beach for the dory and we were just getting it hauled out of the water when about a dozen of these characters pounced on us.' He looked over the bulwark. 'I think they were expecting us. We tried to speak to them but they just kept prodding us with their guns and demanding that we anchor the boat inside the inlet.

Crespin clenched his fists. 'But are they . . .?'

'Partisans?' Preston studied him thoughtfully. 'Could be. Come to that, they could be anything. But they've kept Captain Coutts as an insurance policy. The rest is up to us.'

Ross said gruffly, 'Don't be so big-headed, young fellow!' He looked at Crespin. 'It is surely up to *you*, sir?'

Crespin nodded. It was the first time Ross had called him *sir*. He must be more worried than he showed.

He said, 'If we stay out here we shall be asking for trouble.' He made up his mind. 'Break out the anchor and start up the engine, Skipper.'

The newcomer had been standing in silence watching them with obvious interest. As Ross moved towards the wheel he unslung the carbine and worked the bolt noisily. Then he squatted on the bulwark and pointed the gun at the shore. He spoke briefly, and Preston spread his hands before interpreting unhelpfully, 'He just says to go on in, sir!'

As soon as the anchor broke free the schooner seemed to dance sideways out of control. But with the engine coughing and roaring Ross managed to bring her round until the bows were pointing directly towards what looked like a solid wall of rock.

It was some small comfort to see the partisan, or whatever

he was, was sitting unconcernedly on the bulwark smoking a cheroot and swinging one foot as the schooner bucked and rolled beneath him.

Ross muttered, 'Ah, I have the feel of it now.' He said no more, but spun the wheel hard over as two tall rocks reared out of the darkness and slid away over the starboard quarter like a pair of browsing sea-monsters.

All at once the engine noises became louder and the sea less choppy, and Crespin could feel the land closing around him, like a blind man walking into an empty room.

The Yugoslav grunted and gesticulated sharply with the carbine.

Preston said, 'Anchor, sir.'

Crespin waved his hand and from forward came the answering ring of metal as the slip was knocked free and the cable roared once more through the fairleads. Ross stamped his foot twice on the deck and obediently the engine sighed gratefully into silence.

Crespin said, 'Tell your friend that we'll wait for first light. Then we'll go ashore in the dory.'

He did not have to understand the language to know what Preston was going to translate. He saw the little Yugoslav's teeth gleaming in the darkness, heard the taut anger in his throaty voice.

Preston said, 'He says *now*, sir. You are to go with him right away. I am to go, too, apparently.'

It was pointless to argue. If the whole German army was poised on the island it could not make much difference now. They needed help, and these people, whoever they were, must know it by now. So perhaps the villagers Coutts had questioned had not been so dumb and helpless as he had imagined.

He said flatly, 'Right, Skipper, you'll stay in charge. If there's any trouble you'll up anchor and try and run for it. But if this is a trap and there's no way out, then don't try and fight. There's no sense in getting killed for nothing.'

Ross followed him to the side. 'At least they are wanting to talk with you. That must be a good sign, surely? The Germans are less inclined for such things!' Then he stood aside while Crespin lowered himself into the dory alongside.

Preston took the oars and pulled strongly towards the over-hanging side of the inlet. He said between pulls, 'Let's hope they're not cannibals!'

As the boat ground awkwardly into some rough sand several figures moved swiftly from the rocks, surrounding it and shutting it off from the sea. It must be getting lighter already, Crespin thought grimly. He could see the dull gleam of levelled weapons, the cold watchfulness of the bearded men around him. He climbed over the gunwale and then turned as a hand darted out and dragged his pistol from its holster.

Preston said sharply, 'That's all right, sir. Let him take it.' There was an unusual crispness in his tone and Crespin let his arms fall to his sides.

Someone prodded his spine with a rifle, and in single file the little party began to climb a steep narrow path which seemed to lead directly up and through a split in the cliff above the beach. It was hard going, and in the greying light Crespin saw that some of his companions were without footwear of any kind and their weapons varied from old Russian rifles of the First World War to new German Schmeissers. No attempt was made to blindfold him or stop him from looking around the narrow path, and he guessed that they considered it quite un-necessary. If he failed to convince their leader there would be no return journey for him or any of the schooner's crew.

At the top of the path he paused and looked back. The water of the inlet was like black silk, and around and above the tall sides he could see the craggy ridges and hills of the island, bare and very forbidding. The schooner was still hid-den in deep shadow, but beyond the narrow entrance he could see the white wave-crests gliding past driven by the wind and current, so that it looked as if the island was swivelling on a giant pivot.

Another rifle jabbed his spine and he moved forward again. It was even colder on the top of the cliff and the path was rough and treacherous with loose stones and small stunted patches of scrub. Bare feet or not the men kept up a steady pace with no sign of breathlessness or discomfort.

They followed the side of the cliff without a pause, and Crespin became aware of the size of the inlet beneath him.

Long and sheltered, like a Scottish loch, with the merest hint
of a tiny crescent-shaped beach every so often to break the
monotony of the cliffs along the sides.

They walked for an hour, and by the time they had reached
a bend in the path Crespin could see a great towering hill
which must be almost the dead centre of the island itself.
Five thousand feet or more, he decided, its jagged crest already
pale grey in the morning light.

Then he looked down and saw the village. It seemed about
to slide down a steep-sided gully into the water below, the
small houses one above the other, huddled together as if for
support. A few boats were hauled clear of the water, and as
the party tramped down another narrow path he heard dogs
barking and caught the strong scent of burned wood on the
damp air.

But they were not going to the village. They turned on to
another, even narrower track, and after walking for about
fifteen minutes arrived at what looked like a barricade of
stone blocks. In fact, it was a massively constructed wall
which had been built across the entrance of a cavern, so that
once through a narrow entrance they were standing inside a
man-made bunker. It was lit by oil lamps, and the rock sides
were glistening with moisture from the mountain above it.
Crude partitions had been built with ammunition boxes and
old crates, and as the men pushed Crespin deeper into the
cavern he saw figures wrapped in blankets sleeping in rows
beside their weapons, oblivious to the dripping moisture and
the crude rock beneath them.

One man pulled a curtain aside and gestured with his rifle.
Crespin walked into this smaller cave and heard the man at his
back lower the rifle to the ground. He was alone now, for
Preston had been escorted past the cave and he could hear the
footsteps dying away, as if being swallowed up inside the solid
rock.

There was a screen at one end of the cave, and from behind
it came a tall figure dressed in a black leather coat. He was
wiping his hands very carefully on a towel, his close-set eyes
gleaming in the lamplight as he seated himself slowly behind
a trestle table. His features were tanned and deeply lined, and

he could be almost any age from thirty to fifty. He had a neatly trimmed beard, and as he thrust his long legs beneath the table Crespin saw that he was wearing a beautifully made pair of German jackboots.

Then the man looked up from the table and studied him for several seconds. His features were impassive and devoid of expression. By the rough doorway the escort said something in a low voice, and there was something in his tone which told Crespin he was in the presence of the real leader.

The man at the table laid the towel carefully on a pile of grenades. When he spoke it was in a flat, measured voice, again quite devoid of animation. Crespin stiffened. He was speaking to him in German. The sense of failure and despair swept over him in an uncontrollable flood. He thought of Ross and the others waiting aboard the schooner, still holding on to hope. Trusting in his judgement.

He replied bitterly, 'I am Lieutenant-Commander John Crespin, Royal Navy. I do not speak German.'

The man at the table glanced at the sentry and grimaced slightly. Then he said, 'Very well. We will speak in English, if you wish to prolong this little game.'

Crespin felt something like blind anger sweeping through him. The confidence of the man, the cold indifference of his tone made him want to jump the last few feet and choke the life out of him. The man at his back must have sensed this and he felt the rifle nudge him warningly.

He said harshly, 'I am a British officer and my men are members of the armed services.'

'I see.' He nodded distantly. 'Yet your approach and the garb of your men would suggest otherwise.' He smiled gently. 'But I see that by wearing the correct uniform you at least hoped to retain the safety of convention.'

Crespin did not reply. He thought of Coutts and Preston. They were probably dead already. If they were lucky.

'My name is Soskic.' The dark eyes studied Crespin's face searchingly. 'I am the commandant here. Whether you live or die could depend on my final opinion.'

'I have said all I intend to say.' Crespin felt the walls closing

in on him. 'If you are a German officer you will know that is
all I can say.'

Soskic touched his small beard and put his head on one side.
'Then you are *not* a German?' He smiled again. 'That is interesting. It is also what your man Coutts has told me.'

'What have you done with him?'

'I will ask the questions!' The smile vanished. 'I have been
told of your presence here in the islands. I wondered what
sort of story you might bring. Now that you have arrived all
you can do is accuse me of being a German!' He spat the word
out like an obscenity. 'I am Soskic. I command here, not because of the Germans, but in spite of them!'

He gestured sharply with his hand and Crespin felt a stool
being thrust against his legs.

'Please sit down, Commander Crespin.' Soskic rested his
hands on the table and stared at them gravely. 'Yes, I knew
about your coming, but I could do nothing to help you until I
was sure. Sure of you, and what you bring. This is a different
war from yours. There are no rules and no single goal but
victory, no matter at what cost. Our leader, Comrade Tito, is
fighting his own war on our mainland, but out here we have to
manage as best we can. Survival is only a beginning.'

Crespin watched him, noting the strain in his close-set eyes,
the carefully controlled tenseness of his body. So Soskic was a
partisan, or so he said.

He said, 'I expect that Captain Coutts has told you of our
mission?'

Soskic eyed him calmly. 'You are asking or telling? No matter. I have spoken with, er, Captain Coutts. He is an interesting, and I suspect a very dangerous man. But you are, he tells
me, in charge of this matter, so now that you have made this
somewhat hazardous visit perhaps you would be good enough
to enlighten me?'

Crespin felt his wound throbbing in time with his thoughts.
'If you knew we were coming, why all these questions?'

Soskic pressed his fingertips together and looked at the
table. 'I was once a schoolmaster in Dubrovnik. It is a habit
with me still. That is how I speak your appalling language so
well, eh?' For once his smile had some warmth in it.

He hurried on, 'Two days ago we had another visit. Not from the Germans, for they have learned it is too costly to embark on such foolishness.' His eyes hardened. 'Since they invaded my country they have had to fight to hold on to every piece of land. Month by month we have struck at them until now they are fearful to stray away from their garrisons and their strongpoints. We have almost driven them from the islands, but our victories have a double edge. They cannot reach us without great loss, but neither can we help our comrades on the mainland.' His voice became distant. 'So our visit was not of the Germans. They were fellow countrymen, at least by birth. They came with promises, high-sounding pleas for mutual trust in our common fight against the invader.'

Crespin asked carefully, 'The Chetniks?'

The eyes fixed on his face. 'You have been doing some study of our problems?' He shrugged. 'It is so. They are scum, more so because they belong to my country. They remember their king and they dream of the time he will return after *we* have rid the country of the enemy!' He shook his head violently. 'But we want no king, nor do we need their old way of serfdom and bourgeois oppression! So they made up their wretched minds that it was better to retain power under the Germans than to fight for a free Yugoslavia!'

Crespin said, 'It has happened in other countries, too.'

'It has. But in Europe the oppressed people know that soon now they will be freed by an Allied invasion. Out here we have still a long way to go, and there are not many left with the strength and the power to fight. In a year, maybe in months, these Royalist carrion may have recovered control, so no matter which side wins your war, my people are lost forever.'

'When they came here, what happened?'

Soskic stood up and walked to the doorway. As he pulled aside the blanket curtain he asked, 'Did you smell the smoke? It came from the houses those swine burned before we drove them back into the sea!' He returned to the table and sat down heavily. 'I hold myself to blame. I trusted them even though I knew they could not move so freely without the knowledge of the Germans. But I *hoped*, and hope is an empty thing without the backing of deeds. The Germans are like maggots. They devour and corrupt everything they touch, but even so I chose to hope that some of these men were genuine in their desire to help us.' He shrugged. 'And I need help, even from them. I can hold this island against a force fifty times as big as mine, but where is the point of that? *I* am the prisoner in a cage, not the enemy!'

Crespin said, 'I came here to offer you that help.'

The other man studied him without speaking. Then he said slowly, 'For what purpose?'

'Does it matter? We have a common enemy, that must surely be enough.'

Soskic nodded sadly. 'When this war is finished we may find ourselves on opposite sides again.'

'When it is won there may be no sides left to take.'

'As you say!' Soskic walked round the table and held out his hand. 'Captain Coutts has already told me all this, but I wanted to hear it from you.'

Crespin grasped his hand. 'Then you did not really think I was a German at all?'

Soskic laughed. 'You? A German?' He laughed again and the sentry joined in without understanding a word which was said. 'If you had been, I think you would have gone away as soon as you heard I had taken Coutts as a hostage. Only an Englishman would look on the matter of loyalty with such foolish seriousness and disregard for his own safety!' He shook his head. 'Oh no, I merely wanted to hear about you. If you are the sort of man who *can* help us.'

The curtain moved aside and Coutts walked into the cave, a bottle of wine poking from his goatskin coat.

'Well, have you finished yet?'

Soskic eyed him gravely. 'Finished,' he said. 'And well satisfied.'

Crespin felt slightly dazed. 'I would like to see the inlet properly as soon as it's light enough. I think we should be able to use it as our forward base.'

The commandant studied him thoughtfully. 'First you will sleep. Then we will unload the cargo you have brought me and which neither of you has so far mentioned.' He clapped his hand on Crespin's shoulder. 'And *then*, Commander, I will show you our rhinoceros.' Without another word he strode from the cave, his footsteps fading almost at once beyond the curtain.

Crespin looked at Coutts' grubby face. 'Rhinoceros?'

Coutts shrugged. 'Christ only knows, old chap, but let's have a drink and forget it!'

Then he grinned. 'Well, we made it.' He pulled the bottle from his coat. 'It's not much, but it's a beginning, wouldn't you say?'

11 Rescue and Revenge

THE three men stood in silence on the steep hillside with the northern coastline of the island spread below them like a map. The noon sun was high in a clear sky, yet the fresh sea breeze which ruffled the hill gorse like coarse fur gave the air a keenness and made Crespin feel more alert and alive than he had done for some time.

After a few hours' sleep and a hurried breakfast of cooked meat and black bread he and Coutts had followed Soskic at a brisk pace along what was little more than a goat track. It wound between the hills and steep-sided gorges, and Crespin was surprised to find that he was able to keep up with the long-legged commandant who strode ahead with the sureness and the confidence of a cat. They had soon left the inlet and village far behind, but when they finally reached this crumbling hillside Crespin realised just how small the island really was. For the sea was waiting to greet them once more and the scenery, like the air, was a tonic.

The distant islands reached out from every direction, overlapping and shimmering in the pure sunlight, separated by ribbons of deep blue water like the arms of some giant river. In fact, everything seemed to be painted in different shades of blue. The sea and the sky, and the hills and mountains of the other islands which shone in the sun with the paler, more delicate hue of ice.

Soskic turned to look at them. 'Over there is Korcula. There are still some German troops but they are less willing to move far from their base.' His arm swept towards the north-east. 'And that is the Peljesac peninsula, not another island.'

Crespin shaded his eyes against the glare and followed the direction of his arm. The peninsula did indeed look like just another island. The fine air made it seem so close, yet he knew from the chart that it was all of ten miles away. Korcula was about half that far, but a man less used to the sea's deception would probably imagine he could row a boat there in a matter of minutes. It brought a cold sensation to his spine to realise the enemy was so near, so rooted, and he was better able to understand Soskic's bitterness because of it. To see that shining peninsula, part of his homeland, almost within reach, yet to know that it was remote as another world.

The tall commandant added slowly, 'When the Chetniks attacked us they succeeded in one thing. They destroyed our last large boat. They might just as well have cut out our hearts.' He turned back towards the sea. 'There is a small village some twenty kilometres from here. For weeks we have been sending word for our comrades to gather there. All who can bear arms or who wish to come and join us. A secret is hard to keep for long. Now without a boat to bring them I am afraid that they are already as good as dead. When word reaches the Germans, and it will, they will be quick to make an example of those people. It will make up for their reverses at our hands. In their perverted minds the murder of women and children is totally justified.'

Coutts was puffing a cheroot, the smoke streaming behind him in an unbroken plume. 'How many men do you have here?'

'I have two hundred fighters.' Soskic did not turn. 'Men *and* women.'

Crespin studied the firm set of his shoulders and thought of the girl who had died as Porteous had tried to bind her wound. He said quietly, 'If we can help you, I will be happy to put the schooner at your disposal.' He saw Coutts' eyebrows lift with surprise but added firmly, 'What would be the best time?'

Soskic swung on his heel and stared down at him. 'The earlier the better. We may already be too late.' He thrust his

hands into his leather coat as if he did not know what to do
with them. 'I should warn you that your action might lead to
your own death. I could add that if the schooner is destroyed
then you, too, will be a prisoner here on Gradz. I could say all
of these things, but I will not.' He gave a small smile. 'You
would not listen, and I would not want you to.' He pulled out
a gold pocket watch and flicked open its cover. 'Time to move.
You must reach the next headland within the hour.' Without
waiting for questions he turned and hurried down the slope,
his boots sending the stones bouncing towards the sea with
each stride. Over his shoulder he said, 'I got the watch from the
same German who wore these fine boots.'

Coutts said quietly, 'I hope you know what you're doing!
What are you hoping for? A private war all of your own?'

Crespin smiled. 'I think you would have done the same.'

The soldier lapsed into silence. Then he said, 'He's a proud
bastard. That was the nearest thing he's done to thanking anyone for a long, long time, I shouldn't wonder.'

Crespin slipped and struggled back on to the rough track.
'Did you know he was once a schoolmaster?'

Coutts nodded. 'I got it from one of his men. The Germans
wiped out over fifty hostages. His wife and family were among
them.'

When at last Soskic called a halt Crespin was gasping for
breath. He had pulled out his watch again and was studying it
intently.

'Now we shall see, comrades. But I am sure that the German
dedication to routine and punctuality will not disappoint us!'

Crespin lowered himself gingerly on to a flat rock and stared
at the blue water beneath him. Near the shore it was so clear
that even from the tall hillside it was easy to see the jagged
outlines of rocks and pieces of fallen cliff lying far below the
surface.

He found himself thinking of the partisan women he had
seen that morning by Soskic's bunker. Young girls for the most
part, but with all the stamina and determination of regular
troops. Coutts had told him that they lived and slept beside the
men without embarrassment or any fear of being molested.
For the moment their sex had been put in reserve and their

presence was accepted with neither surprise nor compromise.

He thought, too of what might have happened if the Germans had succeeded in occupying Britain. It was not difficult to picture Penny sharing the risks and privations like these partisan women.

Crespin heard Coutts scrambling on the stones as he struggled to get to his feet, and his sudden gasp of surprise. When he looked up to see what was exciting the normally unruffled soldier he imagined for a moment that his eyes were playing tricks, or that the sun's glare had presented a strange mirage above the placid water.

As he pulled his binoculars from inside his shirt he heard Coutts exclaim, 'Well, I've seen some odd ships in my time, but this one beats them all!'

Crespin steadied his elbows on his knees and trained the glasses towards the far side of the channel where the blue ridges of Korcula Island appeared to reach out and overlap the jutting spur of mainland. The ship had come around the end of the island and was altering course in a wide sweep towards the open sea. Her hull was heavy and businesslike, and he guessed that she had once been a sizable cargo or passenger ship, and even the grey paint could not completely disguise the outdated cut of her bow with its heavy crest which told of more leisurely days.

But above the level of the main deck she bore no resemblance to any ship he had ever seen. The bridge and superstructure had been completely enclosed in steel plating, each piece angled in such a way as to make a direct hit almost an impossibility.

Crespin was reminded of the old pictures he had seen of the American ironclad *Monitor* in the Civil War. It looked indestructible, and even the ugly appearance could not detract from an overwhelming sense of danger and menace. Two tall funnels jutted from the steel canopy abaft the bridge, and the smoke which poured busily astern gave the only visible sign of life. She was like some remotely controlled juggernaut which might at any second change to a submarine or take to the air.

Soskic was watching him, a small smile playing about his

lips. He said, 'Well, Commander, what do you think of her, eh?'

Crespin moved the glasses slightly as the strange ship completed her turn and began to head for the channel below the cliffs. Now he could see two massive guns, each independently mounted at either end of the superstructure, again heavily protected by additional steel plate. Other, smaller muzzles jutted from dark slits cut along the side of the lower bridge, and right aft on her deserted poop he could just make out some sort of small railway which was obviously used for mine-laying.

He asked slowly, 'Is *this* the rhinoceros you spoke of?'

Soskic nodded. 'She used to be the *Morava* before the Germans seized her. She is forty years old, and until before the war ran between Greece and our own ports with general cargo and a few passengers. The Germans took her to Split and transformed her into what you now see. They even call her the *Nashorn*, and she is very similar to a rhinoceros in many ways. Awkward to handle, and because of her massive layers of armour she must be almost blind except for the most elementary movements.' He sighed deeply. 'But as you see, Commander, she is indeed formidable. We used to attack coastal shipping and cause havoc with German convoys between the islands. The *Nashorn* put an end to most of that. She steams around the islands as regularly as my watch. She can shoot down any attacker with ease, can smash a wooden craft without even reducing speed.'

Coutts said, '*This* is a problem.'

Crespin lowered the glasses and studied the ship for several seconds. She was pushing very slowly inshore and would pass within a mile of the headland.

He asked, 'Where is she based?'

Soskic pointed towards the peninsula. 'Beyond there. Forty kilometres from this island the Germans have set up a special headquarters just for the *Nashorn*. It is a small place called Tekla, not really suitable for a ship of her size, but it does have the advantage of a railway. You see, the *Nashorn* is coal fired, and every piece of fuel must be carried to her base by rail.'

Coutts said sharply, 'She is training one of her guns!'

Soskic grimaced. 'Every time she passes she fires a few rounds at us.'

There was a bright orange flash which seemed to dart straight out of the steel mass like a tongue, and seconds later the shell exploded somewhere far to the left, the roar of the detonation echoing around the cliffs like thunder.

Crespin wondered if anyone on the *Nashorn's* bridge could see the three figures watching from the hillside.

'I am surprised the Germans haven't used her to force an entry to your inlet.'

Soskic smiled. 'One good rifleman with endless ammunition and no need for sleep could hold an army from landing. The Germans are probably afraid that once inside the inlet their rhinoceros might be trapped in some way.'

Another shell slammed into the cliffs and brought down a great mass of rock and earth into the water below. Although hidden from view Crespin could see the sea churning back from the foot of the cliffs as if from some submarine explosion.

The gun swung back to train once more towards the bows, and with the haze of the explosions drifting to mix with her funnel smoke the ship swung away from the headland and continued towards the end of the channel.

Soskic climbed down from his rock and pulled out a cigarette. 'That monster is commanded by one, Kapitan Otto Lemke. He is twice your age, Commander, and as wily as a fox. He served aboard a commerce raider in the First World War, and I am told he often boasts of the ruses he used to beat your countrymen. I think he only got this appointment because the German Navy did not really know what to do with him. But he came here, and he used his wits when most of his colleagues were using their firing squads!'

The ugly vessel vanished beyond the headland leaving only a smudge of smoke against the clear sky. Soskic led the way back along the path adding, 'The *Nashorn* was his idea. He thought it out by himself, and *made* it work!'

Crespin glanced at Coutts and wondered if he was thinking the same thing. That Lemke sounded exactly like a combination of Admiral Oldenshaw and Scarlett. He had invented a

new craft of warfare. Now he had to make it useful if only to
prove his own worth.

Soskic turned and looked at Crespin's thoughtful features.
'Whatever you are planning, let me warn you. Lemke will
have thought of it already. His only weakness is his coal, and
even if we managed to delay his supply he would still have
sufficient to steam north to Split.' He shook his head. 'If we are
to defeat him, then we must find a way to destroy him. There
is no other way.'

Crespin followed the others in silence. The sudden
appearance of the armoured giant had meant a change in
everything. As Soskic had realised, the ship did not need to be
fast and manoeuvrable. She merely had to *be* here. A policeman and executioner rolled into one.

If the Allied invasion proved successful it would not take
many more months to install bases along the Italian east coast.
From Bari or Brindisi for instance they could operate a separate striking force which would soon hunt down and destroy
Lemke's juggernaut. But in those precious months the partisans would be unable to move and the Germans would be free
to release more and more troops to throw against the battle-
worn Allies. Just that one stupid fact might turn the whole
progress of the war, and with winter drawing inexorably
closer there was no saying what the enemy might pull out of
his hat. They had done it before in North Africa, but this time
it would be far worse. The Allies had the sea at their backs, and
in any case the damage to their morale which such a reverse
would bring might postpone any further eagerness for invasion
for years to come.

Coutts looked sideways at him and smiled gravely. 'Don't
worry about it too much. You've done what you came to do.
Leave the policy-making to the great brains of Whitehall!' He
rolled his eyes. 'And God knows what sort of mess *they*'ll
make of it!'

Crespin found no comfort in his words. Running guns and
landing small parties of raiders was no way to finalise a war.
It had to be faced from the opposite viewpoint, as Lemke had
so clearly done. His experience astride the British shipping
lanes in that other war must have taught him the vital im-

portance of communications and supplies, without which whole armies ground to a standstill and nations lost the will to withstand the shortages and privations which followed.

And while the *Nashorn* maintained her vigilant patrols the enemy had nothing to fear. No wonder they could send troops from their occupation forces without bothering to hide the fact. Those who remained in Yugoslavia might be unable to move about as freely as they would have wished, but as Soskic had remarked, they were like maggots. They could live and grow fat on what they controlled. If anyone suffered it would be the Yugoslavs themselves.

When they reached the bunker Soskic said, 'I suggest that you get some rest. I have to select a raiding party for the schooner. We will head for the mainland as soon as dusk makes it safe enough.' He looked hard at Crespin. 'That is unless you have changed your thoughts about it?'

Crespin shook his head. 'I shall be ready.'

The commandant nodded. 'Good.' Then he turned on his heel and walked briskly towards the village.

Coutts said, 'And I was supposed to see that you kept out of trouble!' He took off his goatskin and laid it on the floor like a rug. 'I'm not making a very good job of it!'

Crespin watched him settle down on the coat as if he had been sleeping in this fashion all his life. He replied quietly, 'The partisans need us. But if we're going to do any good out here we have got to make them trust us, too. You can't buy trust with a cargo of old guns and a few boxes of salvaged ammunition.' But when he looked down again he saw that Coutts had fallen asleep.

He smiled and walked across to a crude wooden bench. He sat for several minutes massaging the pain in his wounded leg and thinking about the armoured ship.

Whichever way you looked at it, the *Nashorn* seemed to be the key. She had to be destroyed, but how?

Then he lolled back against the rock wall and he, too was asleep.

*   *   *

As the first shadows of evening darkened the sides of the in-let the little schooner hoisted her anchor and headed purpose-fully into open water. Crespin, who had at first thought it safer to wait for complete darkness, soon realised that an early start was not only sensible but essential if their mission was to have any chance of success at all. For with the coming of night to the islands the wind had immediately dropped, so that once more Ross had to rely on the schooner's tired engine alone. In addition to thirty heavily armed partisans the ship was further hampered by the last of the island's sizable boats which yawed astern on a towline, and after a full two hours at sea the engine began to overheat so that they had to reduce speed still more.

But if the partisans were troubled by the delay they were certainly not showing it. They sat or lounged about the schooner's deck smoking and chattering as if they were on some kind of holiday. Perhaps they were just glad to be leav-ing their isolation and heartened by the chance of doing some-thing instead of merely surviving.

One of them had taken the wheel, and while the schooner pointed her bows eastward into the darkness he stood beside Ross in companionable silence, turning the spokes gently this way and that while the bearded skipper watched him with quiet approval. Crespin had discovered that the helmsman had also been a fisherman like Ross, so in spite of their lack of com-munication they had a complete understanding which isolated them from all the others. Ross, it seemed, had served for so long in deep-sea trawlers that he had an inbuilt mistrust of charts and the more sophisticated methods of navigation, and was more prepared to use his fisherman's instinct in such matters.

Soskic passed the time by moving amongst his men, speaking to them individually, checking their weapons and making sure that each one knew what he had to do. But he seemed a changed man from the one who had stood on the headland to watch the *Nashorn's* methodical bombardment of the island, and Crespin thought perhaps his restlessness was more to cover his uncertainty than for any other purpose.

Shortly after midnight they crept slowly beneath a great

overhang of black cliffs. It could have been Gradz again, or any other landfall in the Adriatic, but both the helmsman and Soskic seemed quite satisfied.

The commandant crossed to Crespin's side. 'It would be better if you anchor now. You are in twenty metres of water here and it is good holding ground.' He moved his pistol holster to the front of his belt. 'I will send a patrol ashore in one of the boats. I am not happy that it is so quiet.'

Crespin signalled to Ross, and after the customary stamp on the deck the engine rattled into silence. By comparison the sound of the outrunning anchor cable seemed terrifying, but Soskic said briefly, 'It is safe here. The village is around the next headland. I know this place well.'

Crespin did not ask him why he was still apprehensive or the reason for anchoring the schooner so far from the picking-up point. Time was short, but Soskic did not seem the sort of man who would waste it unnecessarily.

One of the two heavy fishing dinghies was warped along-side and six partisans jumped down into it. They seemed to have little idea of stealth, and Coutts groaned as one man dropped his machine-pistol and another shouted curses at him for his carelessness.

He said, 'I'll go with them if you like?'

Soskic studied him in the darkness. 'You will please stay here. You may think that my men are amateurs and unfit for their work, yes? But what they lack in training they have much to offer in experience.' He brushed past Coutts and barked an order to the dinghy. The oars splashed noisily until the men picked up some sort of stroke and almost immediately vanished beneath the blacker shadow of the cliffs.

Coutts said irritably, 'I suppose he thinks I'll have them all forming threes or something!'

Crespin sat on the hatch coaming and tried to pitch his ear above the sluice of water around the swaying hull. The first part, in spite of the primitive arrangements, had gone well. At any staff college this sort of operation would have been ridiculed even if it was considered, he thought. It was all a question of trust and knowing the individual strength and weakness of each man involved. He felt the heavy pistol dragging at his hip and thought of the small partisan who had returned it to him. It had been the same man who had so neatly whipped it from his holster as he had climbed from the dory. He would probably have killed him without hesitation if Soskic had so ordered, but he had handed back the pistol with the eager simplicity of a child who had been proved wrong. There were no words. Just a cheerful grin, and the fact that the weapon had been carefully oiled and cleaned as an additional mark of mutual respect.

A full hour dragged by with nothing but the sea noises to break the silence. Coutts sat slumped against the bulwark staring at the deck, and Crespin wondered if he could ever get used to this way of fighting a war. There was always uncertainty. Always an overriding sense of danger and helplessness.

Then two of the partisans stood up and cocked their weapons, and Ross said, 'Here they come!'

The big dinghy bumped against the hull, and breathing heavily the returning patrol climbed aboard.

Soskic spoke with the leader for several minutes, his head bobbing in time to the curt questions and answers, the descriptive gestures of the other man's hands.

Then he looked at Crespin and said harshly, 'We are too late. As I feared, the Chetniks have discovered our purpose here. I do not know how it happened, but someone must have betrayed us!'

He spoke with such bitterness that Crespin could feel his despair.

He replied quietly, 'What did your men find?'

'There is a German patrol in the village. Those Royalist swine would not have dared to attack unless there was help nearby. Most of our people are penned in some sheds under guard. No doubt they will be transported elsewhere for interrogation very soon.' He drew one hand across his mouth. 'Some have already died. They are lying at the roadside like slaughtered animals!' He seemed to take a fresh grip on himself. 'There is nothing for us to do but return to Gradz. There will be other days, and when the time comes we will not forget.'

Crespin saw the other partisans standing round them, listening in silence. Theirs was to have been a small gesture, but to men who had already lost families and friends and were condemned to death for their resistance, it must mean a great deal.

He said, 'Do you know who is in charge of these Chetniks?'

Soskic nodded. 'His name is Kolak. He was a colonel in the Royal Guard before the occupation. He was the one who attacked my village on Gradz. Whose word I wanted to trust. Now he has shown his hand as only his sort can. He is outwardly working with the Germans. For that he has lost the right to live!'

Crespin touched his arm. 'If he found out about your plan it must have been *after* his attack?'

'That is so. But how can that help?'

'Then he cannot know about the schooner.' Crespin could feel the man's mind grappling with his words. 'He knows that your one large boat was sunk and that you are not the kind of man who would attempt to rescue these people in a few oared dinghies.'

Soskic looked at him closely. 'That is true! And he knows *me*. Any such plan would have been out of the question!'

Crespin continued, 'If you were in his position, what would you expect?'

Soskic's hand rasped over his beard. 'I have the village. I have the hostages. I would expect that any attack would come from inland. A mass escape rather than a rescue attempt, eh?' He gripped Crespin's wrist tightly. 'How does that sound to you?'

Crespin nodded. 'I think you're right.'

'But why are we talking like this?' Soskic's hand dropped helplessly to his side. 'If we make an attack from the sea we must do it in daylight. Even if we succeeded there is still the voyage back to Gradz. And how long do you think it would be before Kapitan Lemke's ship came looking for us?'

Crespin felt the excitement running through him like madness. 'I still believe it is worth a try! You said yourself that the *Nashorn*'s movements are measured by the clock. Maybe we were wrong to think that Lemke has no weakness. Perhaps his devotion to punctuality *is* that weakness.'

Soskic stared at him. 'He is not due to pass Gradz until mid-day tomorrow.'

Coutts interrupted, 'It's tomorrow now!'

Soskic ignored him. 'You're right. We might just succeed.' He rapped out another question to the patrol leader. Then he said, 'The Germans are few in number. Just one half-tracked vehicle and maybe half a dozen men.'

Crespin wondered how the patrol had found out so much in so little time. Their efficiency obviously far outweighed their lack of precision and smartness. He said, 'I suggest that you land most of your men right away. Get them in position above the village.' He thought suddenly of the marine major who had died on the Sicilian raid. '*Plenty of noise and confusion,*' he had said.

He continued, 'As soon as it gets light enough you can start a mock attack. Use everything you've got, grenades, anything you can lay hands on, but don't show yourselves. Make them think you've roused the whole partisan army!'

Soskic asked, 'And what will you do?'

'Sail this old tub right into the cove by the village.' It sounded so simple that he wanted to laugh. Anything to release some of this rising insanity. 'They won't know which way to run!'

The commandant nodded, suddenly calm. 'That is what we will do.' He beckoned to several of his men and began to explain what he wanted.

Coutts blew out his cheeks. 'Now I've heard everything. You actually *told* him what to do.' He looked at Ross who was grinning broadly. 'Not only that, but he *listened*!'

Crespin shrugged. 'Well, you said it was your job to bring me here. After that it was up to me, remember?' He pushed through the chattering men beside the hatch. 'Now haul up that other dinghy and get ready to start the engine again.' He put an edge to his voice. 'If that bloody relic breaks down I'll have your guts for garters!'

Ross prised the Yugoslav helmsman's hands from the wheel and grinned. 'You go with your lot, matey! This time it's a job for the professionals.'

Preston sauntered back from the bows, his hands in his

pockets. To nobody in particular he exclaimed, 'It just goes to show, doesn't it? There are a few regular officers about who know what's what after all!'

Coutts eyed him coldly. 'Thanks.' He pulled out his Lüger and rubbed it against his leg. 'Thanks for damn all!'

*   *   *

'Keep as close inshore as you can!' Crespin saw Ross's hands ease the spokes over and watched as the small bow wave creamed away to break across the fallen rocks at the foot of the cliff. The schooner was steering parallel with the land, so that the cliffs seemed to hang directly overhead, catching the sound of their passing and throwing back the engine's throaty growl in a never-ending echo. From high, unseen ledges flocks of disturbed gulls rose flapping and screaming, and then dived down over the two vibrating masts before circling back to their nests to stare after the intruder with ruffled annoyance.

Crespin looked at his watch and then up at the cliff top where already the sky was changing to a hard grey. In the dull light he could see the schooner's crew and the remaining handful of partisans crouching along either bulwark, their weapons trained outboard and ready. In the bows Preston lay beside the rusty cable, a Bren cradled against his cheek while he poked the muzzle through a fairlead and stared at the dark line which marked the edge of land around which lay the cove and the village.

The engine was throttled right down but it was still too noisy. Before they could swing to starboard and head for the beach they would have to turn slightly to seaward to avoid one isolated pinnacle of rock which rose against the murky sky in a towering black triangle. Those would be precious minutes lost. Time for a sentry to hear their engine and raise the alarm. Time for the enemy to realise what they were trying to do.

He asked quietly, 'How much water between that pinnacle and the cliffs, Skipper?' He saw Ross staring over the bows. 'At a guess?'

Ross put his weight on the wheel and swung the stem slightly away from a telltale flurry of white spray. 'There's about sixty feet between them.' His eyes narrowed with professional interest. 'Not much depth though.'

'Enough for us?'

Ross seemed to realise what Crespin meant. 'It'd be a tight squeeze, sir. Aye, there'll not be a lot under her keel.'

Crespin bit his lip. It had to be done. 'In a minute I'll want full speed. Everything that mechanic of yours can give you! We'll head straight between that gap and go hard astarboard.' He saw Ross nodding imperturbably. 'Then, and only then, we'll cut the engine completely and go for the beach. If we don't hit anything she should have enough way on to reach it without using any more power at all.'

He heard Ross shouting through the engine hatch and found time to wonder at the mechanic's lonely existence. Unlike Magot, he had no one to talk to, nobody to explain the happenings of the world above his head.

Ross grunted. 'Ready when you are, sir.'

'Right. Full ahead, Skipper!' Crespin gripped the coaming and felt the deck begin to shiver and vibrate as if it would collapse beneath him. They were so close inshore now that the cliff seemed to be tearing past at an impossible speed, although he guessed it was probably less than ten knots. Faster and faster, with more enraged gulls sweeping around them in a noisy escort.

Coutts stood beside him, his pistol in his hand. He watched the great rock pinnacle creeping out to port and murmured, 'Too late to change your mind now. So here we go!'

All at once they were churning between the two walls of rock, the water seething and leaping over each bulwark like a millrace as the schooner ploughed through the narrow gap. One partisan was pointing over the rail, his voice lost in the sounds of engine and backwash, but Crespin did not have to look to know that he had seen the sea's bottom gliding up to meet their onrush, the littered fragments gleaming through the churned water like black teeth.

Coutts said, 'Christ, we're through!'

Crespin did not even hear him. 'Hard astarboard! Cut engine!' He almost fell as Ross put the wheel down and sent the little schooner pivoting around the last outflung arm of headland. And there was the cove, a wide crescent of beach at the far end, already grey in the dawn light, and beyond it, in a jumbled mass of stone and shadow, was the village.

Somewhere on the hillside beyond the cove Soskic and his men must have seen the schooner's erratic appearance, for in the seconds which followed the remaining shadows were split apart by murderous bursts of automatic fire, while from somewhere to the left came the heavier explosions of grenades.

As the schooner's keel cut a fine line across the sheltered water and the cove opened out to meet her more firing started from beyond the low huts and cottages, sporadic and vague at first, and then as the alarm was raised, heavier and with more controlled purpose.

Crespin ran forward as Preston squeezed his trigger and sent a stream of tracers flicking across the water towards an open space between the houses. Like Crespin he had seen the crouching shape of the German half-track, and as he emptied his first magazine he saw sparks fly from the steel while more bullets ploughed into the sand around it, making it spurt into the air like jets of steam.

Crespin seized his shoulder and shook it. 'Not the half-track!' He had to shake him violently before he understood. Beside the parked vehicle Crespin had seen a small camouflaged tent where the German crew had no doubt been enjoying a sleep, safe in the knowledge they were in an occupied village. But now they were stumbling out of the tent, their bodies pale in their underclothes as they staggered towards the safety of the half-track. 'Get them! If they reach that thing . . .'

His words were lost in the renewed burst of tracer from the Bren as Preston shifted his sights. Three of the Germans fell kicking on the sand and another turned and ran back into the tent. The muzzle moved very slightly, and even in the poor light Crespin saw the bullets ripping it apart until it hung from its frame in tattered fragments.

He yelled, 'Stand by to beach!'

Beyond the houses the hillside was criss-crossed with gun-flashes and the sharp orange detonations of the grenades. There was smoke, too, and occasionally Crespin could see figures running from cover to cover, shooting as they ran, some falling, others crawling blindly until the next shots cut them down.

With a groan of protest the stem drove into the beach, and as the schooner sidled awkwardly on the hard sand the men were already leaping over the bows, wading through the water with their weapons above their heads.

Crespin shouted, 'Covering fire with the Bren!' Then he, too was over the side, the sea dragging at his efforts to wade ashore, like a man in a nightmare. The water was surprisingly warm, and this fact seemed to steady him. Salt splashed across his face, and he realised that bullets were now coming towards the schooner. Behind him he heard the Bren rattle into life once more and felt the bullets fanning overhead in a hot wind.

A partisan reached the beach first and lifted his Schmeisser to fire. Then he fell forward on to his face, and another man dropped almost by his side.

But they were well up the beach now, with figures and objects looming out of the smoke, faces distorted and unreal as the Sten guns and pistols threw them back on to the sand, their blood making strange patterns which looked black in the dull light.

Crespin saw Leading Seaman Allan fall on one knee, blood gushing from his mouth, and a partisan snatch his Sten as he ran past the dying seaman with hardly a pause before he reopened fire. One of the Germans in the tent had survived after all. He dashed out between the running figures, his hands above his head, his cries unheeded until a stray bullet brought him, too, kicking to the ground.

Coutts saw him fall and fired two shots into his body as he ran past.

Inside the tent the remaining German soldier leaned against a small field radio set, the microphone still gripped in one bloodied hand. The lower part of his face had been shot away, but his eyes stared up at Crespin with an expression of incredible hatred. The radio was buzzing beneath the corpse until Crespin fired his pistol directly into it, the crash of the shot dragging his mind back from the edge of nausea and insanity.

As he walked out of the tent he saw more people than ever

surging around him, but this time they were strangers. Men and women, even children, clutching the grim-faced partisans, weeping and cheering, oblivious to the danger and the bullets which still whimpered towards the sea.

Through the fog of his reeling mind Crespin realised that the firing was less and the bang of grenades seemed muffled and much further away.

Coutts strode towards him, the Lüger replaced in its holster. He paused as he saw Crespin and threw up a salute which would have done credit to any Palace guard.

'The village is ours, *sir*.' His teeth showed white in his grimy face. 'Any orders?'

Crespin lifted his arm. 'Don't let the partisans blow up the half-track. There's a four-barrelled Vierling gun on it. They could use it on Gradz.' He wiped his forehead with his wrist. He felt dizzy and sick, yet something was still making him go on. He did not even recognise his own voice. 'Tell Ross to send his mechanic here. He should be able to strip it.'

Hands were pounding his shoulders, and a dark-haired woman with a deep cut above one eye was holding up a baby towards him like a talisman.

Then Soskic came out of the smoke. 'You did well, comrade!' He was watching Crespin gravely. 'Those carrion have run for the hillside.'

Crespin gestured towards the tent. 'That German may have had time to send a signal. We must get the schooner floated off immediately.'

He swayed and Soskic steadied his arm, shouting above the voices which surged around them in a tide of excitement and relief. 'My men will do it. She is only a little ship, but worth caring for, eh?'

Crespin nodded and then walked back towards the sea's edge. He could hear occasional shots and what sounded like screams. Perhaps those Germans had been the lucky ones after all.

Coutts joined him and stopped to slash some water against his face and hands. He said, 'I saw what the Chetniks did here. They butchered about thirty of the villagers. They raped the women first before killing them, of course.'

Crespin said harshly, 'Do you have to keep on about it?'

'Yes, I think I do.' Coutts half turned as another terrible scream echoed down the beach. 'You're sickened because of what the partisans are doing. Just remember how you'd feel if it was your girl up there by the road in a pool of blood.'

Ross waded up the beach and looked at both of them impassively. Then he said, 'We'll be afloat again any minute, sir. If we fill the boats with people we should be able to manage all right.' He sniffed the air. 'Maybe we'll get a wind to blow us home this time.'

Crespin made himself turn and look at the village. 'We'll take all who want to come with us,' he said slowly. 'Reprisal leads to reprisal, and I don't want to cause any more suffering in this place.'

Ross looked at Coutts who gave a brief shrug. Then he said, 'If I may say so, sir, you did well. Very well.'

Crespin realised that he was still carrying the pistol and with a sigh thrust it into his holster.

'We all did, Skipper.' He walked slowly along the beach, his eyes on the rock pinnacle. 'I suppose that has to be enough.'

12 Crespin's Promise

WITHIN half an hour of refloating the schooner every
foot of space was filled in readiness for the return
voyage to Gradz. The frantic preparations went on at
full speed unhampered by the enemy except for an occasional
stray bullet from the hillside beyond the village where Soskic's
rearguard stayed to cover the final withdrawal.

Crespin watched the last of the Yugoslavs being hauled
aboard from the dinghies which had been used for ferrying
them from the beach, and wondered how they were managing
to find any more space. They must be jammed like sardines,
and he could feel the hull yawing uncomfortably as the last
group struggled over the bulwark and were guided or pushed
towards the hatch.

He saw a partisan jump clear of the abandoned half-track as
a great tongue of flame licked greedily along its side before
engulfing the whole vehicle in a mass of fire and smoke. The
motor mechanic had managed to dismantle the Vierling gun
which was now stowed in the schooner's bilges. Its extra
weight above the keel might help to give the hull some stability
and make up for the packed humanity between decks, Crespin
thought.

Some of the rearguard ran down the beach and launched one
of the dinghies. They were yelling and cheering with excitement, and one of them was able to stand up and shoot towards
the hills in spite of the crowded figures around him.

Crespin said, 'We shall have to tow that lot behind us. Make the line fast and signal for the others to fall back now.'

He saw Ross staring at the sky, and when he turned he saw to his astonishment that it had clouded over in the space of minutes. When he had last found time to look it had been clear and pale blue, with a hint of morning sunlight already warming his face. Now there was just a low blanket of cloud, and the sea which had looked so placid and inviting had changed to a hard, threatening grey.

Ross called, 'I'm not happy about this! I think we're in for a blow!'

Crespin did not answer. He had heard of these Adriatic gales. The 'Bora', as it was known, could come with the force and the suddenness of a tropical storm. He thought of the wretched people crouching below deck and the miles of open water beyond the cove.

'Make another recall to those people ashore. We must get under way immediately!' He crossed to the other rail and lifted his glasses. Beyond the headland and its protective pinnacle he could see the nearest island on the far side of the channel. But that, too had changed, and the top half of it seemed to have been cut off by low cloud or a belt of fast moving rain. And the channel itself was already breaking into ranks of short-ridged rollers, their crests crumbling in the face of the growing wind.

A bullet, almost spent, thudded dully into the hull and brought a chorus of muffled cries from below. Some children were weeping pitifully, but whether from fear or hunger, Crespin did not know. Maybe their parents were amongst those corpses beside the road which Coutts had described so brutally.

He breathed out slowly as some running figures came down the beach and jumped into the last boat. They were pulling strongly for the schooner when more shots came from the village, the gun flashes almost completely hidden by smoke from the blazing half-track.

In the bows Preston returned fire with his Bren, sweeping slowly back and forth, the empty magazines mounting beside him in a steady pile.

Crespin watched narrowly as the other boat picked up the tow and then shouted, 'Up anchor! Get under way, Skipper!'

Soskic managed to jump to the schooner's bulwark before the last dinghy yawed away on the end of its line, and Crespin saw that his eyes were shining with grim satisfaction.

Crespin asked, 'How many did you lose?'

'Seven.' Soskic pulled up his coat collar and watched as the seamen struggled amongst the crouching refugees to loose the two big sails. 'But we made *them* pay ten times over!'

Ross shouted above the din of banging canvas and engine noise, 'I'll make for the middle of the channel. We must get a bit o' sea room, sir!'

Crespin nodded. The old schooner was fore and aft rigged, and would not be easy to handle with so much dead weight aboard.

Soskic clung to the hatch coaming and said suddenly, 'You have seen the weather signs, eh? It is not good for us.'

Crespin looked at him. 'We have to get away from here. There's no damned choice in the matter.'

Soskic shrugged. Then he said simply, 'We are in your hands.'

As soon as the schooner was clear of the headland the wind came down across her quarter with a smashing impact which heeled her over until the lee bulwark was almost awash. Astern the two towed boats were veering away diagonally, and Crespin could see the partisans baling frantically, even using their hats as they struggled to stay afloat. It was bad, and the wind still rising.

Coutts shouted, 'God, the headland has disappeared!' It was true. Within minutes the visibility had fallen to yards as wind and sea lifted and surged together into one insane symphony. 'Those two boats are pulling too far round!'

Crespin had to yell above the shriek of the wind. 'If you stay here you might as well shut up! But if you want to do something useful then go and help calm those poor devils below!'

Coutts seemed about to protest. Then he gave a shrug and clawed his way to the hatch. The deck was heeling so badly that he appeared to be standing at a forty-five-degree angle.

'And start the pumps, Skipper! This hull can't be too good after all these years.'

Ross's face was streaming with spray but he managed to

shout back, 'Just the *one* pump, sir!' He bared his teeth as a big wave lifted over the rail and sluiced down the full length of the deck, sweeping some partisans into an untidy heap of limbs and weapons below the foremast.

Soskic was watching through narrowed eyes. 'What do you intend, comrade?' He sounded neither worried nor critical. Merely interested.

'I *was* going to cling to the island on the far side of the channel. But unless this wind drops we'll have to go about and try to beat straight for Gradz.'

Crespin swung round, ducking, as the mainsail exploded above his head with the force of a gunshot. It was split from head to foot, and as he stared he saw the wind paring it away, so that within a minute the canvas was reduced to a garland of tattered ribbons.

He yelled, 'Get the other sail off her, Skipper! We must use the engine alone!'

All around him men were struggling and cursing as they fought with the spray-swollen halyards and tried to remain on their feet.

'Come *round*, Skipper!' Crespin watched the deck tilt over once more, and stay there, with the water creaming inboard as if the schooner was already rolling on her beam ends. 'Hard astarboard!'

Ross spat some of his beard from his mouth. 'Wheel's hard over! She's not answering!'

Another crested roller cruised from the mist of spray and broke hissing over the weather side. The schooner shuddered and settled more firmly on her side. Below his feet Crespin could feel thuds and scrapings, and imagined the trapped people falling helplessly in blind, terrified confusion.

The foresail came down in a sodden, flapping tangle, and as if released by a hidden spring the deck began to swing upright again. Crespin watched as the bows lifted and lifted, so that Preston and his Bren appeared to be pointing straight up towards the skudding clouds. Then down she dropped, the smashing vibration shaking every timber and throwing more men bodily against the bulwarks.

But she *was* turning, crashing into the advancing rollers,

then lifting wildly before careering down again into the next trough, and the next after that.

Crespin peered astern. It was a miracle, but both boats were still there, tossing like leaves on a whirlpool. One of the partisans even managed to wave to him before falling back into his boat, his legs sticking unheeded above his frantically baling companions.

Ross had tied himself to the wheel and was hauling at the spokes with all his strength. 'She's taking it well. Just so long as the engine keeps going!'

Crespin needed no reminding. In spite of the wind and sea his ear was constantly listening to the engine's labouring beat with its steady accompaniment from the pump. If it failed now the schooner would broach to and capsize in minutes. The people crammed between decks would know little about it until she was already on her way to the bottom.

He had lost all sense of time and distance. His world had become confined to the next eager line of waves, his reflexes reduced to withstanding each sickening climb and jolting descent, while he waited for the old schooner's seams to burst apart and surrender to the onslaught.

As if in a daze he saw two figures emerge from the hatch, a dripping corpse between them; man or woman he did not know for its face was masked in blood. The men waited their chance, rising and swaying with their lifeless burden as if in some macabre dance, then as the last wave receded along the deck and gurgled from the streaming scuppers they heaved it overboard and ran for the hatch again without a backward glance.

Crespin tried not to think of the others. And the children. He yelled, 'Any sign of land?'

Soskic replied, 'We must be clearing the Mljet Channel!'

Crespin stared at him. Surely Soskic was mistaken. But in his heart he knew that he would know these waters like the back of his hand. And if he was right it meant that they still had the full ten miles of open sea to cross before they could reach the inlet at Gradz.

He peered at his wrist with amazement. His watch had gone, torn from the strap without his knowing. In spite of the gale

raging around him he had a sudden picture of his mother when
she had given him the watch as a present. It had been when he
had received his commission at Dartmouth. Now, like her, it
had gone forever. Another link wiped away.

He said harshly, 'Well, we shall just have to stick it out!'

Twice more Crespin saw bodies thrown over the side, but
they were soon forgotten when Ross informed him that the
pump had given out and the water was gaining in the bilges at
an alarming rate.

Coutts came on deck soaking wet and covered with oil and
slime. 'Some of those people will drown if we don't get 'em up
here!'

Crespin shouted, 'If they come on deck we *will* turn turtle!'
He grasped Coutts' sodden coat. The goatskin felt slippery with
oil. 'Just get down there again and organise a bucket chain!'
He added savagely, 'Do as I say and quickly. Try *saving* a few
lives for a bloody change!'

He saw Coutts' sudden anger and knew that he would kill
himself now rather than give in to the sea.

As the soldier slipped and fell through the hatch Soskic
shouted, 'You have a fine way of doing things. I could use you
in my little army!' He was grinning as if it was a huge joke.

Crespin turned as a man tipped the first drum of water over
the hatch coaming and wondered how Coutts was managing
to cope with translating his orders into deeds in the confusion
and darkness below. He said, 'The sea has taught me one thing.
If you turn your back for a moment you're finished!' He saw
Preston staring back from the bows to listen and realised with
a start that the roar of wind and water seemed to be fading.

Soskic gripped his arm. 'You see? The sea is ashamed, your
words have had a fine effect.'

Crespin wiped his streaming face. It was incredible. With
the same suddenness of its arrival the storm was already moving on and away, the wave-crests flattening in its wake as if
spent with the fierceness of their efforts. Astern the clouds
were thinning, and through the curtain of spray the cliffs of
the mainland stood out with sudden brightness as the sun broke
through once again.

In the towed boats the partisans paused in their baling to

cheer and wave their arms, and even as he watched Crespin saw the cloud shadow moving rapidly across the water, like a trapdoor being raised, until with eye-wrenching brilliance the sun swept across the schooner and opened up the sea ahead of her pitching stem. First one and then another island appeared, shining momentarily in the sudden glare before fading again in a drifting haze which masked the bared horizon in a long curtain of fine vapour. The schooner, too, appeared to be wreathed in steam as the heat explored the streaming planking and rigging, soaked into the exhausted men and made them stare at one another as if witnessing some kind of miracle.

And there, dead across the schooner's bows was Gradz. It was little more than a purple hump in the filtered sunlight, but as the word was passed below Crespin heard a chorus of shouts and cries, while in the open hatchway he saw bearded faced and dark-haired women staring up at the tattered sail, their eyes filled with wonder and disbelief.

Coutts emerged from the hatch dripping and filthy. He looked guardedly at Crespin and then grinned. 'You'll be glad to know that I've got the pump going again.'

Crespin ran his fingers through his hair. 'Thanks.' Then he smiled. 'For everything.'

Ross pointed suddenly. 'Aircraft, sir! Red four-five!'

Crespin wiped his glasses on his shirt and followed the line of retreating clouds. Then he saw it, glinting brightly as it flew into the sunlight, like a child's toy.

He said slowly, 'Reconnaissance plane.' Around him he could sense the sudden tension. 'Might not see us.'

But it did. It was a very small, high-wing monoplane, and as it turned into the sun it began to lose height until everyone on deck could see the bright arc of its propeller, the twin black crosses on the wing.

Coutts snapped, 'You men on deck! Hold your fire until I give the word!'

Crespin lowered his glasses and glanced at Soskic. 'Have you seen it before?'

'Occasionally.' The commandant was lighting a cigarette, but his eyes were following the approaching aircraft. 'The Germans use it for patrolling the main roads usually.' He threw the match over the rail. 'But this time I think they look for us.'

Crespin could hear the plane's high-pitched engine now above the schooner's heavier beat. It was taking its time. Making quite sure. Then quite suddenly it dived steeply towards the sea, the sunlight flashing across the perspex windshield as it levelled out above its own reflection.

Coutts glanced questioningly at Crespin. 'Shall we shoot at the bastard?'

Crespin raised his glasses again. 'Wait a bit longer.'

The little aircraft flashed down the port side less than a cable away, making the water shimmer below it in a miniature shock-wave. Then it pivoted neatly and began to climb again, turning and rising until the sunlight blotted out its silhouette and its tilting wing gleamed in the glare like burnished steel.

Coutts said half to himself, 'Watch out for the Hun who comes out of the sun!'

'Here he comes!' Preston swung the Bren round and jammed the bipod on top of the capstan.

With a sudden roar the spotter plane swept straight across the schooner's poop, the shadow floating over the water like a black crucifix.

'Open fire!' As Crespin shouted above the engine's roar the air quivered to the onslaught of gunfire as every man who was in a position to shoot poured a sporadic burst after the plane. Machine-pistols, the Bren, anything, even though there was almost no chance of scoring a single hit.

Coutts grinned. 'That'll teach him, the cheeky bastard!'

Crespin did not watch as the aircraft grew smaller and smaller against the clearing sky. He said, 'Full power again, Skipper. You know why this time!'

Then he sat on the hatch cover and tried to light his pipe with some damp tobacco. It was useless to keep looking at the island. You could not make it get any nearer just by willing it so. And the harder you stared, the further away it seemed to be.

Coutts crossed to his side and offered him his lighter. 'Try this. You'll run out of matches in a minute.' He waited until Crespin succeeded in getting his pipe going. 'Pity about the spotter plane,' he said quietly. 'It could have been worse. No bloody Messerschmitt would have been put off by our pop-guns!'

'What time is it now?' Crespin watched the pipe-smoke drifting across the rail.

'Half past eleven, if my watch is still all right.' Coutts held it to his ears. 'In case I don't get time later on, let me just say that I think you've been bloody marvellous. The way you got us out, and in a poor old relic like this!'

Crespin said, 'Tell me again, when we're in Malta.'

The minutes dragged by without anyone saying a word. When he looked towards the bows Crespin saw the island had already grown, so that it spread out on either hand, with the paler shadows of Korcula overlapping beyond. He could see the tallest hill and the deeply shadowed headland where they had anchored the schooner and waited for Coutts to return in the dory.

It all seemed so long ago. And here they were, with a clapped-out old schooner and over a hundred bewildered but grateful people, going from one uncertainty to another.

Something like a deep sigh came from the watching men in the bows, and when he got to his feet Crespin knew the reason before he reached them. He saw the smoke first, a dirty brown smudge peeling from the edge of the channel, hanging against the washed-out sky as if it would never move. He raised his glasses as the men stood aside to let him pass.

He said flatly, 'It's the *Nashorn*.'

Coutts murmured, 'What do you think?'

Crespin tried to picture the islands as he had studied them on the chart so many times. 'She's doing about eight knots. Our speed is no more than four.'

Coutts looked away. 'So that's it then.'

Crespin moved the glasses very slightly. The German was altering course already, so that he would pass around the op-posite side to his usual patrol. Jutting out from the dark cliffs was the steep spur of headland. In the powerful lenses he could see the fine line of broken water at the foot, around which lay the inlet, and safety. It was pointless even to consider it. The headland was like a magnet, towards which both vessels were

being drawn. Even in spite of the German's massive guns they
might still have made it in safety, he thought bitterly. But for
the storm and the great weight of passengers they could just
have scraped through.

Soskic spoke at his side. 'The German will cut off your chance
to enter the inlet. You are too much hampered to make up the
required speed, yes?'

Crespin was still watching the other vessel. How strange and
menacing she looked with her massive covering of armour.
His glasses enabled him to see the false bow wave which had
been painted below her anchor. It was an old trick and gave
the impression of far greater speed.

He replied, 'Something like that.'

Soskic grunted. 'As I thought.' He rapped an order to one of
his men, and when Crespin looked round he saw the tall commandant striding aft, a long knife gleaming in the sunlight.

Coutts said tightly, 'He's going to cut the boats adrift!' As
Crespin made to move after him he caught his arm. 'Leave him.
Don't take away their pride now. You *need* that extra speed.
Otherwise they'll *all* be killed.'

Soskic reached the taffrail and called something to the
nearest boat. Then very deliberately he began to saw through
the towrope. As it parted the two boats seemed to fall astern
with terrifying speed, their hulls rising on the schooner's growing wash. Nobody spoke, nor was there any display of emotion
or despair. Most of the men in the boats had risen to their feet
and merely stood swaying in tight groups. Just watching and
saying nothing. As if they were already dead.

The schooner dug her stern more deeply into the sea as she
drove forward unhampered by the tow, and when Crespin at
last tore his eyes from the two dwindling shapes he saw that
the headland was already creeping out to meet them. There
was a bright flash from the *Nashorn*'s bows and a shell screamed
overhead, the shock-wave pressing them down like some
physical force. They saw the shell explode far abeam, throwing
up a column of broken water and brown smoke. It was a badly
aimed shot, and he guessed that the German gunnery officer
had been caught out by the sudden change of events. The next
shell ripped overhead with the sound of an express train, and

another column of water lifted and shone in the sunlight like virgin snow.

Through his glasses Crespin saw the black line of headland cutting across the *Nashorn's* superstructure, the sudden twist of her bow wave as she began to turn seaward and away from the lurking reefs. Then she was hidden completely, and he knew that by the time she had curved right round the entrance to the inlet the schooner would be safe inside.

Nobody was looking at the entrance any more. Sickened, Crespin lifted the glasses and watched as with methodical care the *Nashorn's* gun shifted to the two drifting boats. It was all the more terrible because the enemy ship was still hidden from sight by the headland. In the small, silent picture of his binoculars he saw the water-spouts rising nearer and nearer to the boats. He could see the faces of the partisans, some of which he knew and remembered, their mouths calling to one another as they waited for the end.

Coutts spoke his thoughts aloud. 'The bastard is taking his time. He's *playing* with them!'

It was true. The shells seemed to explode all around the boats, playfully, cruelly, until some of the men on the schooner's deck were openly weeping with anger and despair.

But as the *Nashorn's* ugly bow crept around the headland the game was finished. A shell ploughed alongside the two boats and exploded with a livid orange flash. When the spray and smoke drifted clear there was nothing to be seen. Not a plank or a fragment.

Then the *Nashorn's* siren bellowed across the glittering water and boomed into the inlet like a great howl of triumph. As she steamed across the opening and around the next headland Crespin found that he was shaking so badly that he could hardly hold the glasses.

'You bastard!' He was oblivious to Coutts and Ross who were watching him. 'If it's the last thing I do on God's earth I'll get you for what you did!'

Ross dragged his eyes from Crespin's strained face and stared towards the end of the inlet. He could see the village, the people already running down to the water's edge to see the returning ship.

'Stand by to let go the anchor!' But even his voice seemed hushed, and in his ears he could still hear that siren, obscene in its petty victory.

Soskic crossed to Crespin's side and watched the people thronging the waterfront and the black rocks above the village. Together they saw the others scrambling through the hatch and running to the bulwark as the anchor splashed down into the clear water, letting the joy and the sense of release wash over them, cleansing them, as if to free them from the horror they had left behind.

Then Soskic said, 'This was our war until you came. Now, whatever happens, we will know that we are no longer alone. Let the *Nashorn's* captain and those like him enjoy their tyranny while they can.' His voice was taut with suppressed emotion, but still he kept his eyes on some point above the village. 'In another world or a different time I might find it in my heart to pity them. But there is no more room for compassion. They made sure of that themselves.'

The first of the small dinghies from the village were alongside and the work of unloading was begun.

By nightfall the schooner's deck seemed strangely deserted, and the stream of men, women and children had vanished into the village as if it had never been.

Outside the inlet the moon cast a pale reflection on the unruffled sea, and at the foot of the forbidding headland a mere handful of charred fragments bobbed amidst the rocks to make the end of a gesture.

*   *   *

The schooner remained at her anchorage for a full week before Crespin decided to risk trying to leave. There was no doubt in his mind the enemy was fully aware of what had happened, but it was essential they should go on believing the raid and the rescue of the other Yugoslavs from the mainland was solely a partisan affair. If the Germans realised what the schooner's presence really represented it was unlikely that they would leave any escape route unguarded.

Every day the *Nashorn* paid her customary visit, firing a few shells into the hills before continuing her patrol amongst the islands. But now when she passed Gradz she never failed to sound her siren. It was like a taunt, as if to drive the partisans to some act of senseless daring which might place them squarely across her gunsights.

The small spotter plane made several visits, too, and it was all Crespin could do to prevent the partisans from firing at it with the newly assembled Vierling gun which he had sited above the village. There was only limited ammunition for it, and it was not to be wasted.

On the seventh night Crespin decided to make a move. The spotter plane had not been over the inlet for two whole days, and it seemed likely the enemy was satisfied that Soskic was still licking his wounds and would be content to stay at arm's length for a while.

Their departure was strangely moving, not least because of the silence. As the schooner slipped quietly towards the entrance she was escorted by every available dinghy, each of which was filled to capacity with partisans and their new companions in exile.

Soskic stayed aboard until the schooner was almost up to the headland. As a dinghy came alongside he joined Crespin beside the rail and held out his hand. 'When you return we will make some history together.' He looked towards the moonlit water beyond the cliffs adding, 'Take good care of yourself. You have many miles to go.'

Crespin thought of the voyage ahead and the uncertainty of what he might find. 'I will be back.' He in turn looked round at the place he was leaving behind. The watching people in the boats, their tribute more stirring than if they had paraded a regiment and military band to send the schooner on her way. 'And I will not forget either.'

Soskic nodded and threw one leg over the bulwark. He paused and thrust something into Crespin's hand. 'To keep that memory alive, my friend!' Then he was gone, and as Ross stamped his foot on the deck Crespin saw the dinghy bobbing astern on the rising wake before it, too was swallowed in the shadows below the headland.

He walked to the binnacle and held the gift against the shaded compass light. It was Soskic's watch.

Coutts murmured, 'Now that really is something.'

Crespin thrust it into his pocket and turned away. He did not want Coutts or anyone else to see his face at that moment.

Ross said, 'Bringing her on course now, sir. West-south-west.'

When Crespin stared back along the schooner's pale wake Gradz had vanished.

Before dawn they had Pelagosa Island abeam, that last lonely point on the chart which marked the centre of the Adriatic between Yugoslavia and Italy, then they turned again and headed south-east, the daylight bringing an empty sky and bare horizons as far as the eye could see.

Thirty-six hours after leaving Gradz Crespin was dozing in the bright sunlight when Preston shook his arm and announced, 'Fast surface craft to the south-west, sir! Could be E-boats!'

Crespin climbed to his feet and saw the others already lining the bulwark, their faces set with tired despair. They had come so far, had seen so much. To be caught now would be too hard to bear.

But Crespin did not even use his glasses. He dropped one hand on Coutts' shoulder and said, 'The war must have moved quite a bit while we've been away.'

Coutts stared at him as if he thought he was suffering from sunstroke or delayed shock.

Crespin smiled. 'I'd know *that* sound anywhere.'

There were in fact four of them. Two M.T.B.s and two motor gunboats, their ensigns streaming, the black gun muzzles already swinging to cover the little schooner as they swept down on her with a roar of power which brought back so many memories to Crespin.

A loudhailer barked some attempt at Italian across the narrowing strip of churned water, to be greeted with great shout of laughter from the schooner's crew. Coutts was pointing at Crespin, the tears pouring down his cheeks as he tried with sign language to sweep away the last of their deception.

When one of the boats came alongside Crespin found his hand being pumped delightedly by the M.T.B.'s captain, a face vaguely familiar, but in the mist across his eyes he was no longer sure of anything.

The man was shouting, 'Where the hell have you been, John? Christ, I thought it was a ghost.'

Crespin heard himself say, 'I never expected to see any of our boats this far up the Adriatic.'

The officer grinned and pumped his hand even harder. 'You must have been out of circulation, old chap! My unit is already based in Taranto! We're right across southern Italy now, from Sicily to Brindisi!'

Coutts said, 'We'd better go with them.'

Crespin nodded. 'The sooner we get our information to Scarlett the better.' He saw Ross watching him and nodding in silent agreement. To the grinning M.T.B.'s captain he said, 'I'm with the Special Squadron now. Can you get us back to base?'

The officer looked at the battered, listing schooner and said, 'I'd never have believed this.' Then he said firmly, 'Hop aboard. We're going to Taranto anyway.'

The farewells were brief but strangely sad. Ross and Preston, the weary motor mechanic, and the rest of the small crew.

As the boats formed into line and growled noisily across the glittering water Crespin looked astern and watched the little schooner until it was lost from sight.

He was back now in a world he understood, but when he thought of Gradz and what they had achieved together, he knew that he would not rest until he returned there.

13 Expendable

ON the evening of the following day the frigate in which Crespin had obtained passage from Taranto slipped past the protective guns of Malta's coastal batteries and picked up her moorings. The anchorage was filled with heavy ships, and while Crespin waited impatiently for the accommodation ladder to be lowered he was conscious of the feeling of release, a freedom from fear which these big ships represented. As the Allied line hardened across southern Italy, Malta could at last face each day and night without dread, safe in the knowledge they were no longer in the centre of the enemy's net.

The few hours spent in Taranto had left him with a confused picture of a town which appeared glad to be occupied. While he had searched for some suitable naval authority and had composed a signal for Scarlett, he had been aware of the mixed emotions all around him. There seemed to be Italian sailors everywhere, pathetically eager to salute him, to bar his way if necessary until noticed, as if to prove that they at least were not just members of a beaten enemy, but new allies with a common cause. It was as comic as it was sad.

After sending his despatch he had enjoyed his first bath for over three weeks, resting and dozing in a grand, marble-walled room and letting the water soak into his tired body, like a sensuous embrace. A harassed staff officer had given him a clean shirt, and in spite of the fact he was still wearing the same crumpled battledress in which he had lived and slept since first stepping aboard the schooner, his revival felt complete.

Coutts, on the other hand, seemed happy to stay as he was, and when they had received authority to take passage aboard a Malta bound frigate he remained unrepentant and indifferent to the wardroom's obvious disapproval.

Now, at Crespin's side, he was puffing at one of his black cheroots and studying the bombed houses above the harbour with something like affection.

'Nice to see the battered old place again. I wonder what Scarlett has been cooking up for us?'

Crespin watched the frigate's motor boat casting off the falls and chugging astern towards the ladder. The whole time he had been away he had not thought much about his own command. Now that he was here he could hardly wait to get back aboard.

He said, 'I expect he'll be waiting for a full report.'

The frigate's captain climbed down from the bridge and walked stiffly past his busy seamen. He was wearing a stained duffel coat and his eyes were rimmed with fatigue. A typical commanding officer, Crespin thought. The Navy seemed to produce such men without effort, yet to the world at large they were nameless parts to the whole.

The captain said, 'Nice to have you aboard. Pity we didn't get more time to yarn about it all.' His eyes flickered towards the motor boat, his mind already busy with the hundred and one things waiting to be done before he could retreat to the sanctuary of his cabin.

Crespin held out his hand. 'My pleasure.'

As he ran down the ladder the other captain called after him, 'And get your smelly friend to take a bath! The wardroom stinks like a goatshed!' But he was grinning as the boat cast off and headed up the anchorage.

Purple shadows were darkening the harbour as they surged past the cruisers and neat trots of moored destroyers, and Crespin found himself looking towards each ship in turn, as if he still could not believe he was back. Just over three weeks, yet it felt as if he had been away from the only life he knew for months.

Then he saw the *Thistle*, almost end on and swinging gently
at her own isolated buoy. Even in the deepening shadows there
was no mistaking her stubby stern, the jaunty rake of her solitary funnel.

Across the water a voice called, 'Boat ahoy?'

The boat's coxswain cupped his hands. '*Thistle!*'

Coutts said, 'You look like a lad with a new toy.'

Crespin saw figures gathering at the corvette's gangway and
grinned. 'I feel like one!'

The bowman hooked on, and with Coutts slipping and cursing quietly at his heels, Crespin ran up the short ladder to the
side deck. In the shaded police light he saw Shannon standing
stiffly at attention with the gangway staff by his side, their eyes
watching their returning captain with something like awe. The
frigate's boat had already dashed away, but Crespin did not
even notice.

Shannon said awkwardly, 'Welcome back, sir.'

Crespin controlled his sudden elation as something in Shannon's voice sounded a warning. Without speaking he looked
around him, and as his eyes probed beyond the little circle of
blue light he saw the uneven patches of new paint, some discarded pieces of plating, each pockmarked with telltale splinter holes.

'Has there been an air raid?' A chill of anxiety moved
through him. 'Where is Number One? Is he all right?'

Shannon looked uncomfortable. 'I think you'd better come to
the wardroom, sir.' He glared at the watching seamen who
seemed to shrink back into the shadows. 'It would be easier to
explain there.'

Crespin walked to the ladder, but once they had reached the
deck below he caught Shannon's arm and swung him round.

'I'm waiting for an explanation. From *you*!' He knew his
voice was unnecessarily harsh, but the sudden sense of fore-
boding pushed everything else aside.

Shannon said dully, 'We returned to harbour two days ago,
sir. We'd been sent on patrol to look for a Special Service
M.L.' He dropped his eyes under Crespin's flat stare. 'There had
been a raid by some commandos, but the M.L. got separated
from the group and shot up. We found her all right, but we

were jumped by six Ju. 87s. The M.L. was sunk, and *we* lost five men killed.'

Crespin asked tightly, 'And Number One?'

Shannon reached for the wardroom door and pushed it open. 'He's here, sir.' Then he stood aside to allow Crespin and Coutts to enter.

Wemyss was seated at the table, his head resting on one hand while he played with a full glass of gin with the other. A bottle, two-thirds empty, stood within easy reach.

Crespin stared at him. He had steeled himself to believe that Wemyss was dead, or at best wounded. His mind was still grappling with the discovery that *Thistle* had been sent to sea in spite of what Scarlett had promised, and to see Wemyss, obviously drunk, made him explode with sudden anger.

'Just what the bloody hell do you think you're doing, Number One?'

Wemyss turned his head very slowly. There were deep shadows beneath his eyes and he did not seem to be able to focus properly. He did not get up or even attempt to.

'You're talking to the wrong officer, sir.' He poured some more gin into the full glass, so that it ran unheeded over his hand. '*He* is the first lieutenant at the moment, *Mister* bloody Shannon!'

Crespin looked coldly at the lieutenant. 'Is this true?'

Shannon bit his lip. 'Temporarily, sir.'

Wemyss was muttering thickly, 'All my life at sea and never lost a man or a bloody ship without trying to save both. And that pompous, stuck-up bastard tries to tell *me* what to do.' He wagged the glass dangerously. 'I've been watching, y'know, Shannon. You and God Al-bloody-mighty Scarlett!'

Crespin said coldly, 'Put that drink down and listen to me.'

Wemyss replaced the glass very carefully and tried to rise to his feet. If he had further lost his temper or passed out completely Crespin would have known what to do. But when Wemyss faced him he saw that his stubbled cheeks were running with tears.

Wemyss said between his teeth, 'Sent them to their deaths, he did! They never stood a bloody chance!' He wiped his face with his sleeve. 'Scarlett told us it was just a patrol. To look for an M.L. which he had bloody well mislaid somewhere.' He shook his head slowly from side to side. 'They weren't lost. They were damn well sacrificed to his bloody mania for glory!'

The curtain across the door moved and Crespin heard footsteps in the passageway. At any minute a seaman, anyone, might come in and see Wemyss like this.

He said to Coutts, 'Get him to my cabin. I don't care what you do, or how, but get him there *now*!'

Coutts was slim, and beside Wemyss looked almost delicate. Yet with the ease of a fireman with a limp woman he pulled Wemyss' arm over his shoulder and thrust him towards the door. They cannoned into the sideboard as Wemyss tried to turn, his eyes already glazing over like those of a corpse.

He said, 'I know what you're thinking, sir. But I did it for you, *and* the ship. I've seen too much already, too much waste and bloody incompetence. I'll not let a bastard like him throw what's left on the bloody fire!'

Coutts grimaced. 'Come on, old son. Let's be having you then.'

Together they staggered through the door and Crespin breathed out very slowly.

Then he asked quietly, 'Well?'

Shannon looked away, his cheeks flushing. 'I didn't ask for this, sir, you must believe that. Captain Scarlett ordered him to take the ship inshore, near an occupied harbour, to try and get the raiding party away.'

'How far inshore?'

Shannon frowned. 'About a mile, I think, sir.'

'What time of day was it?' Crespin kept seeing Wemyss' stricken face and knew there was worse to come.

'In the forenoon, sir. There was a coastal battery, but it was supposed to have been knocked out.' He licked his lips. 'It wasn't.'

'What happened next?'

'Captain Scarlett was with us. When the battery opened fire he ordered Wemyss to pull out, but he insisted on trying to reach the last M.L. It was aground on a sandbar, in broad daylight.'

'Go on.'

'Well, sir, the battery straddled us, but we managed to silence it after about twenty minutes. And all the time the marine commandos on the M.L. were standing there, cheering us on, as if it were a football match.'

Crespin thought of the partisans waving to him from the boats towed astern of the schooner. The way they had stood in silence to be slaughtered.

Shannon said dully, 'Then the bombers came. They blew up the M.L. and killed a few others who were floating about from another boat. We lost our men when a bomb exploded alongside.' He ran his hand over his hair, trying to remember. 'Some of our fighters came over after that. They shot down one of the German kites.' He shrugged. 'And we got the hell out of it, sir.'

Leading Telegraphist Christian tapped on the door, and when he saw Crespin his face split into a grin.

'Nice ter see yer back, sir.' He held out a flimsy. 'Telephoned signal from Captain Scarlett, sir. Report when ready.'

Crespin looked past him towards the ship's crest above the sideboard. Wemyss had said, 'I did it for you, *and* the ship.'

'Very well. Call away the motor boat's crew. I'll change my uniform and go across.' As the man left he added to Shannon, 'I suppose the whole ship knows about this?'

Shannon shrugged. 'Hard to say, sir. We came in just two days back and we've been working like hell to put things right. Captain Scarlett had it out with Lieutenant Wemyss here in the wardroom. I don't know exactly what happened, but when the captain left he said I was to assume his duties, and Lieutenant Wemyss was suspended until further notice.' He shook his head. 'Could be serious for him. A court martial would not only ruin his chances in the Navy, it would also finish his career outside the Service.'

Crespin clenched his fists tightly. Once, during a middle watch, he had heard Wemyss discussing his life with young Porteous. He had pointed over the screen towards the black water and said, 'This is my home. A ship and a suitcase is all I need.' Now, hearing Shannon dismiss his past and his future with such smug indifference filled him with blazing anger.

'In case you had forgotten, *Mister* Shannon, I am in command of this ship. Until such time as I order otherwise, Lieutenant Wemyss will remain as my Number One!'

Shannon said, 'I was only doing as I was told, sir.'

'Good, well keep on doing it! You may think you're God's gift to the Navy because you've got two pieces of gold lace on your sleeve, but as far as I am concerned you are still a half-trained, conceited and thoroughly irresponsible officer! I know Wemyss is drunk, and I also know that what he said in front of me amounted to putting his head into a noose. I also happen to believe that he is one of the most honest and reliable men I have ever met.' He looked at Shannon with cold anger. 'So remember that! A ship is a unit. Men and steel all bound up as one. There is no room for petty ambitions or lack of trust, you'll do well to remember *that*, too!'

Barker, the steward, peered in the door and said nervously, 'I got yer shoregoin' uniform ready, sir.'

Crespin tore his eyes from Shannon's dark face. 'Good. Now fetch a pot of black coffee to my cabin on the double, and a large bottle of brandy!'

Barker's eyes were popping. 'Yessir. Right away, sir!' He fled.

Crespin took a deep breath. 'I'll go ashore in fifteen minutes. But before I leave I want to see the action chart and the log.' He turned and strode from the wardroom without waiting for an answer.

Barker came down the ladder carrying the coffee-pot and almost collided with Petty Officer Joicey.

The coxswain caught his arm. 'The Old Man's back then?' Barker nodded vehemently. 'Back. And *how* he's back!'

Joicey watched him go and then plucked his lower lip. Not a bloody minute too soon either, he thought grimly.

*   *   *

The spacious room above the harbour was just as Crespin remembered it. But it was no longer cool, and with the windows sealed by shutters and blackout curtains it felt oppressive and humid, so that his shirt clung to his body like another skin. It was very quiet, and beyond the shutters the street noises seemed muffled and far away, a constant, unchanging murmur.

As the minutes dragged past he could barely control his impatience. Apart from the guards and a poker-faced steward who had ushered him to this room, he had seen nobody, and he wondered if it was just part of Scarlett's policy when receiving returning officers. He could feel the brandy rasping on his stomach lining and thought suddenly of Wemyss' strained face as he lay tossing on the bunk, his words slurred and confused, between reason and oblivion. As he thought about it he became angrier, mostly with himself for not understanding Wemyss' despair from the start. He had never seen him drunk before. That alone should have prepared him.

The double doors swung inwards and Scarlett hurried across the room, a file of papers beneath his arm. He reached the big desk in a few strides and threw himself into the chair. Then he looked hard at Crespin and said. 'You're here then.' His voice was devoid of expression.

Crespin reseated himself and replied, 'I came as soon as I could, sir. There were some matters aboard the ship which needed my attention.'

Scarlett looked unusually tired. On edge.

Crespin added, 'I have brought a full report as ordered. Captain Coutts has prepared one of his own also.'

Scarlett nodded abruptly. 'I see. I have studied your brief appraisal which you despatched from Taranto. I shall want to study the matter more fully before I can assess its value.'

Crespin eased his back against the cane chair. Then he said, 'I should like to know why my ship was sent to sea while I was away, sir. I was given to understand she would remain here until I returned.'

Scarlett leaned back and stared at him coldly. 'What I decide to do or not do with the vessels and personnel under my command is my concern and not yours, Crespin. I see that you have heard all about the patrol, the appalling handling of the whole affair. It was a stroke of pure luck I was there to stop it turning into one godalmighty shambles!'

'In my opinion Lieutenant Wemyss did exactly what I would have done.' Crespin controlled his voice but his hands gripped the chair until his knuckles shone white. 'As far as I can tell from the log, a force of marine commando was sent to raid a small Italian harbour in two L.C.I.s with an M.L. for escort. It wasn't even certain if the harbour was still occupied by the Germans!'

Scarlett said, 'It was a reconnaissance in strength. There are always risks to be faced. You don't win wars by sitting on your backside!'

Crespin replied evenly, 'Nor can you win them by throwing away lives, *sir*!'

Scarlett jumped to his feet, sending the file skidding across the floor.

'Just who the hell do you think you're talking to? I told you at the outset that your ship is just a weapon, not a way of life! Do you imagine that your officers and men are exempt from taking risks? That they deserve some special consideration?' He was shouting. 'The operation failed due to poor intelligence reports. When I saw what was happening I ordered your first lieutenant to withdraw at once. He refused, do you hear? He bloody well disobeyed my direct order!'

Crespin watched him steadily. 'He was not the first lieutenant, sir. He was in acting command. Upon his judgement depended not only the ship's safety, but the lives of everyone there.'

Scarlett banged the desk. 'Well, he didn't damn well save those marines!'

'But he tried. He is too good an officer and seaman to leave them without attempting to save them.'

'So that's your attitude, is it?' Scarlett strode to the wall map and stared at it for several seconds. 'You think you know better than I do!'

'I just think you've not been entirely open with me, sir.' Crespin watched Scarlett's shoulders. 'About the use of the ship in my absence.' He paused. 'And certain other matters.'

Scarlett swung round, his eyes flashing dangerously. 'What *other* matters?'

'Able Seaman Trotter for instance, sir.' Crespin saw a brief shaft of surprise before Scarlett recovered himself again. 'He was once one of your men, yet you said nothing. I might have been able to help him if . . .'

Scarlett sat down again. 'Is *that* all? Really, you amaze me, you really do! Every hour men are being killed, yet you pause to bother about one stupid seaman who lost his will to live! Of course I knew him. But you wanted to run your new command in your own way, and I approve of initiative.'

'I think he was murdered, sir.'

Scarlett did not even blink. 'I read the report by the military police. I also spoke to Porteous about it. He did mention something about Trotter's being left-handed, but in God's name that doesn't mean he was murdered!' He tapped his fingertips together and studied Crespin calmly. 'In any case, you should have spoken out. Your total lack of interest in this affair makes me think you are just using it to cover up the more important issues of your officers; Wemyss in particular!'

'It was merely my opinion, sir.'

'Well, I'm too busy to worry about it now. The matter is closed as far as I am concerned. And if you want to avoid a court of inquiry you'd better forget it, too.'

'I will be ready to face one if required, sir.'

'Well, I'm not!' Scarlett picked up Crespin's report and weighed it in his hands. 'There's a lot to do. I'm understaffed, and everyone's screaming to get things done. I cannot do everything myself, nor can I afford the time to listen to your sort of arguments.' He was speaking very rapidly now, as if to avoid interruption. 'I sent you on this mission, not because you're the most perfect man for the job, but because you were the best *available*. Yet you speak of your ship as if she was something special.' He gave a short laugh. 'Why do you think she was chosen, or for that matter, her entire company?'

'I shall be interested to hear, sir.'

'Will you? I doubt it!' Scarlett looked away from Crespin's cold stare. 'Just think about it. For the most part they are men who have failed at everything else. They have become a means to a useful end and nothing more.'

Crespin was surprised that he felt so calm. It was as if Scarlett's words had at last removed the deception.

Scarlett added, 'I mean, they're expendable!' He turned and looked at him. 'We've got a war to win, as you've said yourself often enough. If these men prefer to believe they are hand-picked then so much the better. Just so long as you stop deceiving yourself as you are doing now!'

Crespin replied quietly, 'That is how the *enemy* behaves, sir. It is also why he will lose in the end.'

Scarlett laughed. 'Rubbish! And I thought you were different from the rest, but it seems I was wrong. You've been too long a regular, too long on the little straight rails of tradition and "playing the game".'

'Well, I *do* care what happens to my men, sir. Not just to their lives, but to their minds after it's all over and done with.'

'*Very* commendable.'

Crespin stood up slowly. He could feel his career falling in ruins but he could no longer stop himself.

'You don't give a damn about any of them. It's just a game to you. Just a senseless bloody game. A few men die because some fool has misread the instructions, but what does it matter? There are always more to fill the gaps, and throw away later.' His voice was shaking with anger. 'It just so happens that some of these *expendable* human beings *do* care. I'll say it now, and if necessary at my court martial, you're no better than the people we're fighting!'

Scarlett stepped back as if he had been struck. 'How *dare* you speak to me like this? I knew you had been through a bad time before you got this command, but I had no idea that your mind was affected, too!'

The door opened again and Crespin swung round expecting to see Penny, and suddenly fearful that she would become caught in the bitter crossfire.

But it was a small, balding man in a crumpled lounge suit, his pale eyes already darting across the room as he looked from one to the other. Then with a start Crespin realised it was Rear-Admiral Oldenshaw, and yet it was difficult to understand it was the same person. Without his uniform he seemed to have shrunk to a stooping, wizened old man.

But his voice was as sharp and incisive as ever. 'Glad to see you arrived back in one piece, Crespin.' He crossed to a deep chair and sank into it. 'I see from your expression that you did not know I was here?' He sighed. 'I was in Alexandria when I heard of your return. I flew in a few hours ago.' It seemed to be an effort to turn his head. 'Is that your report? Good, good.' He nodded vaguely. Then he looked at Scarlett's angry face. 'I heard a certain amount of disagreement going on. Thought I should put in an appearance. Arguments between brother officers are inevitable, even necessary, if we are to remain sane.' His tone hardened. 'However, there are limits.'

Scarlett said, 'Crespin has been complaining about Lieutenant Wemyss, sir.' He glanced at Crespin. 'Amongst other things.'

'I see. Quite so.' The admiral watched them bleakly. 'I, too have read your account. Interesting. Still, it's nothing that can't be sorted out, is it?'

Crespin said stubbornly, 'I want to keep him as my first lieutenant, sir. If I had been aboard I would have acted as he did.'

The admiral said dryly, 'I can imagine. I do not know if that is a defence or an admission.' He hurried on, suddenly impatient, 'I think that can be arranged.' He glanced at Scarlett. 'All right with you?'

Scarlett opened his mouth and closed it again. Then he said, 'If you say so, sir.'

'Then that's settled.' Oldenshaw crossed his thin legs and peered at Crespin. 'Now what about your mission?'

Crespin sat down. It was incredible. With a few words the ancient admiral had taken the heat out of the battle, with the merest effort. He said, 'As I have explained in my report, sir, the partisans on Gradz are ready and eager to fight. But they need a lot of good weapons, and much more beside.'

Scarlett said abruptly, 'I heard that Colonel Kolak has a much larger force at his disposal. He's a good soldier, and his men are well drilled and disciplined.' He was not speaking to Crespin.

The admiral nodded. 'My intelligence reports have said something like that.'

Crespin thought of the butchered villagers, the children crying as they were lifted aboard the schooner.

'He's a Chetnik, sir. He's no longer interested in helping anyone but himself. He was working with the Germans when I was there.'

Scarlett could not hide the sneer in his voice. 'And what was your precious Soskic doing? They're all bloody communists, whereas Kolak has already proved his loyalty as a Yugoslav officer.'

The admiral seemed to sense the return of tension between them.

'Crespin's report does seem to bear out what I have heard from other, wider sources. There is a military mission over there now, and I have no doubt that we will be able to send more help to the mainland in the very near future.'

Scarlett said, 'If the communists are allowed to take over from the Germans they'll never let go!'

The admiral smiled gently. 'Well, they are Yugoslavs, too, Captain Scarlett. They must decide what to do with their own country.' His eyes flashed. 'But that will be *after* the Germans have been driven out!' He stood up and hobbled to the chart. 'All over the Adriatic it is the same story. The patriots and partisans are holding down more enemy divisions than all of our troops in Italy at this moment! If we are to be any use we must act right away, before they are crushed or drained of supplies. I have the authority to tell you that as far as our government is concerned we will help those who are actually fighting the Germans. The overwhelming vote seems to come down in favour of the partisans!'

Crespin shot a quick glance towards Scarlett. He expected another protest, some new attack, but his face was quite blank again.

The admiral added slowly, 'But *our* immediate task is to help clear the offshore islands. To do that the partisans need arms and medical supplies as well as military aid.' He looked steadily at Crespin. 'In your Taranto despatch you told of this German ship. The *Nashorn*?'

'Yes, sir. I have made some sketches of her. She mounts two big guns, probably five point nines, and a lot of smaller ones.' He took the drawings from his shirt and handed them to the little admiral. 'But as you can see, she is not just another armed merchantman.'

The admiral placed a pair of steel-rimmed glasses on his nose and peered at the papers.

'Hmm, quite impressive, I must say.' His eyes gleamed above the frames. 'You did not waste your time on Gradz, it seems.'. He added to Scarlett, 'You were wise to choose Crespin for the task. Very wise indeed.'

Scarlett's eyes were like stones. 'Thank you, sir.'

The admiral folded the drawings and placed them on Crespin's report.

'Would you be so good as to take these and have some copies made. I will study them on my way back to the U.K.' He watched as Scarlett gathered up the papers and added, 'I'll leave you to fill in the details, but this time I want an all out effort.'

'I shall need extra facilities, sir.' Scarlett stood looking down at the admiral's shoulder. 'I intend to move' my headquarters up the east coast to Brindisi, and I must have some more vessels and equipment.'

The admiral smiled calmly, 'One thing at a time. Results first. Then we shall see what we can do.'

He spoke very gently, yet Crespin could sense the strain between him and Scarlett, and guessed that Oldenshaw had come to Malta for reasons other than to welcome his return from Gradz.

The door closed and the admiral said, 'I'll not detain you much longer. You will have a lot to attend to, I expect.' He seemed to come to a decision. 'Don't like it when my people start getting at odds with each other.' He smiled crookedly. 'I heard most of what you two were saying, and I can guess the rest.' He leaned back in the chair and closed his eyes. 'Captain Scarlett has been doing this sort of work for a long time. He's pushed hard, and spared nobody, least of all himself. But'—he lingered over the word—'there comes a time when we all need a change, if only to obtain a different viewpoint.' His eyes opened and fixed steadily on Crespin. 'I may be taking him away from this theatre of operations. At home, his experience could be invaluable, whereas if he goes on pushing himself to or beyond the limit out here,' he shrugged, 'he might be doing less than his best, and that would be a pity.'

Crespin asked, 'May I ask why you are telling me this, sir?'

The admiral's answer was indirect. 'I listened to you talking about your work on Gradz. Also I have had other information from different sources, about things you did *not* recount. You did well. You could easily have ended up dead. It is quite obvious to me that you believe in these people and what they are trying to do. To have a cause is one thing. To believe in it, another entirely.' He frowned. 'I'm wandering again! What I was going to say was, would you be prepared to take over this sector of operations if need be?'

Crespin nodded slowly, 'If you think so, sir.'

The admiral looked at the overhead fan. 'Everyone says that. But I have to *know*. Do you think you can help these people?'

He nodded. 'I do.'

'That's settled then.' The admiral lurched to his feet. 'Getting too old for this sort of thing. Like trying to lap Brooklands in an Austin Seven!'

Crespin smiled, feeling a sudden warmth for this strange, wizened man. 'They are noted for a good performance, sir!'

The admiral was already on his way to the door. Then he stopped and looked back at him. 'This war may last a long while yet. It has already gone on so long that some people tend to forget its purpose. It will be effort wasted if we end with the same bloodied hands as the enemy.'

Crespin stood looking at the closed doors for several minutes, the admiral's last words hanging in his mind like an epitaph.

Oldenshaw seemed to know everything. Perhaps that was his real strength. Old he might be, difficult he certainly was, but he knew the power and the weakness of his own people like the steel of a well-tried blade.

Crespin took out the gold watch and looked at it. He wondered how his visit would have ended if Oldenshaw had not been there, listening and testing in his inimitable style.

Then he closed the watch with a snap. When he thought of Scarlett's eyes he did not have to search far for an answer.

*   *   *

A heavily shaded lamp enclosed the bed in a small circle of warm yellow light, leaving the rest of the room in darkness and distorted shadow. Crespin lay on his back, the crumpled sheet pulled down to his waist, while his mind floated between drowsiness and the fierce recollections of the last hour. Or was it longer?

Through the half open door to the other room he could hear a drumming beat of music from the radio, and he could picture the bottle of wine and two glasses on a small table, also ignored as he had taken the girl in his arms. Now their two uniforms lay entangled beside the bed, disordered and limp, as if they, too, were spent by the intensity of their embrace.

Crespin propped himself on his elbows and peered at the open window. She had thrown back the shutters and he could see her naked body outlined against the stars, her hair moving in a slight breeze as she stared down at the street below.

'Come back to bed. You'll get pneumonia over there.'

He heard her laugh quietly. 'You were asleep.'

'Never!'

She crossed to the bedside and stood looking down at him. 'You were, and you were snoring!'

Crespin reached out and touched her thigh. The edge of the lampshade left the upper part of her body hidden in darkness, but her thighs shone in the light like pale gold. He felt her body quiver as his hand moved gently around the soft skin.

She said quickly, 'I'll get that wine if it's the *last* thing I do!' She sidestepped away from his hand, and seconds later he saw her push open the door and walk fully into the light of the other room.

He called after her, 'Suppose your friend the nurse comes back unexpectedly, what the hell will she think if she finds you like that?' He had to speak, if only to clear the sudden dryness from his throat. She was beautiful, with a teasing innocence which went to his head like a fever.

She walked slowly towards him, the light at her back making a halo across her hair and bare shoulders.

'I'd tell her it was none of her damn business who I have in my bed!' She sat on the side of the bed and handed Crespin the wine, her eyes searching his face across the rim of her own glass.

Impulsively she added, 'I have been sick with worry. Week after week and no news. And now that you're back at last it's just to say goodbye all over again.'

He touched her shoulder and ran his fingers lightly down the length of her spine.

'We're not going to talk about it. Not now.' He saw her brush her eyes with the back of one hand and continued gently, 'Here's to us!'

She lifted her glass. 'To us!'

Then she said, 'But promise me you'll take extra care. Things have been going very badly for Scarlett since you went away. He seems desperate to make a success of this new operation. He appears to *need* it, like some personal thing.'

Crespin replied, 'To him it is personal. But don't worry, Scarlett isn't going to do anything to jeopardise his whole position just to get his own back on me.' He slipped his arm round her waist and cupped her breast in his fingers. It felt smooth and warm, and he sensed the same desperate longing coursing through him again like fire.

She shivered and then reached across him to put the glass beside the lamp.

'Darling?'

He pulled her closer. 'What is it?'

She shook her head and then kissed him lightly on the mouth. 'Nothing. Just *darling*.'

Somewhere in the far distance a man laughed, and from the harbour came the mournful toot of an outgoing tug. The sound seemed to break through the girl's inner thoughts, and placing her hands on Crespin's chest she levered herself away from him and stayed for several seconds just staring at his face. Then she gripped the sheet and pulled it down between them. She seemed to sense Crespin's sudden tenseness and said quietly, 'You mustn't mind the wound now. Not now, or ever.'

Crespin lay back, feeling her fingers on the savage scar along his leg, her hair brushing like silk over his thigh. Then the warm, firm pressure of her lips, and from a great distance her voice, husky and strangely gentle. 'Now you'll never worry about it any more, my darling.'

Crespin's wineglass fell and shattered beside the entangled uniforms, but, like the girl, he heard nothing.

14 Watch them Burn

WITHIN a few days of Crespin's return Scarlett began to put the next phase of his new operation on the move. Under cover of darkness the *Thistle* and the rest of Scarlett's special force, the armed yacht, two M.L.s and the old schooner, slipped through the Otranto Strait, and after hugging the protection of the Italian mainland entered their advanced base at Brindisi. The port, situated as it was sixty miles deep into the Adriatic, came in for fairly regular bombing raids, and hardly a day passed without the seamen running to their stations, only to find the sneak raiders had been and gone almost before they could uncover the guns.

But the advantages of the new base far outweighed the discomforts. Gradz and the other islands in which Scarlett was now so interested were less than one hundred and forty miles away. A day's steaming, and well within reach of future operations.

What those future operations were going to involve nobody seemed to know. Except possibly Scarlett, and he was saying nothing. Crespin saw little of him in the days which followed, and for that he was thankful. But as days began to drag into weeks if became obvious to everyone aboard that the first expectation of action was falling once more into anticlimax. It was made worse by the fact that Brindisi was bustling with naval activity, which only helped to give the ship's company a further sense of frustration and disillusion.

Motor torpedo boats and gunboats, which had already moved

their base up from Taranto, were constantly on the move, and most days saw them snarling back into harbour, their battle flags and bullet scarred hulls proclaiming another clash with the enemy on the other side of the Adriatic.

Whenever Crespin saw Scarlett the latter was curt and formal, and seemed content to keep his officers at arm's length by passing all orders and instructions through his small collection of assistants. He spent many days away in either Taranto or Malta, and each time he was careful to take the girl with him. When Crespin did manage to see her she said it was just a way of getting his petty revenge. For when she accompanied him on his tours to see the 'powers that be' he hardly spoke to her at all, and only confided in matters of routine and fleet communications.

Coutts had vanished completely, and although he had gone without a word, Crespin guessed that Scarlett had sent him back to Gradz to pave the way for his final move into the enemy's own territory.

As the long days followed on each other Crespin found himself almost praying for action. Anything which would jolt the ship from her torpor and gloomy resignation. Morale was very low, and unless something happened soon it would get even worse. The lengthening string of defaulters and men under punishment told their own story. Fights ashore, drunken brawls with other seamen, even acts of insubordination aboard the ship herself showed how bitterly the *Thistle*'s men felt their lack of purpose.

Even Wemyss seemed different. Whether it was guilt or resentment which had changed him, Crespin did not know, but the first lieutenant spent most of his off duty time ashore, and made a point of going alone. Altogether, the atmosphere aboard ship was brittle, to say the least.

Shannon, on the other hand, was thriving. He carried out his daily duties with obvious relish, and though he, too, went ashore alone, he always returned bright-eyed and sleek, and Crespin thought that he at least had found a new interest somewhere in the town.

The two sub-lieutenants rarely left the ship, and were usually to be found at the end of each frustrating day sitting in the wardroom, either in companionable silence or engrossed in some complicated discussion which always ceased immediately when Crespin appeared.

Instead of feeling more used to Crespin they seemed almost afraid of him now, and he guessed it was because of Wemyss' strange withdrawal. A first lieutenant, good or bad, was the essential link between captain and junior officers. Without it the gulf became uncrossable. For this and so many other reasons Crespin craved to get back to sea. If they were never going to Gradz, then he wanted to go somewhere, anywhere, if only to drag the ship back into a single entity again.

The weather was worsening, while to the north there had already been reports of heavy rain which slowed the Allied advance to a painful crawl. Tanks were bogged down, and while the wretched infantrymen probed the yellow mud for mines and slogged through one battered village after another, the retreating Germans fought a savage rearguard action without let up, knowing, as did everyone else, that winter would soon grind the campaign into a stalemate.

And then, one month to the day after Crespin's return from Gradz, Scarlett sent a signal. Shore leave was to cease forthwith. All officers of the special force were to muster in the *Thistle*'s wardroom at 1900. Scarlett's Circus was, it appeared, in business again.

A few minutes before the arranged time Crespin stepped into the wardroom and watched the assembled officers. The place was filled almost to overflowing, and it was hard to imagine a more mixed or a tougher-looking collection, he decided. Their clothes were as varied as their faces. Battledress and khaki drill, sweaters and coloured scarves, they did indeed look like a bunch of pirates.

Scarlett arrived a few moments later, and Crespin was immediately aware of the change in him. Not so much a change as a return to the old Scarlett he had first met, jovial, confident and shining with good health. Even the lines of strain had gone, and as he strode to the wardroom table he flashed a broad grin around the assembled officers, his teeth white in his tanned face.

Following him, tired and dishevelled by comparison, came

Coutts. He saw Crespin's glance and gave a brief shrug. He
looked gloomy and a trifle irritated, and stared at the other
officers with obvious dismay.

Scarlett said cheerfully, 'Well, gentlemen, the waiting game
is over!' He gestured with his thumb. 'You all know Captain
Coutts, our scruffy Guardee!' There were a few laughs. 'He
has just returned from Gradz, and the news he has brought is
almost too good to be true.'

He unrolled a chart very carefully across the table and
leaned over it, his face set in a frown of concentration.

'The partisans have been stepping up their attacks on the
enemy's communications, so that the Germans are having to
withdraw more and more troops from the islands to reinforce
their garrisons on the mainland.' He tapped the chart with his
finger. 'Apart from our little island of Gradz, the larger ones
of Hvar, Korcula and Vis are almost completely in the hands
of the Yugoslavs. In the near future, the very near future,' his
smile moved round the table, 'the partisans will link up into
one solid force, and with our help will tie the whole occupation army into knots!' He swung on Coutts. 'Do you wish to
say something?'

Coutts stood looking at the chart, his hands in his pockets.
'The real stumbling block is the *Nashorn*.' His eyes flickered
towards Crespin. The merest glance, but Crespin could almost
feel the strain and the anxiety of his words. 'At present the
Germans can still prevent any unified action amongst the
partisans merely by keeping this ship patrolling the channels
between the islands. In the last two weeks the *Nashorn* has
destroyed three partisan schooners and has shelled several villages as reprisals for sabotage.'

Scarlett wagged a finger. 'Now then, let's not be pessimistic
again, eh? The *Nashorn*'s presence is a great problem, but it is
not an insuperable one.' He looked around the intent faces.
'She has a base, as you should all know by now if you have
read my intelligence reports. That base is her weakness. It is
also the most perfect place for a full scale attack by the
partisans.'

Crespin stared at him. For a moment he imagined he had

misheard, but when he saw Coutts' lined features he knew he
had not.

Scarlett beamed. 'Destroy the base, and the *Nashorn*'s immediate usefulness is curtailed. By the time the Germans have
made other arrangements the partisans will have linked up
with their comrades on the mainland, and we will be home and
dry.'

Everyone started to speak at once. Questions and doubts
flooded around Scarlett with as much effect as spray breaking
on the Barrier Reef. He seemed able to overcome every objection almost before it was voiced. He was actually enjoying
himself, swinging between buoyant confidence and crushing
sarcasm as he demolished every argument or counter-proposal.

Even Crespin was aware of the excitement which was growing around him. It was only when he remembered the
Nashorn's ugly bows jutting past the inlet, the thunderous roar
of her heavy guns as she smashed the drifting partisans to
bloody pulp, that he realised the danger of Scarlett's proposal.

He said suddenly, 'If the *Nashorn* attacks us during the
actual raid we will be cut off, sir.' Scarlett's eyes swivelled towards him, smiling, but ice-cold. 'The German base is beyond
Tekla Point and hemmed in by islands. She could approach
within a mile of us before we even saw her.'

Scarlett replied calmly, 'If you'd let me finish?' He smiled
at the others. 'I have not been idle you know. The M.T.B.s have
been attacking shipping in the Otranto Strait for several weeks
now. Particularly in the Valona Bay area where the enemy's
coastal shipping is busiest. I have explained my task to the
F.O.I.C. and he has instucted the M.T.B.s to step up their
raids, and the effect is already showing around the islands to
the north. Practically all the German patrol ships have had to
move south to counter these attacks. The *Nashorn* will remain
in the islands, but this time, gentlemen, I think the enemy is
placing just too much faith in her!'

Coutts shrugged and said wearily, 'That is true. However, it
is now known that the Germans are despatching additional
troops down from Trieste.' He tapped the chart loudly. 'And
they are sending them to the *Nashorn*'s base, probably with
any such raid in mind.' He gave another tired shrug. 'They are

coming by sea, and are timed to arrive at the base two days from now.'

Scarlett ran his fingers through his thick hair. 'So there you have it, gentlemen. The facts and the figures.' He grinned. 'What Captain Coutts omitted to add is that the *Nashorn* is going into Trieste for a boiler clean. They know that the partisans would never attack a troop convoy. It is just the moment to choose for an overhaul.'

Crespin felt a chill run down his spine. He knew what was coming next.

'So, gentlemen, we will disappoint the Germans a little. The special force will move at once to Gradz.' He lifted his gaze to Crespin, paused, and then added calmly, 'The *Thistle* will attack and destroy the troop convoy.'

There was a stunned silence. No one present seemed to know whether it was the most daring or the most lunatic idea ever conceived. Then a bearded lieutenant, the captain of one of the M.L.s said grimly, 'That's a hell of a job, sir. Couldn't *we* give a bit of support?'

Scarlett eyed him coldly. 'The convoy will consist of *one* ship, Lieutenant. One ship and maybe two small escorts.' He looked again at Crespin. 'The *Thistle* should be able to cope with them all right, eh?'

Crespin nodded. Then he said quietly, 'But the surprise element will be lost, sir. After this the Germans will know exactly what we're up to.'

There were several nods and grunts of agreement.

Scarlett sighed. 'It will not matter very much. I intend to launch the raid on the German base as soon as the convoy is destroyed. It will be too late for the *Nashorn*, or any other damn ship, to do anything!'

This time there was no objection. Scarlett's reasoning was as breathtaking as it was convincing.

Crespin asked, 'Does Soskic know about this yet?'

Scarlett sounded evasive. 'More or less. He seems eager to move, and I will explain the rest when I get to Gradz.' He looked round the wardroom. 'Anything else? Right.' He picked up his cap. 'Orders will be circulated immediately. Return to your commands and prepare to get under way.' As they shuffled through the door he looked at Crespin and added smoothly, 'I'll give you all the dope on the troopship. You find it and sink it. If you don't, we might just as well pull stumps and go home.' He walked after the others adding, 'I'm going to see Rear-Admiral Oldenshaw. He's dropping in here on his way back to the U.K. again. He'll want to hear that you all know what to do, and share my enthusiasm.'

Crespin watched him impassively. There was more to come.

Scarlett said casually, 'I shall be sending Third Officer Forbes back to England with him of course. Can't take her to Gradz with us, eh?' He grinned, his eyes shining coldly beneath the oak-leaved peak of his cap. 'Still, that's the way of things.' Then he was gone.

Coutts said calmly, 'The bastard!'

Crespin looked past him, not even hearing what he said. He had known it was coming. They both had. But if only . . . If only they had been given just a bit more time.

He said abruptly, 'What do you think about this plan?'

Coutts watched him, his eyes thoughtful. 'It's all too perfect, too pat. Everything must go like a clock, and in war it very rarely does.' He looked across the wardroom where Wemyss and Porteous were studying the chart. 'Of course, it's the sort of hair-brained scheme which just might succeed. If it does, Captain Scarlett will be on velvet. And if it fails, he'll probably be dead with the rest of us.' He grinned and clapped his hand on Crespin's arm. 'But as he so rightly said, that's the way of things!' As he turned towards the door he said quietly, 'You'll be getting under way immediately, so I'll clear out.' He hesitated. 'I'll be going to the airfield, so if you want me to give her a message?' His face softened. 'It might be a while before you see her again.'

Crespin shook his head. 'No. But thanks. I'll wait until this affair is over.'

Coutts shrugged. 'You could be right, old son.' He sauntered out of the wardroom, humming to himself.

Crespin turned. The *Thistle*'s officers were all watching him. They were dependent on each other now. And the ship depended on them as she had never done before.

Wemyss said, 'Shall I send for Magot, sir?'

Crespin shook his head. He was thinking of the girl. The plane which would drop her on some rain-washed English airfield. The distance and perhaps the years which would come between them.

He said, 'First, ring for Barker. We will have a drink together.' He looked at Porteous and Shannon, at Defries, the pale ex-submariner, and lastly at Wemyss.

'It may be the last chance we get for some time. I just wanted to tell you that when the operation starts there can be no letting up until it's completely finished, one way or the other.' He let his words sink in. 'You may think that the war you're going to is too remote to matter, the people too different from us to count. You'd be wrong to believe that, as you will discover.' He smiled. 'Do your best, and give every encouragement you can to the people who depend on you.' He remembered Scarlett's scathing remarks. Expendable. He added harshly, 'They're all worth it.'

At midnight the *Thistle* slipped her moorings and headed once more for the open sea. The stars were hidden beyond deep-bellied clouds, and the waves parted across her stubby bows in low, sullen breakers.

But as Crespin sat on the bridge chair, his oilskin buttoned tightly round his throat, he was aware of the changed atmosphere around him. Even the ship's movements seemed easy and controlled, as if the little corvette shared his own perception. It was like a sense of destiny, when there is no more time for looking back, and little use in remembering.

The only reality was the present, and what lay beyond the hidden horizon was like the future, and never got any closer. It was a small moment of peace, and he felt content to share it with the ship beneath him.

*   *   *

An enamel cocoa mug rolled from a flag locker and clattered noisily across the gratings. Crespin twisted round in his chair, startled at the sudden sound and surprised that he had been asleep. He heard Griffin muttering threats to the young signalman who had allowed the mug to fall, and knew from the tone of his voice that he, like the rest of the bridge party, must have known he had been drowsing in his chair.

He cleared his throat and saw Wemyss' dark shadow shift slightly on the opposite side of the bridge.

'What is the time now?'

Wemyss replied, 'Just after midnight, sir.'

Crespin levered himself forward in the chair and peered over the spray-dappled screen. It was pitch dark, but his eyes were so accustomed to it that he could see the paler outline of the forecastle, the black pointer of the four-inch gun and the sluggish arrowhead of broken water creaming back from the stem. The slight movement made his body protest. Every fibre and muscle ached, and the pain from his wound throbbed, as if it had just been kicked.

It was the second night at sea, and apart from occasional visits to the chart room he had not left the bridge. Around and below him the ship creaked steadily to the short, choppy swell, and he could almost feel the men tensed and waiting at their action stations. He lifted his face towards the leaden sky, feeling the hint of rain across his skin, the creases of strain around his eyes.

Without consulting the chart he could picture the ship's position, creeping nearer and nearer to the overlapping masses of the two large islands, Hvar and Brac, between which ran a twenty-five-mile channel of deep water. He gritted his teeth and tried to shut out the possibility of some mistake, some fault which he had overlooked. Even supposing the intelligence report was correct, it was still possible he had missed the troop convoy. The whole area was covered with scattered islands. Suppose the Germans had decided to take another route, or had altered their timing? The convoy might have passed into the channel already, could perhaps be inside the Tekla base while he and his ship waited in vain for the rendezvous.

Wemyss said quietly, 'The western tip of Hvar Island bears one-two-five, sir. About nine miles clear.' He sounded doubtful. 'We will have to turn shortly, or we'll start running into the channel.'

Crespin nodded. If they were ahead of the convoy and they entered the channel first, it would mean going about and fighting back again to the open sea. In total darkness it would be inviting disaster.

He snapped, 'Tell Willis to keep a close radar watch, Number One. With all these back-echoes from the islands he might miss something.'

'I have just told him, sir. He's a good hand and I don't think . . .'

'Tell him again!' Crespin's voice was harsh. 'Even a good operator only sees what he expects to see!'

He heard Wemyss speaking over the voice-pipe and settled down again to stare across the screen. There was no point in taking it out of Wemyss. But the waiting and the uncertainty were paring away his resistance, and the tiredness was doing the rest.

It would have been better if they could have steamed down parallel with the coast, instead of darting straight in amongst the islands. But the first day out they had been spotted by a high-flying Dornier bomber. It had circled the ship for over an hour, careful to stay out of range, but close enough to watch and if necessary report the course and appearance of this small, solitary corvette.

Crespin had had to assume that the German pilot knew his business, so he had been made to alter course away from the Yugoslav coast on a wide, frustrating detour, which even Magot's hard-worked engineers had been unable to make up with extra speed.

Now it was almost too late, and he was blaming himself. The German pilot was probably just curious and nothing more. He should have ignored the Dornier. He ought to have maintained his course and to hell with the consequences.

Wemyss returned. 'I've told him, sir.'

Crespin lifted his glasses and moved them slowly back and forth above the screen. It was very cold, yet within the clinging oilskin his body felt as if it was sweating from a fever.

He said, 'There's nothing else for it. We'll alter course and make one more sweep to the north-west.'

His words seemed to come back at him like a mocking echo of defeat. An admission of failure.

Wemyss said, 'Very good, sir.'

As Wemyss stooped over the screened chart table Willis's voice came across the open bridge like a chant.

'Radar . . . bridge!'

Crespin almost knocked a lookout from his feet as he ran to the voice-pipe.

'Bridge! Captain speaking!' He could hear Willis's sharp intake of breath.

'I think I've found them, sir. Two echoes, bearing green oh-four-five. Range oh-eight-oh.'

Crespin swung round and pressed his forehead against the rubber pad on the bridge repeater. In the small enclosed screen the echoes and outlines swirled before his eyes like candles in a breeze. Again he felt the surge of despair. There was nothing new. The spiky, smudged shape of the island's tip creeping out on the starboard bow. Another, heavier blob to port where Brac Island marked the opposite side of the channel entrance.

Then he stiffened and held his breath, hardly daring to blink.

The two small blips winked back at him, vanished, and then reappeared, the large one dead in the centre of the channel, the smaller one close astern of it.

He snapped, 'Take a look, Number One. It's them all right. It must be.'

The tiredness seemed to have dropped away like a blanket. His brain was suddenly steady and like ice.

'Starboard fifteen!' He waited, watching the ticking gyro, his mind working with it. 'Midships. Steady!'

Joicey's voice came up the brass tube, calm and wide awake. 'Steady, sir. Course zero-eight-zero.'

Willis again. 'Target's course is due east, sir. Steady at oh-nine-oh.'

Crespin kept his voice calm. Willis of all people must not be confused now. 'What about their speed?'

'Hard to say, sir, but it's very slow. Not more than a few knots.'

Crespin walked a few paces to the wheelhouse voice-pipe again. 'Starboard ten. Steer zero-nine-zero.' To Wemyss he added, 'We'll have to crack it on, slow or not. The Oerlikons are useless beyond a thousand yards, *half* that in this visibility.' He felt suddenly relaxed. It was a strange, remote feeling. 'Full ahead. We'll have to risk him seeing the bow wave.'

The telegraph clanged below his feet, and almost at once he felt the ship begin to tremble, as if she, too knew what was expected of her.

Joicey sounded unruffled. 'Course zero-nine-zero. Engine full ahead, sir.'

Wemyss was watching the radar repeater. 'No sign of the other escort. Maybe he's sniffing about on the other side of Brac, sir.'

'Perhaps.' Crespin watched the growing banks of white spray peeling away into the darkness on either beam. The deck and bridge fittings were shaking and vibrating madly, and from the funnel he saw the smoke pouring astern, as straight as the ship's knife-edged wake.

He said, 'Tell Shannon to be ready to fire star-shell. He'll only have time for one, so it had better be dead right!' He groped for the red handset and waited until Magot's voice echoed tinnily in his ear.

'More speed, Chief!' He could picture Magot's expression of painful resentment. 'All you've got and more!'

Magot asked, 'We goin' to fight, sir?'

'Yes.' He slammed down the handset and walked back to the chair. But he could not sit down. It was all he could do to stand still while the voice-pipes muttered and squeaked on every side.

Willis reported, 'Range is down to oh-four-oh, sir. Bearing constant.' He sounded completely absorbed, like a commentator at a race meeting.

'Good.' Crespin tried to picture the troopship creeping through the deep channel. The captain would feel safe so close to his new base, he thought. He would be concentrating on his navigation, leaving the rest to the escorts. And *they* would be sweeping the channel for partisans with any luck at all. It was, after all, unlikely for a single enemy warship to be right out here amidst their own offshore islands.

He felt the sweat like ice rime across his forehead. Another minute. Just one more minute and they would have turned away. Or Willis might have left his set for a few seconds and missed those tiny, flickering blobs of light.

Wemyss said, 'The old girl's getting her head.'

The *Thistle* was certainly moving. Fourteen, fifteen, then sixteen knots, and still the speed mounted. Her builders would have been proud to see her, Crespin thought.

'Target's range oh-two-oh, sir!' Even Willis sounded vaguely surprised.

'Stand by star-shell.' Crespin gripped the rail below the shivering glass screen. Surely someone on that escort would see them soon? Two thousand yards was a long way at night, but the *Thistle*'s great bow wave must be standing out in the darkness like the crest of an iceberg.

Below the bridge the Oerlikons shifted uneasily, their thin muzzles clearly etched against the frothing water on either beam. The *Thistle* mounted six all told, and at close range their rapid fire was murderous. But it had to be *close*.

'Tell Porteous to set depth-charges at minimum, Number One. Just in case we get a chance to drop them.' He thought suddenly of that other time, when Porteous had been unable to move. But that was a long time back. A hundred years. An eternity.

'Escort ship is turning, sir!' Willis's voice was shrill with suppressed tension.

'We don't want to waste time with him.' Crespin saw the faces watching him around the bridge, pale and unreal. 'The trooper is the one we want.'

He wondered briefly if the troopship's captain had noticed anything. He doubted it. It was said to be an old, three-thousand-ton coaster, and being crammed with troops and their equipment her captain would be too eager to reach port and get rid of his human cargo to care much about the activities of his escorts.

A diamond-bright light flashed across the water, and for an instant Crespin thought the escort had opened fire.

Leading Signalman Griffin said, ' 'E's makin' 'is challenge, sir.'

Crespin nodded. 'Reply to it.'

Griffin sucked his teeth and cradled the Aldis on his forearm. He was too old a hand to be flustered, and the shutter clicked rapidly on his lamp as if he was indeed replying to a friendly ship.

The other light came again, the escort's signalman probably confused by the meaningless jumble from Griffin's lamp.

He showed his teeth in a grin. 'Agin, sir ?'

Willis called, 'Troopship's range is now increasing, sir. He must have called for full speed.'

That decided it. Crespin snapped, 'Open fire !'

The bell jangled briefly before Shannon's gun lurched back on its mounting, the thunderclap of the detonation smashing across the bridge and blotting out every other sound.

Shannon must have heeded Crespin's warning very carefully. The range and bearing was perfect, for as the flare exploded against the low clouds Crespin saw the troopship, almost stern on, less than a mile away. She looked high in the water, and in the brilliant light the smoke from her two funnels writhed above her propeller wash in an unbroken brown fog.

The escort was little more than a converted trawler, high bowed, with a gun mounted right forward above the stem.

Crespin saw the cream of her bow wave as she swung hard over, the glass of her wheelhouse windows glittering in the flare like eyes. Tiny figures were running aft, and he knew that the captain would try to drop smoke floats to shield his ponderous consort.

Shannon's voice was incisive. '*Shoot!*'

This time it was no star-shell. Crespin gripped his glasses against his eyes and flinched as the water-spout rose like a ghost in direct line with the escort's bridge.

Shannon snapped, 'Up two hundred !' An empty shellcase clanged unheeded on the quivering plating. 'Shoot !'

The shell smashed into the little ship's superstructure and exploded with a bright orange flash. Fragments and jets of escaping steam burst through the smoke, and above it the single funnel swayed and then pitched down like a tree under the axe.

The next shell hit the escort somewhere on the waterline, and there was hardly any flash at all. But the ship stopped instantly, the bow wave falling away to nothing even as the *Thistle* swept out of the smoke, her Oerlikons ripping across the short waves with bright lines of tracer, tossing aside the

German gunners who were still struggling to train their weapon towards them, then creeping still further along the escort's listing hull.

Crespin swung his glasses to watch the trooper. She was turning to port, making for the protection of the island.

'Port ten!' He crossed the bridge, shouting above the rattle of gun-fire, the splintering detonations from the sinking escort. 'Stand by to shift target!' He pounded the screen with his fist. 'Midships!' God, the trooper looked damned big in the dipping flare. Big and old.

He heard Shannon yelling, the click of the breech block, and then the ear-probing bang of the four-inch. He saw the shell explode under the trooper's poop. Just a pinprick of glowing light, like an ember from a fire. But below decks, with troops crowded and hemmed in by chaos and awakened crewmen, it would be enough to start a real panic.

'Shoot!'

Crespin saw a thin line of tracer coming at him from the trooper's bridge. Probably a light machine-gun. Some of the bullets cracked and shrieked against the bridge and others whispered overhead like souls in torment.

Another of Shannon's shells exploded somewhere on the troopship's boatdeck, and instantly fanned into a wall of dancing yellow flames. A paint store or some carelessly stowed cargo had caught alight, and marked the ship's progress better than any flare.

The *Thistle* was overtaking her, steadily and remorselessly, so that as the careering troopship drifted across her port bow the Oerlikons, and then the harsher thump, thump, thump of the pom-pom, joined in the din of battle.

'Second escort closing, sir! Green two-oh!'

An arc of red tracer lifted from the darkness and floated down across the forecastle.

From aft Crespin heard Sub-Lieutenant Defries calling to his gunners and the sporadic response as the disengaged Oerlikons returned fire.

He felt the bridge shudder, the telltale whine and crash of cannon shells hitting home. A man was screaming, another called desperately, 'Fred! Help me, Fred, for God's sake!'

Crespin wiped his streaming eyes and peered at the troop
ship. She was still turning. God, to lose her now, after all this
'Port twenty!' He felt the rudder pulling the ship over
'Midships!'

Water swept over the rail and surged unheeded along the
side deck.

'Stand by depth-charges!' He craned over the swaying
screen as a messenger spoke into the handset. He saw Porteous
crouching by the quarterdeck thrower with his small crew
watched him as he lifted his hand to point as the trooper rose
out of the dark sea like a cliff.

A young signalman was hanging to a voice-pipe, his voice
cracking with shock. 'Look! Look at them soljers!'

Crespin steadied the glasses again. What he had taken for
deck cargo suddenly blossomed in the lenses in a great seething mass of figures. They were everywhere. On the blazing
boatdeck and down on the hold covers. On every ladder and
part of the bridge. Like one, undulating, living thing.

A seaman called, 'Depth-charge crew ready, sir!'

Crespin felt the tracers whipping over the bridge but could
not drag his eyes from the scene of terror and desperate confusion. Some of the soldiers were even leaping or falling over
the side, small feathers of white spray to be lost and swallowed
in the ship's churning propellers.

He held his breath, counting seconds. The *Thistle* surged
past the other ship's side, so close that it was possible to hear
the crackle of flames and isolated pistol shots, and above all
the combined roar of hundreds of voices, like a sea breaking
on reefs.

'*Fire!*'

The depth-charges jerked away, hardly noticed by the sweating gunners as they fired and reloaded with the fierce intensity
of madmen.

The explosions were hollow and metallic, hammers on an
oil drum. As the pyramids of water leapt skywards Crespin saw
the troopship give one great convulsive shudder and then appear to fall sideways in a welter of falling spray.

Wemyss was yelling, 'God, that was close!'

Crespin realised dully that there was a thin line of surf right across the bows. They were driving headlong for the nearest island with hardly room left to turn.

Another great explosion jarred the hull beneath him and as he ducked over the voice-pipe he saw the troopship sagging on her beam, vehicles and crated equipment thundering across her tilting decks before smashing on and over the rail.

'Hard astarboard!'

He ran back to the side as the deck tilted wildly and threw the lookouts into a tangled heap of arms and legs.

The troopship had broken her back, and as the bows lifted wearily through the smoke and the pressurised haze of escaping steam he saw the soldiers falling and kicking like animals as they fought to escape the flames.

An Oerlikon fired a long burst from aft, and the low clouds were painted afresh with even brighter colours as the savage tracer ignited some drums of fuel below the troopship's bridge.

Sickened, Crespin watched the fire running like glowing lava down the broken ship's side, spreading across the water, isolating and consuming the screaming men, devouring them and driving them mad in those last few moments of horror.

He pulled himself against the gyro, feeling the bile in his throat, the sick disgust for what they were doing.

'Midships!' He heard a mumbled reply and knew that it was a quartermaster on the wheel and not Joicey.

He snapped, 'Is the coxswain all right?'

But it was Joicey's voice again. 'I'm here, sir! Wheel's amidships!'

Crespin knew Joicey had left the wheel. To see the Germans burn. To watch them die in such a frightful horror.

'Steer two-four-five!' He left the voice-pipe and crossed to the screen. The flames were already dropping astern, the last half of the broken ship black in their middle like a dying whale. Of the second escort there was no sign, and with a start he realised he had not even seen it when it had first opened fire.

Wemyss was watching him, his face like bronze in the fires.

'Report damage and casualties, Number One.' Crespin met his gaze and added flatly, 'Mission accomplished.'

Wemyss nodded. As he moved back to the chattering voice-pipes his shoulders were hunched, so that he looked like an old man.

Crespin leaned his forehead on his arm and swallowed hard. They had died as his men had died. He should have felt nothing but satisfaction.

He heard a man whimpering with pain and the sounds of more cries from aft. There was still a great deal to do before making the dangerous passage to Gradz, and Scarlett.

But he had to wait a little longer. To wait and think. He tried to remember that small moment of peace when he had left Brindisi just two nights ago, but it was gone. It left him sick and empty.

Wemyss was speaking on a voice-pipe and he heard feet clattering up the bridge ladders. Demands and requests for instructions. Casualties or men to be buried. It was no use. The ship could not wait. So nor could he.

He straightened his back and turned to face the others. 'Very good,' he said. 'A very successful attack!'

15 The Letter

T HE *Thistle*'s arrival at the inlet was both impressive and
emotional. After the short, savage attack on the convoy
and the nerve-racking dash through the remaining darkness, the greeting which awaited the weary sailors was staggering.

From every niche and ledge on the towering sides of the inlet, from headland and half-submerged rocks they were
cheered by what seemed to be hundreds and hundreds of men,
women and children. Some even waded thigh-deep into the
shallows by the village, ignoring the ice-cold water as they
stared and waved at the approaching ship.

Next to a torpedo boat, a corvette was just about the smallest
warship in commission, but to the Yugoslavs, so long starved of
help, isolated and faced by an overwhelming enemy, the little
Thistle's two hundred feet must have seemed like a battle-
cruiser.

Crespin stood high on the gratings as he conned his ship
slowly through the narrow entrance and up the side of the
overhanging cliffs. Even for the *Thistle* it was a close fit, and
as he edged the ship ahead and astern, using the single screw to
turn her almost in her own length, he was all the time conscious of the growing sunlight and the need for haste.

Along the Dalmatian coast telephones would be ringing,
senior officers would be called from their beds to hear the news
of the sunken troopship. The word would be flashed to airfields and coastal patrols alike and begin a massive search. At

any second a spotter plane might come down across the inle
and *Thistle*'s secret would be out.

He watched narrowly as the entrance swung slowly acros
the bows once more. It was better to have the ship pointin;
seaward, just in case.

'Let go!' He saw Shannon drop his hand and heard th«
rumbling response from the outgoing cable. It was difficult t«
concentrate, hard to accept that they had arrived, especiall)
as the ship seemed hemmed in on every side by dinghies, fishin;
boats and anything else which would stay afloat, while thei;
cheering occupants stared up at the bullet-scarred corvette
heedless or unaware of their own danger from her swingin;
bow and the urgent thrashing of her screw.

Crespin had already dropped the motor boat as he had en
tered the inlet, and now as he craned over the screen he coul«
see Petty Officer Dunbar and a small party of men drifting
astern, laying out one more anchor to stop the ship from swing
ing against some projecting rock or into the cliff itself.

'Stop engine!' He felt the vibrations idle into stillnes:
and heard the shouts and cheers intensified in the sudde»
silence.

The ship's company seemed too dazed to understand wha'
was happening. Dirty and smoke-stained, they just stood a¹
their stations staring at the upturned faces, conscious vaguel)
of their new importance, but still too shocked from battle tc
accept it.

Crespin said sharply, 'Number One, break out the canva:
canopies and get 'em rigged before our people fall asleep or
their feet!'

At the far end of the inlet he had already seen the twc
M.L.s and Scarlett's armed yacht snugged down at improvised
moorings, their shapes almost hidden beneath grey-painted
canopies and camouflaged netting. From the air, moored a:
they were so close beneath the cliffs, they might stay invisible
even to the most vigilant pilot.

Wemyss hurried away and Crespin heard him shouting hi:
orders with something of his old vigour.

Shannon cupped his hands and yelled up at the bridge, 'Sir!
These people are coming aboard. Shall I stop them?' He

sounded vaguely upset that the Yugoslavs should be allowed
to swarm up the ship's side unchecked.

Crespin smiled wearily. 'Let 'em come!' He swung round
as Soskic, followed by a grinning Coutts, clambered on to the
bridge.

Soskic took both of Crespin's hands and studied him with
something like affection. 'You came back! Everyone is speaking of what you did!'

Crespin felt dazed. It was impossible to accept that they
were moored within twelve miles of the nearest mainland. Yet
here they were, and Soskic already knew what they had
achieved. The *Thistle* had come from the slaughter at her
maximum speed, and still the news had preceded her. How, or
by what means, he could never know.

Soskic said, 'And tomorrow the coastline of my country will
be ringed by floating corpses. It will give my people fresh
heart to see them.'

He seemed to sense Crespin's sick tiredness and added in a
more controlled tone, 'Perhaps I shock you? But you must
understand that to an oppressed and tortured people these are
the only signs which matter any more. It is our war.' He held
Crespin's arm tightly. 'Maybe you see *your* war through a gun-
sight or a telescope. Perhaps the damage you must do is even invisible beyond an horizon or under the water. It is the same in
the end. But close to, it *feels* dirtier!'

Crespin nodded. 'I understand.'

Coutts watched as the first mass of canvas and netting jerked
its way up and over the forecastle. 'They take to it in a manner
born,' he said slowly.

Crespin looked down at the side deck where five still forms
lay in a neat, canvas-sewn row awaiting burial. 'They did well,'
was all he could find as an answer.

Coutts followed his glance and said, 'You never get used to
it.'

Crespin looked across at the bare hills beyond the cliffs. They
would have to be buried there. There was no time for honours
at sea.

He said, 'I wonder if anyone from England will ever visit
Gradz in years to come and see their graves?' He watched the

motor boat pushing back between the bobbing dinghies, the seamen grinning like schoolboys. 'If they do, they'll probably wonder why anyone had to die for a place like this.'

Coutts smiled sadly. 'Well, *we* know, don't we?'

Porteous climbed on to the bridge and saluted. He looked worn out and drooping with fatigue. 'Camouflage secured, sir.'

Crespin nodded. 'Very good.' He added, 'I understand that your Leading Seaman Haig was killed?'

Porteous stared at the deck. 'Yes, sir. We had just fired the charges. He was actually smiling at me. He said, "This time you did it on your own, sir" or something like that.' He shuddered. 'Then a tracer-shell came from somewhere and he was dead. Just like that.'

Magot appeared at the top of the ladder and glared for a few seconds at Soskic. Then he said, 'Will you pass the word for these foreign buggers to keep out of my engine room, sir?'

Crespin felt his face twisting into a smile. 'Very well, Chief.' He added, 'Have you hurt your mouth?'

Magot looked from Coutts to Soskic and then opened his mouth wide. 'When we done that quick turn I slipped an' fell, sir. I dropped me bleedin' teeth an' Gawd knows where they are now!'

Leading Signalman Griffin clapped his shoulder as he hurried down the ladder. 'Never mind, Chief. When they break the old ship up for scrap they'll likely find your mashers still down there. Probably send 'em to the bloody Maritime Museum!' He was laughing as he followed the fuming engineer from the bridge.

Soskic shook his head. 'Remarkable men!'

Then he became serious. 'I have met your Captain Scarlett. I am impressed with his energy. Most impressed.'

Coutts said dryly, 'He came ashore with me last night when we arrived. He's been a ball of fire ever since.'

'I can imagine.' Crespin thought of the job they had come to do, the enormity of the problems still to be faced.

He asked, 'Any news of Lemke's *Nashorn*?'

Coutts replied, 'They say the ship is at Trieste as reported. That is all we know at present.'

Soskic waved his arm towards the village. 'I have three more

schooners since you were last here. Also we have gathered
nearly three hundred men from the surrounding islands to help
us. We are armed and ready. Your Captain Scarlett says we
are to attack Lemke's base. What do you think of that?'

Crespin saw Coutts look away. 'It depends. It will not be an
easy task.'

Soskic plucked his beard and grinned hugely. 'That is what
you said before, my friend! When you took your schooner and
drove the pigs from that village!'

Crespin saw some of his men giving food to the partisans
and replied, 'There's more to lose this time.' What was the
point of trying to explain to Soskic? To him the war was too
personal, too close. But Coutts would be thinking about it. He
of all people must realise that Scarlett was only interested in
the raid as a single, glowing episode. He would never see it as
what it really represented to Soskic and his people.

Or was *he* the one who was unrealistic? Had he allowed his
mistrust, even dislike of Scarlett to get the upper hand? Like
that business over Trotter. After all which had happened, did
it really matter how he had died? To know that he had been
driven out of his mind for causing the death of a German
prisoner should be enough.

Soskic sighed deeply, 'I will leave you now. I must go and
see Captain Scarlett again. There is much to plan and prepare.'

They watched him return to his boat, his beautiful boots
shining in the sunlight.

Then Coutts said, 'I saw her at the airfield.' He fumbled inside his coat. 'She gave me a letter for you.'

Crespin took the envelope and looked at it. 'Did she get off
all right?'

'It was raining.' Coutts was watching him. 'Yes, she was all
right. She's a damn fine girl.' He shrugged and glanced at his
watch. 'Better get back to Scarlett's H.Q. Don't want young
Preston doing a wrong translation for him.'

Crespin followed him to the deck and stared unseeingly at the
covered corpses.

'Thanks for the message.'

Coutts saluted casually. 'My pleasure, old son.'

In his cabin Crespin sat down and turned the letter over in

his hands for several minutes. Around him he could hear the usual shipboard noises, yet the cabin retained the stench of smoke and cordite. He slit open the envelope and read the unfamiliar handwriting very slowly.

It was a short letter. At the top of the second page it continued: '. . . and I expect Captain Scarlett let you believe he had ordered my return to England? The truth is that I *asked* for the transfer myself. I knew Admiral Oldenshaw was on another tour and I made my request to him. You see, my darling, I think I am pregnant, and I could not tell you, knowing you as I do. If you still want me, it must be because of us and not because of what has happened. When you get home again, I, or maybe we, will be waiting. Think about me sometimes. I love you. Penny.'

Crespin laid the letter on his table. It was almost as if he had heard her own voice, and he looked around the cabin like a man emerging from a dream.

Wemyss peered into the doorway, his cap beneath his arm. 'Excuse me, sir, but there's a messenger from the village. Captain Scarlett requests your presence at the bunker for a briefing.'

Crespin stood up, his movements heavy and barely controlled. 'Thank you, Number One. Call away the motor boat.'

Wemyss said slowly, 'Shall I attend to the burial party, sir?'

Crespin nodded. 'If you would.' He was only half aware of what Wemyss was saying. She had gone. Afraid that he would marry her because he had to. In his tired mind the distance between them seemed to build up until it was limitless, like black space.

'Is there anything I can do, sir?' Wemyss was watching him anxiously. 'Anything at all?'

Crespin walked past him. 'Nothing.'

Wemyss followed him to the gangway and saw him into the boat. He watched the little motor boat curving away towards the village and wondered about the letter.

Sub-Lieutenant Defries appeared by his side. 'Was that the captain, Number One?'

Wemyss nodded. 'Why do you ask?'

'Signal, sir. Just been decoded.' Defries moved the pad into the sunlight between the draped netting. 'I think he should know about it, although it's addressed to Scarlett.'

Wemyss looked at Defries's pale face. 'What does it say?'

'From Admiralty, Number One. The aircraft carrying Rear-Admiral Oldenshaw is overdue and presumed missing. Captain Scarlett will return to U.K. and assume control of Special Operations until further orders. Ends.' He looked up at Wemyss' lined face. 'What does it mean, d'you think?'

Wemyss turned and stared after the motor boat. The letter on the desk and Crespin's face. That was what it meant.

He said harshly, 'When the boat comes back I'll go ashore. Tell Shannon to take charge of the burial party. He ought to be good at it!' Without another word he walked aft and leaned heavily against the depth-charges.

Porteous saw Defries and asked, 'Another flap on?'

'Oldenshaw's been killed.' Defries was still staring towards Wemyss' slouched figure. 'Still, I suppose he would have died anyway pretty soon.'

Porteous looked at the dead seamen being lowered into the waiting boat, the small firing party, embarrassed in their best uniforms. He thought of Haig, the competent leading hand who had died at his side. Now he was going ashore for the last time. He wondered vaguely how they would manage to scrape out the graves in that rocky hillside.

He said quietly, 'That's a comfort, I suppose. But not much.'

*　　　　*　　　　*

It was very cold in Soskic's bunker, and the silent figures around Scarlett's improvised map table huddled together for mutual comfort. As Crespin stepped through the rough sacking curtains Scarlett looked up, his face gleaming in the glare of several oil lamps.

'Good.' He gave Crespin a ready smile. 'You made a bloody potmess of that troopship to all accounts!'

Crespin saw Coutts translating Scarlett's remarks to the partisans and there were several nods and grunts of approval. He noticed that there were many more partisan leaders than on his other visit, leather-faced, tough-looking men in thick jerkins, their bodies festooned with weapons and ammunition of a dozen makes and sizes. Almost without exception the partisan commanders wore German jackboots, their late owners having no further use for them.

He said, 'We lost five killed and three wounded, sir.'

Scarlett regarded him searchingly. 'Hard luck. Still, it could have been worse.' He took a bayonet from one of the partisans and used it like a pointer across the map. 'We must get on with it if we're to make use of our advantage.'

Crespin rested his palms on the table. He must push the other thoughts from his mind. He had to concentrate. The tiredness was dragging at his brain like a drug. It was hard even to see straight.

Scarlett said crisply, 'Up here we have the Peljesac Peninsula, beyond which is the main channel to the coast and Tekla Point. We will keep fairly close to Korcula Island and thereby avoid the other island of Hvar. There are still German forces on the latter and we don't want an alarm to be raised before we get within reach of our objective.' He paused and tapped the map with obvious impatience as Coutts translated for the benefit of the partisans. 'Surprise and quick action are the mainsprings to this attack. The Germans obviously imagine that the troopship was sunk by forces from Italy. Otherwise we'd have seen more activity around here by now. So much the better. I have decided,' he paused and shot Soskic a warm smile, '*we* have decided that the attack should be in two parts. The schooners under Captain Coutts' command will land the main body of partisans three miles from Tekla Point to approach overland. *Thistle* in company with the two M.L.s will enter the base from seaward for a frontal attack and destroy all installations and any local shipping which cannot be taken for our own use.'

Crespin watched the tip of the bayonet as it stabbed at each objective. It was a daring plan, but simple enough to work, if only the Germans had no surface forces in the area.

Scarlett said abruptly, 'And if anyone is worrying about the so-called *Rhinoceros*, he had better forget it.' He looked calmly at Crespin. 'If we smash the base, the Germans will be forced to withdraw from this section of the coast. The island of Vis is already in partisan hands, and the other local ones will follow as soon as we complete this raid. After that,' he paused to allow Coutts to finish translating, 'we will have more offensive craft based on Vis, M.T.B.s to be precise, and they will soon take care of this German monstrosity which has been tying everyone down here.'

Crespin breathed out slowly. Scarlett had been saving that piece to the last. Torpedo boats would indeed put an end to the slow and ponderous *Nashorn*, once a base was secured for them.

He said, 'What about the armed yacht, sir?'

Scarlett pouted. 'She will remain here as, ah, communications ship so to speak.'

Soskic looked at Crespin. 'A good plan.' It sounded like a question.

'You have my word for it!' Scarlett's smile had vanished. 'Just make sure that *your* people don't jump the gun, eh?'

Coutts said flatly, 'He means, keep them from attacking before the signal!'

Scarlett's frown eased slightly. 'Very well then. I suggest you gather your men together and put them in the picture. I intend to leave Gradz at dusk and attack at first light tomorrow.'

The partisans stared woodenly at Coutts' mouth, and as he finished speaking gave a great shout of excitement and obvious satisfaction.

The rough curtains moved slightly and Wemyss appeared within the circle of lamplight.

'Signal, sir.' He glanced quickly at Crespin and then back to Scarlett. 'Immediate.'

Crespin watched Scarlett's eyes moving quickly over the pencilled signal, but it was impossible to gauge any sort of reaction.

Then Scarlett said curtly, 'Carry on then. I'll be coming round to make a last check in two hours' time.' His eyes shifted to Wemyss and he added, 'You can carry on, too, Number One. I don't need you here.' It was a cold dismissal.

He waited until most of the partisans had followed Soskic from the bunker and then said, 'Bad news, I'm afraid, Crespin.' He held out the signal. 'It makes things all the more urgent.'

Crespin read the neat printed letters and felt the bunker moving around him as if in a mist.

Scarlett's voice seemed to come from a great distance. 'A great loss to the Service.' He sounded more preoccupied than charged with any sort of emotion.

Crespin placed the crumpled signal on the table, amazed that his mind had become so clear. Clear and empty, like a void. There should be pain, some words to ease the shock and agony of the brief report. A plane down, lives lost. It was common enough. He should have been able to accept it.

He said, 'I would like to return to my ship, sir.'

Scarlett nodded slowly. 'Best thing. No use brooding at a time like this.' He added, 'Too much depends on all of us.'

Coutts had been standing in the shadows. 'What's happened?'

Scarlett gestured towards the signal. 'I'll be leaving after the raid. I shall be needed for other work now.' His eyes gleamed as he turned towards the lights. 'France, and then Germany.' He moved restlessly. 'Our work out here is almost finished anyway.'

Coutts said quietly, 'I'm sorry about this, old son. Damned sorry.' He followed Crespin into the harsh light of the hillside and added, 'There aren't any words. There never are.'

Crespin heard himself say, 'She was having a baby.'

'Hell!' Coutts pulled out a cheroot and then replaced it in his pocket. 'You were right for each other. I knew that.'

Crespin saw the motor boat cutting a fine line towards the shallows below the village.

'If it hadn't been for me she'd still be alive. She didn't *have* to go on that bloody aircraft!'

Coutts looked at him and then replied simply, 'You're wrong, you know. You must stop thinking like that. It won't help her, or you either.'

Crespin started to walk down the stony track, his eyes fixed on the flat water of the inlet. Coutts watched him go, his eyes troubled. Poor bastard, he thought. Poor, lonely bastard.

Scarlett emerged from the bunker and stood beside him staring at the village below.

Coutts said slowly, 'Pity about Oldenshaw, sir.' He waited, watching Scarlett's face for some sign of regret.

Scarlett thought about it. 'I agree. Still, it will make hard work for the rest of us.'

Coutts felt vaguely satisfied by the comment. You're starting to feel glad the plane crashed, he thought bitterly. It will mean promotion for you, and a firm place in history to gloat over when you go back to your other world.

He said, 'I'll go down to the schooners, sir. Time's getting a bit short.'

Scarlett was still staring around at the hills. 'You know, Coutts, I think I'll be *sorry* to leave here.'

'Sorry?' Coutts turned his face away. 'I hope I never see the place again. Ever!' Then he swung on his heel and walked quickly down the slope, leaving Scarlett staring after him.

*   *   *

At dusk the same day the *Thistle* made ready to leave the inlet. Beneath the deepening shadows of the tall cliffs it was already as dark as night, and only the swirling water showed any sign of movement, and shone in the fading light like black steel.

The schooners had sailed an hour earlier, their decks crammed with armed partisans, their patched hulls swaying uncomfortably as they edged between the headlands to meet the swell of the open sea beyond. Theirs would be a slow passage, but via a shorter route, hugging the islands and slipping through even the narrowest channels to rendezvous before dawn with the rest of the group.

The stream anchor had been recovered, and as the main cable clanked slowly inboard Crespin stood by the screen watching the pale shape of the stern swinging towards the middle of the inlet, pushed steadily by the wind until it seemed to point directly at the village. Below his feet the deck trembled impatiently, and he heard the squeak of blocks and falls as the motor boat was run up to its davits and made fast. The stern was still swinging, and he wanted to yell at Shannon's anchor

party to get a move on. But it might only fluster him, he decided dully.

He knew that Scarlett was still sitting on the bridge chair,
crouching forward to watch the seamen around the bows, but
he did not look at him. Any sort of forced conversation seemed
beyond him, and all day he had confined himself to the business of preparing for the raid.

Looking back over the day it was hard to remember any real
sequence of events. He had slept for maybe three hours at the
most and spent the rest of the time going round the ship, speaking briefly to the heads of departments, checking, and then
re-checking. It had all been interspersed with endless cups of
coffee and little else to sustain him. But he knew he had to
keep going. It would be fatal to stop and think beyond the
necessities of preparation and work.

'Up and down, sir!' Shannon's voice sounded frail on the
wind.

Crespin breathed out sharply. Just in time. 'Slow ahead!
Starboard ten!' He could not wait for the anchor to break surface. A few more minutes and the ship might drift against some
of those rocks. He could see them quite clearly, shining like
jagged metal below the cliffs. There were no watching villagers
or partisans there this time. The old and the sick, the women
and the children would be in their huts and houses, waiting
and praying.

'Anchor's aweigh, sir!'

'Midships!' Crespin groped for the voice-pipe. 'Steer straight
for the centre of the opening, Cox'n!'

'Aye, aye, sir.' Joicey needed no unnecessary orders. He
knew the feel of his ship as a rider knows his horse.

Griffin snatched up his lamp as a shaded light flickered
briefly from below the headland. 'Signal from senior M.L., sir.
Request permission to take up station.'

Scarlett stirred. 'Granted.' He lifted his glasses to watch the
sudden flurry of foam as the two lean M.L.s gathered way and
pushed through the arms of the headland. They would sweep
ahead of the *Thistle* in the wider channel beyond Korcula
Island.

Scarlett said suddenly, 'Make to M.L.s "Good hunting!"'

His teeth shone in the blinking Aldis light. 'It'll cheer 'em up
a bit, eh?'

Crespin did not speak. Good luck. It was like a schoolmaster
handing out a present for the smartest boy in the class. He felt
sick.

Wemyss climbed up beside him. 'Motor boat secure, sir.' He
stared up at the fast moving clouds. 'Glad to get shot of those
damn nets.'

Crespin said, 'Tell Willis to secure the radar, Number One.
I want no transmissions of any sort from now on. The Germans
are not supposed to have any detecting gear hereabouts, but
we'll not take chances. Then go round the ship and check every
last fan and watertight door yourself.'

Scarlett watched Wemyss clatter down the ladder before
he spoke. 'Taking no chances, eh?' He sounded calm and
relaxed.

'No, sir.'

The headlands opened up on either beam and then slid past,
their protective reefs coming into sudden life as the ship's bow
wave surged over them.

'Starboard ten.' Crespin buttoned his oilskin over his binoculars as spray drifted above the bridge and spattered against
the screen. 'Midships. Steer two-eight-zero.' He watched the
gyro's luminous dial ticking round and then steady itself.
Away from the island, away from the mainland. They would
circle round in a wide turn before making that final approach
up the unmarked channel.

The bosun's mate looked up from a voice-pipe. 'Anchor
secure, sir!'

Crespin nodded. 'Very well.' He reached out and pressed the
red button below the screen, hearing the shrill clamour of bells
echoing around the ship, knowing that the men who now ran
quickly to their action stations would remain there until the
ship returned to Gradz. Some would come back to Gradz and
stay to join those five graves above the village.

He half-listened to the muttering voices, the slam and crash
of watertight doors, the scrape of ammunition and steel hel-
mets. After this raid was finished, what would happen? he
wondered. The little *Thistle* would perhaps go back to her

proper role of escorting helpless merchantmen, and her company scattered and lost from each other for ever. And himself? He thought of the M.T.B.s which would soon be coming to the Yugoslav islands. Maybe he would go back to them. Go on fighting in the Adriatic, further and further north until . . .

'Ship closed up at action stations, sir.'

'Very good.' He turned as Scarlett eased his tall frame from the chair.

Scarlett said, 'I'm going to the chartroom. I'll be there if you need me.'

'Yes, sir.'

Scarlett paused below the gratings and dropped his voice to a fierce whisper. 'I know how you feel about that plane crash, but you mustn't let it get in the way of what *we* have to do. This raid must succeed, it *has* to!'

'You'll find me ready enough, sir.' Crespin looked down at him, surprised that he could feel neither anger nor resentment any more.

'I'm glad to hear it!' Scarlett seemed eager to go, yet unable to leave without saying more. 'I had a feeling it might come to this, you know. Right from the start. I was prepared to accept that you might resent serving under a temporary officer, one who has commanded nothing larger than an armed launch. I was ready to accept it because I thought you were different. But your attitude in the past, your very upbringing has made future possibilities in this section out of the question.'

'Is that all, sir?'

'No, it's not!' Scarlett pushed his face closer. 'Admiral Oldenshaw told me that he might be considering you for this command in my place. I was against it, of course, but I suppose he had his reasons.'

'And now he's dead.' Crespin looked past Scarlett's head towards the ship's small wake. Gradz had already disappeared in the gathering darkness.

'Exactly.' Scarlett checked himself. 'And that's an end to it.' He turned his back and made for the chartroom.

Wemyss came back, dragging his feet noisily across the gratings.

Crespin asked, 'Everything all right?'

He nodded. 'All positions checked, sir.'

'Good.' Crespin walked to the chair and leaned against it. 'After the attack we will return to Gradz. Coutts will pick up the partisans and withdraw to Korcula Island. It's nearer for him and no Germans left there to hinder things.' His voice sounded toneless and he added sharply, 'By that time the Germans on the mainland should be too busy to bother about us. The raid and demolition of the Tekla base is the general signal for other partisan attacks up and down the coast. It'll be a long day all round.'

Wemyss said quietly, 'I heard about Third Officer Forbes, sir. We all got to like her a lot. She was sort of part of our little community.' He was fumbling for words. 'And I know what she meant to you.'

Crespin gripped the chair with all his strength. 'Thank you.'

Wemyss added, 'It's different from the Atlantic. Out here it's women and kids, everyone. Coutts was telling me how the Yugoslav children climb on the Jerry tanks to ask for food and then drop grenades or petrol bombs into them.' He faltered. 'That's why it was good to have her out here with us, sir. It evened the score in some way.'

Crespin closed his mind like a steel door. 'Thank you, Number One, and now let's forget it, shall we? Later there may be time, but right at this particular moment there's no damned time for anything.'

He saw Wemyss move heavily back to the chart table and felt sickened by what he had said. He wanted to call him, to tell him that he felt just as he did. That his heart was aching with the pain of loss and despair.

In the same instant he knew it would be useless, even dangerous. Just as he had known it was pointless to argue with Scarlett, to tell him that he knew the true reasons for the dead admiral's decision to remove him. Tired, overworked, they were old words. Scarlett's role had gone when the tide of Allied defeats had started to turn the other way. Gestures and brave headlines were no longer enough. Four years of war had pared away the glamour and the frail beliefs in such things. Perhaps Scarlett belong to another era, when war was kept at a distance, when women and children were spared, and the harvest of battle was confined to casualty lists and a yearly service around the Cenotaph.

When Wemyss spoke again he sounded quite normal. 'Time to alter course, sir. New course is three-three-zero.'

Crespin climbed into the chair and felt the steel arms pressing against his ribs as the ship heeled gently to an offshore swell. 'Very good. Take her round, Number One.'

Below in his wheelhouse Petty Officer Joicey spun the polished spokes in response to the first lieutenant's voice from the bell-mouthed tube by his face.

He said, 'Steady on three-three-zero, sir!'

Feet scraped on the deck overhead and he could imagine the officers and lookouts swaying and crouching below the screen. By comparison the wheelhouse was snug and warm, and to a stranger it would seem almost oppressive. The steel shutters were clipped over the windows, and the unmoving air was heavy with damp and the mixed smells of oil and Brasso, the latter being kept to maintain the binnacle and fittings in perfect order.

In the glowing compass light Joicey could see the telegraphsman and a bosun's mate squatting on lockers, their bodies rising and falling with the ship, their heads angled to avoid the condensation which ran from the bulkhead like rain. It was all familiar and strangely comforting. For Joicey had stood on this very grating for more times than he could remember. In and out of harbour, under air attack, and chasing the elusive U-boats. He almost knew what the ship was going to do before an order was passed to him.

He thought suddenly of the one moment when he had left the wheel. The first time ever in his life he had broken his code of discipline. But he had needed to see the Germans die. Burn and die like so many tortured shapes in hell.

But every time he tried to build a picture in his mind he kept seeing instead the communal grave, with her name up there with the rest. He was still not sure what he had expected to feel when he had watched the dying soldiers. Elation? A sense of release? But there had been nothing at all, and *she* was as far away from him as ever.

He swung the spokes angrily as the gyro ticked a degree off course to mark his momentary lapse.

He saw the bosun's mate's head begin to droop and snarled, 'Git up on the bridge, you idle sod!' The man jerked upright as if Joicey had kicked him. 'An' ask Jimmy th' One if we can stew some char, right?'

The seaman nodded. 'If you say so, Swain.'

Joicey glared at the telegraphsman who was again fully awake. 'An' *you* can stop gawpin', for a bleedin' start!'

Outside the wheelhouse it was now pitch dark with no division between sea and sky. But the *Thistle* pushed her bows through the short waves without effort, seemingly indifferent to anything which might lie across her path. Perhaps, like the men who served her, she understood that the future was no longer quite so far away, and accepted it.

16 A Face in the Past

REACHING the rendezvous was a feat of navigation and sheer concentrated effort. As the *Thistle* wound her way between the larger islands, groping from one channel to the next in total darkness, it became a matter of stop-watch timing for each alteration of course and every change of speed. Wemyss hardly left the hooded chart table for more than seconds at a time, and as Crespin concentrated on the business of conning the ship he found time to notice how they had all become a team, probably without being aware of it.

Scarlett left the chartroom and took his position in the steel chair, his body craned forward as if to sniff out the invisible land across the bows. His return seemed to symbolise the inevitability of action, and as the ship slipped through the last narrow channel with the mainland barely two miles abeam, the tension on the upper bridge became almost unbearable.

Crespin wiped his forehead with the back of his hand. It had gone far better than he had dared hoped. No flares, no awakened coastal batteries to bracket the ship as she edged so close inshore. Somewhere ahead the two M.L.s were presumably on station, and as there had been no sudden activity ashore it was to be assumed Coutts had landed his partisans without incident.

Wemyss' voice was muffled beneath the hood. 'Tekla Point bears three-two-one degrees, sir. Five miles.'

'Very good.' Crespin leaned over the voice-pipe. 'Starboard ten.'

'Starboard ten, sir. Ten of starboard wheel on.' Joicey sounded tenser than usual.

'Midships.' Crespin thought of Wemyss' complete confidence in his own work. A thousand watches at sea on a dozen different bridges. The *Thistle* was reaping the benefit of that experience now. 'Steady!'

'Steady, sir. Course three-two-zero.' Joicey must be reading his mind.

'Steady as you go, Cox'n.' Crespin moved back to the screen and pulled his glasses from inside the oilskin. The sky should be brightening by now, but the clouds were holding back the dawn, as if trying to delay the inevitable.

Scarlett said, 'I only hope that fellow Soskic knows what he has to do.'

'He'll be all right, sir.' Crespin moved the glasses slightly to port and saw a huddle of floating gulls bobbing jerkily up and down, probably on the wake of one of the M.L.s. They looked like a garland of lilies left after a sea burial.

Scarlett grunted. 'He *must* be in position and ready to take all his objectives when we give the signal. Telephone wires cut, railway blown, and the road guarded at both ends.'

Crespin thought of the three hundred odd partisans who were now fanning out along the hills and cliffs beyond the jutting headland. There was a concrete pillbox on the southern end of the road which led into the *Nashorn*'s base. Soskic's men must have passed it by now, and there had not been a single shot. He could almost find pity for the Germans in that pillbox.

'Light, sir!' Griffin sounded very calm. 'Starboard bow!'

Three blue flashes, very low down on the water.

Scarlett massaged his stomach vigorously. 'Thank God for that!'

The brief signal came from Coutts' schooners which lay somewhere below the headland waiting to follow *Thistle* into the bay.

Griffin said, ' 'E's landed 'em all right then, sir.'

'I should *hope* so!' Scarlett was peering at his watch. 'How much longer?'

Wemyss said flatly, 'Forty-five minutes, sir.'

Crespin pulled off his oilskin and laid it by the chart table.
It was very cold, but the coat's clammy restriction was
making him sweat.

'Warn all guns to stand by, Number One. Not a sound out of
anybody.' He heard Wemyss speaking quietly on a handset and
then thrust his head under the hood and leaned over the chart.
It was a last look. In a few minutes he would have all his work
cut out. It might be the last time he looked at a chart at all,
he thought grimly.

He pushed the possibility from his mind as he ran his eyes
over the wavering lines and bearings, the beak of the headland
and the little horseshoe bay beyond. It was a well protected
place. Mountainous hills at the back, a steep headland and
shelving cliffs on either side of the entrance. A very suitable
lair for the ponderous *Nashorn*.

Crespin withdrew his head and shoulders from the hood and
stood up. The bridge already seemed lighter, with faces and
hands standing out against the grey steel and the dark water
beyond the screen. He tensed. This time it was not all water.
The land was climbing out of the darkness, and against a paler
wedge of cloud he could even see a pointed hill, perhaps far inland. And there, fine on the starboard bow was the end of the
point. Sloping and sharp-edged, it ploughed into the sea like
the bow of an old ironclad, the surf leaping at its foot and
giving the additional impression of movement.

He could see the M.L.s, too, falling back, their engines only
giving steerage way as they waited for the corvette to lead the
attack. They were both rolling heavily in spite of the sheltered
water, their frail hulls shining with spray, the slender guns already trained round towards the land.

Somewhere below the bridge a man began to bang his hands
together. From cold or nerves, Crespin did not know. In the
damp stillness it seemed like gun-fire. Shannon's sharp tone
reduced the unknown seaman to silence.

Scarlett stood up and gripped the rail below the screen.
Against the greying clouds his face looked impressively calm.

The jutting stem of land was sliding towards the starboard
bow now, very slowly, for the ship was still at minimum speed.
There was a dull coloured hump at the top of it, and as Crespin

trained his glasses he saw that it was another pillbox, the
weapon slits black in the wet concrete like eyes. A man was
waving to the ship far below him, a rifle above his head. It was
one of Soskic's men. One more objective taken.

Scarlett said shortly, 'Right then. Let's make a start!'

Crespin turned and looked at Wemyss. 'Full ahead.' He
heard the telegraph and added to Griffin, 'Get ready with the
flare.'

Magot must have been poised above his throttle for the ship
responded immediately. It took the M.L.s by surprise, for by
the time they had swung round to take station on either quarter the *Thistle* was already pushing past the point and swinging
in a wide arc towards the bay.

Crespin snapped, 'Carry on, Bunts!'

Griffin fired his flare and stepped back to watch as it burst
in a bright green star above the cliffs.

Crespin stood on the gratings and tried to steady his glasses
against the throb and rattle of the bridge as the revolutions
mounted and the bow wave streamed away in twin white
banks of foam. The bay was just as he had expected. Grey and
dispirited looking in the dull light, with a stone breakwater
and an unlit beacon away to port, and almost dead ahead the
telltale pale blobs of huddled buildings, below which lay the
jetty and the extended railway where the *Nashorn*'s coal was
delivered whenever needed.

A Very light drifted in the wind, masked immediately in
smoke as a great explosion boomed across the bay and echoed
around the hills like an approaching storm.

Wemyss said tightly, 'Soskic's men must have blown the
railway.'

One of the M.L.s swung away and opened fire on two
moored tugs, the tracers darting across the choppy water and
beating it into a mass of white feathers before fastening greedily
on the deserted vessels.

From the buildings at the top of the bay came a sudden
rattle of Spandau fire, and more tracers floated over the roof-
tops to join with those already stabbing from a dozen different
angles.

In the growing light Crespin saw a strange, bridge-like structure clearly framed against the flickering tracer.

He shouted, 'Tell Shannon to open fire on that! It's there to
carry coal from the railway to the ship's side, and should make
a good target!'

It did. After one miss the four-inch gun landed a shell
directly beneath the towering mass of cross-beams and steel
rails, setting it alight and bringing the seaward end crashing
down across two moored lighters in a shower of yellow sparks.

The small German garrison, so rudely awakened, had at last
realised the attack was coming from the sea and not just across
their tried and tested positions along the road. More tracers
flickered over the water, faltered and then swung back to concentrate on the nearest M.L.

Crespin called, 'Shift target to red four-five! Hit those
machine-guns!'

He waited until the four-inch had reopened fire and then
snapped, 'Port fifteen!' The ship tilted and came round like a
stubby dancer, the pom-pom beating the Oerlikons as it sent a
necklace of flaming tracer over the M.L. in a protective barrage. The enemy guns fell silent, but more shots were coming
from further inland.

Scarlett yelled, 'The Jerries have got some flak guns up there
by the railway! Try and get them with the four-inch!'

Crespin crouched over the compass, watching the ticking
dial, judging the moment.

'Midships!' He ran to the forepart of the bridge again. 'Give
Shannon the range and bearing of that battery if you can! I'm
going round the bay again!'

A sinking fishing boat loomed out of the smoke and rocked
sluggishly on the corvette's wake. Crespin hardly noticed it as
he gauged the moment to make his next turn. When he looked
up again he saw that the nearest hills were already silver in
the morning light, but the clouds were as thick as ever. Or it
could be gunsmoke, he thought vaguely.

'Port ten!' The *Thistle* was almost back at the breakwater
again and turning for another run-in. As he glanced quickly
astern Crespin saw the spindly shapes of the four schooners

coming round the headland, Coutts no doubt impatient to be in at the kill.

'Midships! Steady!' He winced as the four-inch lifted, settled and fired again. The shell burst far beyond the buildings, throwing up a bright scarlet ball of flames which grew and spread until several of them appeared to be sucked into it.

'Fuel dump!' Griffin was using his telescope.

Scarlett rubbed his hands. 'That'll show the bastards!'

The tracer from the buildings by the jetty was getting sparse and more sporadic now, but Soskic's efforts appeared to have redoubled as grenades and mines exploded in every direction. Crespin saw a German army lorry charge from between two sheds and head for the coast road, slewing from side to side to avoid the hidden marksmen. A figure ran directly across the road, pausing only to throw something before diving headlong to escape the front wheels. It must have been a petrol bomb, for as the lorry swung crazily across the road it burst into flames and smashed out of control into a pile of rocks before rolling drunkenly on to its side. Burning petrol ran over the road, setting alight to bracken and writhing men alike before the lorry exploded and dense smoke drifted down to blot out their final anguish.

Both of the M.L.s were close inshore now, so near to the jetty itself that Crespin could see their gunsmoke rising in a brown wall between their hulls and the moored lighters as they fired again and again into the crumbling defences.

Wemyss yelled, 'W/T office has a signal, sir!' There was a black smudge on his face. 'Immediate!'

Crespin stared at him. It was hard to realise that far away, in another world, men were sitting in their offices coding and decoding, having cups of tea, planning a night out . . . He checked himself. 'Very well. Tell Defries to get it decoded! Things seem to be under control here.'

Scarlett snapped, 'That's bloody *typical* that is! I suppose it's a signal to tell us that war has been declared!' He swung round to watch as another thunderous explosion rocked the waterfront buildings and brought down a gantry almost across the stern of the nearest M.L. 'Tell that idiot to pull away! There's a lot to do here yet!'

Defries appeared on the bridge and saluted. He seemed quite oblivious to the din and smoke around him. 'Here's the signal, sir.' Even his voice was detached.

Crespin stood down from the gratings and read it quickly. 'Intelligence report, sir.' He looked up at Scarlett's back as he swung his glasses from bow to bow with obvious excitement. 'It says that the *Nashorn* left her berth yesterday afternoon. Destination unknown.'

Scarlett seemed to have difficulty in tearing his attention from the destruction ashore. Then he snapped, 'Yesterday afternoon? What are the bloody fools playing at?' He swore savagely. 'Intelligence officers? *Stupidity* officers, I call 'em!'

Crespin thought of the obvious difficulties, the agents risking their lives to transmit or carry this vital information. And all Scarlett could do was behave like a spoilt child.

He said, 'We must give the signal to withdraw, sir. *Nashorn*'s obviously coming back to her base. Lemke will have realised what the sinking of the troopship could mean. He's even cleverer than I thought.'

Scarlett scowled. 'For God's sake! We're not half finished here yet!'

Crespin said stubbornly, 'We have to pick up the partisans and get them to safety, sir. It all takes time, and the *Nashorn* could be within twenty miles of us now.'

Scarlett licked his lips and then said excitedly, 'God, that was a good shot!' He came back to Crespin's words with another effort. 'We will press on with the attack.'

Crespin saw Wemyss watching him, his mouth pulled down in a tight frown.

'If we don't withdraw, we could be caught inside the bay.'

Wemyss said, 'That's right, sir. The German ship will use the channel we were going to take. It will be a head-on clash!'

Scarlett turned on the chair and glared at them. 'Just attend to handling the ship. I'll decide what we will or will not do!'

Crespin walked to the opposite side of the bridge and watched the distant schooners moving slowly towards the entrance of the bay. To Wemyss he said, 'Slow ahead. We're in no more danger from the base.' He pulled the hood from the chart and bent over it. It was light enough to see it quite clearly, yet the whole attack had taken less than fifty minutes.

He worked with the brass dividers, shutting his mind to the crash and rumble of explosions and Wemyss' grave voice as he took over the con and started the ship on one more slow circle around the bay.

Scarlett could be right, and yet . . . He measured off the distance very carefully. The *Nashorn* was old and heavy and probably did little more than twelve knots at best. An anxious captain could be here within four more hours. A chill ran down his spine. Lemke was not the sort to be anxious, from what Soskic had said. Suppose he had not followed the normal route, but had come south through the complex of offshore islands which he must know so well? The dividers glinted as he tried to put his idea into reality. When he stood up again his face was set.

'Sir, I suggest you make that signal *now*!' There was a lull in the noise ashore, and in the sudden silence his voice seemed unnaturally loud. He saw Scarlett's returning anger but persisted calmly, 'I think the *Nashorn* will be taking the inner channels. She *could* arrive within the hour.'

Scarlett looked at the watching faces around him. 'Think? Could? What value is there in these words?' He shrugged and tried to smile. 'This is a very successful operation! The whole thing has gone like clockwork. I don't suppose the enemy even knows about it yet. We'd have seen some air activity by now if he did.'

'I'm thinking of Soskic's men, sir.' Crespin did not smile back at him. He felt ice cold, helplessly calm, even though his whole being was crying out to take Scarlett by the throat and shake some sense into him. 'The schooners can only manage a few knots. In any case it will take time to recover the raiding party.'

Scarlett opened his mouth as if to speak and then turned his back to watch the drifting smoke above the shattered buildings. A white flag was being waved from one house, but it was hastily withdrawn as a savage burst of machine-gun-fire plucked it with invisible fingers.

Crespin climbed up beside him. 'We have done what we came to do . . .'

He swung round as Griffin shouted, 'Signal from Cap'n Coutts' boat, sir!' He trained his telescope to watch the feeble light as it stabbed through the haze.

Then he said, 'Funnel smoke to the north-west, sir!'

Wemyss muttered, 'Christ Almighty!'

Scarlett edged round in the chair, his eyes opaque. 'Very well. Signal a general recall. M.L.s to cover the schooners until Soskic's men are lifted off.'

Crespin licked the dryness from his lips. 'Tell Captain Coutts to get alongside the jetty immediately and fire the signal for Soskic's recall!' He watched the flare burst above the smoke and then, thankfully, an answering one from the hillside by the road where the German lorry was still blazing furiously.

Scarlett slipped off his seat and said briskly, 'Not to worry! It's all going well, eh?' But he was no longer smiling.

Wemyss said quietly, 'It'll be a close call, sir.'

Crespin watched the schooners chugging past, their crews already in the bows with mooring lines and grapnels. He did not want Wemyss to see his eyes in case he should read his anxiety.

He replied, 'Well, here come the partisans.'

They were running through the smoking ruins, some carrying captured stores and weapons, others firing as they ran, or pausing to shoot into some last possible hideout.

He saw Coutts standing beside Ross aboard his schooner as the first of Soskic's raiders swarmed over the bows, and he thought he saw Preston with his Bren staring across at the *Thistle* as she edged round in another slow turn.

Crespin tried not to look at his watch or count the dragging time it was taking for the partisans to make their way to the jetty. Thank God the Germans were either dead or hiding. It would take just another few shots to get Soskic's men on the rampage again. This was their moment. What they had waited and trained for.

He looked round for Scarlett but he seemed to have vanished. Griffin saw his expression and said quickly, 'Chartroom, sir.'

Crespin nodded. 'Signal Coutts to start pulling out now.' He leaned over the screen and waited until Shannon looked up at him. 'I want those two coal lighters sunk as we leave!'

When he turned again he saw that the schooners were already carrying out his order and backing slowly from the shell-scarred jetty.

He said, 'Now signal the M.L.s to take off the rest of 'em!'

Griffin grinned. 'Cor, some of 'em think they was bein' left behind.'

The excited gestures changed to cheerful waves as the first M.L. glided inshore to recover the last of the partisans.

Scarlett was back again, and as he brushed past to reach the gratings Crespin smelt whisky across his face and saw the new brightness in his eyes as he peered at the slow-moving schooners.

Then Scarlett rubbed his hands. 'Right, I see you've carried out my orders!'

Crespin was about to reply when he saw Scarlett's face freeze to a tight mask. Even as he turned he heard a sound like a great wind, and then the glass screen shivered in its mounting and the whole bridge lit up with a bright orange flash. Sickened, he saw the nearest schooner rocking wildly amidst a falling curtain of spray, her hull covered by drifting smoke, while the crowded figures on deck stared around as if mesmerised.

Scarlett said, 'God, that was close!'

Crespin ignored him. He had expected it, in spite of all his reasoning if not because of it.

'Half ahead, starboard fifteen!' He looked at Scarlett. 'She can't see us yet, but she'll be coming up the channel at any moment now.'

Scarlett's voice sounded like a record. 'Not to worry. We'll make it in time!'

Crespin snapped, 'Midships! Steady!' To Wemyss he added, 'Hoist battle ensigns!' He saw the numbed understanding on his face and added shortly, 'It might give our people over there a bit of heart. And Christ knows, they're going to need it!'

Scarlett caught his sleeve. 'What the hell are you doing, man? Are you mad or something?'

Crespin replied calmly, 'The schooners and the M.L.s will

need time to reach the channel we came in by, sir. We must hold the *Nashorn* in *her* channel until they're clear.' He studied Scarlett, aware for the first time that his face was utterly empty of understanding. He added slowly, 'It's the *only* way, sir.'

'Only way?' Scarlett seemed unable to drag his eyes from the big ensigns which Griffin and his signalmen were hoisting. They looked clean and remote above the battered little ship.

Then he said vaguely, 'It was a very successful raid. We can't be expected to throw everything away now.' His eyes swivelled down and fastened on Crespin's face. 'Signal the schooners to scatter. Then take the *Thistle* at full speed to the original channel. There's nothing we can do for these boats now.' He gave a great sigh. 'I'm sorry, Crespin, God knows I'm sorry, but there's nothing else for it.'

Joicey's voice echoed up the tube. 'Steady on two-five-five, sir.'

Crespin did not take his eyes from Scarlett's. '*Steady as you go!*'

'I don't think you understood me, Crespin?' Scarlett stepped back a pace. 'I am giving you an order!'

With a piercing shriek another shell passed overhead and exploded in the centre of the *Thistle*'s wake. It was well clear, but even so the hull shook violently.

Crespin replied, 'Then I am disobeying it, sir.'

Scarlett swayed on his feet as if he had been struck. 'I'm giving you one last chance, d'you hear me? Then I'm going to put you under arrest!'

A messenger called, 'Sir! Sub-Lieutenant Porteous is requesting instructions!'

Crespin did not turn. 'Tell him to come up here.' To Scarlett he continued in the same level voice, 'We both know why Admiral Oldenshaw wanted you back in England, sir. If we leave here now and let these people die, you'll have that shame for the rest of your life. This raid may be just one more operation to you, I don't know, but to these people it is an essential victory, can't you see that?'

Scarlett's eyes seemed to fill his face. 'The raid's over!'

'Well, if you can leave all these people to be slaughtered, *I* can't!'

Porteous climbed on to the bridge, 'Sir?'

Crespin said, 'How many charges do you have left?'

Porteous looked at Scarlett and replied uneasily, 'Just four.'

'Right. Get the damage control party and lower both boats to deck level. Put two depth-charges in each boat, with a setting of fifty feet.'

Porteous stared at him. 'Yes, sir.'

'Rip out all the buoyancy tanks from the boats, too, while you're at it.' He saw Porteous's confusion and added sharply, '*Jump* to it!'

To Scarlett he said, 'The admiral offered me this command out here not because I was the best man for the job, but because you have reached a point where you can no longer make a detached judgement . . .'

He got no further. Scarlett seemed to forget the men standing around the bridge. 'Well, the admiral's dead! When I get back to England I'll see that you're broken!'

A great crash shook the bridge and a lookout shouted, 'One of the schooners, sir!'

It was a direct hit. The schooner had been about to pass the stone breakwater when the five-point-nine shell, fired by gunners who could not even see a target, smashed it into oblivion. There was only the bow section left and that was already sinking rapidly in a great whirlpool of fragments and splintered wreckage. It must have been crammed with men, for as the *Thistle* pushed the remains aside Crespin saw that the water was covered with a great crimson stain, spreading and writhing above the sunken remains as if the schooner itself was bleeding.

Scarlett seized his arm, but he was no longer shouting. His voice seemed suddenly small and pleading. 'I know you mean well, Crespin. But you don't understand. The act of attack is important. We can't always gauge the cost, or measure the losses!'

Wemyss turned away, unable to watch.

Scarlett continued, 'You can't fight the *Nashorn*, you know that!'

'I said from the beginning that the base was the secondary objective, sir. While the *Nashorn* stays afloat our whole operation is wasted. Even the torpedo boats won't be able to reach

Vis while she patrols these channels.' He shook Scarlett's hand away. 'Too many have died already because of her!'

Scarlett staggered as the four-inch opened fire, the muzzle trained hard round towards the receding jetty. The nearest coal lighter lifted to the shellburst and then settled down to sink, dragging the other lighter with her.

Then he yelled wildly, 'You *fool*! You're trying to ruin me!' He was unable to check himself now. 'You're like all the rest! You think you understand war, but when it comes to getting your hands dirty you can't stomach it, can you?'

Crespin said nothing. Scarlett was destroying himself. It was terrible to watch.

'Like that idiot, Trotter! *He* was like that. Wanted to be a bloody hero, until that night . . .' His legs buckled under him and he collapsed into the chair. 'I *tried* to reason with him. Make him understand.'

Crespin looked over the screen and saw the M.L.s following the three schooners out of the bay. Smoke was drifting above the water, shutting out the burning buildings and reducing the visibility to less than a cable. His mind recorded all these facts, just as it noted that the German ship had ceased fire. The *Nashorn* must be in the main channel now. One door was closed, the remaining channel—barely three miles wide—was a long way away.

Scarlett was going over it all again, the words flooding out, confused and disjointed. Crespin thought of the girl and what she had meant to him. Perhaps because of her influence alone he was still able to accept what he now understood. All those months of suffering and anguish, the nightmares, the regular pattern of terrible pictures which mocked him as he slept. That face, that one face which came back over and over again. It was difficult to understand why he had not realised it had been Trotter's face. The dream and the reality had become stark and clear in Scarlett's words.

He heard himself ask, 'Why did you kill Trotter, sir? Just tell me that!'

Scarlett stared at him, his eyes suddenly eager. 'You see? You *do* understand!' He reached out and seized Griffin's arm as if to emphasise his words. 'It was just an accident. We captured the launch behind enemy lines. It was our first really successful raid. Then, coming back, we came on these people in the water.'

Crespin said quietly, 'You didn't have to fire on us. You could have left us.'

Scarlett nodded sharply. 'That's what Trotter said. When he joined your ship and realised who you were, he wanted to come right out and tell you.' He laughed, without making a sound. 'Imagine that! After all my hard work, and all that I've done, he'd have spoiled everything because of *one bloody mistake*!' He lifted his chin and yelled, 'I did not know the men in the water were our own people!'

Crespin said, 'What difference does that make?' He turned away as Wemyss said, 'Senior M.L. is signalling, sir!'

Scarlett followed, dragging Griffin with him. 'I *had* to shoot him! The fool, he was making a written confession about it!'

Crespin raised his glasses. The channel beyond the nearest islands looked clear and blue. It would be a fine day after all.

He said, 'Tell the M.L. to escort the others to Korcula as fast as he can manage.'

To Scarlett he added flatly, 'I am relieving you, sir. You will go below to my quarters, *now*!' He wondered why he did not care more. Scarlett was the man who had mercilessly butchered his own men without reason. Had then shot Trotter and made it appear like the confession he had been looking for. It was strange how the obvious had eluded him.

Now Scarlett was speaking to Griffin, grasping his arm, his head lowered in some confidential explanation, while the leading signalman stood quite still, his face like stone.

Crespin realised that Scarlett was more victim than culprit. He had seen and done too much in a short time, and the veneer had worn away. Now he was a whimpering, useless thing, as much a casualty as all the others he had helped to make.

The M.L. was gliding nearer, her skipper staring up at the *Thistle*'s bridge and shouting, 'We'll stop and give you a hand!'

Crespin said to Wemyss, 'Tell him to obey my orders.'

He watched Griffin guiding Scarlett to the bridge ladder, the expressions of shock and contempt recorded on the watching faces.

Wemyss spoke to a signalman but kept his eyes on Crespin's face. Then he asked, 'Did you *know* all this, sir?'

'Perhaps I didn't want to know.' Crespin levelled his glasses on the breakwater. A German steel helmet lay quite alone near the beacon at the end. Its owner probably dead with all the rest.

Wemyss said half to himself, 'I'd have sent him across to one of the M.L.s!' Then he said harshly, 'Still, I suppose he might as well stay with us and see what he's got us into.'

Porteous reappeared on the bridge. 'I've moved the depth-charges to the boats, sir.' He glanced at Wemyss who gave a brief shrug. Then he said awkwardly, 'I've heard what Captain Scarlett did, sir. I think . . .' He faltered under Crespin's gaze then said quickly, 'I think you should send him with the other boats, under arrest!'

Crespin looked over the screen. The senior M.L. was already curving away, her wash rising as she hurried back towards the other slow-moving craft.

He replied, 'He'll have enough to answer for later on, Sub. Just forget the legal side of it for five minutes and try to imagine how you would feel in his position. It's bad enough to be ordered off the bridge, for God's sake let us spare him the indignity of being hauled across to another ship like some bloody piece of cargo!'

Wemyss muttered, 'He wanted to do it to *you*, sir.'

Crespin grimaced. 'Forget it. Let me know the exact distance to the secondary channel.'

To Porteous he added quietly, 'But thanks all the same. I know you meant well.' He smiled sadly. 'If it makes you feel easier, I suggest you put the steward on guard outside Scarlett's door.'

Wemyss said, 'Ten miles, sir.'

Ten miles. Two hours steaming for the schooners and their escorts. Two hours to hold the *Nashorn* from pounding them to scrap before his eyes.

He looked at the sky, the growing tinge of blue around each cloud. It was grotesque. All the more so because the *Thistle* would probably sink within a mile of where they had destroyed the troopship.

It was useless to think about it. Perhaps that was the real reason for keeping Scarlett aboard, just as Wemyss had suggested. To hold him here, if only to witness what he had caused.

He snapped, 'Full ahead! Course two-five-five!'

To Griffin he said, 'Signal the M.L.s to drop smoke-floats. It will help give them some cover.'

He wondered briefly what Scarlett was thinking down in the sealed cabin. Perhaps something inside him was even thankful it was all over, that the pretence and deceit was no longer necessary. As he had left the bridge he had looked as if he only half understood what was happening, as if the enormity of events had finally unhinged him so that he felt nothing any more.

Crespin walked to the front of the bridge again, feeling the breeze across his neck. Smooth and clean. Like her touch. Like the big flags which made a twisting shadow above the bridge.

Porteous spoke again. 'Any orders for me, sir?'

Crespin lifted the glasses and scanned the channel carefully. It was made misty blue by the nearest island and seemed so peaceful that it was almost impossible to believe this was all happening.

'Tell the Buffer to check the boats, Sub. We will drop them when we make our turn. A few shots should sink them and let the depth-charges blow up on their own.' He sounded tired. 'It might give the *Nashorn* something to think about.' Then he said, 'You can come back here after that.' He waited until Porteous had gone. 'You take his place aft, Number One. If I'm bumped off I want you in one piece to get the ship out of this.' He smiled. 'If you can.'

Wemyss licked his lips. 'You can rely on me.'

Crespin turned again to study the channel as the ship's speed continued to mount. It saved him from seeing the other boats and their slow progress towards safety. Perhaps they were all watching the *Thistle*, he thought. Soskic and Coutts, Ross and Preston, and all the others he could not put names to.

It would be a sight to remember. David and Goliath. The little corvette and the armoured giant.

They had at last caught up with the future, and it felt as if

To Risks Unknown

all the other things had just been part of a build-up for this one particular episode.

He was about to climb on to the chair and changed his mind. He wanted to remain standing, to keep the feel of the gallant little ship beneath him.

Apart from the racing engine and the sluice of water against the hull there was a great silence, and he found time to think of all the men around and beneath him who had been brought to this moment of time to share it as best they could. His officers. The mate of a merchant ship, a shop assistant, a barrister, and whatever Defries had once been. And the rest. Magot, who should have been living out his years with his grandchildren. Joicey, who had waited to see his enemy suffer but had found only understanding. Griffin, standing calmly and without fear, watched by his signalmen who were little more than boys.

Expendable they probably were, but *Thistle* could have wished for no better company, he thought.

The next shell came without warning, screaming overhead like something unleashed from hell. It exploded far astern, lost in the drifting smoke.

Crespin wiped some spray from his glasses and lifted them once more. The waiting was over.

17 The Name of Action

LIEUTENANT MARK SHANNON walked round the gunshield and then stood with his back against its rough steel staring straight across the bows. It was a strange, exhilarating sensation, as if he was being carried quite alone by the ship which lifted and ploughed so eagerly beneath him. His crew were hidden by the shield, and there was not a living soul between him and the invisible enemy.

He heard the shell scream overhead, and after a moment's hesitation walked slowly back around the shield. As he glanced up he saw Crespin's face to one side of the bridge, set and impassive, and other heads, motionless like statuary, parts of the ship's structure.

He turned his back and looked searchingly at his small crew. 'Don't forget, this is to be a close action. The enemy has two big guns, but if we can keep her end on she can only use one at a time, right?'

Leading Seaman Kidd, the gun captain, rubbed a gloved fist over the breach lever and grimaced. 'Won't do much with *this* pop-gun, sir.'

Shannon glared at him. 'It's all we've got!' He grew impatient. 'When that gong goes we open fire and keep on firing!' He raised his voice so that the other gunners turned to watch him. 'Nothing else bloody well matters, see?'

He saw the layer and trainer exchange quick glances across the breech but decided to ignore them. They were good enough hands, but as unimaginative as the rest.

He thought suddenly of his shells slamming home. One target after another. The first tension which he had suspected might be some sort of fear had been nothing of the kind. It had been only the fear of failure, and the success of his gunnery had wiped that away as if it had never been.

Like a mist clearing from his mind, he thought. All the other hopes and doubts had been quite pointless. You could only depend on yourself. He thought, too, of Scarlett. A case in point. To think he had lowered himself to the extent of expecting a man like Scarlett to help him. He was no better than those patronising bastards he had been forced to serve over a shop counter so long ago.

He looked around the shield and watched the blue mist floating above the channel. Everything was blue. It was like being in space.

As he thrust his hands into his reefer pocket he felt the hard outline of the jewelled crucifix. He had almost forgotten about it and the touch brought a sudden smile to his lips. He was not religious in any way, but the cross was the most beautiful thing he had ever seen. It was also worth a great deal of money.

But its value went even deeper than that. During the ship's first week at Brindisi he had met Carla. Her husband was a major in an Italian artillery regiment, but she did not know if she was a widow or not, for he was one of the unlucky ones, caught beyond the Allied line and forced to hold his allegiance with the Germans.

She had a small house on the outskirts of the town, and after their first meeting in a restaurant Shannon had become a regular visitor. It was not just a case of going to bed with her. Her need of him, her desperate desire to do anything and everything to please him had made him realise his new power. She was ten years older than he and hardly spoke any English at all, yet she seemed to understand him better than he did himself.

Only when he had made her wear the crucifix around her neck while he had made love to her had she shown any sort of protest. For that reason he had made her suffer, to teach her a lesson. He had placed the cross between her heavy breasts and had knelt astride her, watching it, seeing the shame in her eyes, yet knowing her passion was returning in spite of it.

Now she was back there in Brindisi, probably still waiting for his return. He would never see her again, no matter what happened. She had served her purpose, and for the first time in his life he felt complete. The crucifix would always be there to remind him of the past. But now, the future was the only thing which counted.

A thunderous explosion rocked the hull, and as he clung to the ammunition hoist he saw a great column of water shooting skyward barely a hundred feet from the port bow. The deck and fittings shook in protest, and as water began to fall hissing alongside he realised that Bullen, the gunlayer, was sprawled at his feet, his eyes wide with astonishment and a gaping hole dead in the centre of his chest.

The others were all staring, stunned by the suddenness of death in their own crew, and he felt the same gripping excitement sweeping through him like ice water.

He dragged the man's body clear and jumped forward into the seat. 'Stand by!' He looked at Kidd. 'It'll be any second now!'

Leading Seaman Kidd glanced at the staring corpse by the rail. He had been his friend, and in a matter of a split second he had become something without personality or meaning. Then he looked across at the lieutenant, seeing his insane grin, the quick, deft movements of his fingers on the sights. Between them they seemed to symbolise his own fate, and as he stood clear of the breech Kidd knew that he, too, was going to die.

From his position in one corner of the bridge Crespin saw the gunlayer fall, but his mind barely recorded it as the thrown spray cascaded over the port bow in a solid sheet.

The speaker behind him intoned, 'Enemy in sight! Bearing green two-oh! Range oh-six-oh!'

The last of the spray drifted clear, and as he steadied his glasses once more he saw the *Nashorn*. It was strange how they had managed to draw so near to each other without becoming visible, he thought. She seemed to detach herself from the side of the island on the starboard side of the channel, materialise out of the blue mist even as he watched, her ugliness making it all the more unreal.

Three miles away, yet already he could see the massive

hump of her armoured bridge, the two funnels streaming
smoke as evidence of her captain's efforts to reach his base.
There was another long flash, and seconds later a tall water-
spout burst directly in the *Thistle*'s wake.

'Starboard ten!' Crespin gripped the screen tightly. 'Midships!'

Another scream and crash, the whirlpool of the falling shell
appearing dangerously close to the last one.

But perhaps it was too close, he thought. Any one of those
shells could destroy an M.L. or schooner without even having
to obtain a direct hit. The corvette must be a more difficult target.

He shouted, 'Hard aport!'

Clinging to the screen he pulled himself along the tilting deck
to watch as another shell exploded in direct line with the
others. Good shooting, provided the target remained on a set
course, or was too small to withstand a near miss.

He looked at Wemyss. 'Midships!' He added, 'We must close
the range! If we can give Shannon a chance we might be able
to do some damage.'

A bosun's mate looked up from a voice-pipe. 'Four-inch requests permission to open fire, sir!'

Crespin nodded and pressed the button. The crash of the gun
drowned the gong, and he guessed that Shannon had been itch-
ing to fire, although at this range and in the hazy visibility any
hit would be pure luck.

When he peered astern he saw that the land had vanished
behind a low wall of brown smoke. It was a screen put up by
the floats and momentarily effective. The German gunners
would be more inclined to concentrate on the *Thistle*.

The breech clicked home and he heard Shannon rasp, 'Re-
peat that deflection, you fool!' Then, 'Shoot!' Another
armour-piercing shell tore away from the gun, and seconds
later the speaker intoned, 'Short! Up five hundred!'

Crespin said, 'We will close the range and then turn away.'
He saw Porteous nodding, his face pale beneath its tan. 'I will
make smoke and then drop both boats with the depth-charges.
When the enemy enters the smoke I am hoping the charges
will explode close to her. While her captain is making up his

mind about the cause, I'll go about and have another crack at him!' He grinned to try to reassure Porteous. 'Just so long as we can stop him from turning away. If he does that he can bring both guns to bear on us. A straddle would buckle this little hull like a soup tin!'

There was another slamming crash and a column of water towered above the bridge like a solid thing, gleaming in the sunlight, hanging there as if it would never fall.

Crespin felt the jarring clatter of splinters against the side, the demoniac scream of others as they whipped overhead.

'Starboard fifteen!' He felt the spray across his neck as he groped for the compass. It tasted of lyddite. '*Midships!*' He had to keep zigzagging if he was to avoid one of those massive shells. But the turns must be as haphazard as possible. Any sort of mean pattern would soon transmit itself to the German gunnery officer.

'A *hit*!' Shannon was yelling like a maniac. 'Jesus, we hit the bastard!'

Crespin steadied his glasses, feeling the ship canting in response to the helm. He was just in time to see the brief red glow below the *Nashorn*'s boat deck. Then it was gone.

'Range oh-five-oh!'

Griffin muttered, 'We'll be close enough to board the bugger soon!' It brought a smile to one of his signalmen and he was satisfied.

Crespin said, 'We will close to three thousand yards and then turn . . .' He looked round for Porteous and then flinched as the next shell exploded right alongside. For the smallest part of a second he had felt it coming. Like a change of hearing, a brief shadow, it was all and none of these things.

When it burst the bridge was plunged into shadow and the world was confined to a crushing onslaught of falling water, of screaming metal and the overall feeling of helplessness.

Crespin felt himself slipping and falling, his feet knocked from under him, his hands and knees scraping against steel as the deck tilted violently and then staggered upright.

For an instant he thought he was the only one left alive. Then, as Griffin and Porteous scrambled to their feet and another man tried to claw his way from beneath an upended flag locker, he looked up and saw the jagged remains of the radar cabinet, the gaping holes in the funnel, and tried to gauge what the damage would be like below, nearer to the explosion.

When he attempted to stand he felt a pain lance through his side, sharp and agonising, and he looked down, expecting to see blood, to know that he had been hit. There was nothing.

Porteous gasped, 'Are you all right, sir?' He looked dazed.

Crespin nodded, biting back on the pain. 'I think it's a rib.' He pointed at the ladder. 'Get down and see what has to be done.' He ducked as another explosion shook the hull and more spray soaked down across them, shocking them into movement and thought again.

He saw Porteous dragging himself to the ladder and then walked back to the gratings. One of the young signalmen lay face down beside the chart table, his fair hair moving in the following breeze. Griffin was on his knees beside him. Then he took Crespin's discarded oilskin and covered him.

Griffin returned to his position at the rear of the bridge. He said nothing, but his eyes spoke volumes.

'Port twenty!' Crespin waited, holding his breath, then he heard Joicey's voice, 'Twenty of port wheel on, sir!' Thank God the wheelhouse had been spared. 'Midships!'

'She's turning, sir!' A lookout was pointing wildly, his forehead covered with blood.

Crespin craned over the screen. 'We are going about!' He saw Shannon and the gun captain staring up at him. 'We can't allow him to pull over and use the other gun!' He noticed Shannon was grinning, his teeth white in his grimed face. He swung round as Porteous reappeared on the bridge. 'Well?'

Porteous said, 'Starboard side, right on the waterline, sir. But mostly superficial, except for some splinters.' He gestured above the bridge. 'Radar gone.' He shuddered. 'Willis and his mate, well, there's nothing left of them.'

'What other casualties?'

'Two stokers from damage control, sir.' Porteous held up his hand as if to shield his face as a shell screamed above the bridge, pressing them down with its shockwave and cutting away some signal halyards as cleanly as a knife.

It exploded, and Crespin saw the waterspout far away on the

port beam. He wiped his glasses and trained them over the screen as the *Nashorn* fired again. But it was her after-gun, and he saw her ugly outline lengthening still further as she completed her turn and headed for the opposite side of the channel. It was now or never.

'Hard astarboard!' He ran from the voice-pipe and dragged Porteous towards the ladder. 'Tell Number One to lower the boats and get ready to slip them!' He hurried back to the side and snatched up the red handset.

'Chief? Captain speaking. I want you to make smoke . . . *now*!' He slammed the handset on its rack and clung to the compass as the ship continued to swing round in a wild turn.

Order and timing seemed out of place now. The corvette strained round, her deck almost awash as the sea sluiced up over the side. It was a world gone mad. Made worse by the billowing fog of oily smoke which gushed from the funnel and a dozen splinter holes as well, it was like a new nightmare. At regular intervals the shells arrived. Tall white columns of water, they appeared to be all round the ship; this side and that side, until it was almost too hard to count the seconds between each one.

'Midships!' The hull bucked hard beneath him, and more jagged splinters hammered the side. 'Steady!'

The smoke came down in a choking cloud, blotting out the sun, while the *Thistle* plunged into her own screen. Then she was through it, and as the drifting fog mounted astern she pushed back into the sun, her screw still racing at full speed.

Crespin wiped his streaming eyes. 'Slow ahead!' He could imagine Magot's surprise, but there was no time to delay now. He must get rid of those depth-charges. Another shell burst somewhere astern. He waited, biting his lip, feeling the pain in his rib, as if his ship's own agony had reached out for him also.

He said tightly, 'Just one shot! She's turned again and is after us!' It had worked. He clung to the top of the ladder and peered down at the litter of punctured plating and the snaking patterns of fire-hoses.

Both boats were swinging on their falls barely a foot above the dying bow wave. Wemyss and the damage control party were staring up at him, and he saw Defries right aft by the pom-pom tying a bandage on a seaman's wrist as if it was the most normal thing in the world.

Crespin cupped his hands. 'Slip the boats, Number One! One at a time. You'll have to cut the falls, so get a move on! I don't want to hang about!'

He saw Wemyss wave and then felt himself being hurled backwards on to the bridge. He had heard nothing. One minute he had been watching Wemyss, the next he was falling, hearing his own voice cry out in agony as his ribs crashed against an unyielding piece of steel, seeing the sunlight through the smoke, his reeling mind registering, as if in a dream, that the foremast was falling, the battle ensign suddenly near and very white as it was dragged down and out of sight below the bridge.

He had reached the plating below the compass and could even see the neat rivets beside his mouth, but he still seemed to be falling. With the falling came the darkness, the sunlight drawing away. Like dropping down a well, he thought vaguely. Then it was completely dark, and the noise and pain ceased abruptly.

*   *   *

The *Nashorn*'s shell exploded halfway down the port side, less than ten feet from the hull. The men working by the davits were killed instantly, and the boat itself, splintered in a dozen places, sagged to the full extent of the remaining falls so that it scooped water over the bows, while the two depth-charges rolled and banged unchecked from their severed lashings.

Sub-Lieutenant James Porteous had just left Wemyss and his lowering party at the starboard boat when it happened. But for the shelter afforded by the superstructure abaft the bridge he, too, would have died, and as he seized a stanchion to stop himself from being hurled overboard he felt the blast from the explosion ripping at his body with the force of a pressure hose. He must have been momentarily deafened, but as his hearing returned he heard the crash of breaking metal, and through the smoke he could hear someone screaming.

He groped his way back to the davits and saw Wemyss crouched on one knee, his thumbs pressing into his leg as he tried to stop the bleeding. Two seamen lay beside him, and another, unmarked but quite dead, sat propped against the guardrail, his eyes fixed on the others with something like hatred.

Porteous shouted, 'I'll get the S.B.A.!'

Wemyss shook his head, gritting his teeth against the pain. 'Get to the bridge! Never mind these damn boats!'

It was then that Porteous remembered seeing the captain fall. Up to that moment it had been shut from his mind by shock. Totally excluded, like a page ripped from a book.

He nodded and began to pull himself up the bridge ladder. Another shell exploded somewhere, but he hardly noticed it as he concentrated all his strength on getting up the ladder. It seemed to take an age. Every steel rung stood out with stark clarity, while other things below and around him stayed hidden in a mist.

When he passed the wheelhouse he saw more bright-edged splinter holes and spurting jets of smoke from the opposite side.

As his face lifted above the bridge coaming he almost dropped back to the deck below. His eyes were level with something which moved its arms and legs like a living person, even though its face had been wiped away.

Sobbing, Porteous heaved himself on to the bridge, his shoes crunching across broken glass and woodwork and other hideous fragments which made his mouth choke with vomit.

Griffin was squatting by the voice-pipes, his head on his hands. He looked up suddenly and tried to grin. Then he croaked, 'Skipper's down 'ere, sir!'

Porteous dropped beside Crespin's sprawled figure below the compass. His face was very pale, and when he tried to move him he felt blood on his fingers.

Griffin crawled across the deck and gasped, 'Take over, sir! For Gawd's sake, *do* somethin'!'

Porteous suddenly realised the significance of Griffin's words. For the first time he became aware of the voice-pipes, the cries and curses which seemed to be aimed at him, the crash of explosions beyond the bridge plating, and above all the fact that he was entirely alone. Crespin seemed to be dead, and Wemyss too badly wounded to get here and help him. God alone knew what Shannon was doing. He felt his mind giving way to sudden terror and he knew that in a few more seconds he would be quite unable to move. It was then that he looked down and saw that Crespin had opened his eyes.

Griffin struggled round, heedless of the broken glass, and lifted Crespin's shoulders across his knees.

Porteous asked thickly, 'Are you all right, sir?' It was a stupid question and he knew it. But just listening to his own voice again helped to steady him.

Crespin said, 'Cut those boats adrift!' He winced as another shell roared close to the ship. 'Then, and then . . .' His head lolled and fell against Griffin's chest.

The leading signalman said fiercely, 'You 'eard 'im, Mister Porteous!'

Slipping and lurching through the smoke Porteous scrambled to the screen. A few seamen were coming down the port side, and he saw Wemyss hopping on one leg, his arm around a stoker's shoulders as he made for the damaged boat. Porteous watched, knowing that if the boat slipped the two charges into the sea now the *Thistle*'s back would be broken instantly.

An axe flashed in the filtered sunlight and the after-falls parted. Wemyss glanced up at the bridge and shouted something, his voice lost in yet another explosion. But the enemy's shells were falling wild. The *Nashorn* must be steaming into the smoke now, shooting as fast as ever, and even though her gunners were blind they knew it was just a matter of time. The *Thistle* had nowhere to go but back to the end of the channel, and when once the smoke was clear the *Nashorn* would still be able to finish both her and the escaping boats.

A man shouted, 'There it goes!'

Porteous saw the boat drop sluggishly into the trough of the bow wave and begin to scrape down the port side. But it was sinking too fast. It would never clear the hull in time. With a sob he ran across to the opposite side. If the motor boat was still hooked on it would be better to hoist it again. There was no time left.

He stopped and stared incredulously. The motor boat was already in the water, the engine coughing and spluttering as it moved clear of the severed falls and idled astern into the smoke. It was impossible. Porteous could feel the hair rising on his neck. But there was a man actually at the helm!

He pushed himself from the rail and almost fell on to the voice-pipe. 'Full ahead!' He paused, his nerves screaming. '*Full ahead!*'

Joicey replied harshly, 'Engine full ahead! I've only got one set of 'ands, for God's sake!'

It was so unlike the imperturbable coxswain that Porteous stared at the voice-pipe with disbelief.

But then everything was crazy. He rubbed his forehead and looked around at the splinter holes. Nothing made sense any more. This little ship which had taken so much was still afloat. Even the engine was responding. The motor boat had gone, even though the lowering party lay dead or wounded, with some lunatic at the tiller.

He swung round and gaped. And there was the captain, completing the madness. He was not dying as he should be, but actually on his feet, pulling himself along the screen, his eyes fixed on the smoke rising above the bridge.

Crespin asked, 'Boats gone?' He had one hand pressed to his side and there was blood spreading down the front of his shirt.

Porteous nodded dully. 'I've rung down for full speed again.'

Surprisingly, the captain grinned. 'Good for you, Sub! We'll give the boats time to drift astern and then head back into the smoke.' He seemed to sense Porteous's disbelief in spite of his pain. 'What is it?'

'The motor boat was *manned*, sir!'

'The what?' Crespin swayed and would have fallen but for Porteous's arm as a great explosion boomed hollowly against the hull. Then as a towering wall of water burst through the smoke astern he gasped, 'The charges! God, the charges have blown!'

Porteous helped Crespin to the chair, and as he released his hold he was astounded to find he was no longer frightened. If it was possible to stay alive after today he knew he would never be the same again. A shell burst above the water far abeam with a bright orange flash, and he felt more splinters clanging against the hull. Yet he was able to watch and consider these things without flinching. Perhaps later . . . He shook his head and walked quickly to the voice-pipes.

'Report damage!' His voice sounded like someone else's, crisp and confident. He grinned across at Griffin. 'S.B.A. to the bridge on the double!'

*   *   *

As the *Thistle* steamed back along her original course, her billowing smokescreen spreading protectively over either quarter, her company fought their own battles in their own way. Some, cut off by watertight doors and sealed deep in the trembling hull, clung to their voice-pipes and telephones, their only links with that other world above. Those at the guns crouched behind their shields, which as time wore on seemed to get smaller and thinner, while they waited for the ship to turn and fight back once more. The crews fought from their little steel islands isolated by smoke and the din of shellfire, calling to each other and shouting curses, but never turning away from their guns when a man fell or some awful cry came back at them through the fog of battle.

Some men did what they had always been trained to do, because as their minds cracked under the onslaught they worked more by instinct than with any sense of understanding.

And a few did what they had sworn never to do. Sub-Lieutenant Jocelyn Defries was one of these.

The boat with its depth-charges would have exploded right against the hull but for Porteous's prompt action. If it had, the engine room would have burst wide open to the inrushing water, and Magot, who had stayed toothless and shouting from his footplate throughout every phase of the action, and all of his weary, deafened men would have been fried alive in the scalding steam.

As it was, the boat capsized in the ship's wake and sank like a stone, the shock of the twin explosions lifting the stern like a surfboard on an incoming roller and then dropping it again so that the sea roared hissing along both side decks, plucking

at the corpses and whimpering wounded before sighing back
again to wait its next chance.

Defries was at his station by the pom-pom. The gun did not
have the range for this sort of fight and he had been forced to
stand with his men and watch the destruction like a helpless
onlooker. He was better at it than most. Submarines had taught
him that, if nothing else. In a stranded submarine lying on the
sea-bed there was nothing to watch except the faces around
you. Each face watched the other, gauging and measuring his
own resistance in what he saw there.

A seaman at the handset yelled, 'Sir! Tiller flat's floodin'!'

Defries took the phone and spoke into it, his pale eyes
fixed on the smoke astern. The ship was racing as if her heart
would burst, yet because of the screen she seemed to be held
motionless. He said, 'Quarterdeck! What is it?'

This time it was not Porteous but the captain. Defries
smiled faintly. That was good. He had imagined Crespin killed
or too badly wounded to help them any more. And he liked the
captain. He was quiet and understanding, with the compassion
of a man twice his age.

The voice said, 'The tiller flat's been punctured, Sub. The
Chief says the pumps can hold it, but I'd like you to take a
look.'

Defries nodded, 'Aye, aye, sir.'

Crespin's voice was fading as he prepared to drop the phone.
'Easy now. No unnecessary risks.' Then he was gone.

The oval hatch which led to the small steel flat in the ship's
stern was right aft by the empty depth-charge racks. A seaman
from the damage control party, hatless and soaked with spray,
looked up at him, his eyes flooding with relief.

'Wot'll I do, sir?'

Defries knelt down. 'Is it bad?'

The man nodded. 'The Buffer's down there. I was with 'im
but 'e sent me back.' He licked his lips. 'The 'ole place is
floodin', sir.'

Defries kept his face wooden. Petty Officer Dunbar had
beaten him to it. The flat was flooding, there was nothing else
to do but seal this hatch. In time the pumps would cope. If
they stayed afloat long enough.

He looked over the towing hook into the deep, clean furrow of the ship's wake. No one would blame him. They might not even know. He ignored the warnings and stood up, his legs straddled to the swaying deck.

'Open it!' He made himself keep watching the frothing water leaping up from the racing screw. Then he lowered his eyes and stared at the oval hole with something like nausea.

The trapped water was ebony black and he could see his own reflection in the one oval piece of sunlight. Then, apparently right aft, he saw a flashing light and knew it was a torch rolling back and forth across the deck below. There was no sign of Dunbar.

He could feel the sweat running down his spine, and it took all his strength to hold back the growing fear.

He snapped, 'I'm going down. He might be holding on to an overhead pipe or something.'

Without looking at the seaman he lowered himself on to the steel ladder, feeling the cold water dragging eagerly at his thighs as he ducked below deck level. The water was half way up the tiller flat, but it must be rising slowly, he thought.

To the seaman he called, 'Lower the hatch. I'll knock with my torch when I'm ready to come up.'

The man hesitated and then slammed down the weighted steel, shutting out the sunlight. The sound from the racing propeller, the shake and quiver of the shaft were all the more intensified, and Defries knew it was pointless to call Dunbar's name. He clung to the ladder swinging his torch round, his mind reeling as some of the water sloshed over his head and shoulders. They had warned him that he would break down completely if he ever went back to submarines. One more incident like the last and he would go mad. He moved the yellow beam slowly and then laughed, the sound coming back at him from all sides.

He was not going mad. *He was all right.*

The torch jerked and he felt a shockwave hammer against the ship as a shell exploded in the sea nearby. But he was still chuckling as the light played round and then fastened on Petty Officer Dunbar. He was floating face down under water, his grim features shining in the beam of his own torch.

Defries sighed and waded back to the ladder and began to climb. He banged sharply on the hatch, noting that the water had risen two rungs within the last few minutes.

On the quarterdeck, huddled between the depth-charge racks, the seaman crouched above the hatch, his fingers still locked around the clips. He seemed to be listening, so intent was his expression. But he was dead. Killed by a splinter from that last haphazard shot.

Defries hammered again, the chuckle held in his throat like a rattle.

Then as the water surged around his neck he began to scream, the sound lost in the urgent thunder of the screw.

*   *   *

Crespin sat back on the steel chair, breathing deeply and allowing the cold wind to play across his bare shoulders. Lennox, the Leading Sickberth Attendant, took another turn with his bandage around Crespin's ribs and then muttered, 'That should do it, sir.' He had blood all over his arms, but his face was quite impassive, or shocked beyond any more feeling. 'I'll see to the cut now.'

A piece of flying glass had cut Crespin's right breast with the smoothness of a knifeblade. Lennox secured the dressing and shook his head. 'Still, you ought to be taking it easy, sir!'

They stared at each other and grinned. Then Crespin said, 'Thanks, but I'm a bit busy!'

Porteous called, 'No sign of the motor boat, sir!'

Crespin slipped his arms into his jacket. Even before Lennox had told him about the steward, he had known it must be Scarlett in the motor boat. Poor old Barker, the wardroom steward, had been lying dead outside the cabin. Above him was a line of splinter holes and a smudge of drying blood which told their own story. Scarlett would have seen him fall, or heard his last cry before he died. He had left the cabin, pausing only to take Barker's revolver, the symbol of his last status as a sentry, and must have burst out on to the starboard side deck. It would take a man like Scarlett about two seconds to see the possibilities of the motor boat. Cutting the trailing falls had been easy, and in the death and confusion aboard the *Thistle* no one had seen him go until he was well clear.

He was probably chasing after the M.L.s by now. While the *Thistle* turned to face certain destruction he would be back there, charming and explaining, rebuilding his own delusions so that more men might die because of them.

Crespin looked around the bridge, past the covered corpses and the great bloodstains which appeared to be on every foot of space. Perhaps the depth-charges would have made no difference at all, but at least they might have given them a little more time.

His eyes moved on, and he could feel them pricking with pain and despair as he saw what was happening to his ship, to the men who were still able to understand what he must do.

A halyard squeaked and he saw Griffin clipping another ensign ready for hoisting to a makeshift staff behind the bridge.

A lookout said, 'Let one of yer buntin' tossers do that! You look done in!'

Griffin carried on with his work. 'They're both dead.' A tear splashed on the back of his hand and he added savagely, 'Anyway, they could never do a proper splicin' job!'

Crespin looked away. 'Warn all guns. Stand by to turn!'

There was a crunch of glass and he saw Wemyss hopping clumsily across the bridge. He swept the mess from the chart table and squatted himself on it, his leg with its bloody bandage sticking out in front of him.

He looked at Crespin and nodded. 'A fine day for it, sir,' was all he said.

18 'Just as if She knew!'

'PORT twenty!' Chespin gripped the compass, feeling the deck cant steeply as the wheel went over. It was very quiet, and he could almost picture the enemy ship groping her way into the fringe of the drifting smoke. He heard Shannon calling more orders to his gun crew, while from aft a man cried out with sudden agony as he was dragged into some remaining piece of shelter. When he looked round the bridge he saw that fresh lookouts were already in position, facing outboard, their feet almost touching the bodies of those they had come to replace. One of the machine-guns had vanished, plucked away by the same savage blast which had flung him across the bridge, stunning him and knocking him senseless, but nevertheless saving him from the splinters which had cut the other exposed men to pieces. The remaining machine-gun was manned by a telegraphist and the assistant cook, their faces frozen into masks of tense concentration as the ship swung round and headed back towards the smoke.

Crespin felt the sun moving across his neck as he looked down at the gyro repeater for the hundredth time. 'Midships!' By turning the opposite way they might at least hold on to a small piece of surprise. 'Steady!'

Joicey called, 'Steady, sir! Course two-seven-zero!'

The ship settled on her new course, and Crespin saw the smoke coming rapidly towards the bows. With the sun following from astern the smoke seemed to shine like something solid, so that as the stem bit into the first billowing layer he almost expected to feel some sort of impact.

Then they were inside their own screen, the sunlight blotted out, the bridge filled with smoke, making it difficult to breathe without coughing.

Crespin stayed on the fore gratings, his eyes pressed against one of the last remaining pieces of glass as he tried to see beyond the bows. But visibility ended within feet of the hawsepipes, and Shannon's four-inch gun appeared to be floating on the smoke, completely detached from the deck below.

He shouted, 'Be ready to shoot! Don't wait for any orders from me!'

It would be very close this time. But Shannon seemed to be in complete control of his wits, for he saw him turn and grin up at him.

The smoke was already thinning, so that small patches of blue sea stood out on either beam, the sunlight confined and mocking as the ship hurried past.

Porteous was the first to see the enemy. He was standing with his bulky figure jammed against the port wing of the bridge where the torn steel curved inboard, the blackened edges twisted into fantastic shapes, like wet cardboard.

'Enemy at red four-five, sir!'

Crespin raised his glasses and then let them drop against his chest. There was no need for them this time. As the ship pushed steadily into the bright sunlight and the smoke thinned and peeled away like a mist, he saw the *Nashorn* less than two thousand yards away. She was directly across the port bow, steaming slowly towards the smoke, as if reluctant to take that last plunge into it. She was on a diverging course, so that her whole ugly length was quite clear in the glare, the dull grey paint reflecting on the water like a slab of rock. Abaft her armoured bridge the scarlet ensign with its large black swastika made a bright patch of colour, while the hull itself was still patched and daubed with red lead, evidence of the haste with which her captain had quit the dockyard.

The four-inch fired immediately, and Crespin saw the shell burst right alongside, throwing a thin plume of spray and smoke right over the enemy's bridge.

Shannon was yelling, 'Come on, man! Reload!' A pause, then, '*Shoot!*'

The second shell slammed into the *Nashorn*'s side, making a bright orange star and another small cloud of drifting smoke.

But the ponderous ship steamed on, while from its massive shield forward of the bridge the big gun was already training round towards the corvette with something like tired irritation.

The four-inch lurched back on its mounting, and Crespin felt the sharp detonation scraping the inside of his skull like a hot needle. But it was no use. He watched the shell burst behind the enemy's bridge, the fragments of steel and wood lifting in the air like so much blown paper, but it was making no real impression at all.

Then the *Nashorn* fired, and the shell seemed to explode almost before he heard the shot.

She was turning very slowly, her false bow wave giving an impression of tremendous effort, and possibly for that reason alone the shell missed the *Thistle*'s forecastle by a matter of feet.

Crespin felt the ship reel drunkenly and saw the sea surging over the port side in a creamy flood while the air came alive with screaming splinters. It seemed as if they would never stop, and he could hear the white-hot metal tearing into the hull, crashing through frail plating and ripping crazily into the empty forecastle where countless men had once lived, dreamed and hoped.

'Port ten!' He was conscious of the lightness in his limbs. There was no pain from the diagonal scar across his chest, and beneath his bandages he could not even feel his whole ribs, let alone the fractured one. It was like being under drugs, or mesmerised by some madman and forced to watch one's own murder.

The enemy was turning, too, so that both vessels were approaching each other on invisible parallel rails.

God, Kapitan Lemke was *that* confident! He cared so little for the *Thistle*'s puny armament he was not even bothering to haul off and use his other big gun. He must be up there now behind those tiny slits in his armoured bridge, biding his time, knowing that whichever way his enemy turned or acted, he was finished. Once abeam he would use the secondary armament, but if one of his big shells hit the *Thistle* squarely before that moment he could just keep going, ramming her perhaps, and then brushing her aside with no more thought than a man who crushes a gnat.

What was he feeling? Crespin wondered. Elation or contempt? Admiration for an enemy, outgunned and overwhelmed by his own ship, or just the cold satisfaction of seeing them die? Remembering perhaps all those years of brooding over that other defeat and wiping away the bitterness in the *Thistle*'s death agony?

He shook himself out of his fixed concentration and shouted, 'Tell the secondary armament to open fire.'

The port Oerlikons and then the pom-pom responded at once, but like the four-inch gun on the forecastle they seemed ineffectual and totally useless against the other ship's massive armour. The tracers were ripping and ricocheting in every direction, the gunners yelling and sobbing as they fired magazine after magazine, until the muzzles were glowing with heat, the decks littered with expended shells and cartridge cases.

The *Nashorn*'s next shell burst in the air almost level with the bridge. It was probably old, like the gun which had fired it, or maybe in their haste the German gunners had mismanaged the fuse, otherwise it would have blown most of the structure into scrap.

But it was bad enough, almost too much for the ship to take. Crespin had been bending over the wheelhouse voice-pipe and felt the blast searing over his shoulders like flames from an open furnace. Splinters were smashing into the side of the bridge, and he saw a man's arm whirling above the screen alongside the sheared-off barrel of an Oerlikon. Smoke and fumes were everywhere, and all around he could hear men crying out, screaming and calling to each other, their voices mingling into one confused chorus.

He saw Wemyss struggling to his feet and ran quickly to the rear of the bridge. It was a miracle that anyone could live through this. But as he peered down through the smoke he saw seamen with axes and extinguishers climbing over the littered deck, and Lennox's blood-spattered white coat bobbing amongst them like a ghost.

There was an Oerlikon gunner just below the bridge,

strapped to his weapon but fighting it with his hands and feet, his words rising to a scream as Lennox scrambled up beside him.

'Help me! I'm blind! Oh, Jesus bloody Christ, *I'm blind*!'

It's no use. We're finished. Crespin did not know if it was a thought or if he had spoken aloud. One Oerlikon was still firing steadily from aft, the bright tracer fading in the smoke above the sea which still shone so placidly in the cruel sunlight.

The four-inch, which had fallen silent after the explosion, reopened fire, but the intervals between shots seemed longer and disjointed. Not that it mattered now, he thought wearily. The enemy would soon engage with her automatic weapons and drive the rest of the *Thistle*'s men back and down into the shattered hull before ending her hopeless fight, finally and without mercy.

As he stared over the rim of the bridge he saw her outline looming through the smoke, made larger and more formidable because of it. A solitary machine-gun had already started to fire from somewhere below her boat deck, and he heard the heavy calibre bullets smacking into steel and whimpering viciously through the swirling smoke above his head.

Forward of the bridge Shannon twisted on his steel seat and stared wild-eyed at the crumpled figures around the gun.

'Kidd! *Clear the breech!*' But the gun captain was lying back over the side of the rail, his mouth open, his face screwed into shocked agony and frozen there in a death-mask. Robbins, the trayworker, was on his knees, one gloved hand still reaching up for the breech, the other pressed to his stomach. He, too, was dead.

Shannon screamed, 'Reload! Jump to it, you bastards!' With crazed desperation he threw himself round the gun and dragged open the breech. The empty cartridge case clanged past him, sending the dead Robbins sprawling, but he hardly noticed as he lifted another shell from the rack and thrust it into the smoking breech.

Muttering and cursing to himself Shannon ran to the trainer's position and pulled the huddled man bodily from his stool. When he pressed his eye against the sight he felt blood sticking to his forehead, and saw a bright scar on the steel where a flying splinter had cut the trainer down.

Breathing fast he adjusted the sight and then scurried back around the gun to his own seat. He had to blink several times to clear his vision and his head felt as if it was bursting.

More than anything else he was filled with an overwhelming anger. This was the moment he had waited for, but just when he needed everything to run like clockwork he had been left to manage on his own. The drills and the reprimands, the persistent instruction of men who seemed incapable of following his quick mind, were all in vain.

He looked round at the silent shapes and yelled, 'Useless! You're all bloody useless!'

The communications rating was still sitting in his little steel compartment beside the ammunition hatch, his earphones knocked askew across his head and one eye hanging from its socket.

Shannon saw all and none of these things. He pressed his head to the rubber pad again and watched as the *Nashorn's* hull misted over in the sight, hardened and then settled firmly on the crosswires. He would make it at last. Hang on to this moment which he could now share with no one. It was, after all, the only shell within reach. Perhaps the very last one in the ship.

The range was down to a thousand yards, maybe less. In the confusion of shell-fire and smoke it was impossible to judge any more.

As one more water-spout shot above the starboard side Crespin looked at Wemyss and asked, 'How long?'

Wemyss knew what he meant. The expression on Crespin's face was enough.

'It'll be half an hour yet before Coutts and the others can reach safety, sir.'

Crespin said bitterly, 'Then we're dying for nothing, after all!'

Wemyss dragged himself across the bridge, his face grey with effort and shock.

'We tried, sir!' He shivered as another explosion cracked against the hull. 'God, we *tried*!'

Crespin turned away, almost afraid to look as Porteous shouted, 'Sir! On the port beam!' He was cracking with disbelief. 'It's a boat!'

Crespin wiped his face with his sleeve and tried to understand what he saw. At first he thought Porteous's new strength had at last failed, or that he himself was finally breaking under the strain.

The little motor boat was coming steadily out of the smoke, her small bow wave cutting a neat arrowhead as she turned slightly and headed towards the *Nashorn*.

Every gun fell silent, and as the two ships continued towards each other Crespin saw tiny figures appearing on the *Nashorn*'s upper deck for the first time. They were running towards the foredeck, and as he watched a machine-gun began to stammer from one wing of the upper bridge.

He could see bullets splashing around the motor boat, but whatever damage they were doing seemed to make no difference either to her speed or direction.

Wemyss said thickly, 'God, it's bloody Scarlett! He must be raving mad!'

Crespin lifted his glasses. It *was* Scarlett. In the lenses of the powerful glasses he could see him crouched beside the tiller, his oak-leaved cap pulled hard down over his eyes as he stared fixedly across the small cockpit. Perhaps in his crazed mind he had not realised that the *Thistle* had turned to re-engage the *Nashorn*. He might have cast off the motor boat and steered astern in order to catch up with Coutts and the others, only to find as he broke through the wall of smoke that he was heading straight for the enemy. Or it could be one more wild gesture, one last effort to prove himself. But whatever his earlier intention might have been, there was no mistaking his present one.

As more bullets spattered around the boat Scarlett half-rose to his feet, and Crespin realised he was firing his revolver directly at the enemy's bows. Scarlett's mouth was tight with concentration, and he did not even duck as pieces of the gunwale were splintered in another burst of machine-gun fire.

Porteous yelled, 'Look! There are more men coming on deck!'

Crespin saw the German seamen for just a few seconds before they vanished below the big gun mounting. It was useless
to shoot at them. They were on the opposite side of the ship by
now, no doubt marksmen sent by Kapitan Lemke to finish off
the motor boat before it got any nearer.

Wemyss muttered, 'He'll never make it!'

Crespin held his breath as Scarlett reeled back over the gunwale, one hand clutching his shoulder. He could see the blood
spreading down his side, the useless way his arm and the empty
revolver hung straight down by the tiller. More bullets smashed
into the small hull, but Scarlett was dragging himself across
the cockpit, his mouth opening wide as he yelled something at
the *Nashorn* which was now within thirty yards of him.

Surely the Germans must have realised this was something
other than the madness of one man? The *Nashorn*'s bow wave
increased slightly, and she began to turn slowly and heavily
to starboard.

Crespin lowered his glasses. Scarlett was bleeding from
several wounds and his agony was terrible to watch. The motor
boat was losing way, the engine silenced at last by the machine-
gun.

Wemyss said quietly, 'He's down, sir. I think he's bought
it.' He, too lowered his glasses. 'The poor, crazy bastard!'

Porteous was saying, 'They couldn't even leave him like that,
could they?' The words were torn from his lips.

Crespin's reeling mind seemed to fasten on his words like a
blind man feeling something old and once familiar. He raised
his glasses, his brain registering what Porteous meant and remembering what Soskic had once told him about the *Nashorn*
ramming defenceless boats. Just for the hell of it. He could feel
the cold realisation running through him like ice and he had
to force himself to move and act.

'Stand by on the four-inch!'

He seized Porteous's arm and shook it, pulling him from his
sickened concentration on the bobbing motor boat with its
bloodied helmsman as it waited to meet the *Nashorn*'s towering bows.

'He's going to ram the boat!' He shook him savagely. 'Don't
you see, *that* was Lemke's weakness!' He ran back to the

screen and yelled, 'One shell on her poop!' He saw Shannon staring at him. 'The *Nashorn* was afraid to turn and use her other gun!'

Why was it taking so long to make them understand? Lemke's one real weakness was his cruelty. It was blinding him to the danger of those depth-charges and to the real menace of those mines he always carried. The mines on their little poop railway which Crespin and Coutts had once seen and sketched as the ship had steamed contemptuously past Gradz every day on the same punctual hour.

Perhaps even now Lemke had realised his one and only error. Smoke gushed from the twin funnels, while from beneath the counter the screws threw up a great welter of foam as the engines went to full astern.

The motor boat had disappeared, hidden by the great wedge of the swinging bows, but its pitiful progress could be judged by the moving heads of the German seamen on the fore deck, the sudden panic as they at last understood the truth of their small conquest.

The actual explosion was quite dull and muffled, but the shockwave rumbled against the *Thistle*'s bilges, keeping time with the great pinnacle of water which rose high above the *Nashorn*'s bridge before falling back slowly alongside.

Crespin felt his eyes watering with strain and concentration. 'Half ahead!' He must not close the range now. The enemy was still turning, her upper deck wreathed in smoke and darting flames. Across the narrowing strip of water he could hear a strange grating sound, and guessed that one of the coal bunkers had fractured, and with the ship turning at the moment of the explosion it was ripping the inner plates away like paper.

While the *Nashorn* continued to turn the big after-gun swung slowly on its mounting, the long barrel shining in the sunlight as it reached out towards the small ship which still managed to stay afloat.

Wemyss said between his teeth, 'It's a race!' He cursed as a line of tracer darted from the enemy's bridge and ripped along the *Thistle*'s upper deck. He banged the plating with his fist, murmuring fiercely, 'Come on, old girl! Come *on*!'

Crespin watched the gun. It was trained as far round as it

would bear, and as soon as the ship completed her turn it would fire. From a corner of his eye he saw some black specks drifting near the German's hull and guessed they were fragments of Scarlett's boat. He had probably died long before the boat had reached the enemy's side. That was a pity, for this was something Scarlett would have undoubtedly enjoyed, he thought bitterly.

Shannon let out a sudden yell. 'Got it!'

Crespin shifted the glasses, seeing the big gun muzzle pointing almost directly towards him. He was just in time to see the lip of the enemy's small railway appearing beyond the poop ladder before Shannon squeezed the trigger.

The German fired a split second later, the shell exploding some fifty feet from the *Thistle*'s port bow. Maybe the *Nashorn*'s gunnery officer had been concentrating so hard that Shannon's sudden challenge had made him react too soon.

Crespin heard the splinters clashing against the hull plates, but was too stricken even to take cover. He saw Shannon's last shell explode with little more than a puff of smoke and a few pieces of whirling wreckage from the poop. Then, as he turned to face Wemyss to acknowledge that he had failed, the world seemed to come apart in one prolonged and ear-splitting explosion.

Smoke tinged with orange fires, spray and fragments had completely hidden the other ship from view. And as dazed men poured from bridge and guns alike, Crespin saw a miniature tidal wave sweeping towards his ship, lifting her almost carelessly before cruising away towards the nearest island.

Like something from a nightmare the *Nashorn* moved slowly out of the smoke. In actual fact she was quite stationary now and only the smoke was moving. But for those few minutes it seemed as if she was still as unbreakable and terrible as ever. Until the smoke at last cleared her bridge and revealed that there was no more of her to see.

There were more internal detonations, and flames darted out of the torn plating to mingle with smoke and escaping steam as with tired dignity she began to heel over towards the watching corvette, machinery tearing loose and crashing through the inferno between decks.

Just when it seemed as if she would turn right over, one great explosion sent a wall of flame shooting a hundred feet above the listing bridge, and as Crespin clung to the screen he could feel the heat across his face, could imagine the horror of that final moment.

In his wheelhouse Joicey gripped the spokes and listened to the roar of the last explosion, and knew it was the end of the *Nashorn*. It was strange, but this time he had no desire to leave the wheel and watch. Even if he had been able to. He stared wearily around the shuttered compartment. It was almost as light as if the scuttles had been wide open. Smoky sunlight made fine yellow bars through a dozen splinter holes and played across the telegraphsman, a messenger and a bosun's mate, all of whom lay in the various attitudes of sudden death. One other man appeared to be sleeping. He was lucky, Joicey thought. Brought in badly wounded, he had been too drugged to feel the final pain when it burst in on him.

Joicey did not know how he had survived. Throughout the action he had stayed at the wheel, shouting at his companions, cursing and responding to Crespin's constant demands, and all the time holding to his trade with the tenacity and fury of a wild animal at bay.

Magot heard the explosion, too, and ran his fingers over his controls with something like love. Across the pounding machinery he saw his stokers watching him, red-eyed and soaked with oil and water from leaks in the hull and several severed pipes. Magot had been so long in the noisy world of an engine room that he had little use for words, and when he tried to shout what he wanted to say to the men he had so often chased and cursed, he could not find any at all.

The little ginger stoker, the bane of Magot's existence, held up a small bundle and grinned.

'Yer teeth, Chiefy!'

Magot seized them and looked away. The stoker hurried back to his demanding dials, proud of what he had endured, but ashamed at seeing the tears in Magot's eyes. It was like stealing someone's secret, he thought.

The bells clanged and the needle of the dial swung round once more to 'Full Ahead'.

Magot turned and glared up at it. 'All right, you impatient sods! Here we go again!' He threw his spindly body across the throttle wheel, cursing and muttering into the din of his racing machinery.

The stokers looked at each other and grinned. The old Maggot was back again.

Shannon did not hear the explosion. As he had released his grip on the trigger a splinter from the *Nashorn*'s final shell had hit him squarely in the chest, killing him instantly. His dark features were still twisted with anger and disappointment when Lennox and his stretcher bearers arrived, possibly because the last thing he saw on earth was the apparent failure of his shot.

Lennox looked around at the spread-eagled corpses and then dropped on his knees beside Shannon. Something had fallen out of the lieutenant's pocket and lay glinting brightly in the widening pool of blood beside him.

One of the seamen said, 'A crucifix? Didn't know 'e was a Catholic!'

Lennox picked it up and turned it over in his hands. Then he looked at the dead men by the splinter-torn gun, at the battered bridge beyond, with its tattered ensign still jaunty and clean above all this horror. 'Well, it didn't do him any bloody good, did it?' Almost savagely he hurled the cross over the rail and picked up his bag. 'Come on then! Spare a thought for the living!'

Crespin climbed on to the bridge chair and leaned forward to watch the mounting bow wave.

He heard Wemyss say quietly, 'Just as if she knew!' He laughed shakily. 'She was even pointing in the right direction for home!'

Crespin did not trust himself to reply. The anguish of battle was fading with the smoke astern, all that was left to mark where *Nashorn* had finally vanished. Now as he gripped the rail below the broken screen he could feel his limbs beginning to shake, the pain in his chest and side coming back, as if he was emerging from a drugged sleep.

Feet crunched on the glass behind him and he heard Leading

Telegraphist Christian speaking urgently with Porteous. One more man who had somehow survived.

Wemyss joined him by the screen and studied him anxiously. 'I think you should go to the chartroom, sir. You've done enough for ten men this morning.'

Morning? Crespin stared listlessly at the clear sky. Was it still only that? The same sky and sun, the same glittering water.

Porteous's face swam across his vision. 'Well?' How small his voice seemed.

Wemyss took a sheet of paper from Porteous's hand and said slowly, 'Signal, sir. *Thistle will return to base forthwith. Air cover will be provided immediately*.' He touched Crespin's arm and added quietly, 'It says to cancel the last signal, sir. *Aircraft recovered. Rear-Admiral Oldenshaw and party safe*.'

Crespin looked up slowly, fearful in case he was drifting back again into unconsciousness. He saw Wemyss and Porteous staring at each other and grinning, and beyond them Griffin and the telegraphist, who still did not realise the importance of his message.

Then he said, 'Thank you.' He reached out and touched the smoke-stained steel by his side. He could have been speaking to the ship. 'Thank you very much.'

Christian asked, 'Any reply, sir?' He sounded tired.

Wemyss took his arm and guided him clear of the gratings. There was still a long way to go and there were a hundred things to do in the next hour or so. But as he looked around the riddled bridge he no longer had any doubt in his mind that she would get them there. His eyes fell on the figure in the chair. Crespin was lolling in time with the ship's easy roll, and he guessed that he had at last given in to sleep and total exhaustion. When he awakened he would remember. And he would know that life had again something to offer.

He said, 'As soon as we meet with our escort you can make this signal.' He paused, conscious of the moment, for himself, and for the little ship around him.

'*Thistle* will enter harbour as ordered. Enemy destroyed.'

Epilogue

IT was a cold February morning, and although the rain had all but stopped the low clouds above Portsmouth harbour showed that there was plenty more to come. The harbour was crowded, and the sleek grey frigate which had just passed through the entrance picked up a berth on the outside of two other ships, the oilskinned seamen pausing at the mooring wires only to whistle at two perky Wrens who were already climbing aboard with the ship's mail.

Then, as the rain came back again the seamen dispersed to their quarters to read letters from home, to change into shore-going rig, to enjoy themselves once more and forget the last patrol.

In the captain's day cabin Commander John Crespin unslung his binoculars and handed them to his steward before sitting down at his desk and stretching his legs. Both cabin scuttles were uncovered, but because of the ship alongside the place was in semi-darkness. Crespin yawned and switched on the desk light, then after a slight hesitation picked up a newspaper which with several official letters had just been left by the mail boat.

The headlines were glaring and optimistic, as they always seemed to be these days. The Allies were across the Rhine and smashing deep into Germany. Everywhere the enemy front was collapsing, and what had once seemed like a hopeless dream was now becoming a reality.

He heard the steward whistling to himself and the clatter of crockery. The coffee would be very welcome just now, he thought. With the war so nearly finished it was more necessary than ever not to relax and take unnecessary chances. Like the last patrol, for instance. Dull and almost without incident. But the danger was always there just the same. He froze in his chair and leaned forward, imagining for a moment that his tiredness was playing tricks on him.

It was just a small paragraph, a few lines right at the foot of the second page.

'Yesterday the Secretary of the Admiralty announced the loss of the corvette H.M.S. *Thistle* (Lieutenant-Commander Douglas Wemyss, D.S.C., R.N.R.) The announcement was delayed for two weeks in the hope that some further information might be made available. It is understood that the *Thistle* was one of the escorts of an Atlantic convoy en route for America and was detached to search for survivors from another ship. She was never seen again. Next of kin have been informed.'

Crespin sat back in the chair, the brief announcement moving through his mind, as if he was hearing it spoken aloud.

He had last seen the *Thistle* in Brindisi sixteen months ago, since when so much had happened, and yet as he read the paragraph once more it felt as if it was yesterday. Now she was gone, taken by the Atlantic which she had fought for so long and with only one pause. And that pause, her efforts and disappointments, her final victory over the *Nashorn* had not even been mentioned. Perhaps, like all the other acts and sacrifices, hers was just a brief episode after all. An episode which he had shared, and now, would never forget.

He stood up and walked unseeingly round the cabin, his mind filled with pictures and memories, of faces and names, of all the things which had made that one battered little ship so different.

Perhaps she had never really recovered from the wounds she had received, and when she had again challenged her common enemy, the Atlantic had triumphed.

He thought, too of Wemyss and Porteous, Magot and Joicey, and all the others. She was in good company wherever she was, and would keep her last secret forever.

He realised that someone had knocked at the door, and when

he turned he saw his first lieutenant framed in the entrance.

'Just wanted to discuss arrangements for leave and so forth, sir.' He saw Crespin's eyes and added, 'I'm sorry, sir. Is something wrong?'

Crespin looked away from the lieutenant's sleeve with its interwoven gold lace. Like Wemyss. Wemyss who had loved the ship, perhaps more than any of them.

He said, 'Nothing wrong.' He had even replied to Wemyss like that when he had received Penny's letter. Now Penny was over there in the hotel with their child, waiting for him, as she always did. He recalled too how Wemyss had tried to comfort him when the aircraft had been reported missing. Perhaps in his own way he had wanted to share his grief.

He picked up his cap and looked slowly round the cabin. 'I just read something in the paper. About an old friend.' He broke off. Who did he really mean? 'I'll tell you about it one day.'

Then he brushed past him and walked out into the rain.